# THE
# FETCH

A NOVEL

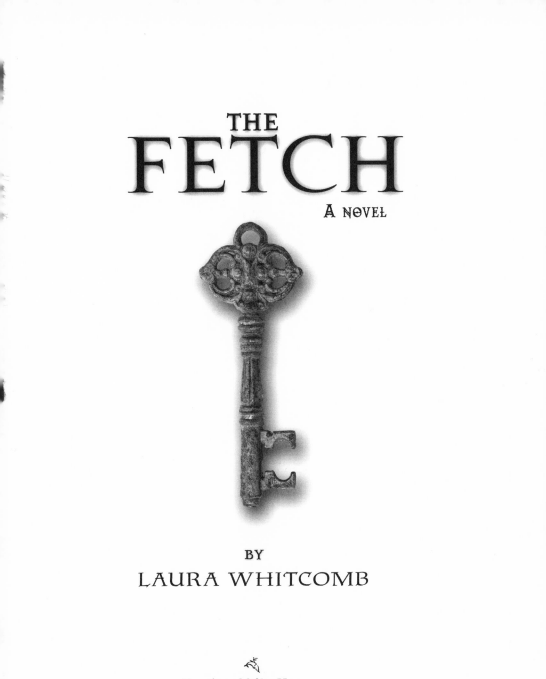

BY
## LAURA WHITCOMB

Houghton Mifflin Harcourt
Boston 2009

FOR MY FATHER,

MY HERO—MY FIRST EXAMPLE OF MASCULINE STRENGTH

AND HOW THAT POWER SHOULD CHAMPION PEACE.

THANKS TO—my family, especially Cyn for being my first reader, my writers support group, my Chez sisters, professor Edward Segel of Reed College, the research librarians of Lake Oswego Public Library, Penn Whaling, my fabulous agent, Ann Rittenberg, my entire Houghton Mifflin team, including Alison Kerr Miller, Ann-Marie Pucillo, Sheila Smallwood, Michael Nelson, Karen Walsh, and especially my brilliant and diplomatic editor, Kate O'Sullivan.

Photo of Imperial Family, page 380 © Getty Images.
Photo of Alexis, page 380 © 1992 KEA Publishing Services Ltd./CSAOR
Photo of Ana, page 380 © 1992 KEA Publishing Services Ltd./CSAOR

www.hmhbooks.com

The text of this book is set in Fournier.

Library of Congress Cataloging-in-Publication Data
Whitcomb, Laura.
The Fetch / a novel by Laura Whitcomb.
p. cm.
Summary: After 350 years as a Fetch, or death escort, Calder breaks his vows and enters the body of Rasputin, whose spirit causes rebellion in the Land of Lost Souls while Calder struggles to convey Ana and Alexis, orphaned in the Russian Revolution, to Heaven.
ISBN 978-0-618-89131-3
[1. Future life—Fiction. 2. Death—Fiction. 3. Anastasia, Grand Duchess, daughter of Nicholas II, Emperor of Russia, 1901–1918—Fiction. 4. Aleksei Nikolaevich, Czarevitch, son of Nicholas II, Emperor of Russia, 1904–1918—Fiction. 5. Rasputin, Grigori Efimovich, ca. 1870–1916—Fiction. 6. Forgiveness—Fiction. 7. Russia (Federation)—History—Revolution, 1917–1921—Fiction.] I. Title.
PZ7.W5785Fet 2009
[Fic]—dc22
2008013307

Manufactured in the United States of America
MP 10 9 8 7 6 5 4 3 2 1

# Part I

## The Aisle of Unearthing

# One

CALDER WAS A FETCH, a death escort, and had been since his own death at the age of nineteen. He had been a Fetch for three hundred and thirty years, and so had seen many women in the Death Scenes to which he had been sent. He'd watched women drowning, one with seaweed twisting her gown into a mermaid tail, another in a pond surrounded by lilies that glowed like funeral offerings about her floating hair. He'd seen women lost and broken in ivy-choked woods and in open fields where they lay fallen in the snow, half covered like gravestones. Some died safe in their downy beds, some forgotten in alleys.

He had also seen many women who tended to the dying—this one washing her sister's face with lilac water, that one praying and weeping with her father. Some had been nursing soldiers, others dreaming beside husbands they did not realize had ceased breathing.

For the last three hundred and thirty years Calder had seen thousands upon thousands of mortal women, so he did not understand why, on this day, the sight of this particular woman afflicted him.

❊ ❊ ❊

On earth it was the winter of 1904. The Death Door had opened onto a nursery, and the dying body was that of a baby boy whose swollen belly was bleeding from the inside. The sight of a dying infant did not shake Calder, for he'd escorted hundreds of them through the Aisle of Unearthing. He had seen babes die alone in their cradles at night, or surrounded by doctors and priests, in dirty huts, in palaces, from cold or from fever, and he had often seen their mothers trying to breathe life back into their small mouths. Calder, like all Fetches, felt sympathy for this pain, but when a human soul—even an infant's—reaches for its Fetch and slips out of its earthly shell, the cries and shudderings of those left behind are closed on the other side of the Death Door. No mortal terror, sorrow, or anger could ever rattle that portal open again.

The Fetch holds the only Key.

So though it was not the first time Calder had seen a beautiful woman, when he first beheld this woman's halo of reddish-gold hair, he was stung with recognition. And although he had seen many women devoted to their children, when he saw the way this woman held her baby in the nest of her white dress and whispered to him words that were not words but tiny prayers and magic charms, he was mesmerized. She sat, gently rocking in the lamplight, like a ghost singing in a forbidden language. She pulled at Calder's heart, almost unfurling the stiff pages of his memory—so familiar, but he knew he had never set eyes on her before.

Calder tried to remember if this woman looked like anyone he had seen during his nineteen years on earth, but just as the sorrow of the earthbound is shut on the other side of the Death Door, the memories of earth are drawn away from the dying soul. When Calder died and became a Fetch, his old life was eclipsed by his new one—he could remember being human in a distant way, like viewing a painting on a wall through an open door one room removed. Whether the picture of a Fetch's past life was heavenly or hellish, it appeared serene and remained motionless.

Calder's own painting of his human life was a rich and shadowed thing, deep with color and detail but as still as any canvas mounted on a wall. Before a theatrical arch, under the warm glow of a paper lantern, with his audience of gentlefolk standing or reclining about him, Calder played an ornate drum and sang so sweetly that everyone stopped to listen. At his feet lay a fur cloak, perhaps a gift from his noble patron. What songs he sang and the name of his benefactor were distant to him now in both time and interest.

But sometimes as he traversed the Aisle and heard the pulse of music in the Theatre or Feast of the soul in his charge, he would almost recall some snippet of tune or line of poetry that had been known to him on earth. A note that leapt up and hovered, a simple lyric of love unrequited. The memory would flare, then fade before he could repeat it. When this happened, Calder wondered if under this perfect picture of his human life there might not be another painting hiding in pentimento, its darker and forgotten shapes waiting to be drawn to the surface.

Calder tried now to recall women he had known on earth, but he could not remember any sisters or his mother. He imagined what the women might have looked like, those that listened to him sing. Graceful ladies in satin and pearls, nodding with admiration. But none of the feminine visions he could conjure brought him joy like this woman in white.

Calder stood still so as not to disturb her, though he couldn't be seen or heard by most mortals. She must have been the nursery maid or governess, for she was wearing a simple cotton dress with the sleeves rolled to the elbows, in contrast to the room, which was richly dressed with brocade curtains, cushioned chairs, and a brass crib filled with lace bedding. Perhaps the baby was only her charge, but it was clear that she loved him as though he was the only child on earth. Calder studied her delicate fingers as she cupped the baby's head and lifted him to her lips. He watched her heartbeat tap an almost invisible rhythm at her throat. He felt despair pulsing through her, but only the slightest trembling was visible in her shoulders. She was calling all her strength to the task; Calder could feel it as distinctly as he felt his own tremors: she was trying to still her nerves and calm her breathing so that the dying child would sense no fear. Calder watched with a confounding sense of loss. And this was when he did something he had never done before in all his years as a Fetch.

He hoped the child would live.

Calder, like all Fetches, was supposed to be indifferent to the outcomes of Death Scenes, and usually that came naturally. Some souls chose to cross over; others chose to stay. And it was not always the sickest who chose death or the one with the slightest wound who chose life. A Fetch was to respect this choice without question and without judgment. Calder had never wished to stop a Death, but when a Death Scene held a single mourner, one human left alone with no relative or friend as comfort, Calder felt an instinct to stay with him, though, of course, he could not.

As Calder gazed down on these two mortals, he could hear men's voices coming from the corridor—hushed, apprehensive whispers—

perhaps doctors, perhaps holy men. This family could afford the best physicians, but some hurts cannot be healed.

A gentleman, with dark whiskers and fine clothes, came to stand in the nursery doorway. A woman peered over his shoulder. These were the baby's parents, perhaps. Calder paid little attention to them, for he was reluctant to turn away from the governess since he would have so little time with her. He knew a good Fetch would not stare this way at a human, but he could not help himself.

Moments later the father and mother had gone, but a child appeared in their place—a girl of no more than four, peeking around the door frame. Calder had no intention of looking at the girl, but she had a strong presence, like a bit of mirror-reflected light flashing in the corner of his vision. Her hair was as reddish-blond as that of the governess, but her face was not angelic—she was like a storybook elf, with pointed chin, a short, round nose, and curious eyes beneath brows arched in a kind of challenge. Calder suspected she was lonely since her governess needed to spend so much time with her baby brother. The girl watched the governess for a moment, then turned to Calder and set her tiny fists on her hips. He regarded her, unruffled. Though Fetches were invisible to most adult humans, very young children could often see them—some animals could, as well. But since the children able to see Fetches were usually too young to describe their visions with any clarity, and since they would forget the incident within a few months, the Order of the Fetch remained a secret.

As the elfish child glowered at him, Calder felt a familiar movement in the spectral air, the spirit wind that accompanied a soul's indecision.

The wind circled the nursery, rippling Calder's hair but leaving everything tangible in the room undisturbed. This was the turning point in a Death Scene, the secret discussion between the body and the spirit. Next a stillness fell over everything, the sign that the decision had been made: The baby would stay. He had chosen life. Calder felt almost sick from the pleasure. He wanted to stay until the governess realized the baby would live, but he knew he could not. She wouldn't feel the relief of it for hours, but the little girl in the doorway knew something had changed. She dropped her hands to her sides as if any threat Calder had brought with him was now past, then slipped out of sight, the flip of her petticoats flashing like a white rabbit through the dark hole of the doorway.

Calder felt the Death Door appear again in the air behind him. Though he longed to, he did not linger. He took his Key from a chain about his neck and unlocked the Door, opening it without another glance back. He couldn't stay with the governess, but neither could he leave her behind. He set the memory of her in a secret drawer of his mind, like a tiny locket he could open at will, though he did not know her name.

# Two

CALDER HIMSELF, LIKE EVERY FETCH, had only one name, but he had two ages: his Earth Years numbered nineteen and his Death Years numbered three hundred and thirty. Though it was no excuse for what he would do, for a Fetch, Calder was young.

The Order of the Fetch, on the other hand, was old—it began when the ruins of the first garden could still be found hiding in the desert beside a river, a blanket of green vines having grown over her like a shroud, and, in this moist cave that was once Eden, at the heart of her darkness, the Tree of Knowledge bowed to the earth. Abel, the second son of Eve, the first to die in Eden, became the first Fetch—he was there, in a rocky field east of the garden, standing over the body of his father as Adam took his last breath.

The Order of the Fetch had no written history. By the time Calder was Squired, in the English year of the Lord 1574, no one in the Aisle knew how many Fetches there were. Some said thirteen hundred, some said thirteen thousand.

The Vows of the Fetch numbered seven:
    To honor the Order of the Fetch by loving others
      above one's self and God above all.
    To strengthen the Order through prayer and pure thoughts.
    To open all Death Doors and to accept each soul's choice
      to live or die.
    Never to alter a soul's journey through the
      Aisle of Unearthing.
    To choose and mentor at least one Squire.
    Never to upset the world of the earthbound.
    Never to interfere with the duties of another Fetch.

When Calder stepped through his Door into what he assumed would be his next Death Scene and found only blackness ahead, he should have been afraid. Every Death Door led to either a new Scene or his nightly Prayer Room. He should have seen the darkness as a warning, but instead he was thinking about the governess. And he did an odd thing then that should have alerted him that he was about to venture down the wrong path.

He gave the woman a name. He called her Glory.

※ ※ ※

Calder reached his hands into the blackness but felt nothing. He tried to purify his thoughts, to put images of Glory away, to help him cross into the next Death Scene. He recited from the second Fetch Psalm.

    *Many worlds, but one God.*
    *His power is the sun in every land,*

*His forgiveness the moon watching over every night,*
*His love the stars in every corner of the heavens.*

Still he was blind. He prayed for guidance and recited his Vows. But Calder was afraid that Heaven had finally figured out what he had known all along—he was unworthy to be a Fetch. A mistake had been made when he was Squired. Other Fetches were calm and wise. They were gifted with an egoless self-assurance and poise that he had never possessed. Instead, Calder was restless and lonely. He felt always as if he were searching for someone and waiting, as if he had left someone behind or been abandoned.

Calder was afraid of being found out, and would certainly be ashamed if the Captain were to discover how unfit he was to be a Fetch, but perhaps Calder would be relieved to be unmasked. It was a burden to be the only one that knew he was a misfit. Still Calder prayed for the next Scene to appear, for in the same way a human fears the unknown in death, Calder was afraid—what place in Heaven would there be for a banished Fetch?

Finally Calder heard soft waves sighing on the shore. Gratefully he entered the new Death Scene, stepping onto a night beach, where a young man ran past him clutching his side. His clothes appeared to be Elizabethan—a costume, perhaps: a torn pair of tights, no shoes, his shirt half open and bloody, his vest dragging behind him by one arm. Perhaps it was only his garb, but Calder felt a great affinity with him, as if the lad could have played Calder in a drama of his own human life. Calder had been close to this young man's age when he died, and the clothes seemed familiar. But the theatrical face paint was not what a musician would wear. This young man was an actor, though his wound was real.

Calder followed him along the sand, listening to him gasp for breath, watching him stumble and fall. The young man crawled on hands and knees as if being pursued by an invisible attacker. No moon or stars lit his path, only a faint light from a village on the hill above and the delicate glow each time a wave crashed. The actor finally collapsed and curled onto his side, a dark puddle forming under his belly.

Instead of hovering over him with divine calm, Calder was thinking about Glory. If she was a governess, surely she would not be married. The actor shook at Calder's feet. Both the spirit wind and the earthly one blew over the sand and around the dying man. Calder knelt beside the actor and waited for the decision to be made. Even then Calder was not paying attention.

He was wishing that God had chosen Glory as a Star Fetch, a Squire chosen from the ranks of the living. A rare thing, but beautiful. A Star Fetch was a mortal who is present at a Death Scene and gifted to see and hear the visiting Fetch. Star Fetches were always souls of deep empathy. Calder had met only a few, but they were all radiant beings, like Glory. He'd been looking for a Squire since nearly the beginning of his Fetch life, but he was too careful. Not just because he did not want to choose unwisely and apprentice an untalented soul like himself, but because he would be seated with this Squire later in the Afterlife. Calder would be proud to sit beside Liam, his master Fetch, but was always searching the eyes of the dying, looking for a sign, waiting for a somehow familiar face.

The actor had stopped breathing, his heart had stopped beating, but the soul was still quivering inside the painful flesh. When Calder realized that he was prolonging the actor's suffering, he closed his mind to Glory and leaned close to the young man's ear.

"Don't be afraid," he whispered. Finally the wind dropped and relaxed around them. The actor sat up from his body and reached for his Fetch the way a startled baby grabs at the air when it wakes.

"Come with me," Calder said, and took his hand. It didn't matter what language the actor had learned on earth; all words were understood equally in the Aisle of Unearthing. The dead man gazed at Calder with delight as he was lifted out of his discarded flesh. The actor's spiritual form remained his death age, but it was whole and strong, his wounds healed.

When a soul leaves the world behind it chooses its own form. Some remain in the likeness of their bodies at death, others become younger, some heal withered limbs, others grow as beautiful as statues. The only ones that cannot seem to change form are infants, so Calder would carry the souls of babies through the Aisle cradled in his arms.

The actor had dressed himself in a fine black suit. Calder brought him to his Death Door, and because the young man was an actor, the Door appeared as a green velvet curtain hung in a golden proscenium. Every soul saw the Aisle through its own eyes, with the colors and scents and textures of its own ideas. But the Fetch Key opened every Death Door— rice screen or iron gate—with equal ease.

Like an excited child, the actor gasped at the beauty of the Door. Some souls entered the Aisle sick with fear, others in unsteady confusion, but many greeted the parting from life as an adventure.

"Are you an angel?" the actor asked, as so many others had before him.

"I'm a Fetch," said Calder. "I'm your escort."

Calder locked the Death Door behind them and dropped the Key chain back into his robes. Each parting soul costumed his Fetch in the form most comforting, and this young man clothed Calder in silk robes the color of wheat. Sometimes Calder found himself in full armor like a warrior and other times with white wings fanning from his back like great sails. In the same way, the Aisle itself changed its outward appearance depending on the soul that was being escorted. For this one the Aisle was formed from red clay, for that one mossy logs, or perfectly flat black marble, or painted wood, or even gleaming with jewels. The floor went from Indian rugs to sand, to grass, to polished cedar, to straw mats as each different soul passed through.

Yet some things about the Aisle of Unearthing never changed: the Theatre, the Feast, the Gallery, the Garden, and the Cell.

As they moved into it, they found the Aisle covered in marbled paper, and the floor was a thick crimson carpet. First, as it always did, the soul's Theatre appeared. The actor watched as a small stage opened on the left. Three masked figures pantomimed a tragic scene in which a pair of lovers was interrupted by a man with a sword.

The actor stopped and watched as the intruder stabbed the male lover and left him crawling toward the wings. Although the actor did not comment on the play he was watching, he asked Calder, "Am I dead?"

"Yes," he told him.

The actor followed Calder farther down the Aisle. Next the Feast appeared on the right side of the Aisle. This was where the souls of dead humans saw and remembered the people they had left behind: their families, their comrades, their lovers, even their enemies. It was always a meal—a great celebration with huge platters of wild boar in a glowing great hall, or dry bread on a wooden table beside a tiny fireplace, or a picnic of sweets and wine on the clovered bank of a stream.

The actor turned to his right as a smoky tavern appeared, a noisy room full of laughing and singing men and women drinking ale and eating roasted chicken with their fingers. They wore mismatched costumes, feathers, and fake gems. The actor raised a hand to them in greeting. The faces of the crowd turned to him, girls throwing kisses, men lifting their cups in a toast.

Calder led on. Next, to the left, the papered wall was hung with a series of framed paintings—scenes the actor understood, because he stopped and gaped at them—a dead horse, a coin in an open hand, a half-burnt candle. This was the Gallery, where souls saw their mistakes, their worst regrets, on display–a mural in polished lapis and jade, or a tapestry, great figures carved into the walls, or delicate ink strokes on papyrus. Whatever these memories were, they brought tears to the actor's eyes. After looking at them, he turned away.

"I'm sorry," he whispered.

"It's finished," said Calder. "Now look."

On the right they approached the Garden, where souls saw the fruits of their life. It could appear as a great tree, or a vast plain of green wheat, a carefully planned circle of topiary, or a wild, blowing field of flowers. For the actor, his Garden was an orchard of almond trees, each one, though disguised in the poetry of nature, a message to the dead man: *In this way the world was made better by you.*

The actor gasped and tried to reach for one of the branches.

"Do you see?" he whispered. Whether these trees were good deeds or well-received plays, Calder could not know. Only a human soul can read his own Garden.

"It's beautiful," said Calder.

And then, at the end of the Aisle, as always, the Cell appeared. For the actor it was a jail cell, the walls blank, the tiny window barred. Some souls saw locked closets, others dungeons with chains, even the bottoms of deep, dry wells.

The Cell always held a Prisoner—sometimes tied to a post, other times locked in shackles, strapped to a bed, or caged like an animal. The important thing was for the soul to feel empathy for the Prisoner and recognize him.

In the actor's Cell, a naked man sat in the corner, shivering. He had dust in his hair and scrapes on his knees. He moaned and flexed his hands.

"Are you hurt?" the actor asked him when they had stepped into the Cell.

The Prisoner turned his face to the wall.

"Don't be afraid," said the actor, then added, "Don't be ashamed."

The actor squatted down close to the Prisoner and they spoke in hushed tones—the inscrutable, intimate conversation that no one, not even a Fetch, could overhear. Finally the actor stood and smiled down at the Prisoner. "I'll help you."

"There's no way out," said the Prisoner.

"But the door's standing open," said the actor, offering him his hand and gesturing to a place in the Cell wall where a passageway opened. The Prisoner let himself be lifted to his feet, and as the Prisoner looked into his eyes, the actor understood and began to laugh. "What a fool!" He hugged the Prisoner and the Prisoner disappeared.

In these moments some wept, some trembled, and others danced with delight.

As soon as a soul discovered that he himself was the Prisoner, they became one and the Cell vanished, as it did now. Calder and the actor were standing on the shore again, only now, it was light.

Even the Great River appeared different to different souls. To some it was a small lake as silver as a mirror, to others a babbling brook or a vast ocean. And the Captain and his ship changed form with each soul, from a hollow log or an Egyptian barge with a feathered canopy, to a Viking ship with a dragon's head pushing through the waves or a Venetian gondola, painted black and gold, rocking in the mist. The Captain appeared in every form imaginable—in satin robes or black sackcloth. Fierce as a pirate or gentle as a priest. Giant or leprechaun. But to Calder he was always his Captain, the eternal constant.

Now, as the actor gazed out to sea, a small ship with a mermaid figure-head moved across the soft waves of the bay, hissing up onto the sand, magically nesting on the beach. The Captain, wearing a uniform of purple and red, stood before the white sails like a bright banner.

"I pass this soul into your care," said Calder.

"I will take him the rest of the way," said the Captain. "God be with you."

"And also with you."

These words were always the same. But the releasing of the soul was different each time—some souls had already forgotten Calder by the time they stepped onto the Captain's boat; others clung to him and begged the Captain to let them take their Fetch along. In this case the actor took Calder's hand and shook it.

"Thank you," he said. "Thank you for taking me first, before the woman."

Calder pulled his hand away. This had never happened before. Souls could not see other dying souls and Fetches were never made to choose between one Death Door and another. But the actor was smiling.

"You can go to her now," he said.

Calder saw nothing in the Captain's face that made him think they were being overheard.

"What woman do you mean?"

The actor ran over to the boat, jumping on board in one boyish leap. "The one with the reddish-gold hair," he called.

As the boat glided into the waves and away from the shore, the Captain turned and the gaze he set upon Calder was curious and dark.

*The man was speaking nonsense,* thought Calder. *The Captain will dismiss it.* Calder wanted to believe this, but he was shaking with fear as he unlocked the Door at hand. Calder usually felt sad at the end of the Aisle, when he had to give up the company of the soul in his charge and watch him sail off with the Captain, but now he was glad to disappear through the next Door. Despite the disturbing turn of events, it seemed that Calder's day was done, for the Door opened into his Prayer Room.

※ ※ ※

Because it was his own, Calder's Prayer Room never changed. The only person who ever came into a Fetch Prayer Room other than its Fetch was the Captain. Calder had never asked his fellow Fetches what their Prayer Rooms were like. It seemed too personal a question.

Calder's Prayer Room was small and square. A window opened to the south, the shutters flung wide, and a door to the west stood ajar— this was where the Captain entered. It was always twilight, with the sky still holding a little color from the sun, with a breeze from the Great River and the sound of waves in the distance. The room was empty and the walls, floor, ceiling, all plain white. It was the most peaceful place Calder could imagine, and that was why it was his Prayer Room. But this night he was not at peace.

Great rewards were granted the Fetch. Daily, a Fetch shared the dying soul's joy as it was set free. And once in Heaven, Fetches were awarded an honored position, seated at the left hand of God, like the favored Knights of Camelot.

But the Fetch also suffered hardships. Some, like solitude, came daily. And one hardship was fused to the final reward. In Heaven, the Fetch would become anonymous. No one but his fellow Fetchkind, the

Captain, and God would know the Fetch and his great works. Not one of the souls that the Fetch helped through the Aisle would remember him. Some said it was created thus to banish vanity and pride. Liam, Calder's Master Fetch, told him that it was not really a hardship because once one steps through the Gates of Heaven, acknowledgment is no longer desired. "You may walk the streets of gold and visit any soul you wish, but your past glories will become mythic tales only in the halls of the Fetch." The Scotsman stood a head taller than Calder and looked down at him with a smile. "Be assured, though—it won't matter to you." Liam gave him an affectionate thump on the back. "Trust me. You will be content."

But this enlightenment seemed worlds away. Now Calder waited with eyes closed and head bowed, fearing the Captain had heard and understood the actor's words about Glory. Or even if the Captain hadn't heard, that he would easily read his heart. But when the Captain came to the doorway, he simply stood with the purple sky behind him and listened to Calder recite his Vows as he did every night. The only unusual thing that occurred was that before listening to Calder sing a psalm, the Captain asked him a question.

"Did your last soul fight you?"

It had been years since a soul had tried to escape Calder. Had the Captain asked the same question then? He couldn't remember.

"No, he did not fight me."

Calder was sure that the Captain sensed something had gone wrong—that the actor had suffered needlessly at his death because Calder had been distracted and neglected his duty. Just as there was no place more peaceful than his Prayer Room, there was nothing better than pleasing the Captain. It wasn't that the Captain rewarded him with boons when he'd done well, or threatened him or scolded him if he failed. But an unspoken approval in the Captain's temperate gaze made Calder hunger to better himself, and the nobility in the Captain's bearing reminded Calder of all that was most desirable and gratifying about being a Fetch. The last thing Calder wanted was to displease him.

The Captain asked no more about the actor's death. He listened to Calder sing the Evening Psalm with his usual tranquility.

> *My Captain, my master,*
> *My work this day is done.*
> *Alone in my chamber,*
> *I pray and wait on thee.*
> *Be thou the way before me.*
> *Be thou a banner above me.*
> *Be thou the peace within me.*
> *To God I give praise.*
> *To you I give my life.*
> *To every soul my guiding hand,*
> *To every Door my Key.*
> *Bless me as I cross this night,*
> *My Captain. So shall it be.*

When he was done the Captain said, "As we overcome them, these battles with weakness make us stronger."

Calder froze. *He knows what I have done. That I wished the child to live, that I made the actor suffer, that I was thinking about a mortal woman. That I have never been a proper Fetch.*

"Do you understand?" asked the Captain.

"Yes," said Calder. He thought of feigning confusion but feared he would be caught in the lie. "My thoughts were not on my work," he confessed. "Forgive me."

"It is done." The Captain placed his hand as a blessing on Calder's bowed head, as he did every evening, and was gone.

Calder felt a great guilt for having told his Captain only part of the truth. He hadn't only let his mind wander. He'd coveted a mortal as his Star Fetch. And the greater secret, that he was not worthy of his station, he held back as he always did, a stone of imperfect metal, cold and heavy in his chest. These lies should have been a warning to him that something was not right. But he reasoned that he would forget Glory in time.

That night he meditated on the honor of being a Fetch. To be a witness to the transformation of souls over and over again, a multitude of riches. What could be a more beautiful setting than the Aisle of Unearthing and the shores of the Great River? Glory had been merely one of the many beautiful sights he had beheld along his way. This comforted him.

Until the next morning, when he found her again.

# Three

TIME IS NOT THE SAME EVERYWHERE. On earth it is as constant as the planets pulling against one another in their dance around the sun, but in the Aisle of Unearthing time stops and starts, stretches, and flies forward depending on how many earthlings are dying at any given hour. Time in the Aisle rushes, crawls, or sleeps, though it never goes backwards. In the Aisle, a Fetch always knows what earth year it is when he opens a Death Door, even though for the Fetch it may be 1703 first thing in the morning and 1710 by nightfall, or 1865 for a thousand days. So it was not surprising that several human years had passed in one Fetch night. On earth it was now 1912.

It was only Calder's second Door of the morning, the first having opened beside a sinking ship where he had waited with many of his own kind while the huge vessel split and tilted down into the night sea. As usual, Calder craved the companionship of his fellow Fetches, but felt guilty for it, because of the human suffering. The man Calder had come to escort was one of the first to die, but as the vessel dropped under the waves, nearly a thousand Death Doors opened at once, their brightness flaming like a sun, glowing through the water for miles around.

As Calder stepped through his second Door, the infant that he had seen the day before was now eight years of age. The boy lay in bed in a darkened room, his skin pale and wet, his thin body shaking, his eyes narrowed and fixed on the ceiling. Pain lay thick and heavy over him like chain mail. Calder did not recognize him.

The door across the room opened and four girls walked in, hesitating at the sight of the dying boy. They came to stand in a row at the foot of the bed, the boy's sisters no doubt. They resembled each other, these beautiful young women. Except the one on the end. She was shorter than the others, clearly the youngest, perhaps twelve. Although she would still certainly be considered pretty, she was neither as slender nor as poised as her sisters. And there was a familiar impish glint in her eyes.

Something floated out of the shadows then, the vision of a woman forming in the low lamplight like an apparition. Frightened and incredulous, Calder turned away and then back again. She was no dream. It was his Glory, radiant and unchanged, though the boy was half grown.

He was stunned by the miracle of it. Weak and dizzy, he reached out for help but, finding nothing he could grasp, fell to his knees. Never before had Calder been sent to the same human twice. When a Fetch is summoned to a soul's Death Scene, he is that soul's Fetch for the journey at hand. But a person who has come close to death several times might have been visited by one Fetch at age ten when he almost drowned, another when he was thirty and nearly died of pneumonia, and then another at eighty when he finally entered the Aisle. The parceling out of Doors all depended on who was dying that day and which Fetch was not already in a Death Scene. But there was a deliberate hand in this meeting. It was implausible and shocking but *true:* he and Glory were meant to find each other.

Glory seated herself in a chair beside the child's head, directly across from where Calder was kneeling. Most Fetches chose dying humans as their Squires. Calder's Master Fetch, Liam, had chosen Calder in that way. But Glory had been ordained as Calder's Star Fetch, he was convinced of it. That's why he had been sent to her— it was his second chance. As a Star Fetch, she would be able to see Calder and hear his voice. He would offer her the Key and take her into the Aisle, body and soul. To the boy's family it would seem as if she had vanished. Then Calder would train her and one day, when her Fetch years were done and she had passed the Key on, she would be seated forever at Calder's side in the Afterlife.

Calder was sure Glory was ordained as his Squire. As she stared across the room, her eyes were resting on him.

As the girls bowed their heads in silent prayer, Calder got to his feet. This movement, which should have been invisible, pulled the gaze of the youngest sister. She searched the air beside her brother's bed, peered into the shadows where no moon came through the window, and looked Calder straight in the eye.

The girl made no sound of alarm—she didn't appear in the least surprised, though clearly she could see Calder. And when one of her eyebrows arched, he knew who she was. She had been the little elfish girl in the nursery doorway the day before.

He had never been observed by any child older than four. It was as if this girl were half cat or bird. The older girls were not gifted like their sister, for they prayed silently over folded hands. Calder frowned at the youngest girl and willed her to disregard him, but she continued to stare.

He whispered, "I am not here."

She lowered her face in prayer.

Calder turned to Glory, who gave all her attention to the boy. Calder was surprised to find the boy gazing back at him, as it was rare for humans to see their Fetches before they left their bodies. When they did, they often saw them as angels or in the form of dead friends or relatives. Once in a while a soul, heavy with regret, might glimpse his Fetch and mistake him for a person he had wronged or a minion of the devil come to drag him to Hades.

Calder wondered now in what form he appeared to this dying child. The boy's eyes were narrowed, nearly closed, and glassy with pain, but they focused on him markedly. Calder understood better now than when the boy was an infant what was killing his body. The child's blood was diseased so that it could not stop once it had broken from a vein—whether it was a cut on the finger from a tin soldier or a tear deep inside him from a tumble down a grass lawn, the blood flow would not stop and in its path it would leave swelling, deformity, and great pain.

Calder felt empathy for the boy, but there was an even more important reason he had been sent to this Scene. He watched Glory stroke the boy's hand and took a step closer to the bed.

"Do you hear me?" he whispered to her.

Glory sat up and wrapped her arms about herself as if she were cold.

"Don't be afraid," said Calder. Glory was staring at him, or at least at his shoulder, so Calder moved to the left until his face was directly in her line of sight. Her eyes flickered, he was sure of it, but when the boy groaned she looked away.

The air began to move—the boy would soon decide whether to live or die. Though he was still completely imprisoned in his body, the boy lifted the hand closest to Calder and reached out for him, another thing that rarely happened. His pale fingers hovered over the quilted coverlet, quivering inches from Calder's own hand.

"I want to die," the boy whispered.

Glory hurried the girls out of the room. The three older sisters left quickly, but the youngest paused in the doorway and gave Calder a warning glare before she slipped out of view. Glory took a wet cloth from a bowl under the lamp beside her and lay it across the boy's forehead.

The choice had been made, yet the spirit wind gusted around the bed. There was no sudden calm.

"Don't," Calder whispered to the child. And when he saw a flash of surprise in the boy's face, he knew he had been heard. The thin arm lowered to the bed again, but the boy's attention stayed on his Fetch.

Calder leaned close to his face. "She wants you to live." He didn't realize at first what he was asking.

"Help me," the boy whispered, and this time Calder could hear the horror of it. The child's voice was hoarse from screaming—his pain must come in waves and this was only a respite. *He'll be well soon,* Calder told himself, *and enjoy a long life.*

The Key hanging at Calder's chest vibrated a silent caution, but he ignored it.

"Live for her," Calder whispered, and the air lashed at him from all sides.

The boy's eyes closed and he rolled onto his side, his back to Calder. Then the air dropped into a sudden stillness. The curtains at the closed windows gently fluttered and the bed gave one tiny shudder as if they had been part of the spectral tempest, although it was impossible for a spirit wind to actually disturb the world of the earthbound.

And yet today impossible things kept happening.

Calder was shocked by what he had done. The boy would live, but he had been forced to stay. And to Calder's dread, the boy moaned and began again to weep. Glory lifted his head and shoulders in her arms, closed her eyes, and softly rocked him until he relaxed.

"My lady," Calder whispered. "Show me that you hear my words."

Glory's eyes opened suddenly. She had heard, Calder was certain. He knelt beside the bed across from her so she looked into his face.

Calder's Key began to shake and jerk on the chain about his neck. He tried to reach out and touch her, but he was pulled back as if he were swimming against the current of a river. The Door was summoning him too soon. She had gazed into his eyes, heard his voice, but he had still to give her the Key. He was horrified that the Aisle was betraying him. God had given him this woman as his Squire. She was a Star Fetch, he knew it.

But Calder did not trust God now as he was being pulled away from Glory. He had been waiting for this woman since the beginning of time, and he deserved to be with her. A wicked thought flew through his mind—he wished it had been Glory and not her charge who was dying—it would've made the passing of the Key simple.

The Fetch Key slid up Calder's chest and over his shoulder, levitating on its tether, pointing over Calder's back straight to the Fetch Door behind him as if a spectral whirlpool was sucking at it from the other side. The Door stood, invisible to the earthbound but all too solid for Calder, huge and silent between the bed and the window.

"I know you hear me," said Calder. Glory wasn't staring through him—she saw him. She had to. "And I know you can see me." He could read her heart. She wanted nothing more than for the boy to survive and be well. She was the child's guardian and once she had saved him, she would be released from her torment. He reached across the bed again and held out his hand to her. "The boy will live. You can leave him now."

A tear ran down Glory's cheek. Her stare was fixed somewhere beyond Calder's face, yet she reached up with one hand just as the pull of the Door dragged him backwards, out of her reach. Instead of touching his fingers, her hand grasped the coverlet and pulled it closer around the child.

Calder pushed away from the Death Door, but he was overpowered. Drawn backwards in a rush, he stood pressed to the Door, shaking with frustration, watching Glory whisper to the boy. Calder put his Key in the lock, and as he crossed the threshold, sick with disappointment, the Door slammed. No final glimpse of her, but he did catch one word:

"Alexis."

# FOUR

No Prayer Room was waiting.

Calder stepped through into a new Death Scene. On earth it was 1916. He could see that it was winter by the frost on the windowpane before him. He was in a small and dimly lit room. In the street below a scene played as if in another world. Horses and carts, an occasional motorcar, heavily coated people, hurried along. Calder appeared to be alone. He found a sink, a commode, and bathtub piled with dirty laundry, but no dying human. He had forced the boy's choice to live and thrown off his Death Door and now he was stranded. That he had saved the boy and lost Glory weighed heavy on his spirit.

A hand reached out and gripped at the side of the bathtub. What had appeared to be a pile of clothes was in truth a person. Calder leaned in to watch as the man tried to roll onto his side. He was large, with a long dark beard and wild black hair in great abundance. Calder saw now that his clothes were soiled but expensive—they had been stained and ripped in some recent adventure. The man slid onto his back, disoriented, most likely drunk. He reached out with both hands now, trying to pull himself up but only sliding around in the porcelain tub. His hands were scarred and filthy, his breathing labored. He kicked out his feet, fighting to sit up, but with a sharp laugh he fell again to the bottom. His eyes were fervid, piercing, like a wild dog's.

The man vomited and, lacking the strength to sit up or roll over, he choked. In the midst of his struggling and gagging, it seemed to Calder as if he began to laugh again. The air around them twisted in a crooked funnel. He watched the man, wanting to feel sympathy but still only able to feel miserable about Glory. The spectral air dropped so suddenly, Calder nearly fell into the tub himself. The wild eyes were fixed now on the stained ceiling.

"That's funny." The man's soul sat up halfway out of the corpse and grinned at Calder. "I thought I would be murdered." The dead man's soul laughed loudly. "No one will believe it was drink that did it." Then he regarded his Fetch more deeply. "A hand up, friend?" He reached for Calder, who lifted him away from his body. "Where did you come from?" the man asked. In spirit he was just as he had been in life—the same clothes, unwashed, long black hair and beard flying and unkempt, his eyes blazing.

"I'm your Fetch," said Calder. "I've come to escort you."

"Ah." The man appraised him, head to foot, and was probably unimpressed—he had clothed Calder just as himself, in a dirty coat and muddy boots. When the man caught sight of the body, he sighed with no apparent horror. "Pity," he said. "I quite enjoyed the flesh." Then he spun toward Calder with an alarming excitement. "But now I will know everything!" He clapped his hands together. "Lead on!"

# FOUR

Enormous double doors carved with roses and inlaid with ivory stood in the recently solid bathroom wall. Calder took the man's hand with his right and unlocked the Aisle Door with his left. The corridor that greeted them was carpeted in white satin and smelled of sweet tobacco and spiced wine. Warm air washed in around them as Calder locked them into the Aisle.

"Beautiful," said the man. "What is this called?"

Calder had been asked thousands of questions: *Is this Heaven? Where are the saints? Will I grow wings? Why did God not come to greet me?* But no one had ever asked him the name of the passage.

"This is the Aisle of Unearthing," said Calder.

"Is it?" The man grinned, his keen eyes darting about until the Theatre appeared. On the left, the walls that hung with flickering candles became a puppet theater. There, between the small velvet curtains and thin wood painted with gold cherubim, two puppets battled each other in high-pitched frenzy. Both dolls wore dark robes, wild black wigs, and long black whiskers. Both of them had huge dark eyes and grinning painted mouths. One used a wooden cross as a weapon, the other a toy bottle of wine. They chased each other back and forth across the tiny space, screeching and laughing.

The man stopped and watched the show, letting go of Calder's hand to applaud them. The puppet with the cross was being beaten down now by the bottle of wine. He sagged over the edge of the stage and dropped his cross. The puppet with the bottle pushed this fallen man away behind the tiny proscenium and started dancing a celebratory jig.

The man with the wild eyes laughed until the second puppet also fell as if dead. "The little idiot." Then he rubbed his palms together and started again to walk. "This is a strange corridor, is it not?" he asked. "What's on the other side of these walls?"

Calder didn't know how to explain that. Nothing and anything. It wasn't a physical hallway, like the sort that are built into castles or court-houses.

"Is there day and night here?" asked the man. "I'd like to see outside."

Calder followed him until they found the Feast. The wall on the right changed into large windows that blew open to reveal an enormous room. In it there dined every station of folk from peasants in rags to royalty in diamonds, sitting intermingled and chatting away as if this were completely natural. Calder rarely studied these vignettes—they were for the soul that was crossing, after all, not for the Fetch. But in this scene Calder caught a glimpse of something that unnerved him. At the far end of the enormous table, which stretched away from the Aisle in an impossible way, seven figures wearing white sat together—a man with a short beard, a woman with reddish-gold hair whose face was turned away, four young women too far away to see clearly, and a boy. Calder tried to get a better look, but other guests at the table kept leaning forward and blocking his view.

The man was pleased with this Feast and he winked at Calder as they left it. "I knew every soul at that meal," he told him. "Do we eat and drink in Heaven?" he asked.

Calder was weary from listening to these questions. He was too exhausted to answer.

When the Gallery appeared, the man slowed his pace. The wall on the left was covered with pieces of paper that had been pinned up but fluttered like angry locusts. The man read a few, then tried to stop them from flapping. Calder saw that many were notes, all the same. In Russian they were handwritten, *My dear and valued friend, do this for me.* And there were many copies of the same strange drawing—a huge bearded man with wild black hair holding on his lap a naked woman wearing a crown of jewels like a queen. The man turned his back on the wall, tears running down his face, muttering something Calder could not understand.

Finally the man moved on, his boots dragging. He seemed, at least for the moment, done with questions. On the right of the Aisle the walls now opened in a great arch that revealed a huge garden. Flowers, fruit trees, trellises draped with hanging blossoms and grape vines filled the space around a small pond bobbing with water lilies and busy with fish.

The man put a hand to his heart at this sight and smiled. "It wasn't all sin," he told Calder. "I did God's work, as well." His eyes burned with a dark twinkle. "I was a healer." He leaned closer to Calder. "I saved the life of the tsarevich, Alexis."

The man began again to walk through the Aisle, but Calder was too surprised to follow.

"Did you say Alexis?"

"Matushka would trust no one but me," said the man.

"Who is Alexis?" Calder demanded.

The man let out a booming laugh. "Son of the tsar. Surely you know the rulers of Russia."

The child who had asked to die, he spoke Russian. Seeing Glory twice had undone Calder—this new miracle, if it was a miracle, was bewildering. He couldn't put words together quickly enough. He stared at the man and could not move.

The man smiled at him curiously. "Are angels so ignorant of the world?"

"Alexis has four sisters," Calder told him. "He was bleeding on the inside."

"Yes." A startled expression came over the man, as if he believed that the power had shifted and this angel was now at his mercy.

"What is his name?" Calder asked.

"A strange question coming from you, who I had greatly hoped saw the fall of every sparrow." He shook his head at Calder. "Romanov."

Calder repeated the word in his head, pictured it written: *Alexis Romanov.*

"Nicholas the Second, one of the most powerful men in the world—he and his wife, Alexandra, would kiss my hand and kneel in prayer with me. Why, do you think?"

Calder had no answer—he was still hearing the boy's name in his head. Alexis Romanov, son of the tsar, and Glory was his governess.

"I saved the heir to the Russian throne." The man waited for Calder's reaction, but when none followed he asked, "Does that cancel my sins?"

A new thought shook Calder: Could this be a test sent to him by the Captain?

"I said, am I forgiven, guide?"

The Captain wouldn't trick a Fetch—Calder had never even heard a rumor of this in more than three hundred years. And if it wasn't a test, it must be a sign.

"Speak to me, angel," the man demanded. "Am I so wretched that you cannot bear the sight of me?"

Calder tried to speak calmly, but his voice was alive with fear. "You served the tsar as a priest?" asked Calder.

"And a healer," said the man, "and a prophet. The child's bleeding would stop at the touch of my hand or the sound of my voice. I predicted the boy's birth and the Great War."

"And you were welcome in the House of Romanov?" asked Calder.

"I came and went like family," bragged the man. "Everyone in St. Petersburg knew me. I ate with generals and kings," he said, "and called on their daughters. And sometimes their wives!" He gave a great laugh, but was again displeased with Calder's silence. "Why do you leave me here?" He gestured farther down the Aisle. "I want to see more."

A strange and terrible idea came into Calder's mind, so peculiar that he couldn't have created it himself. "Would you like to see the spirit world?" asked Calder.

The man pointed an accusing finger at him. "I knew there was more you were keeping from me." He broke into a grin. "Of course. Show me."

"It would mean keeping Heaven waiting a little longer."

For the first time the man appeared wary. "This isn't a trick to send me to hell, is it?"

"There is no hell," said Calder.

This was not altogether true. Humans could create hell on earth—
it was part of free will. And there was the Cell: if a soul could not forgive himself he had to stay in the Cell until he did, no matter how long
it took. And then there was the place between death and the Aisle.
Each time a Death Door opened, there was a vulnerable place in the
fabric of the universe laid bare. Once in a great while a disturbed soul
would escape its Fetch and fly through this tear between worlds, into
the Land of Lost Souls, a place between earth and the Aisle, where a
Lost Soul could see the living but commune with none of them. Calder
had never let a soul get away, but one Fetch Calder had spoken to had
lost three souls. Each time he had eventually chased them down and
brought them back into the Aisle, but he said that as he searched for his
strays he witnessed many wandering Lost Souls—some were petrified,
some confused or angry, and a few were playing. It was hell to most,
but not all. As Calder now spoke to the man, he tried to picture this last
peculiar scene, Lost Souls frolicking just outside of life.

"I will let you have three earth nights of freedom in the spirit world,"
said Calder, "and I will have three nights on earth."

"A bargain?" Suspicion darkened his piercing eyes, but he held his
hand out as if accepting the terms.

"A bargain," Calder agreed.

He took the man's hand and guided them back the way they had
come. But he worried when as they moved back through the Aisle
everything around them wavered like a reflection in water. Calder had
never before tried to go the wrong way through the Aisle. The Garden

darkened with a sky of black clouds; the notes and drawings from the Gallery tore from the wall and blew past their feet like white leaves. A twisting wind came at them from the far end of the corridor.

"Where are we going?" asked the man.

"Back to your body," said Calder, trying to sound matter-of-fact.

"Will I need my body?"

"No," said Calder. "I will."

# PART II

## THE LAND OF THE LIVING

# Five

*If I am not meant to do the thing I now do*, Calder told himself, *I will not succeed.*

The bearded man watched Calder curiously as they passed the place where the Feast was no more. Oddly, the space was dark and quiet, huge and hollow. Only the first few feet of the hall were visible—the floor where the great table had stood was empty and vanished into black shadows as if the hall were under water. The sight made Calder's heart shrink.

To find his chosen Squire he was being forced to break his Vows. But he was sure that, unlike the Fallen Three, he would be forgiven. God meant for him to gift Glory with his Fetch Key.

The Legend of the Fallen Three was the story of how the Fetch Vows had been broken only three times since the days of Eden. The first to fall was a Fetch called Alphaeta, who, unsatisfied with what Heaven and earth could offer, abandoned his duties and tried to sail down the Great River instead of across it. They say the infamy of this sin thundered through the heavens, tearing rain clouds open in great black mouths, rumbling out of the earth in lava like blood, cracking open sea floors in boiling waves, and raising the waters of the Great Flood.

The second was called Beolucifer, who lusted after power and challenged God for his throne. This arrogance sent a bolt of lightning down from Heaven as bright as day, as thick as a river, so hot and strong that it shook the earth below and toppled the ziggurat at Babel.

The third, the body thief, was called Thresham. He longed to be human again and stole the body of a dying man, leaving the soul deserted in the Land of Lost Souls, that place between earth and the Aisle. Thresham walked many miles on earth, fooling the mortals, but his transgression began a sick and subtle vibration that tapped and creaked through the Aisle, rippled the waters of the Great River, and rattled the Gates of Heaven. It trembled silently down through the air, shriveling the crops of the earth, rotting and uprooting trees, dropping birds in midflight, and quietly grew in Thresham's stolen flesh as the first of the Black Plague.

Calder had heard the tale of Thresham, but he reasoned that what he was about to do would not be theft and it would not be forever.

Calder had heard the Legend of the Fallen Three many times over the years, on those occasions when a Death Door had opened onto a scene where more than one human lay dying. Standing in a burning building, hovering beside beds in a hospital ward, waiting for the victims of a train wreck to choose life or death, Calder could listen to the Fetch beside him and whisper back. Though he was saddened by the mortal tragedy, Calder thrived on the fellowship. He listened greedily to these stories and he believed them.

Now as Calder and the wild-haired man passed the place where the Theatre had been, the small puppet stage stood empty, with an audible draft breathing out of it, making the little velvet curtains hover toward them as they passed.

The man looked behind him as if he heard a voice calling his name. The corridor wavered and a wind blew around them, cold, damp, and smelling of ash. Calder had never been afraid of anything in the Aisle before, but now he was deeply relieved to see the Death Door up ahead. It was as the man's soul had pictured it before, carved with blossoms and inlaid with ivory and mother-of-pearl.

"Are you sure Heaven wants us to do this?" the man asked, his hair flying about his face.

"I have never seen anyone harmed by the Aisle," Calder told him. "Don't be afraid."

But *Calder* was afraid. His fear should have been enough to dissuade him, yet he took the Key on its chain and held it at the ready as they approached the Door. Something inside him was waking, as if he had, for the first time since his death, regained his sight.

The wind made the walls around them quake. They leaned into the gale, heads pointed toward the Door. The man held tight to Calder's sleeve. An odd groan, like the grinding of huge stones, began to grow at their backs.

Calder grasped the Door's handle. He let the man hold him about the waist as he used both hands to unlock the Door. They burst out of the storming Aisle and into the small bathroom where the man's body still lay in the tub. The Death Door slammed shut.

* * *

Calder did not know at first what damage his actions had caused in Heaven. Or what this disturbance would mean to the Land of the Living. But he and the man, and every person in St. Petersburg, felt the first wave of trouble because it was a real wave—a wave of sound so low, it was felt more than heard. No machine recorded it for historians to later note, but every living thing and every man-made structure was rocked for a mile in every direction of the spot where Calder had broken into the Land of the Living. Every human in the city, for one ominous moment, stopped and had the same thought: *Something is not right with the world.*

The man's soul wheeled about. "What was that sound?" he asked.

Calder could not bear the idea that some warning from the Aisle had escaped into the Land of the Living, so he denied it.

"Only thunder," he said.

The man then regarded the body lying in the tub and asked, "What must I do?"

"First," said Calder, "tell me your name."

"Grigori Rasputin."

"Where are we?" Calder asked. "Is this where you live?"

The man gave Calder a reproachful glare, as if he was about to change his mind. "Can I trust you?" he asked.

This shocked Calder—he was a Fetch, after all. No creature was more devoted to duty and honor. "Yes, of course."

"How will I get back to Heaven?" Rasputin wanted to know.

"In the spirit world you can go anywhere on earth, see and hear everything. Come and find me after three nights."

They had an accord, but now Calder would have to do the thing.

Fetches were of one mind about how Thresham stole a human body. You had to fall into the flesh as you lifted the spirit out.

*If this doesn't work,* Calder thought, *I will chase him down in the Land of Lost Souls like the other Fetches do when a soul escapes.* The body, with rumpled clothes and dirty face, lay waiting in the bathtub. The eyes, even in death, appeared wild and burning.

Now that he was about to take the body, Calder thought of a hundred questions he should ask Rasputin before he let him go. He had no idea where the Romanov palace stood. Did Rasputin have a wife and children? But Calder was afraid to ask too many questions, lest the man have second thoughts.

"Do it now while I am still willing," said Rasputin.

According to Fetch gossip, Thresham had kept his Key with him, passing it from his spectral hand to his human hand as he took the flesh. The rumor came from a mysterious passage in the Ninth Psalm: *Thus palm to palm the Key from light to metal passed.* Calder lifted the chain over his head and held the Key tight in his fist.

"Take my hand and go back into your flesh," said Calder. "I will trade places with you and set you free."

Rasputin grasped Calder's hand with the Key in it. Taking one last look at the body, the man shuffled his spectral feet up against the edge of the tub and let himself fall backwards, disappearing into the corpse. Calder held Rasputin's hand, the Key between their palms, and just as the wild eyes of the corpse began to blink, he jerked Rasputin back out of his flesh and flung himself into the body instead. It was like wrestling with a snake made of water—something kept trying to suffocate him, but dissolved to nothing in his grip. Next moment, everything was quiet. He felt heavy and solid, as unmovable as a gravestone. And blind. Everything was white. Above him he heard Rasputin laughing. The sound ended abruptly, as if the candle of his voice had been snuffed out.

Calder panicked, feeling that the body was dead and he was trapped in it. He cried out, a foreign sound that rippled away through the air in tiny waves. He could hear with the new ears—that was a good sign. All sorts of sounds—distant voices and motorcars in the street, his human heartbeat—quivered in his ears of flesh, tickling like insects. When he felt his own hands clutching at his throat and chest, he knew with relief that Rasputin's body was his to control. He blinked the dry eyelids and was astonished at his vision of the human world through Rasputin's eyes. It took a moment to come, like objects revealed through a thick fog.

Soon everything was in sharp detail: the cracks in the stained ceiling, the peeling wallpaper, the colors pale compared to those of the Aisle. Here the sky was gray, the walls a faded blue, the fabric of his sleeve as he lifted his arm and stared at it a dull, weak black. He studied his hand and found there was no replicating the tones, the pinks and golds and browns, of human skin. This was the one family of colors that was not better in Heaven.

Calder did not see Rasputin, as it seemed he had already flown into the Land of Lost Souls. Even before Calder tried to rise, he felt the sickening rhythm of the globe, the speed and spin of it, the pull of the other planets, and the power of the distant sun driving them all. It made him dizzy, but he sat up, forcing himself out of the tub in his first fight with gravity in three centuries.

He opened his fist and found the Key. It looked just as it had in the Aisle, the same size and shape of teeth, only on earth it was formed from dull metal. And the grip was in that same familiar shape. When Calder was first offered the Fetch Key, it was in the hand of Liam, his Master Fetch, and the grip was formed from two leaves, the one on the left had a tiny caterpillar carved on it, the one on the right had two halves of a broken cocoon. But with every new Squire the Key changes, and Calder was disappointed to see its beautiful leaves twist and tangle into a kind of knot as it was passed to him. And here was that same Key, only now solid and heavy as stone. The thin chain was solid, too. Calder slipped it over his head.

He rubbed the coarse hairs of Rasputin's beard, *his* beard now, between his large fingers. He tried taking in a breath of air, marveling at the way the elements were altered in the lungs. He'd forgotten the feel of it. He could smell the damp towel that hung on the wall and his own sweaty clothes and something unpleasant. His mouth tasted sour and his throat burned. Calder spat into the small sink and rubbed his dry eyes.

He took a step toward the door, then fell onto one knee, grappling with the laws of physics. His skin, bones, muscles, could feel everything with astonishing exactness: the hard floor under him, the smooth coolness of the sink as he gripped it to stand.

Everything went black for a moment and when he held his hands before his eyes, the small, grimy fingers that appeared were those of a child. Calder was crouching alone in the dark, so cold he felt as if he'd become something other than a boy. His nose was numb, his fingers stiff, each breath a little ghost in the air. If he could just warm himself, he thought he could feel human again. From the underbelly of the bridge where he huddled, a curtain of cloud veiled the moon so that it hung in the sky as dim as a single lantern.

*I won't die tonight,* he found himself thinking. *Because tomorrow might be the day she comes for me.*

❊ ❊ ❊

When the vision left him, Calder was back in Rasputin's bathroom staring at his new, thick fingers.

*Steady,* he told himself. *It's the shock of being in the flesh.*

He ran his hands over his body, his limbs and neck. He seemed whole and unharmed. But noticing that his coat was covered in sick, Calder took it off and left it in the bathtub. He tried to walk to the door again and this time kept his footing.

*Surely,* Calder thought, *this is not the kind of home in which one would expect to find a favorite of the tsar.* The bathroom opened onto a stark and dreary den. Possibly something monklike in Rasputin's nature drew him to such humble surroundings. He saw now through an uncurtained window that he was on an upper floor of an apartment building overlooking a city street.

The common room was plain with a wooden table and chairs, a dingy kitchen area in one corner, a cabinet, dark and scratched, and, most unnerving, a pair of ladies' gloves on the dining table. It filled Calder with dread that Rasputin had a wife who at any moment might appear, call him by a pet name, and expect to be addressed in some mysterious language of common knowledge. Calder wanted to wash and change his soiled clothes for his first meeting with Glory, but he would have to hurry.

He was distracted by all the new sensations—every hair on his arms and the backs of his hands sending a message through his nerves, the texture of his fingertips, the hinges of his joints, knees, and ankles, shifting as he moved. He scrubbed Rasputin's body and hair with cold water and soap and cleaned his teeth. He found two small bedrooms, his and hers, it seemed. From Rasputin's wardrobe he took fresh clothes.

While searching for a comb in the bureau, Calder found great scores of paper money, some folded, some crumpled into balls, and several gold coins, mixed in with bits of string and theater tickets, as if money were a clutter of trash. Calder also found dozens of small notes printed on slips of paper no bigger than the palm of his hand. Each read the same: *My dear and valued friend, do this for me*. It was the message that had filled Rasputin's Gallery in the Aisle of Unearthing.

Calder found a comb in the bathroom and tried to pull it through his wet mane, giving up when a tooth of the comb broke and left a tiny horn of ivory stuck in his hair above the temple. He studied Rasputin's face in the bathroom mirror, a strange rendering of a bewildered Neptune.

As he opened the apartment door to leave, three people were waiting: a young man, holding a bottle of wine wrapped like a present, who wanted a role in an upcoming opera. A young woman dressed in a low-cut gown and wearing a ruffled cape said she had come for her appointed healing, though she appeared perfectly healthy. And an old gentleman clutching a Bible demanded to know what Rasputin had been teaching his wife.

Calder was so disturbed by the cacophony of their entreaties, he said, "Be still." The heavy tongue and arching palate, the vibration of his voice tingling through his teeth, resonating in his head, were startling. The three humans waited silently for instructions. Calder couldn't face pretending to be Rasputin for them. Before escaping down the stairs, he called, "Come back next week!"

Calder could feel them staring at his back as he descended, and to them his tentative step would be taken for intoxication rather than a Fetch learning the mechanics of walking. He held the banister tightly until he came out into a small courtyard, where he was greeted by two uniformed men he took to be peacekeepers. Though they both bowed and tipped their hats to him, their expressions were less respectful.

A few people waited for Rasputin in the courtyard. A man in a dark coat and hat ran forward, fighting to pull something out of his pocket. "M-my daughter—" he stammered. A gust of icy wind lifted the man's hat from his head and it rolled out of the courtyard and into the street as if not wanting to witness the rest of the scene.

"None of that!" Both police officers lunged at the man as he finally drew a large silver gun from his coat.

"You don't know what he did!" the man pleaded. "She's only sixteen." The weapon was wrenched from his fingers and he was dragged away, his thin hair standing up in the breeze. Calder felt guilty and disgusted, though, of course, he had no memory of Rasputin's sins.

Now a young woman approached cradling a bundle in her arms. "Please, Father, give my child the blessing."

Calder looked beyond the woman's shoulder at a familiar sight, but one that made a chill run through his unfamiliar flesh. He was about to see how his actions had thrown Heaven and earth out of balance, for the Legend of the Fallen Three was a lie.

Before Calder, the Vows of the Fetch had remained unbroken for thousands of years.

# Six

CALDER WATCHED, MESMERIZED by what was invisible to the humans in the courtyard. The shape of a golden door shimmered into place behind the young mother. The Door was visible only to him, Calder suspected, because it was a Fetch and not a human soul that was peering out through Rasputin's eyes. The woman, holding her infant to her chest, had stopped a few paces away from Calder, confused by his expression.

The figure that stepped through the golden Door did not appear as vivid as he would have been in the Aisle; instead, the Fetch glowed as faintly as a yellow rose in a midnight garden. The Death Door blew open wider and Calder was blasted by a gust of spectral wind as if Heaven were furious with him.

The Fetch was called Auben—Calder had seen him several times, most recently that very morning at the sinking of a ship just before he had been sent to Glory. Auben recognized Calder as well and, astonished by the sight of him in the Land of the Living without a Door, seemed to grow pale. The disguise of Rasputin's body fooled humans, but apparently not a fellow Fetch.

The woman holding the baby took another step toward Calder. "Father Grigori, please," she said. "Help me."

Auben slipped in front of her, engulfing the young woman in golden light, then stepped away with the baby's soul nestled in his arms. Calder was fascinated to watch, from his new earthly vantage point, the act of an infant passing into the Aisle of Unearthing. But to his horror, the infant began to cry—an unheard of event.

Calder rushed forward, hoping to help somehow, but the Fetch wind held him back as it had tried to do when he and Rasputin fought their way backwards up the Aisle.

Auben raised a hand in warning: *Keep away*. He stepped through the doorway, and with one last howl of wind, the Death Door slammed shut and was gone. Calder stood mute and shivering, breathing the delicate, floral scent of home that still hung in the air. He hoped it was not his fall from Heaven that had caused the child to cry, but he had seen the hardness in Auben's eyes.

"Heal my baby," the woman said, and offered Calder the small bundle.

"It's too late," he told her. "Your son is dead."

The pain on the earthly side of the Death Door frightened Calder; like a coward, he lowered his head and hurried out of the courtyard, away from the sound of the woman's anguish. He hoped the bustle of the street would mask her keening, but it pierced through the growl of engines and the percussion of harness and hoof. The cry dragged from his memory a scene so piteous, he stopped on the pavement.

Calder was a child again, weeping into his hands. He did not recall the loss that had wounded him, but he felt as if the only person he might have run to for comfort was the friend for whom he mourned. Being a Fetch did nothing to soothe his pain at this memory. And it did not shield him from what he beheld as he looked up at the stream of mortal faces that passed by him along the busy street. He perceived in every countenance a dreadful sorrow buried and unresolved.

Calder counted thirty heartbeats before he felt strong enough to walk. He concentrated on the new sensations of the physical world. He could feel the folds of his clothes under his arms and creasing at the back of his knees with each step. He was unnerved by the pivoting of the orbs of his eyes and felt like a prisoner in Rasputin's skeleton, but he kept walking.

Mortals rushed about, some alone with their coats pulled up to their hats, others in pairs speaking quickly. Many wore military uniforms and carried rifles over their shoulders. The air smelled of chimney smoke, horses, and the strange scent of engines. Motorcar wheels sprayed and churned at the snow and mud; carts rattled through the slush. Calder missed the Aisle so deeply, he began to tremble.

But then he remembered why he had come: to give Glory the Key and take her into the Aisle. And he would find her even if he had to knock on every door in Russia. Though this was more easily said than done. He'd forgotten what time and space truly meant. How long did it take a mortal man to walk a mile?

This idea made him aware again of the whirling planet, the relentless movement of time on earth. Every second, the daylight crept a tiny bit farther across the ground, shadows curled in and then stretched out, and the night slid in behind the day like a trailing veil. There was no stopping it. The longer he stood still, the less daylight he had to find her. The shadows already grew long.

Calder addressed the human closest to him, a man in a gray over-coat who was stepping into a long black car.

"Sir, would you help me?"

The man smiled. "Father Grigori," he said. "What can I do for you?"

Calder drew back when he realized the man had met Rasputin before, but he managed to say, "Will you tell me the way to the Romanov palace?"

"He has his own car." This came from a small woman Calder could now see waiting in the front seat of the vehicle.

"He can't drive," the man whispered to her. "He's drunk."

"He can take the train," the woman snapped back.

But to Calder's relief the man opened the back door of the car and offered to take him to what the man called Selo.

There were three wrapped presents and a bottle of wine on the back seat. The man's wife refused to acknowledge Calder, but the man in the gray coat grinned at him several times as they drove, asking after his health and talking about the weather. Calder was nervous about playing the role of Rasputin. He smiled politely but made sure he appeared captivated by the view from the window.

The buildings of St. Petersburg were grand and straight, weath-ered, but strong. Fringes of ice like lace hung from the moldings and statuary. The country must have been at war, for soldiers marched the streets and stood on corners, watching the civilians as if they were the enemy.

Calder's heart began to pound as he realized he might see Glory in only a few minutes. He tried to imagine what he would say, but when he did his throat tightened up. He would have to tell her the truth no matter how strange it sounded. But he knew what he would say when he passed the Key to her—he would repeat the words that Liam had said to him: *I pass this Key to you, my Chosen One.* And he knew how to summon a Death Door—Liam had taught him. If a Fetch found himself either in a Death Scene or in his Prayer Room without a Door into the Aisle, he only had to hold his Key and summon one: *Beyond this Door, Heaven waits.* Calder imagined standing before Glory in an empty nursery, lowering the Key's chain over her head, taking the Key in their hands together, and a Door appearing in the wall.

Calder watched the train tracks running along the side of the road, sometimes lifting up on trellises where the earth dipped into a small valley, and then leading them right to the corner of the palace walls.

Calder stepped out of the car and gazed in wonder at the high hedges. Through the metal lace of the black and gold gate, he could see the palace grounds—a frosted lake, vast buildings shining blue and white, pristine and ornate, glorious gardens worthy of Elysium, all bedecked in snow.

To his surprise, he was not questioned or hindered by the sentries. On the contrary, the guards nodded with respect and not only admitted him but called for a car, the driver of which opened the door for him with a bow. Perhaps Rasputin truly had performed miracles. He was driven past the small lake of ice, and up a narrow bridge beyond which enormous buildings gleamed. Their pillars and spires, their arched windows like the towers of eastern rajas covered in gold and topped with crosses, made the palace look like a bejeweled ornament.

Calder was driven to one of the smaller buildings and welcomed into a dark vestibule.

"Where are the children?" he asked. He reasoned the governess would not be far from the children.

"Kindly wait in the sitting room," said the servant who had opened the door, "if you please." But instead of showing him the way, the servant went out the front door and left him alone. Rasputin would know which door he was meant to open, but Calder wandered down the corridor, shaking with anxiety. The hallway was lined with tapestries, cushioned chairs, and polished tables. He was relieved to hear the sounds of children laughing—he was close now.

Up ahead double doors stood open and Calder peered in at a library. Large windows faced one of the white, empty gardens, a log crackled in the fireplace, books, dark and leather-bound, lined the walls and stood in disarray on almost every surface—in stacks beside the sofa and chairs, under the lamp stands, and across the enormous table that spanned almost the entire west wall. Electric lights glowed from the chandelier and a huge Indian carpet in reds and golds lay under the sofa before the fire.

There were three females in the room, but none of them Glory. The sisters of Alexis sat at the table with pens, paper, and opened books. All three were as beautiful as they had been when Calder had seen them at the foot of their brother's bed, but they were older now. Their honey-brown hair had been pulled into bows at the backs of their necks. Each wore a pale blue frock of simple design that gathered at the waist under a broad navy sash, the sleeves, lined in buttons, modestly covering the arms down to the wrists. Their faces were sweet and uncomplicated—the eldest was perhaps twenty, the youngest sixteen. But she wasn't really the youngest. Calder wondered where the elfish one was hiding.

A boy sat on the floor with his back to the door, no doubt Alexis—Calder recognized him even from behind, a particular shade of dark blond hair. He wore a sailor suit in white with navy blue stripes and trim. *But he must be nearly twelve*, thought Calder. *How many years have passed between when I refused to let the boy die and meeting Rasputin? Do such children still need a governess?*

The curtains on the far side of the room flew over the globe that was mounted in a large stand beside the window and a fourth girl appeared, the youngest sister, now perhaps fifteen. She was much like her sisters, and yet nothing like them. Here was the same color of hair, but hers was escaping from its bow in little wild tendrils, like a sweater coming unknit. Here was the same dress, but the cuffs had been unbuttoned and the sleeves rolled up past the elbows. The hem was wrinkled and her stockings smudged with what might have been ashes. And here was not the same face. Well, he could not say she didn't look like her sisters: certainly there was a resemblance, but this girl had a mischievous smile, a cheek with an unruly blush, and the arched brows of a sprite.

After making her dramatic entrance from behind the curtain, she performed a manic and silent comedy in which she greeted and flirted with an invisible hero in the empty chair that sat in front of the window. She donned the curtain sash around her head as a scarf and accepted a discarded wad of paper as a flower from her make-believe lover. Her movements were rushed, a wild dance of hand gestures and acrobatics. Soon an invisible villain entered and the girl fought him off with a fire poker. Calder finally deduced that she was imitating a moving picture. He had seen only glimpses of two or three himself.

Her brother laughed loudly as she finished the kill and threw victory kisses. One of the sisters, the oldest, looked up from her book and saw Calder in the doorway. She smiled and nodded politely.

"Good afternoon, Father Grigori."

Calder nodded in what he hoped was a sage manner.

The boy swiveled around with a gleeful expression, but when he met eyes with Calder his face fell. He did not address Calder as Rasputin. He didn't speak to him at all.

"Good afternoon," another of the older girls echoed.

The boy turned away, his back stiff. The youngest girl stopped taking bows and looked to the doorway.

"Father Grigori?" she asked. "Where?"

The moment this youngest girl looked him in the eyes, Calder felt afraid and moved back into the corridor, out of view.

He heard her ask her sisters, "Who was that?"

# Seven

Calder was startled by his own reflection in a gilded mirror. He had Rasputin's face, his eyes, his body, his absurd mane of hair . . . of course Glory and the children would assume he was Rasputin. Humans relied on sight to tell each other apart; on earth people didn't go around transforming from angels to warriors to monks every time a door opened. It made perfect sense that they would believe their eyes.

Yet Calder's confidence was shaken now. He wanted to go back in the library and ask where to find Glory . . . but he was afraid. Glory was the only one to whom he wished to reveal his secret. The idea of the girl in the library exposing him as an imposter made him want to hide.

A servant moved into the reflection behind Calder's shoulder. "The tsarina will see you now, sir."

Calder's skin tightened. The tsar's wife, the empress of Russia, had asked for Rasputin and now Calder would have to face her with no idea what to do or say. He was led to a door near the far end of the hallway. The room was lined with dark oil paintings, portraits on every wall.

The servant left him there, and at first Calder thought he was alone. But someone waited near the hearth.

For a moment Calder did not understand. He saw his Glory in the glow of the fireplace, but she was wearing diamonds at her throat. When she smiled and walked toward him with her hand held out to him, Calder saw her satin shoes, the fine lace of her gown. This was not the way a governess would dress or approach a visitor. The woman who had waited outside the nursery of the dying baby must have been a friend or relative. This woman in white with the red-golden hair had always been the boy's mother, not a governess.

Glory was the empress.

Calder went cold and took a step backwards.

"What is wrong?" Alexandra Romanov waited a few feet from him, studying him with concern. He wondered if she had truly seen him in her son's last Death Scene or if he'd imagined it.

"Do you recognize me?" he asked her.

Puzzled, she said, "Friend, what is wrong?"

Alexandra believed him to be Rasputin. He could see it in her face. She had never seen him in his true form at her boy's deathbed, or heard his words, and she saw only Father Grigori now.

Still, she sensed something out of place. "You've changed," she whispered.

"Yes," Calder agreed. "I've changed."

Alexandra's eyes filled with tears and she rushed forward, taking his hand. "I knew the holy part of you would prevail."

She was a married woman, with five children, and an empress. And

she was much older than Calder had imagined. Her reddish-blond hair was lined with white. She was lovely, and no doubt possessed a beautiful spirit, but it was clear to him at once that she had never been his Star Fetch. It wasn't only that she was many years his senior, and bound to a husband and children, that calmed his desire to offer her the Key. In truth it was the devastating lack of recognition. She did not see Calder beneath his disguise and in her eyes he found no home.

"You've been touched by God," she told him, squeezing his hand and gazing up at him as if he were a saint.

"I'm not Rasputin," Calder confessed, but as soon as the words were out he knew she would not believe his story. And what would be the purpose of convincing her? He would not and could not pass the Key to her and take her away from her family. He tried to think how to comfort her and then escape her company, but he was shaking and his tongue was dry.

"I've made a terrible mistake," he began.

"Don't confess your sins to me," said Alexandra, releasing his hand. "I tell everyone that the rumors our enemies spread about you are lies. I don't need to hear your regrets."

Calder felt a wave of nausea at playing the part of a man who'd been the cause of such scandal. Alexandra brought him to a settee and sat beside him. He tried to steady himself, to sit and smile as Rasputin would, but guilt gnawed at him.

He had broken his Vows for a fantasy.

Calder tried to swallow back the panic rising up his throat. He had forced his way out of the Aisle, misused Rasputin, and abandoned the

Order of the Fetch. He needed to throw himself at the Captain's feet and beg forgiveness. But first he had to call Rasputin back somehow. He'd have to leave the body on earth and take Rasputin's soul back into the Aisle.

A knock at the door startled him to his feet. He expected to see a Death Door standing open with the Captain scowling on the other side. Instead, a servant carrying a folded paper on a silver tray entered.

"Forgive me," said Alexandra, taking the envelope. She read the note and told Calder, "Please excuse me for a few minutes. Look in on Alexis, won't you?"

Calder was relieved to be dismissed. He came out into the hall and searched for a place to be alone so he could summon Rasputin and a Door back into the Aisle. The corridor was empty, and so was the next chamber, a small music room filled with chairs, music stands, and a covered piano. Calder shut himself in and took out his Key. He held it in his right hand.

"Grigori Rasputin," he whispered.

The room remained silent and dark. The only sound was a mysterious hum from the piano strings as if a breeze were stirring them from the inside.

"Rasputin," he said, louder this time. "If you hear me, answer."

A servant opened the door and, facing away from Calder, cleared his throat. "You'll find the tsarevich in the library, sir."

When Calder peered around the edge of the library door, four of the children were playing at blind man's bluff, a game he'd observed in a Death Scene a few years back.

For a moment the library disappeared and Calder saw orange light through a scarf tied around his face, smelled fish frying, stretched out his arms and found only empty air, but heard the laughter still.

This blindness frightened him, but he tried to calm himself. *You're recalling your life on earth now*, he told himself, *because you're back in the flesh. These are images from three centuries ago, when you were a child.* And he did recall, not just playing a game of blind man's bluff, but being poor, living on the streets, singing for ha'pennies and bread. He hadn't been a fine musician, singing for royals and nobility. He thought he remembered himself as a young man sitting under a theatrical arch, with a paper lantern glowing above, with captivated listeners all around. But it had been the underside of a bridge he was seeing, the lantern had been the three-quarter moon, and what he thought were gentlefolk gathered around had been the pier legs and pilings, rocks and debris along the waterfront.

He remembered playing an ornate drum as he sang, but realized now it had been only an upturned wooden box. He thought he'd had an expensive fur cloak at his feet, a token of gratitude from his wealthy patron, but in truth it had been Dog, the mutt that had been his companion for a dozen years, lying across his feet with his ribs pressed to Calder's ankles. It was not shameful to be poor, so Calder felt no loss at rediscovering his true station in life, but he did feel there was something more he was supposed to remember.

He was blindfolded again and as he lifted the scarf from his eyes, a small boy with black hair and startling blue eyes stood before him grinning.

"What would you do without me?" the child asked him. And with shocking clarity Calder breathed in the smell of the roasted potato—felt the weight of it as it was dropped in his cold fingers, the heat through his tattered gloves—and he recalled how these things had delighted him.

Then the scene was gone.

❊ ❊ ❊

When his sight returned, Calder slipped into the library. The eldest Romanov girl sat at her books and tried to ignore the giggles, but the other three sisters were dashing about the room with their little brother, bumping into chairs and tables. The youngest girl wore the curtain sash tied over her eyes and held her arms out in the empty air, stretching her fingers to touch whichever sibling came close enough to catch.

Calder was glad the little sister was blindfolded—she was the one he felt the most uncomfortable being seen by.

"One," said the youngest girl. In turn her two sisters and brother called out, "Two." "Three." "Four." When she heard their voices she rushed at the sounds and grabbed the air, nearly catching one of her sisters' skirts. The others darted about, running into each other and shrieking.

"Be careful," the eldest girl reminded them as her brother nearly tripped. Then she saw Calder and waved him into the room, indicating a chair in the corner near her table. As he stepped forward, an end table and two books crashed at his feet. Calder bent to retrieve them, but before he could right the table, he felt a hand close on his sleeve.

"I have you!" The youngest girl held him fast. The other two sisters gasped.

"Ana!" one scolded her, but apparently Ana was not one to jump to attention at a warning. Too scared to move, Calder let her run her hand over his sleeve.

Ana laughed, but kept the blindfold in place. "Who is this?" She reached up without a care or the least hesitation and felt Calder's face. Her slender fingers tapped at his beard, ran along his cheekbones and forehead, gently pressed his eyelids. She stopped and grinned.

"Father Grigori," she declared. Calder could hear one of her sisters cheer, but he kept his eyes on Ana. She pulled the sash from her head, then took a step back and frowned. "Who are you?"

"Don't be disrespectful," said the eldest sister.

"I know you," Ana whispered. "I've seen you before."

This gave Calder a start. Now he realized the boy, Alexis, was silent and pale.

"You were at my brother's sickbed," she said, confident now that she'd placed him. "You were the ghost doctor."

"I told you it was Father Grigori all along," said the eldest girl. As if in explanation she told Calder, "She used to tell us that Alexis had a ghost doctor that visited him through a magic door."

"Alexis saw him, too," Ana protested. She motioned her brother to come. Alexis still appeared unnerved, but he moved to Ana's side, never taking his gaze from Calder's face. "This is your ghost doctor, isn't it?" Ana asked her brother.

Slowly the boy nodded. "But he feels like Father Grigori," she whispered. "Close your eyes."

Calder was too stunned to retreat. He had no idea what kind of response Rasputin would have had to this strange scene.

Alexis closed his eyes and let his sister, excitement blazing in her face, take his trembling wrists and guide his hands over Calder's cheeks, brows, and hair. After a few moments the boy pulled his hands away and opened his eyes.

"See?" whispered Ana. "He looks like the ghost doctor, but he feels like Father Grigori."

Alexis nodded in agreement, but seemed none too comforted. Ana, on the other hand, appeared fascinated, as if she had uncovered an eighth wonder of the world.

"How?" asked Alexis.

Ana smiled up as if expecting Calder to answer.

"Don't be pests," said the eldest girl. "And please pick up that mess before Mother sees it."

Calder tried to smile at the two youngest children in a paternal manner, but it was clear that he was fooling neither. Ana folded her arms stubbornly, and Alexis studied him with such anxiety that Calder wondered if the boy weren't recalling the pain he had been made to endure when Calder had refused to let him die.

"What are they saying?" one of the older sisters asked another.

Ana turned to them. "Can't you tell he's not Father Grigori?"

Calder hurried out of the room as quietly as possible, but a servant stopped him in the corridor and told him that the empress wished to walk with him in the garden. Since he had no coat, one was brought for him, a thick black garment that came almost down to his ankles. As he waited for the empress in the corridor, he saw a man dressed in a naval uniform standing at the library door. He gave Calder a short bow, and when Alexis came out he escorted the boy away down the hall.

Feeling trapped indoors, Calder waited for Alexandra on the outside step. As he stood in the cold, gray light, a voice startled him.

"Sir!" It was Ana. She did not address him as Father Grigori. She ran out on the front stairs with a small black box of a camera in her hands. With one eyebrow arched at him, she took his picture and just as abruptly ran back into the house.

❈ ❈ ❈

Alexandra, wearing a long brown coat edged with fur, joined Calder, linking arms with him as they descended into the frozen garden. She had changed from her delicate white shoes to sturdy brown ones. The snow had been neatly shoveled off of the paths. Perhaps it was just Calder's state of mind, but the garden seemed sad, as if something more than winter or wartime were holding it prisoner. He had an itching sensation that it was he himself who was having an ill effect on the scene. It looked like either a place that had not been fully created yet—like Eden before God had made the day and night, the animals and the plants—or perhaps a place that had been *unmade,* a painting that had been washed over with white so that the artist could start again. Both of these ideas made Calder nervous, for they spoke of a profound incorrectness, as if his being there had thrown a cloud over everything.

At first, as a shaft of sunlight broke through a cloud and lit the place with gold, Calder thought God was sending a sign of hope, until he saw that every shadow around him pointed east.

All except his own.

# Eight

A<small>T SECOND GLANCE</small>, he saw that he cast two shadows, one obedient and one wild. Calder's rebellious shadow pointed south, wavered on the snow like a dark vapor, and then slithered into place with its twin facing east. Calder tried to appear as if he was listening to Alexandra, but he was unnerved by every glint of light and bush trembling in the breeze.

Alexandra spoke of many things that troubled her, a stream of ideas and unfamiliar names. All over the land there were protests, the war was failing, many officials were not to be trusted. Calder wanted to empathize, but was distracted.

"I had him replaced, as you suggested," she went on.

"I suggested?" Calder had forgotten she was talking to Rasputin.

"Was that not right?" she asked.

"It doesn't matter," he told her.

"It doesn't matter?" She stopped on the path under a trellis. "But just last week you said—"

"I mean—" He hadn't meant to interrupt her. "I mean, what you have done is perfect."

This pleased her. She took his arm again and held it tight. "I wish I could have one day," she said, "when everything was right with the world." As they walked on, the muted shadow of a leafless tree ran over her face like a lace veil being pulled away.

"Let's take a respite by the fire," she said. "My bones ache."

Tea, cakes, and sandwiches were set out on a side table when they came back into the sitting room. A fire crackled in the hearth, and although there were several cushioned chairs arranged close together, Alexandra indicated that he should sit beside her on the chaise.

"Now tell me, do you have a message for me today?" she asked.

Calder wondered if the messages Rasputin had been passing on before he died were about Alexis and his health.

"I'm sorry if your military advice has seemed unwelcome of late," she added, pouring the tea.

Military advice? Rasputin did not seem like someone who would advise on wartime strategies. "What was the last message I gave?" Instantly Calder wished he had waited until he'd found a better line of inquiry, but Alexandra answered without pause.

"Do you mean the transfer of authority to the Ministry of the Interior?"

Calder took a sip of the tea, which felt warm going down but brought him no pleasure. He wanted badly to escape from the conversation. "I will pray about it." He put down his teacup in its fragile saucer, stood, and bowed to her. "I must excuse myself," he said. "If you'll forgive me."

"Will you come again tomorrow?" she asked.

"Of course," said Calder, though he did not expect to be in the Land of the Living the next day. His manners were undoubtedly shameful, but he had to find someplace to be alone so he could try again to summon Rasputin's spirit and then a Door.

Before he could make his way outside, Ana blocked his path.

"I need to speak to you," she told him, her tone commanding. She seemed to think better of it, for she hastily added, "Sir." And then, "If you please." She had come out of the shadows so suddenly Calder could only assume she had been hiding, waiting for him.

"Very well." He put on what he hoped was a venerable expression, but in truth he was afraid of her.

Ana motioned him into a tiny study where a small desk sat beside a cold and empty fire grate. She closed the door and began speaking without offering him a seat.

"I know you're not who you pretend to be." She folded her arms in a guarded way, or perhaps it was a sign of stubbornness.

"Why do you say this?" he asked her, not truly wanting the answer. "Who do your sisters say that I am? What does your mother say when she addresses me?"

"So, you are Grigori Rasputin?"

"Who else would I be?" This was evasive and unfair, but she made him nervous.

"If you are Father Grigori," she said, "tell me about your life.

Where were you born? Did you do all those sinful things they say you did?" She was flushed with anger.

"Yes, I'm sure I did."

"You're lying."

It was a shocking thing to hear, but he couldn't fault her for being perceptive.

"And why, child, would I lie about that?" He hoped calling her "child" would sound like Rasputin.

Instead of calming her, he had stirred her passion. "Do you remember your childhood, Grigori Rasputin? What was your mother's name? Did she sing you to sleep? Did you lose this tooth first or this?" She pointed to her top middle teeth.

Calder had been gathering his wits to answer, or not answer, with what he hoped would be good humor, but now he saw that she was not asking for answers. She was listing the kinds of human details she already knew he did not have in his memory.

"I know who you really are," she said.

"Who am I?"

"You were at my brother's deathbed," she told him, "twice." She put on that elfish expression again, and the right eyebrow lifted. "You didn't think I'd remember the first time we met," she said. "I was three. No one believed me. But I knew what I saw."

"You think I'm a ghost doctor." Calder did not smile or frown; he tried to keep his emotions unreadable.

"No." She seemed a little less sure now. "You're more of an angel, aren't you?"

He didn't answer.

"The only reason I don't tell Mother is that I can see you're . . ." She paused to choose her words carefully. "You're of God."

He knew what she meant: If he were from Heaven his presence held no threat that her mother would need to be warned of. Calder thought it was safe to nod in agreement.

"Why are you here?" she asked.

If he'd had more time, Calder would have thought of a better answer, but as it was, cornered by this girl with the peculiar gift of sight, he decided that the closer he stayed to the truth, the better. "I came because of your mother."

"Before you came to help my brother," said Ana. "Is Mother ill?"

"No."

"Where is Father Grigori?"

Here was a more difficult query. He had no intention of explaining the Land of Lost Souls. "He is in my world." Not a lie, but not strictly the truth.

"Do you swear you will not bring harm to us?"

Calder hesitated, not because he intended harm but because he feared he had already done so. He remembered Alexis reaching to him, his face drawn with pain. He had given Alexandra her son back, but he had not honored the boy's choice.

"I mean no harm."

"That's not the same thing," she pointed out.

Calder felt shamed by her. She was so direct and he was so deceptive.

She gave his hesitation a different meaning. "Are you unable to do harm?"

He couldn't bear to answer that question truthfully.

"Are you not allowed to swear an oath to me?" Her tone had softened. She let her arms unfold and studied his face carefully.

"We have Vows, but they are made in Heaven." He hoped this obscure answer would satisfy her. But still she searched his eyes, perhaps for a glimpse of angelic fire.

"I won't call you 'Father,'" she told him, flatly. "You're hardly older than I am, aren't you?"

Calder was shocked. She must truly be seeing him and not Rasputin's body and face. "I was born nearly four centuries ago." A slight exaggeration.

"No." She shook her head at him, confident in her appraisal. "What are you? Eighteen? Nineteen?" She folded her arms again. "Not yet twenty."

Calder felt humiliated but kept his tongue.

"What should I call you, then?" she asked. "Do you have a name?"

Calder hesitated.

"Speak your true name," she said, "and I promise not to tell anyone."

"And will you tell your brother that I mean no harm?"

Ana smiled at him as if she respected his bargaining skills. "We'll both keep your secret."

"My name is Calder," he said.

"Calder?" She seemed disappointed. "It's so ordinary. What does it mean?"

He'd never known when he was alive, but another Fetch had told him. "It means 'river of stones.'"

"There's something not right about you," she said. She wasn't teasing him. She was concerned about what she detected behind his eyes. This made Calder's skin tingle. "You're not telling me something."

She was uncanny. Calder silently prayed she could not see how he had broken his Vows and upset her world and his own.

"You're lonely," she told him. "It must be hard to pretend all the time."

He felt a wave of sadness, sudden and deep.

"Don't be afraid," she told him. "Everyone has a secret. I'll keep yours." Her voice was gentle now. "We're all pretending to be something we're not." She seemed to take responsibility now for his silence, fearing she had wounded his feelings. "I'm not like my sisters. I try but I can only pretend to be serious and polite. And I don't even bother pretending to be graceful." She smiled again. "I can't be slender and beautiful, so I'm funny. I can't be reverent, so I'm bold. It's how I survive," she told him.

"Are the others against you?" Calder asked.

She thought about this for a moment. "Not intentionally."

She scanned his face calmly and Calder wondered what she saw. He could hardly recall what he had looked like as a human. There were no looking glasses in his world.

"I want to be known for my true self," she said, "not what Mother hopes I become. Before I was born my parents prayed I would be a boy. Marie told me. That's to be expected, I suppose. But it would be a sweet world in which one was accepted without criticism."

She was disarming. The air shifted. Whether she had meant to or not, with her confessions she had created a kind of balance between them. Calder smiled, finally comfortable with her. "There is nothing about you that I wish to change," he said.

And here she blushed. "A truce, then." She held her hand out and Calder took it. Her palm was small and warm, her fingers delicate but strong. They shook hands for a moment.

She turned to leave, as abruptly as she had the first time they'd met. But this time, before she disappeared, she whirled around to face him again, startling him with a sudden smile.

# Nine

W HEN CALDER CAME DOWN THE FRONT STEPS, a servant held open
the door of a car for him. The driver was silent during the trip back
into town, but he glanced at his passenger periodically in the mirror
above the front window. Pretending to rest, Calder slid down to avoid
being watched. He observed the world through the side window: the
sky, the tops of trees, snow-covered walls. He heard dogs howling and
in the distance, a woman's scream. Smoke rose from a burning roof,
flames licking out the attic window. At this Calder sat up, but they were
moving too fast—the scene had flown. Now they passed a body lying
on the side of the road draped with a blanket, a group of soldiers questioning three women, one woman on her knees, weeping.

❋ ❋ ❋

At Rasputin's apartment building, the two officers on guard were different men from earlier, but they wore the same kind of uniform. No
angry husbands or fathers appeared, no women waiting to be enter-
tained, and no one asking to be healed. The shame of breaking his
Vows and the fear that Rasputin had disappeared forever into the Land

of Lost Souls weighed on Calder like an iron shackle. The climb to the third floor was slow, for Calder's legs felt as heavy as stone. He pulled himself up each step by the wooden railing. The other apartments were quiet except for the sound of a Victrola from a room on the second floor.

It wasn't the music of Heaven; Calder knew that. Earthly music, heard through the Aisle, might sound gleeful or melancholy, but it was always muted. Now, with the Victrola only a few feet away, with the waves of sound vibrating in his ears, the song pierced him and forced him to stop where he was on the staircase. The strains were not sad but sweet and ordered—yet the sisterhood of those lines, the painful discords that blossomed into harmony, overwhelmed him with longing. Like a phantom replica of the perfection of Heaven. He sat down on the stair, holding the banister. The beauty of the Aisle, present in every dissonance, shook him from head to boot with remorse.

*Remember from where you came*, it sang. *You deserter who stole and deceived. You can shake that foreign flesh and cry salt tears, but this is as close to the Aisle as you will ever be again.*

Calder tried to tell himself this wasn't true. He would go into the bedroom, call Rasputin back to his body, summon a Door, and be home. But as he dragged himself into the apartment, Calder felt a great misgiving.

No wife greeted him, which was a blessing. Calder wondered if she might be away on a trip. Or perhaps she had left Rasputin—given his reputation it would not have surprised him. Calder could smell supper cooking in a nearby room, but the idea of eating made him dizzy. As far as he could tell, a borrowed body did not need to eat or drink, and he was glad.

Calder shut himself in Rasputin's bedroom, took his Key in his hand, and banished doubts from his mind.

"Grigori Rasputin," he said. "If you hear my voice, answer me."

The air did not stir. The shadows in the corners of the room remained still.

"Please come back." Calder decided to try a more commanding tone. "Rasputin, I summon you to return to your body!"

But Rasputin did not appear.

Calder hoped he might call a Fetch Door even while in possession of a stolen body. He squeezed the Key tight in his hands and said, "Beyond this Door, Heaven waits."

He pressed close to the wall and scanned the room, ready to run to the Door wherever it appeared. He searched the room for gold light and the outline of a portal. But the walls, floor, ceiling, were all solid and earthly. He flung open the bedroom door, just to make sure the Fetch Door wasn't in disguise, but beyond it was only the rest of Rasputin's apartment.

Calder knew what he had to do. He held his Key to his heart and tried to summon his greatest ally. "Captain, please hear my prayers." But again he was answered with silence.

Deciding it was his surroundings that were hindering him, Calder began to transform the bedroom. He took the large chair and set it outside the bedroom door, tore the quilt from the bed—underneath there were white sheets. He draped the quilt wrong-side up over the bureau, hiding its dark wood. He took the top sheet and threw it over the wardrobe. He pushed the bed into the far corner of the room and hid the two pillows under it. It was not as stark as his Prayer Room, but it was closer.

Calder knelt facing the window and tried to imagine the sigh of waves the way he heard them in his Prayer Room. He closed his eyes and could almost sense a lightness where the west-facing door should be, a rich warmth glowing through his eyelids. Calder willed this to be his Captain, standing over him, waiting for his confession.

"Please," he prayed. "Bring Rasputin to me now. Don't make me stay here for three nights."

Calder was jarred by the sound of the apartment door opening. He flew to the bedroom door and found a young woman in the front room, putting a stack of books down on the table and taking off her coat.

"Wife?" Calder hadn't intended to make it sound like a question.

"You know Mama is in Siberia." The young woman frowned at Calder. "It's Maria, Papa."

*His daughter,* thought Calder. He was relieved that he would not be expected to play the role of a husband.

She lay her coat over a chair. "How much have you had to drink today?" She was pale with dark hair and troubled eyes.

Calder was going to tell her he hadn't had anything to drink, but then realized intoxication might be a good excuse to be left alone. Now Maria was looking past him at the peculiar rearrangement of bedding and furniture in his room. He expected her to ask about it, but she only sighed and said, "I'll make you something to eat."

"Thank you, no," said Calder. "I want to sleep." He closed himself again in his bare room and sat on the bed, feeling wretched, listening to the girl putter about the kitchen. When the light was gone and the street outside quiet, when he heard no more footfalls or chair scraping in the outer room, Calder tried to pray again. He knelt in the dark on the bare wood floor, kept his eyes on the faint light from the window, and whispered his Vows. Not wanting Rasputin's daughter to hear him, he sang "The Gentle Crossing" so softly, he felt his own heartbeat would drown out the psalm. *My Captain,* he begged, *please help me.*

No answer came.

He was alone.

But if he was alone, why was there the sound of soft breathing even when he held his breath? It was too close to be the daughter. There was a faint hiss and sigh of a breathing thing—two breaths, then silence.

"Can you hear me?" Calder whispered.

One nearly inaudible murmur.

"Captain?" Calder waited, but no sound followed. "Who is it?"

From inside the wardrobe, a tiny creaking, like a rocking chair for a mouse. Calder crept up to the wardrobe and lifted the sheet. Slowly he opened the closet door and found the hangers of tunics and trousers within gently swinging. The sudden sound of a breath behind him made Calder throw back the sheet and scan the dark room.

As if an invisible moth were batting about the bedchamber, there came a series of soft raps circling through the room, once at the windowpane, once on the ceiling, on the floor, inside the bureau, on the door, from inside the wardrobe behind Calder's head, which made him gasp, and then nothing.

Calder sat down on the bed to think. He didn't remember reclining or falling asleep, but a voice roused him.

"Can you hear me?" A man's voice, low and familiar. Not the Captain. "Escort!"

Calder gazed up into a pair of blazing eyes and a broad grin. Rasputin stood on the end of the bed, hands on hips, boots planted between Calder's own boots. There was no doubt about it, it was Grigori Rasputin. Calder grabbed at his own chest but found he was still in Rasputin's body, lying on Rasputin's bed.

"I tried to get your attention when you were awake," said Rasputin. "It's no easy task, being seen or heard by the living."

Calder sat up, relieved to see the man, but something didn't feel right.

Rasputin hopped down to the floor. "I'll have to try harder." He laughed. "Probably takes practice."

"Am I dreaming?" Calder asked.

"No," said Rasputin. "You're asleep but you're not dreaming. If you were dreaming I'd be saying what you wanted me to say or feared that I might say."

Calder now noticed what was wrong—Rasputin's bedroom, though solid enough to stand in, was transparent. He could look through the floor and see the downstairs couple curled in their bed. Through the walls he could see Maria in her bed, or the empty street below, even the moon through the ceiling, a faint glow, through a clouded night sky.

"You're asleep, but I'm not a dream," Rasputin repeated. "This is simply the only way I can get through to you so far."

To Calder's discomfort, Rasputin sat on the windowsill with his body half in and half out of the pane of glass.

"My old body doesn't need to sleep, of course," said Rasputin. "That's just you. Your spirit needs rest from time to time."

"I'm glad to see you," said Calder. "We need to go back to Heaven now."

"I'm not ready to go yet," Rasputin said. "I find this place to which you sent me very interesting indeed."

Calder wondered if Rasputin, set loose in the Land of Lost Souls by choice, might have greater powers than the truly Lost Souls.

"Have you seen other Souls?" asked Calder.

"Others? Oh, yes." Rasputin's expression was gleeful. "Seen them. Spoken to them." He hopped down from the window. "Did you know that in the Land of Lost Souls you can watch anyone, anywhere on earth?"

"I had heard that."

Now Rasputin walked to the middle of the floor, dipped his boot down, and touched the electric light fixture in the ceiling of the room below, batting at it with his toe. His spectral boot passed through the light without any effect the first few times. Then Rasputin furrowed his brow and grunted as he hit his foot at the light. The fixture shook and swung to a stop. The couple in bed below stirred but did not wake.

Rasputin smiled at Calder, impressed with his own performance.

Calder's skin went cold to think of Rasputin spying on women as they bathed or frightening children with this kind of foolishness.

"You can fly from Paris to the Sphinx in Egypt to New York City as slowly as a bird or instantly," said Rasputin.

There were plenty of reasons to dislike the man: He had most likely misused the devotion of the royal family and wielded a peculiar influence over the entire court; he had given Alexandra undoubtedly foolish advice about a war he probably did not comprehend. And he had apparently deceived women and men alike. All these things made Rasputin unappealing, even repellent, but what Calder found the most arrogant was that he had done it all in the guise of holiness.

Perhaps it was because Calder knew how easy it was to break a promise to God, but he found he could not despise the man. Honestly, he couldn't help liking him. Rasputin had a strange ability to take joy in life, and a childlike curiosity about death. In Rasputin's eyes there was no remorse. Calder envied him and wondered what it must be like to live free, holding nothing back for fear of burning one's candle out.

"You can travel across the land faster than a train and no soldiers can stop you," Rasputin continued. "We can even fly up and circle the moon. We can move underground, as well. I rode a zebra yesterday."

*We*, he'd said. Calder watched Rasputin pace the room. He'd said *we* can move underground.

"We can fly over the clouds or through the seas." Rasputin seemed delighted by this. "Rushing through the oceans, swimming with whales, even *through* them, snout to tail, past every rib."

"Do you fly with other Souls?" Calder asked.

"Not often." Rasputin came and sat on the bed beside Calder. "Many are not easy to talk to. Some are very angry. Those will talk to you if you agree with them. Others are frightened. They tend to run away. Some are quite mad, really. Those are the most fun."

Calder felt ill. It was dangerous for Rasputin to be meddling with the Lost Souls.

"Did you see their Fetches?" asked Calder.

"Their what?" Then Rasputin laughed. "Oh, you mean like you. Their escorts?"

Calder nodded.

"Yes" was all Rasputin would say about that. "I have a message for you," he said, changing the subject.

"From whom?" said Calder. "The Captain?"

"No, from one of the escorts."

"From a Fetch?" Calder was homesick instantly. "What's the message?"

"You will need to put the worlds in balance again," he said. "The Land of the Living and the Land of Lost Souls. You made a great mess of things when you left your post."

"What can I do to restore them?"

"You have to persuade a soul to cross into the Aisle," said Rasputin, "and save the children."

"Convince someone to be my Squire?" Calder asked. This made sense to him at once. He had come to get a Squire and so it appeared he would need to take one back with him. "What children must I save?" he asked. His mind went to Alexis, but the boy seemed perfectly safe. He was in a guarded palace and even had a sailor as a body-guard.

"How should I know?" asked Rasputin. "That is your business."

Calder longed to speak with the Fetch who had given Rasputin this cryptic message. "Why can't I see and hear wandering Souls and their escorts myself?" Calder asked him. It seemed absurd that he should be asking Rasputin how the immortal world worked, but he'd never been in this situation.

"Don't be a fool," said Rasputin. "You're not in the Land of Lost Souls. You're not dead. I'm haunting you."

"But I can see . . . " Calder wasn't sure how to describe it. "I can see through everything. Isn't that how a Lost Soul sees the world?"

"Can you? Interesting." Rasputin shrugged. "It's only like that at first. Just concentrate on one thing at a time."

Calder stared down where the floorboards should have been and kept his eyes still. The color came back into the wood and it looked solid again. Now as he regarded the room it appeared normal until he wanted to look through a wall or a piece of furniture. Then it would fade like a mirage and show him what lay beyond.

"How very strange," Calder whispered.

Rasputin stroked his beard. "You know what else is strange? I wager that you feel like you've only been asleep two hours instead of two days."

This would've been welcome news if Calder had believed it. He wanted Rasputin to agree to come back with him at once. But it was clear to him that Rasputin was either joking or mistaken. He knew he had only been asleep a short while—the moon had moved very little. It was still the middle of the night.

Rasputin did something then that Calder did not expect. He passed into Maria's room. Calder watched the spot where he'd passed through until it dissolved and he could see the man sit on the end of his daughter's bed. Calder was appalled to see that Maria herself was transparent. He could see her skull, the threads of her veins, and even her eyeballs, through the lids, twitching slightly as she dreamed. But as soon as he concentrated on her forehead, Maria became herself: skin, eyelashes, thick waves of black hair across the pillow.

"If she were to wake," Calder whispered, "would she see you, or are you only haunting me?"

"Sometimes we can make ourselves seen," he said, "but it takes no small amount of strength." Then he stood and bent over his daughter, kissing her lightly on the nose.

"So, you say two more nights have passed?" Calder asked him. "Then it's time for you to come to Heaven with me." He decided to tell the truth. "I came to this world to choose a Squire, but I made a mistake. The spirit I wanted to take was not meant for me."

Rasputin held up a hand as if he wanted Calder to be still so he could listen to something in the distance.

"Now I can't get back into the Aisle of Unearthing without you," Calder admitted.

"Wait," said Rasputin. He paused as if listening to a third party Calder could not hear. "You need to make a reckoning first by balancing the worlds. Were you not listening?"

"Who was speaking to you just now?" asked Calder.

"One of your kind." Rasputin shrugged.

"A Fetch is here now?" Calder felt a chill run through his flesh. "Where?"

"They're always flitting about chasing spirits," said Rasputin.

Calder knew now that Alexandra was not his Star Fetch, but there was one obvious solution. "You could be my Squire," he told Rasputin.

The man let out a snorting laugh. Maria rolled over but stayed asleep. Her father's soul moved back through the wall to stand before Calder.

"You want me to do what you do?" asked Rasputin. "Wait upon one corpse after another and follow them around? I think not."

"I would rather stay on earth as a prisoner than try to force some-one to take the Key," said Calder.

"The longer you wait," said Rasputin, his head cocked as if listening again, "the more the worlds suffer."

Calder flinched at the idea. "The Land of the Living suffers because of me?"

"And the Land of Lost Souls," said Rasputin. "And Heaven, they say."

"How does it suffer?" asked Calder, trembling from the weight of it.

Rasputin scowled as if disgusted. "Ridiculous," he said. "They claim that since you set me free I've been stirring unrest among the Souls here."

Calder had been taught about the danger of agitating Lost Souls. "I'll persuade a Squire to take my Key," he told Rasputin. "I promise. But ask what children I'm to rescue."

"Too late," said Rasputin. "He's gone."

Calder felt weak with loneliness that the Fetch had left them. "Will you help me?" he asked Rasputin.

The man scoffed. "I'm far too busy." Then his face warmed a little. "But I'll come see you again soon. And next time I'll bring company."

# Ten

CALDER OPENED HIS EYES AT THE SOLID CEILING. He tried to see into Maria's room through the wall, but to his relief he could not. He was awake, but he wasn't sure what had wakened him. Rasputin was nowhere to be seen and the night was quiet again.

Calder was startled to his feet by a knock at the door. Not a light, ghostly rapping, but a sharp, strong knock. He came out into the main room of the apartment and found a note on the table beside a plate of bread and fruit. It read: "Could not wake you. Gone to Greta's— Maria." Beside it was a stack of letters and a small package addressed to Father Grigori. Calder's heart jumped at the idea that Rasputin had been right and he'd slept for two days. Perhaps it was similar to the way human time often sped up when Fetches were in the Aisle of Unearthing.

The knocking came again, more urgently than before.

Calder came close to the door without opening it. "Who are you?"

"Father Grigori, I've come to bring you to Prince Felix."

"At this hour?"

"Your invitation was for midnight, sir."

Calder opened the door and a smiling man dressed as a driver bowed to him, but it was not the tsar's driver.

"I'm not well," said Calder. "I'll see him next week."

"But," the man thought for a moment, as if trying to speak in a code. "The lady you've been longing to meet with will be there waiting, sir."

"The lady?" said Calder.

"Her Highness is anxious to speak with you."

Alexandra had asked Calder to come back the next day. If he had slept through two days and missed their appointment, perhaps she was sending for him.

"Why all the secrecy?" asked Calder. "Is anything wrong?"

"All will be well," the man assured him, then led Calder downstairs to a waiting motorcar that although as large and dark as the royal car was nothing like it inside. The Romanov car had been plain and empty. This car was filled with strange enticements—a satin pillow, a bottle of vodka, and a glass in a deep tray, even a cigar and matches.

"Will it be a long drive?" asked Calder.

"Not long." The driver seemed awkward. He continually glanced at his passenger, then swerved as if unused to the icy road.

The only things visible from the rear windows were those caught momentarily in the headlamps—the bare road with the snow piled in ridges along the sides, the trunk of an occasional tree, and for one bizarre moment, the underside of a large white owl as it flew in front of the windscreen and then flapped backwards out of the way.

Calder thought he saw the pale underside of a seagull, flapping down to snatch a bit of bread off a stone wall, but it was only a scrap of memory, gone as quickly as it had come.

Finally the car turned onto a narrow drive and through an iron gate. The house was expensive and large, with few lights about. They stopped in a courtyard that was lined with what looked like abandoned stables, and after being escorted from the car, Calder was shown into the house by an underground entrance.

He was taken into a dim antechamber, then through an open arch into a low-ceilinged room, rich with cushioned chairs and piles of beaded pillows like a sultan's harem. The fire in the hearth was too strong, the room hot and smoky. Plates of pastries and an open bottle of wine were laid out on the table. Music filtered down from an upper room and the air was scented with incense and burning candles. A white bearskin rug lay in front of a cabinet covered with holy icons, including a cross made of crystal, an incongruous arrangement. The den was expensively decorated, but an underground room was not the sort of place one would expect to meet with an empress.

"Whose home is this?" Calder asked the driver as he removed his coat.

But someone else answered. "You've been here many times." The young man was handsome, dressed in a silk tunic of deep red; he stood on a staircase. The driver hung Calder's coat over a chair and left them. The young man smiled. "How are you, friend?"

"I am well," said Calder. "Tell me your name again."

"Are you drunk?" the young man scolded. "You know I'm Felix.

And here is Dmitry." A second young man came down the stairs behind the first and grinned at Calder. He was almost as pretty and wore blue.

"Let us make you comfortable." Felix poured blood-colored wine into the solitary glass that stood beside the bottle and handed it to Calder. "Drink."

Calder had no desire to drink, but he wanted to behave like Rasputin. He swallowed the wine down and handed the glass back to Felix.

"More?" asked Dmitry.

"Thank you, but no."

Both men watched Calder, smiling, waiting for something. Rasputin, no doubt, was a colorful storyteller. The idea of having to entertain them for more than a few minutes made Calder nervous.

"Where is the empress?" he asked. He dreaded asking her to be his Squire, but what else could he do? The worlds were suffering.

The young men exchanged a knowing look. "Do you mean the princess?" asked Dmitry.

Calder thought he hadn't heard correctly. "Did you say 'princess'?"

"Are you feeling unwell?" asked Felix.

"No," said Calder. But his face was warm and his arms tingled. Even his toes were prickling. Calder took a few deep breaths and the odd sensation passed.

"Are you tired, Father?" asked Felix. "Rest. Make yourself comfortable."

"Try a cake," said Dmitry, bringing Calder a plate of pastries.

"No." Calder felt a strange warmth in his chest, different from the sensation after taking tea at Selo. "No food, thank you."

"But these were especially ordered because they are your favorite," said Felix.

"You must taste them," said Dmitry. "That would only be polite."

Playing Rasputin was becoming tiresome, but Calder didn't want to be difficult. "How many do I usually eat?"

The young men laughed. "Two," said Felix. "At least."

Calder picked up two of the little cakes. They were ovals of crisp pastry with thick cream inside and sprinkled with powdered sugar. He sensed that eating neither nourished nor upset his stolen body; he saw no harm in it. He ate one cake after the other, not particularly enjoying them. They tasted sweet at first but then vaguely bitter. All the while his hosts watched him, glancing at each other from time to time. Calder brushed the sugar from his beard and wiped his hands on the thighs of his trousers, not having been offered a napkin.

"How are you feeling, friend?" asked Felix. Or Dmitry. Calder wasn't sure which. His vision had blurred and he felt sleepy. His two hosts seemed like one person now, one soul that walked about in two bodies.

"Impatient," said Calder, trying to follow them with his eyes as they paced back and forth. "When is she coming?"

"Princess Irina will be down in a few minutes," said one voice.

"She's so flattered that you wished to meet her," said the other.

Calder closed his eyes—he wanted to ask who Princess Irina was, but he had to rest for a moment. He put his head in his hands. He took deep breaths. He was just beginning to feel better, was about to comment on the softness of the couch, when he realized he was not sitting on a couch anymore. He was lying on the carpet, and he heard three voices close above him. Felix, Dmitry, and the third voice was that of the driver. They sounded concerned but strangely unsympathetic.

"How can he be alive?" asked the driver. "Did he drink the wine?"

"One glass," said Dmitry. "How much did you put in?"

"He ate two cakes," said Felix.

"One should have killed ten men."

Now Calder opened his eyes. The men jerked away from him as if he were a cobra.

"Father Grigori," said Felix. "Are you quite well?"

"We sent for a doctor," said Dmitry.

The driver smiled unpleasantly, backing away and out of the room. The other two kept their distance, pale and nervous.

"You tried to kill me," said Calder. He recalled now that Rasputin was surprised he hadn't been murdered.

Felix and Dmitry were standing beside the table with the cross, out of his reach—they did not advance or retreat.

Calder's hands were sticky from the cakes, but he felt that the poisons were no threat to him. *No wonder my hosts were stunned,* Calder thought. *A mortal would not have survived.*

"The empress is not here, is she?" he asked them, sitting up on the carpet and brushing himself off. "And you want me dead." He got to his feet, not only unharmed but feeling strong and angry now. "Who are you?" he asked them.

"We are cousins to the tsar," said Dmitry, as if this should impress him. "We are princes, and you are a peasant."

Cousins? Calder was shocked—was Rasputin so hated that relatives of Nicholas wished to get rid of him even though he was a favorite of the tsarina?

Now the driver stepped back in through the archway, a pistol held at arm's length and aimed at Calder's chest. The shot rang out and both the young men jumped, Felix knocking the wine over onto the remaining cakes.

Calder felt a sharp pain but it lasted only a moment. He looked down at his body and found a hole in Rasputin's shirt, but no wound in his chest and no blood. Only a small scorch mark. Feathers drifted to the floor where the bullet, after passing through him, had ripped into a sofa cushion. Calder rubbed the gunpowder smudge from his skin and frowned at the driver.

"I think I'll be leaving now," said Calder. He turned away from his executioners and retrieved his coat. Two more shots rang out. Calder was thrown into the wall and fell face-down on the floor. Disoriented, he stayed still, his eyes closed, thinking what to do.

Calder kept as still as a stone and let them poke at him with their boots.

"Enough poison to kill thirty men and it takes three bullets to bring him down?" asked Felix.

"Get the carpet and some rope."

Calder could hear them on the other side of the room moving furniture, opening cabinets and closets, creaking floorboards. Carefully he stood and crept through the arched doorway into the entrance room, slipping out of the door. Calder found himself in the small, deserted courtyard where the car still waited. As calmly as he could, Calder walked toward the gate that led to the street. It was unguarded; he hoped it was unlocked as well. But before he could reach the wall, another shot rang out and he stumbled, a sharp pain cutting into his right leg and then fading. He hesitated, considered seeing how much he could hurt them, but he still didn't want them or anyone to know he was immortal. So Calder decided to humor them. He took another step toward the gate, and when he felt the next shot bite at his back, he fell and stayed down.

# Eleven

Six booted feet crunched through the snow, two more shots were fired into Calder's neck and skull, and, to his humiliation, one of the young men struck him with what felt like a heavy chain. The memory of some childhood beating came back to him with a sickening shock. The confusion and sorrow of it rolled through his limbs. When he was older he had learned not to fear it. Suffering always faded—it couldn't last forever. He'd survived it before. Now pain jolted him at the beginning of every blow. Each time, the sensation could not fade before the next strike, but Calder kept perfectly still and would not let himself cry out.

He stayed limp and kept his eyes closed as he heard scuffling and whispered voices—he tried to understand what was being said, but it was a strain and soon he was thinking about what Rasputin had told him. Calder had to persuade a Squire to come with him in order to enter the Aisle again. He couldn't choose any willing mortal he came across along the side of the road or in the corner of a tavern. A Squire had to be chosen from a Death Scene, had to be either the one who was dying or a Star Fetch. It had to be Alexandra. There was still a chance she had met eyes with him across her son's deathbed. Still a chance perhaps that she was a Star Fetch. It was the only plan he had. He needed to get back to Alexandra and pass her the Key.

Icy water crashed around him, shocking Calder back into the present. He tried to struggle and found his arms and legs bound with rope. He opened his eyes in the murky river and fought with his bindings, managing to free one hand. Above him, a hole in the ice had been cut, no doubt made especially to drop him through.

Calder tried to untie his other wrist, but the ropes were frozen together. Dark hair flowed over his eyes. He was sinking. Calder was oddly unsurprised to see a pale figure floating before him. Rasputin looked exactly like himself in every detail but had a luminescence about him like foam on a midnight ocean.

"Angel," said Rasputin, "I have brought you visitors."

From deep in the dimness of the waters, black clouds appeared beside Rasputin's spirit. Calder felt he should try to be a friend to these Lost Souls, but he was too weary. His eyes closed again, and the instant he went unconscious, the river transformed and the three clouds darted away like frightened fish.

Calder cried out then at the overwhelming transparency around him. Rasputin appeared solid, but the river was no longer dark and murky, and neither did it grow dimmer with distance. It moved like a river, with all the waves and heavy weightlessness of its former state, but the impossible clarity of its new form was terrifying. The ice on the surface was as clear as fine crystal. The contents of the river moved with the current, but every object, from a leaf as big as Calder's hand to a tiny twig as small as a fly, was as transparent as glass. From where he floated, Calder could gaze through every mirror-scaled, clear-boned fish for more than a mile to where the river bent. And even then, he could see through the underwater banks.

As if levitating, bits of buried things hovered in the crystalline earth—rotting nets, bits of broken china, and in the distance a flock of coffins with wooden walls that gave Calder a view, as clear as through newly washed windows, of the finely clothed bones of their occupants.

The world above the river was visible as well. Calder could gaze up into the complexity of the bridge overhead and through the fur and muscle of a dog trotting past. This blizzard of images, layered one on the other, made Calder dizzy.

"Concentrate," Rasputin grumbled.

Calder tried to focus on a leaf that floated past his face, but Rasputin's words distracted him.

"I'm sorry the others wouldn't speak to you," said Rasputin. "They insist you are not an angel."

Calder was floating on his back now. But not in the river. He was lying on a strange sort of bed with a canopy only a foot over his face. And he saw that a few feet over the canopy a rough carpet of coarse hairs levitated, with broken threads dangling down. The air seemed to squirm with unseeable life.

"Do you have any more messages for me?" asked Calder.

"I'm not an errand boy," said Rasputin.

"Where am I?"

But Rasputin was not in sight, and his voice sounded far away. "Wake up and see."

Giant witchy fingers of roots hung under towering ringed trunks above Calder. Trees? He stared at the canopy and it became the lid of a coffin. The carpet had been the grass he could see above his grave. The squirming air must have been the dirt alive with worms.

"I said wake up," Rasputin urged him, "before the insects feast on you."

\* \* \*

Calder cried out and an ooze of gelled river sputtered from his throat. Everything went black. He tried to move but his fists and knees only clattered against the planks. Since he could not be truly hurt, Calder kicked and thrashed at his prison, ignoring the sting of pain, until the hard wood around him was splintered and crumblings of dirt fell into the tiny space in which he was trapped. Calder could feel and smell the earth as he dug up and away from the direction the dirt fell. He was so disoriented that this was the only way he could determine which direction was up. Finally he burst into night air, the ground broken into chunks as large as bricks around his shoulders.

It was the coolest time of the night, a few hours before dawn, but Calder could tell it was summer. The bushes were budding and frostless. Caked with mud, he climbed from his grave, the only one in the churchyard. At least half a year had passed while he was in the ground, yet his stolen body had not rotted. His hair and whiskers had not grown one inch.

A wave of panic squeezed through Calder's being, but to his great comfort his Key was still about his neck on its chain under his tunic. Those who had buried him must have thought it was one of Father Grigori's icons. He stumbled out onto a path he recognized, and what lay beyond was familiar as well—he was at the Selo Palace. But the gardens had run wild and not one window in all the beautiful buildings was lit. Calder went to the wing where he had last seen Alexandra, but every door he tried was locked. He put his face to a window that peered into the library where the children had played at blind man's bluff, but all he saw were empty shelves and furniture draped in sheets.

As he walked back into the city, Calder decided that he couldn't be Rasputin any longer. He was afraid of the attention he would garner if it was discovered he was a Fetch stowing away in a human body, but it would be worse by far to be thought a famous healer risen from the dead like Lazarus.

The windows of Rasputin's apartment were dark. All the windows in the building were. Although he was nervous about being seen, he was covered in dirt from having dug himself out of the grave—he needed to clean himself up before he went in search of Alexandra.

He tried the door to what would now be only Maria's apartment; it was unlocked. The main room was dark and still. He moved with great stealth to the bathing room, where he washed and then found a pair of scissors, carved like a silver crane, too small for his fingers, but surprisingly sharp. He drew the length of Rasputin's hair over his left shoulder and gripped it hard as he sawed through the thickness. After this he began to randomly snip, clipping the coarse hair to an inch or two from his head, letting the clumps fall like wool from a black sheep. It looked as if a bird had begun to build a nest in the sink as Calder leaned toward the looking glass and snipped at his whiskers. Once he had cropped down the beard close to his face, he was planning to shave himself clean, but soon he noticed a difference in the color of Rasputin's skin—brown, as if he had spent many years out-of-doors, on his cheeks and nose, but pale under the beard, where the jaw had been protected for so long. He thought better of shaving and left the beard short, trimming a whisker here and there until it was relatively even. His hair, on the other hand, was untamable. It stuck out in every direction in random spikes as if he had been licked by the tongue of a great beast.

Calder went to Rasputin's old room, where the door stood open. The furniture had been rearranged completely so that the bed had been replaced by a loveseat, the bureau by a desk. He went to the new wardrobe and took clean clothes, a tunic and black trousers and a long black coat. Boots stood under the window. He found none of Rasputin's notes as he searched the desk, but his money, a large stack of it, was now folded and tied with a piece of ribbon. It made him uncomfortable to take the money, but he did.

"I'm not dreaming," came a voice from the doorway. "You are dead."

# Part III

## The Passing of the Key

# TWELVE

It was not Maria who spoke, but an elderly man in his nightdress, barefooted, shifting his spectacles on his nose as if Calder were an optical illusion.

Calder's pulse was drumming fast. "Where is my daughter?" he asked.

The man shuddered at the sound of this voice from beyond the grave. "Your daughter?" he said. "Moved away." His hands were shaking, but he did not retreat. "Do you haunt these rooms?" he asked. "What do you want from me?"

"I do have another question." Calder managed to smile. "Where is the tsar's family?"

"Some say they are being held in Ekaterinburg," said the old man.

"Held?" Calder was disturbed by the image. "Are they prisoners?"

The old man nodded nervously.

"What has been happening since my death?"

"Everything?" The gentleman shifted from one foot to the other, perhaps wondering if his news would make Rasputin's ghost angry.

"After the abdication, the city's been falling apart. Strikes and riots . . . all over, not just here."

"Who rules the land?" Calder asked.

"They're all mad," said the old man. "The Bolsheviks, the Duma."

"And Russia is still at war?"

"The whole world is warring," said the man. "Here it's revolution." He looked anxious now, as if worried he had said the wrong thing and displeased the ghost.

Calder asked, "How long ago was I killed?"

"A year ago last winter."

*Alexis will be thirteen by now,* thought Calder. *And Ana seventeen.*

"Thank you," said Calder. He walked slowly out of the bedroom and toward the door, the old fellow watching him. "You can rest easy," Calder reassured him. "I'll not be back."

❋ ❋ ❋

As Calder walked to the train station he had seen on his first day in St. Petersburg, the city began to wake. But it did not brighten into a healthy summer morning the way other cities might. Most of the businesses were boarded up, doors broken in, windows shattered. Glass lay like ice shards along the pavement. In the distance a child was crying.

Soldiers appeared, prowling in small groups. Civilians scuttered like wanted criminals at the edges of alleys or crouched in ravaged storefronts, searching through the rubble. The air smelled of smoke and on the street blood had dried into dark stains. Calder stumbled as his vision left him. He tried to stand still, but someone thumped into him from behind and he fell onto one knee.

He saw a narrow street before his eyes that he knew was not in Russia. He smelled the stink of the stagnant puddles, heard a gull crying overhead, and saw a small boy in front of him running on ahead, his lame leg making his gait sway and the dark curls on the back of his neck bounce.

When St. Petersburg reappeared to his eyes, Calder got to his feet and walked carefully toward the train station, not knowing when he might go blind again. The closer he got to the depot, the more people he found. They crowded the overwhelmed stationmaster with queries and pleas for help. But only those with money for tickets were allowed to board the train east to Moscow and beyond.

Not wanting to be noticed, Calder stayed in the seat farthest back, pressed himself into the corner. He heard the hiss of the steam as they were away, felt the growl of the engine, then the jerk as each car was brought along. Through half-opened, filthy windows, he caught glimpses of the bleak countryside, saw a train wreck where the cars lay fractured like gutted cattle in the dead grass. The seat under him was burned, the wall beside his head gouged and torn. It was strangely quiet in the train. Soldiers and civilians did not mix, but clustered together whispering or sleeping.

Calder would not let himself sleep, though the pull of his spirit's weariness tried to lull him under. He believed what Rasputin had told him, that it was his soul and not the body that craved rest, but the last time he lay down and meant to stay awake the hours had gotten away from him. He didn't want to miss his stop and end up in Vladivostok.

When the train finally came to Ekaterinburg, Calder saw no

monuments or palaces that set it apart from other cities. To his surprise, when he asked the stationmaster where the tsar's family was being held, he was given directions as if it were of little significance.

It was late in the afternoon and his shadow walked before him like a ghost. He found the prison house within minutes. Although it stood alone, far from other buildings, the house that was being used as the royal jail was otherwise ordinary. The gate was unmarked and guarded by only two men with rifles. People did not stand and stare at the house, waiting for a glimpse of the old tsar, so no one noticed Calder climbing the tree beside the back corner of the fence.

The fence was high and solid, and when he peered over it into the yard, he found that two more men strolled the courtyard. The windows of the house had been painted white, but otherwise it did not appear difficult to break into. The first floor was half underground, with windows at knee level.

As soon as the guards had all turned away from his corner of the fence, Calder jumped into the yard, stumbled to his feet, and ran along the back of the building. He found wooden stairs leading to a back door to the upper floor. It was barred by a plank that slid down into a brace. The shadows of two men rounded the corner of the house as Calder lifted the bar, slipping inside.

The house was stuffy and sweltering. To the left stood a long, empty room, to his right an empty hall. He needed to see Alexandra alone, which seemed impossible if he thought about it, so he didn't think. He heard men's voices from the left. Calder opened the door on his right and ducked inside a small room with four cots and four chairs draped with white nightgowns—perhaps the girls' bedroom. Now the tread of heavy boots was just outside the door he'd come through. He crept to another door across the room, slipping into the dark chamber beyond and hurrying past the bed to the farthest corner. There was no closet or wardrobe to hide in. Only a tall chair where an old jacket, stained and tattered, hung across the back like a seated scarecrow. It wasn't until he was pressed deep into the corner, listening for voices, trying to extract the sound of Alexandra's from the others, that Calder noticed there was someone on the bed.

Nicholas, the tsar himself, was lying on his back on top of the sheets, fully clothed in a fraying tunic and faded trousers, perfectly still, his eyes closed, his hands at his sides. It was such an ominous sight, his weary face and graying beard, the stillness of him, like the carving atop a sarcophagus—Calder stared, not breathing.

The emperor stirred, then opened his eyes at the ceiling so suddenly that Calder dared not move for fear of drawing his attention to the corner where he hid. Nicholas sighed and sat up, facing away from Calder. He hung his head for a moment, then rose and left the room, leaving the door standing open.

Calder noticed then that the objects on the dresser were not a random clutter as he had first thought. The items were set out in a pattern. On the left a Bible, on the right a small wooden cross, in a half-circle a line of pressed clippings from plants, what would have once been weeds to an empress but these days had become treasures—half a dozen dried snippets, flattened perhaps in the pages of the Bible so that they would last, small leaves and a few tiny flowers. At the back of the dresser top, leaning against the wall at the center of this arrangement, was a photograph. Rough at the edges, unframed, beginning to warp, it was a picture of Calder. He was in Rasputin's body, but it was not Rasputin. It was the picture Ana had taken of him on his first trip to Selo.

He dropped to one knee behind the chair when he heard Nicholas walking back toward the door. He kept his head down, hoping that his bulk was hidden. Calder was sure that, even though the weather was warm, the tsar was coming back for his jacket, Calder's only shelter from discovery. But after the footsteps entered the bedchamber, they stopped. He held his breath, imagining that Nicholas was staring at his hiding place, but then he heard a drawer of the dresser slide open.

Calder peeked over the edge of the chair and saw her, Alexandra, lifting the hair at the back of her neck and putting in an extra hairpin. Her dress was plain cotton, threadbare and stained. Her hands were veined and wrinkled. He stepped out from behind the chair and stood so that he knew he was in the reflection with her.

"Don't be afraid," he whispered.

She met his eyes in the mirror and stopped. Her whole frame shook. "Is this a vision?" she whispered.

Calder moved up behind her slowly, gently placed a hand on her shoulder, shaking his head no. If she were to cry out, guards would rush in, so she held in her tears the best she could.

"The angels have sent you back to me," she said. "Thank God." She smiled and tears came down her cheeks.

Calder held a finger before his lips to remind her to be silent.

Alexandra faced him. "You've come to help us escape."

He didn't have time to explain it all. "I cannot take the rest of them," he said, "but I need to take you with me to Heaven."

She was stricken. "Am I to die now?"

Calder took his Fetch Key out of his tunic and lay it across his palm for her. "This is power over death."

She only glanced at the Key. What she was interested in was something in his expression. "Only for me?"

Calder nodded.

She straightened her back and her eyes cooled. "My family would starve to death and I would survive to watch?" she asked.

"No." Calder jumped at the sound of men's voices again on the other side of the bedroom wall. "I would take you away. You won't have to—"

But she stopped him. "How can you imagine I would leave my husband?" she whispered. "I am flesh of his flesh. I will love him even after death." Her face flushed. "And my children," she whispered. "How were you going to persuade me to leave them?"

Calder lowered himself to one knee, hoping to be forgiven. "I am the cause of all this. The blame is mine. You have done nothing wrong." *All you did,* he thought, remembering the day he first saw her, *was love your child.* "I made a grave mistake in coming to you," he confessed. "I caused a wound in the world, and the only way I can make it right again is by taking you with me."

Alexandra gazed down at him, at the Key in his open hand. "Can you force me to take it?"

Calder's stomach curled into a knot. His hands and face felt numb. "No," he told her.

She lifted her right hand as if to touch the thing, but hesitated. "Promise to do something for me?"

Calder jumped again at the sound of heavy footfalls in the hall. "To do what?"

"Promise before I tell you," she whispered.

He had no choice. "I promise."

"Give this power over death to Alexis." She pulled her hand back from the Key. "For I refuse it."

# Thirteen

Calder stood behind the bedroom door as Alexandra went out to the dining room to speak to her family. With the doors in between standing open, Calder could hear that the tsar was reading aloud to his children. The gentle baritone of his voice reminded Calder of the Captain, that tender and learned lilt. It was one of the human psalms, though Calder did not know their numbers by heart.

Alexandra waited until he had finished, then told her husband and daughters that she would stay indoors and play cards with Alexis while they took their afternoon walk. Calder could hear the girls' voices as they left and Ana's husky, childlike laugh.

Alexandra had never been ordained as a Star Fetch, for if she had she would've felt compelled to accept the Key. But, as Calder remembered, Alexis had seen him, had heard his voice. It was Alexis who was meant to be his Fetch.

Silently, Alexandra came to the doorway and motioned Calder to come. In the dim and empty room, the boy was sitting in a wicker wheelchair, his left leg in a brace. He stared at Calder, not with tears of joy, as his mother had when she first saw him, but with a dark wariness.

"He's suffered so much," Alexandra whispered as she guided Calder to the chair. "This life is harder on him than the rest of us." She turned to the boy. "Our friend has come back to help us."

"He's not our friend," said Alexis.

"Hush!" She glanced at the far doorway, as if expecting them to be interrupted. "Guards come into the rooms without knocking. Hurry."

Calder lifted his Key on its chain over his head and showed it to the boy. Alexis regarded it suspiciously.

"This charm will mean you cannot be hurt," she whispered. "You'll never be sick again."

"I don't want it," said the boy.

"But see what it has done for Father Grigori."

"I don't care."

Alexandra stiffened, and although her voice did not rise above a whisper, her tone had changed. "Alexis, do as I say. We have no time."

The boy sighed and held out his hand. Calder lowered the chain over his head as Liam had done when Calder had become a Squire. And he spoke the same words. "I pass this Key to you," he said, pressing the Key into the boy's hand. "My Chosen One."

Calder did not remember feeling any different after having been passed the Key, but of course he had already been dead. Alexis appeared unimpressed for a moment, then an expression of dismay flashed across his features. He lay a hand on his brace and looked from his mother to Calder.

"What's the matter?" asked his mother.

Calder heard booted footsteps nearby. If they were interrupted, how would they have time to call for Rasputin and summon a Door?

The boy jumped off the chair and stood on his left leg, astonished and grinning. But as he began to unstrap the brace, his mother said, "Father Grigori is going to take you to safety now."

Fear whitened the boy's face. "What?"

"It will be all right, darling." Alexandra put her arms around him. "We don't have time to argue."

Calder's breath was knocked out of him as two guards thrust him to the floor and dragged him backwards away from the boy and his mother. The last he saw of them, Alexis was lowering himself again into the wheelchair and Alexandra was hiding the Key under her son's shirt.

Calder was forced down a flight of stairs and into a small room where two of the guards were already telling their commanding officer the news. The man sat at a desk covered with pistols in a row like fish at a market stall.

"This is the rescue party?" The commander was perplexed at the sight of Calder. "This old bum armed with only the dirt under his nails?" The man was thin, with a deeply lined face. "How did he get in?"

"Divine providence," Calder answered.

The commander smiled. "What's your name?"

Hoping it would have some ominous effect, Calder said, "Rasputin."

To his surprise, the commander laughed and his men with him. "Come to rescue the tsar?" The commander shook his head. "Get rid of him."

Being impossible to kill or wound did not make Calder immovable. He was as easy to lift and throw as any man. Though he struggled and tried to tell the guards he was an angel, a prophet, a sign from God, he was carried down the road to where the shops began and to an alley between two closed storefronts. The civilians they passed pretended not to notice. Calder was flung into a puddle. As the guards backed toward the street, the older one said, "We'll give you a chance—I'll count to three." The man drew his gun.

The younger guard, still nearly a boy, motioned to Calder as if shooing off a bird. "Run away," he said, his voice anxious and strained.

Calder stood but did not flee.

"One." The older guard aimed at Calder's chest. "Two."

"Get out of here!" the young guard called.

The older one fired before he said, "Three."

Calder felt a lightning bolt of pain through his breastbone and stumbled, dropping to one knee. The older guard, sure of his kill, walked away. The younger waited to see Calder fall. When he got to his feet instead, the young guard went pale and fled.

* * *

Although he had no plan, Calder knew he would have to get back to Alexis and take him into the Aisle. But he was stopped at the mouth of the alley by a dark cloud. At first he thought it was smoke, but it moved with a living will like a swarm of tiny insects. Calder stepped back, the stink of burning hair filling his nose. When the cloud thrust itself at his face, he ducked backwards and fell down a narrow flight of cellar steps and lay, stunned, at the bottom of a chained door.

Something was moving on the door beside him, so close to his head, if it were a spider it could have reached a leg out and tapped his ear. Calder sat up, spooked by what appeared at first to be a tan beetle. He scrambled up a step as the little lump stretched into a nose and was followed by coarse whiskers on a bearded chin and the twisted hairs on the brows of a broad forehead. The face slid up the door, surfacing out of the wood like a statue from a dark lake. Father Grigori emerged, face first; then his long body unfolded out of the solid door.

"Ah, I have done it." Rasputin laughed. "You see and hear me, I can tell."

"Yes," said Calder.

"It was not easy. I have been trying for hours."

"We'll be going back to Heaven soon," said Calder. "Stay with me."

"Tell me about the Key."

Calder was startled.

"You used to keep it here." Rasputin reached for Calder's shirt, his hand passing through his chest. "Does it open portals into other places?"

Calder climbed a step higher, away from the man, wondering what other places Rasputin had heard of and from whom.

"Come now, don't be selfish. Share your knowledge with us," said the man. "Or have you given it to someone else?"

From one moment to the next Rasputin seemed to Calder to

change alliances—one moment confiding in Calder as a friend, the next feeling at one with his dearly beloved Lost Souls.

"Heaven will be everything you want," Calder told him. "You won't need other portals."

"There is more to the universe than pining for God." Rasputin's voice hardened and the air around him swirled with shadow. "Obedience is bondage—if God wants to be adored he should make himself more loving." As if he were in pain, Rasputin put a hand to his head and sat on the lowest step. "That's not what I mean. I am so clear sometimes—I know how it all works." His eyes were wide and bewildered. "Then I feel confused and ashamed." He leapt up to touch Calder again, this time swiping at his face with a clawlike hand. "And that makes me angry."

"It's the place you inhabit," Calder told him.

"I tried for weeks to appear to my family," said Rasputin, ignoring Calder's words. "But they never did see or hear me." He patted his clothes as if they were dirty and puffs of shadow rose from him like dust. "And I came to Matushka while she prayed, but she never heard me either. But it doesn't matter," said Rasputin. "Now when I recall how passionate I used to be about protecting the empress, and the boy, how much I loved the whole family, it seems absurd." He thought about this and added, "I prefer this new freedom from attachments. Much more natural. But . . ." In a flash his smile fell. "Sometimes the love comes back into me like a sickness." His eyes were heavy and dark. "Are you sure this is not hell?" Before Calder could answer him, Rasputin was laughing again, his face lit with pleasure. "What foolishness I am talking!"

Rasputin was becoming detached from the Land of the Living, while Calder felt himself stricken in the opposite way. The longer he stayed among the earthbound, the more he remembered the human instinct to cling to life and fear death. He was losing the Fetch's remote and reverent ways of love. He knew if the tsar's family was in danger he would do anything to save them. But save them from what? Death? As if death were the enemy?

"You don't look well," said Rasputin.

"Are there any Fetches near you now?" asked Calder.

Rasputin was no more solid than a mirage, but he appeared now to be casting a shadow that wavered behind on the closed door and then split into two forms.

"Angel?" one shadow whispered. The other hissed, "Look at me!"

The scent of burning hair was back, stronger than before.

"I smell blood." Rasputin glared at Calder. "Didn't you see the guns they had gathered? Why do you just stand there? Save them!"

Calder remembered the row of revolvers on the desk of the prison house commander and leapt up the stairs, taking two at a stride. He got out of the alley, around a corner, and across the empty field that led to the prison house, then suddenly the world went dark for him. When vision flew back into his eyes, he saw a sketched path before him as if he were running along a low wall, dashing through a busy street and under a cemetery gate. He heard the shouts of angry men, and his own breath wheezing, the tap of his feet as he ran and jumped. Now he saw that he was following a little boy with dark curls. He had one lame leg but could run faster than Calder. He glanced back and called, "Catch me!" His eyes flashed blue.

Calder's body, still in a field in Ekaterinburg, stumbled in the uneven grass. He ran blindly forward, having no time for the memory to clear from his eyes. He saw the lame boy hop over a tombstone and duck into a hole in the wall of a crumbling church. Calder followed, but all he felt was the grass and dirt under his hands as he tripped in the field. He rose and thrust on toward the prison house he still believed was in front of his outstretched hands. His vision returned with a sickening jolt—a light shone out from beyond the wooden wall as he approached. It wasn't candle or lamplight. It came from beyond the Land of the Living.

# Fourteen

Calder had often seen more than one Fetch in the same place. On battlefields, dozens of Doors might appear and disappear in a gentle, random rhythm. But only once before in all his years in the Aisle had Calder beheld the night go from complete darkness to the light of many Doors opening at the same moment. It happened just before he had found Alexandra the second time. He'd been the first Fetch summoned to a sinking ship, and as he'd waited, sitting on the floating cellar doors that were the man's Death Door, he'd observed hundreds of Death Doors unlock and open at the same instant, as if a great hole had broken through into the blinding resplendence of Heaven.

Now, as he ran toward the Romanovs' prison house, Calder beheld that same light, the light of more than one Door opening at the same moment. From the seams between the boards in the walls, from the edges of the windows—even stretching through the scratches in the painted panes of glass—brilliant beams tilted and slid down from the upper floor to the lower as he rushed through the gate and across the yard. But before he could reach the house, four hands pinned his arms down and forced him to the ground beside a truck that had not been in the yard before.

"They mean to kill them!" Calder tried to wrench himself free. "They're going to kill the tsar!" He was up, but the guards held him tightly. One was the older of the two that had tossed Calder into the alley, the one that had shot him.

"God sent me to stop this," Calder told him. "That's why your bullet didn't hurt me." If he could show them that he was immortal, they would have to listen. He lunged for the man's belt, hoping to take his weapon, but he was kicked to the ground again. The guard pulled out the gun himself and pressed his boot against Calder's neck to keep him down.

A crackling and popping noise, like twigs breaking under the wheels of a wagon, started a dog in the distance to keen at the night. Calder felt the world spinning too fast and yet standing still, so the noise went on and on. The guards stopped to listen.

As soon as the night went quiet again, a figure stumbled from the house. It was the young guard—Calder saw his dimpled chin and the curl of his hair hanging over his brow even in silhouette as he dropped his revolver, fell to his hands and knees, and vomited. A pendant dangled from his neck. His curls swung as he rested there, rocking for a moment before he rose and walked out of the yard and into the street.

The guard who held Calder down called to him. "Ilya, get back here!" When there was no reply he gave his attention to Calder again, then rested the barrel of the gun against Calder's temple and fired.

The crack shook Calder to the bone. Everything was white, and then, as if a dark cloud had drifted overhead, everything was shadowed. He could hear voices but no words. Whisperings. Angry snarling. And he smelled something burning.

But one face drew close and was not angry. A boy with blue eyes and black curls, a coil of rope slung over one shoulder, bent over him and spoke.

"Look at you," said the child. "Where have you been?"

Calder's ears were ringing. He could see through the world around this boy, layers of earth and tree that weren't there, clear clouds and a crystal moon.

Then everything went dark and Calder woke in a ditch, his body covered in leaves and branches. It was still night. He sat up and found an abandoned can of kerosene a few feet away. Something more pressing had taken his gravediggers away from their task.

Calder remembered then the sound of gunfire, crackling like snapping twigs, and flew across the dark field to the prison house. No one guarded the gate; the truck was gone from the yard. Calder recalled the young man who had run from the house—his sickness was not from the execution of a single grown man, not the tsar alone. That kind of repulsion came from the slaughter of women and children.

Calder could hear shouting and orders flying, boots thundering as he stormed into the house. He ran through every room on the top floor. Not only were the Romanovs gone, but their possessions had been taken away. The tsar's bed was stripped and the cots where the girls had slept were stacked in the corner. Most disturbing, Alexis's wheelchair leaned upside down against the dining room wall.

Calder threw off two men who laid hands on him and flung himself down the stairs, bursting into the lower floor. He went room to room there, too, but the family was gone. Finally he stopped in a tiny room empty but for two chairs, one lying on its side on the floor, both splintered. The wall behind them was like a map made up of holes not only in the paper but in the wood underneath as well.

And there were stains.

As he was being dragged from the house, Calder glimpsed a pile of small things swept together like trash—a Bible, a hand mirror, a brush. He tried to imagine that it was not bloodstains he had seen, but he could still smell it.

Calder was taken into the courtyard and forced to his knees. The guard that had shot him in the head was not among these guards. The commander was brought out.

"It's the same imbecile as before," he told his men impatiently. He stood over Calder, smiling. "The prisoners are fine," he said loudly. "They were moved to a safer location. You can tell your friends. The tsar is far away."

Calder was taken out to the street and released. He began to walk but was too stunned to think where he might go. The tsar and his wife and daughters were dead, their souls had already crossed into the Aisle. But their son, where was he? Calder stopped on the pavement and sat where he was, leaning against the wall of some shop. Had they buried the boy with the others in some hidden place? A voice seemed to answer him, though the man speaking was on the other side of the wall from where Calder sat.

"They were meant to burn the bodies, but they didn't."

Calder found he was leaning against the wall of a tavern. The voice was coming through the open window above his head—a conversation that made him sit up and listen.

"They just dumped them into the water." The man who spoke was trying to whisper, but he'd been drinking and his words spurted out in little blasts. There was a general mumbling of awe, then someone asked, "Who told you this? I don't believe it."

But Calder did believe it. He came to the doorway. The tavern was one small room with wooden benches and a bar with brown bottles. Three men and two women huddled together.

"Zinovi, he was one of the guards," said the first voice. "He touched the corpses with his own hands." The man speaking was small with a large creased forehead.

"All gone, even the children?" one woman asked in horror.

"Every one of them, torn open with bullets and thrown down the mineshaft."

This was followed by a flurry of gasps and muttered prayers.

Calder had to go to this grave before the villagers got curious and went to have a look, or before the assassins themselves became aware of the gossip and went to move the bodies. He quietly approached the barkeep and paid the man for whispered directions to the mineshaft.

He found the road he was told to take, and the smaller road that veered off into the woods. It was a damp forest, bedded in rough brush and bracken, elderberry vines, rocks slick with moss hidden half buried in the mud. A moan rose when the breeze stirred, sounding hollowly through the pines like a great harp. The moon offered a little light, but still many times Calder stumbled and twice had to find his way back to the path when darkness obscured it.

Finally he saw ahead a landmark that the barkeep had told him of—a tree stump that had been cut high as a man's chest standing alone. Beyond this Calder could make out the square of a man-made structure on the ground. The idea that the royal family had been tossed down into this open hole horrified him so that his legs began to shake as he approached.

"Alexis?" he called. "Are you there?"

He heard a small splashing, like a dove in a birdbath, and ran to the open shaft. In the darkness he heard water lapping, and there in the depths below, where the blackness seemed inside out and backward, a surreal space lay between him and what he beheld. The surface of the water, a dozen feet below, shone like a mirror, the reflections of stars and tree branches wavered between the pale shapes of bodies that floated there gently, white as cream, bobbing against one another.

A truly unnatural sight, for the corpses that had been left to swell and rot in a muddy hole had once been spirited with royalty. A tsar of Russia, one of the most powerful men of his world and of his time, was floating at the bottom of an open grave, his clothes mostly gone, ripped away, his flesh torn with bullet holes, his face beaten. And Alexandra, he knew, must be there as well, emptied of her soul, her earthly body stiffening somewhere below him in the dark. And the girls, cast away like animals killed for their skins.

Calder made himself look again down into the throat of the mineshaft. He saw two white legs, bare and still, bump the wall of the makeshift grave as the water stirred. And there against the far side of the shaft, just above the surface of the water, not one but two faces, like pale moons. Alexis and Ana, their expressions disturbingly still, with hair wet and clinging to their cheeks, lifted their chins to him and stared up into the world of the living.

# PART IV

## THE MISSING BONES

# FIFTEEN

ALEXIS MUST HAVE PASSED THE KEY TO HIS SISTER, for they were now both solid and present, but neither alive nor dead. They were something other than a boy and a girl. When Ana had stood at her brother's deathbed, she had seen Calder and heard his voice as Alexis had. Both had been granted the sight. But they were not Fetches yet, for they had been separated from Calder, their Master Fetch. As far as Calder knew, no name existed for such creatures—the children of the in-between.

He meant to call comforts down to them, but no words came. And they did not speak at first, only stared at either him as he climbed down to them or at something beyond him in the sky that held more hope than he.

Carefully Calder grasped the damp beams that had once kept the earth back from the deep hole. The soil, slick with moss, fell freely away as he climbed down. A cross board cracked and Calder dropped into the water. To his shame, he cried out as he collided with one of the dead girls, her undergarments torn to ribbons, waving in the water like seaweed. But he did not have to swim—the water was only chest deep on Rasputin's frame. Uncertain on what he was standing, Calder tried to keep his balance and moved slowly toward them, his arms stretched out.

"Come," he whispered, and they each held out a hand to him; both gripped his arm and silently let him guide them to the wall of the shaft that would be the easiest to climb, where there were the most unbroken beams. First Calder lifted Ana, holding her waist where the shreds of a corset dangled and dripped. He held her as she found crevices for her feet and the edges of boards for finger holds. Her hair, which had once been a dark gold river down her back, had been cut to shoulder length. Her torn petticoat lifted out of the darkness like the sail of a sunken ship, pale and running with dirty water. When she was safely out of the shaft, Calder gave her brother his hands as a stirrup to step from and watched him begin the ascent. Alexis still wore the metal and leather brace on his left leg. It was as the boy's dripping trouser legs lifted out of the water that Calder felt an awful anxiety.

Fetches were not usually repelled by the corpses of the souls they escorted through the Aisle, but Calder felt a chill now as something floated up against his back, something he feared was Alexandra's body. When he'd first seen her, he'd been captivated by her reddish-gold hair and white hands, but even more than this he had been attracted to the beauty of her spirit, the tender soul that loved her child so desperately. But both were gone now. Her spirit had flown to Heaven, and her body, which he was terrified to behold, had been reduced to a broken shell of useless organs, filling with muddy water, melting back into the clay from which God had formed all earthly things.

Calder stood shaking in the darkness, and instead of turning to see the corpse, he tilted his head up to the sky. He shuddered, a small movement that made the waters ripple around him and caused whatever was nestling against his back to tip gently away. Ana peered over the edge of the shaft and knelt, offering him her hand, though it was well out of reach. The boy was standing straight, near his sister but seemingly unaware of her, staring into the trees, breathing fast and shallow.

"Come out of there," Ana whispered. She opened and closed her hand at him, calling him to take hold. Calder did not look to see what slid against the back of his arm. He gripped the beams on the side of the mineshaft and began to climb. He didn't take the girl's hand for fear of toppling her over the precipice, but she grabbed his sleeve and pulled at him as he dragged himself out of the shaft and up onto the ground beside her. She tugged at his clothes, trying to sit him up.

"Did you bring nothing with you?" She was looking around them. "We need rope."

"No," he whispered. "We have to leave them."

An inner fire brightened her eyes and he thought for a moment she would slap him, but she only let go of his arm.

"They'll come back to move the bodies. No one can know we were here," he said. "And we must hurry."

He knew men would soon arrive in grinding trucks, with swinging lanterns and shovels, anxious to move the bodies out of a grave that was foolishly easy to find and into a new burial site beneath some unused bridge, along the swamped bank of a fishless stream, or under some secret and rock-strewn acclivity.

"My father lives!" Alexis stood at the edge of the opening. He dropped to his knees, and Calder and Ana looked into the shaft. The tsar's right arm, his body having floated up against the rotting wall of the grave, had pushed up out of the water and rested there, the hand half open.

Ana, beside Calder, too far from Alexis to touch him, gripped Calder's arm instead of her brother's.

As the water rippled, the tsar's hand seemed to tilt inward, beckoning to those above. The face was hidden by shadow, but the white arm and hand, as relaxed as they might have been during a leisurely swim on some summer outing at the shore, rocked and then slipped softly back into the water.

"I'm coming!" Alexis made to dive back into the shaft, but Calder caught him about the waist and held him, though the boy fought to be free. "He lives!"

Ana stood up, her hand over her mouth, unable to take her eyes from the body that floated below.

"He breathes yet." The boy kicked at Calder and thrashed about. "Look at him!"

They looked, and as the waters again rippled, the tsar's body rotated slowly, and the head, where a father's face should have been, came into the patch of moonlight.

Ana made a small sound and turned her back to the sight. Alexis stopped fighting. Ana stood with her hand over her mouth, keeping back whatever words might have been summoned by such an image.

What flowed from the boy then was not rage but a primal mourning. His cry was the heartbreak of a child but was edged with a horror that should never have been part of any childhood. Ana took him from Calder's arms, pressed his face to her chest, and rocked him, breathing sounds of empathy into his wet hair. And the boy let himself be crushed by her strength, gave away every spasm that racked him, until he was limp and barely conscious, sagging against her shredded clothes as lifeless as a doll.

Calder didn't want to disturb them, but he knew they must at least hide themselves before the men came to move the bodies. Carefully, trying not to break their embrace, Calder came up behind Ana and put his arms around her, cupped her elbows in his palms, lifted her slightly, and coaxed her forward. Her feet took a step, and the boy slid with her. In this awkward way, clasped together as one, the three moved away from the mineshaft and into the thick of the forest.

In a patch of tangled thorns by a pair of dead trees, Calder cleared a place for them to rest. The tree trunks tilted toward one another, holding each other up in a kind of triangular cave backed with vines and fallen branches. Brother and sister sat, holding each other, the boy breathing in small, sharp gasps and the girl in long and labored sighs. Calder crouched beside the tree cave and watched them in the dimness as he listened for the others, the men that would soon be dragging bodies from the mineshaft.

Ana let her eyes close as she rocked her brother in her arms, and the boy squinted through tears out at the darkness.

It appeared that both Ana and Alexis were Star Fetches. Calder knew that it was not impossible for Squires to come in pairs. There was a famous pair of sisters who had been passed the Key together, conjoined twins who did their Fetch work side by side, though they were attached only in spirit in the Aisle. And in this way, it seemed, Ana and Alexis would learn to be Fetchkind in tandem.

Soon the boy's tears stopped and his red eyes fixed on Calder. The hatred in those eyes was impossible to miss even in the dark of the shelter.

"Why not the others?" Alexis whispered.

Ana let her embrace drop. She pulled back from the boy to see what he meant.

"Why didn't you come sooner?" He didn't wait for Calder's answer. "You could have passed the Key to all of us."

"Hush." Ana clasped her hands over his mouth and held his head to her. "It isn't safe," she whispered.

"Why?" Alexis struggled to be free. "Will they kill us?"

"Hush!" This time Ana's tone was more forceful and the boy quieted. Still angry, he refused now to look at Calder.

"If he had come sooner," said Alexis, "we'd still have Nagorny."

"Who is Nagorny?" asked Calder.

"Alexis's companion," said Ana.

"He served in the royal navy," said the boy angrily, as if they had insulted the man. "He was my friend."

Ana regarded Calder with a wary expression, sorry that her brother had been rude and at the same time guarded against whatever he might have in store. "What will they think has become of us when our bodies are missing?"

Calder had not thought this far ahead. What *would* the men think who came to retrieve the dead? Surely they would count them to make sure they had not lost one in the depths of the shaft. Would they not think that either villagers had stolen two of the bodies or that two of the children had survived and escaped? They would search the area, but would it not be risky for them to report the missing children? Such incompetence would come at a dreadful price.

"They will wonder, but they will not tell anyone. It might cost them their lives."

"They'll find us here," said Ana.

"I won't let them," Calder told her.

"Why not?" asked the boy. He was slumped against Ana's shoulder, his eyes half closed now as if he might fall asleep. "I want them to come. I'll kill them."

Ana whispered to him something Calder could not hear. The boy eased back into sorrow, a steady trail of slow tears lining his cheeks until he drifted into a dead sleep. Ana gently rested him on the bed of leaves beside her. Now, for the first time, Calder noticed her bare throat. No chain hung around her neck and no Key dangled above her corset.

"Where is the Key?" he asked her, his heart racing. Ana seemed to see herself then, her corset and petticoat in shreds. She covered herself with her hands, and Calder took off his coat. She put it on, holding it closed at the throat.

"It's safe," she said. Then she glanced at her sleeping brother. "Don't think less of him for his eruptions or less of me for coddling him."

It took Calder a moment to realize she was referring to her brother's words. "I don't."

"He may be the heir to an empire, but he's also a boy who lost his family in such . . . " She herself seemed surprised that her words had halted. Her mouth stayed open for a moment, then snapped shut.

"I'm sorry." The ludicrous inadequacy of these words stopped Calder from offering any others.

"What is happening here?" she asked him. "Why would God save the two of us and not the others?" She waited for a moment, but when Calder didn't answer she asked, "What is the journey Alexis spoke of? Are you going to take us somewhere?"

The plan now seemed shameful. "I will take you and your brother to Heaven," he said, "as soon as you give me the Key." He would explain that they were Squires and needed to learn Fetching once they got to the Aisle.

"Are the others in Heaven?" Ana's eyes were shadowed and she seemed very small and young.

"There is no doubt," he told her.

She nodded at this reassurance and checked Alexis to make sure he was still asleep. "It's not right to be left behind." Her voice was timorous, and a quivering began at the corners of her mouth and around her chin. "Father and Mother would never leave us." She moved away from her brother and whispered to Calder things it seemed she did not want to say but had to. "The bullets went through my body. I could feel them burning. One went right through my throat and hit Olga. I tried to stop the bullets with my hands but they passed through me."

Calder didn't know how to save her from the suffering of this story other than to hear her. "Yes," he said. "I understand."

"I closed my eyes," she whispered. "But I could hear—" She stopped and closed her eyes for a moment, then opened them in the dim light. "I lay down with Olga and Maria, touching them, but all the blood was theirs."

"Yes." Calder felt like a criminal, hearing intimacies meant for her loved ones.

"I felt Alexis take my hand in the truck. We were piled one on the other like firewood. I don't know who was beside me or on top of me, but he found my hand. And he didn't make a sound."

"Yes," Calder whispered back to her. "He is a brave boy. And you are a brave girl."

She took in a breath so sharp, it doubled her over. She hid her face in her hands and wept in an agonizing quiet so her brother would not wake. Calder wanted to comfort her, but as he lifted Rasputin's large hand, he shied back from touching her.

"We need the Key," he said. "Did the guards take it when they searched your bodies?"

A distant sound sent a shock through Calder's spine. An engine grinding, less than a mile away, but he thought their place of hiding was safe enough. At a second sound, the pop of an engine's misfire, Ana lifted her head and listened.

"It's all right," Calder said. "We're well away."

She wiped her eyes and kept listening. "And now what?" She placed a hand on her brother's back. "You will take us to Heaven?"

"Yes."

"Why give us the Key, then?"

"I came to earth to take a Squire," he told her.

"You came for my brother? To train him to be an angel like you?"

"I came for your mother."

The fire was back in her eyes, bringing heat to Calder's face and neck. "You wanted to take my mother away from us?"

"I didn't realize who she was."

"What were you thinking?" Ana's wrath was so powerful, Calder crawled back from the shelter's mouth.

Again she demanded the truth from him. "I thought that I loved her," he answered.

"You didn't even know her," she said.

These words stung his ears but rang true in his soul. His fumbling into the Land of the Living in search of his Glory had been no more spiritual than a bear knocking a hive from a tree to steal the honey. But Ana's face softened at his distress.

"When Rasputin was murdered, that was you they were killing," she said. "But you couldn't die, could you?"

He shook his head.

"Where were you all this time?" she asked.

"In the grave." Calder realized it was a far too simple explanation, but the image of it shocked her. She sat back and stared at him for a moment, her eyes still wet. "Now, may I have the Key?"

"What about a Squire?" she asked.

"Let me worry about that." He felt that once in the Aisle they would be willing Fetches. But for now he wanted to soothe her heart.

For the first time she looked guilty. "I didn't understand what the Key meant." She glanced at her brother, who was still sleeping. "Alexis showed me how it made him invincible." She paused, perhaps remembering her brother showing off how his leg had been healed. "And we needed someone to help us escape." She looked Calder in the eyes and away again. "When I chose someone I didn't know what would happen that night."

She didn't understand that the Key couldn't be passed to just anyone, only those from Death Scenes who could see and hear the Fetch. She and her brother had been ordained as Star Fetches—both had looked in his eyes and heard his words. Whoever she had chosen was not blessed in this way.

"If I'd known, I could've saved them all." Ashamed now of her choice, Ana confessed. "I gave it to Ilya in a note where we always left messages for each other."

Calder prayed this man would be easy to find. "Who is Ilya?" He heard how frightened he sounded, but he couldn't help it.

"He was my intended." At this she blushed, more from humiliation, he thought, than from pleasure. "One of our guards."

"We have to find him."

The sounds of men's voices, shouts in the distance but still too close for safety, silenced the two and roused the sleeping boy. He sat up and the three listened, scarcely breathing.

Another shout, then the faint sounds of angry questions, clanging shovels, and the slam of a car door.

"Let them find us here," said Alexis. "I want them to cut me in half. I'll put myself back together and kick them all the way to hell!"

"Keep still," Ana hissed at him. "Do you want to be caught and prodded at and put on display like some extinct animal?" She glanced at Calder with a coldness that hurt him.

"They'd make us into saints," the boy told her.

"Don't you want to go to Father and Mother?" she asked. This quieted him. "We'll be safe in Heaven soon."

"How will we get the Key back?" Calder whispered.

"In town," said Ana. "I'll show you." She started at the sound of another shout, closer than before.

"Come." Calder helped them up and motioned for them to follow. They moved as quietly as they could away from the sounds of the trucks. Ana and Alexis held hands. With her other hand Ana held up Calder's coat, which dragged in the leaves. The forest floor sloped up and Calder led the way through a thick clutch of larch trees.

"Is this Ilya planning to meet you somewhere?" Calder whispered.

"You gave the Key to Ilya?" asked Alexis.

They were alone with the trees, but Calder felt like there were eyes and ears in every bush and fold of vines. He led them along the slope to the place where the trees thinned. He could hear a stream and thought that if they followed it they would find the place where it ran under a small bridge in the road he had taken from town. Calder thought he saw bird shadows cross their path more than once, but he never saw where the creatures lit or heard their calls. He walked in front with Alexis behind him and Ana following, her throat slender and white in the coat's oversize collar.

The boy walked with his head down. "Why did you have to give the Key to Ilya?"

Calder saw and heard the men at the same moment. The crunch of leaves and twigs under foot. The glint of one man's damp forehead, the flash of the shovel blade. There were two of them, only a dozen paces down the slope. Calder spun around and threw his arms around Ana and Alexis, held them to his chest, and kept his back to the men. Both brother and sister were perfectly silent. He stood as their shield and they trembled together under his chin.

# Sixteen

Calder held his breath and could feel Ana and Alexis do the same as they listened to the soldiers tromping through the leaves below them. One coughed and wheezed as he marched; the other sighed as he swatted at bushes with the shovel.

"Maybe dogs had them," said one.

"Dogs? You're an idiot."

"Wolves, then."

And now higher up on the slope, above their hiding place, more footsteps and the swishing of branches and ruffling of shrubs. It seemed they were surrounded by searchers. Calder willed the men to overlook them. Ana hid her face against his shoulder. Calder tried to imagine a wall around the place they stood, making the three of them as invisible to the guards as he used to be before he'd borrowed a body. He imagined the men seeing the white of his tunic and their skin, and the black of his hair and the coat that Ana wore, as the dark and light of a gnarled and mottled tree trunk. The three were so still, they were rooted to the ground as steadfastly as any larch or fir beside them.

One of the guards sighed. "I'm going back."

The voice was so close to them, Alexis jumped. Ana shuddered and Calder rested his chin on the top of her head. The tramping feet began to move off to the east. Calder waited until their voices and shufflings had faded to nothing, then slowly released brother and sister. Ana, still frightened, looked up at him with gratitude, but the boy shook himself as if being protected were humiliating. Calder led them west, sloping down toward where he hoped they would find the road.

"I know Ilya has the Key," said Ana. "I saw the chain around his neck."

The idea still frightened Calder—Ilya could have given it away, lost it, thrown it down a well.

Alexis seemed to notice then for the first time that he was still wearing the leg brace from his former life. The other two waited for him when he stopped and sat on a fallen tree. The boy unlaced the straps with a fury, kicked the brace off, and made to leave it in the mulch of the forest bed. Calder, not wanting the men who were searching the woods to discover it, tucked it under his arm.

They found the road, saw and heard no more signs of men in trucks, and began to walk back toward town. The sun had almost risen, and Calder decided it would be safer for Ana and Alexis to stay out of sight, not just because their faces might be recognized but because they were not fully dressed.

He found a shelter for them under a cart that, having no wheels, had been abandoned in a ditch. It made a kind of lean-to that faced away from the road. He only hoped a child at play or a curious dog would not discover them before he could return.

"I'll discard this." Calder indicated the leg brace.

"I never want to see it again," said the boy, sitting sullenly beneath the tilted underside of the cart. "Wait." He held out his hand. "I want it."

Calder gave Alexis the brace.

"Why?" asked Ana.

"Because it's mine." Turning it over in his hands, Alexis began to take apart the useless collection of metal and leather, his only worldly possession. "Why Ilya?" Alexis asked again.

"He's a good man," said Ana. "Ilya would never hurt us."

"He was in the room," said the boy.

These words shook Calder. Had this guard been one of their executioners?

"He was there," Ana said. "But he couldn't stop them."

"He had a gun."

"He never fired."

Calder imagined the guard who had stolen Ana's heart watching as his comrades painted the walls with blood.

"You chose to pass the Key to me," Ana told her brother. "Why shouldn't I be allowed to pass it to another?"

"It doesn't work that way," said Calder.

But Ana ignored him. "You would like Ilya if you really stopped to talk with him," she told Alexis.

Calder hated to let them out of his sight, but he had to. He walked through the empty streets, having forgotten it was too early for the businesses to be open. He found a store that sold clothing and shoes and broke one of the tiny panes of glass in the front door.

He slipped in and took a dress and a pair of ladies' shoes he thought were the right size for Ana and a boy's shirt and trousers only, since Alexis still had his own shoes. He also saw a simple ladies' hat, round with a small brim, the color of wheat, sitting on a hat stand. He picked it up—it felt so soft, he tucked it under his arm. As he stopped to leave some money, he took a pair of eyeglasses from the counter before sneaking out again.

The city was waking now, but no one had found the fugitives under the cart. Calder stood watch with his back to them as Ana and Alexis put on their new clothes. When Ana told him they were finished and he turned to them, Calder's expression must have been uncertain.

"Is it that bad?" she asked.

Ana's dress, an earthy brown color, was close-fitting, with long sleeves, a rounded collar, and a pocket on each side of the skirt. He was startled by how pretty she looked.

"It's a size too big," she conceded, trying to shift the shoulder seams.

"Very becoming," said Calder.

"I'll break my neck tripping over these." Alexis shook his trouser legs. The cuffs dragged on the ground, but Ana rolled them up. The white shirt billowed out like a Shakespearean chemise.

"Think of it as a disguise," she told him.

Calder was confident that Alexis had grown so much since he'd been in captivity that no one in Ekaterinburg would recognize him. He was less confident about Ana. She had so much of her mother and sisters in her face. He made her hide her hair under her hat and gave her the eyeglasses, from which he broke the lenses.

Alexis studied her up and down and gave a sigh. "Ridiculous."

"Thank you very much," she said.

Calder made them promise to stay hidden. They wanted to go with him to the prison house, Ana to see Ilya, and Alexis, Calder suspected, to get his revenge on the soldiers that had been their executioners. They protested at first, but Calder also saw a certain relief in his refusing to take them. "Do you know what they called that place?" Alexis asked Calder. "The House of Special Purpose. I guess now we know what that purpose was."

❈ ❈ ❈

Only one guard stood at the gate, and in the yard three men huddled together, smoking and leaning against the west wall of the house. They were armed but appeared unconcerned. Calder waited until they were distracted, laughing at a joke. Since this guard was not one Calder recalled from the day before, he walked up to him, smiling, and asked, "Do you know Ilya?"

The guard frowned at him. "Why?"

"He's my nephew. His grandfather is dying."

"He doesn't work here anymore," said the man.

Calder took a step back. "Thank you." But as soon as the man had joined his fellow workers for a cigarette, Calder crept through the entrance and to the open front door of the house. The muffled voices he could hear within seemed to come from the floor below, so he slipped into the hallway and went straight to the tiny water closet, easily found where Ana had described it. Just under the toilet's tank and chain, Calder slid his fingers behind the pipe and found a small hole in the wall as he'd been told he would, but it was empty. Ilya, or someone, had found the letter in which Ana had hidden the Key.

Calder was seen as he walked out of the courtyard, but no one shot at him. One voice called a question, but when he waved in farewell, the guards laughed as if they no longer had real duties to perform.

"He has no reason to stay in that place without our family to watch over," said Ana when Calder told what he'd discovered.

"You make him sound like a guardian angel," said Alexis.

"He lives across from the church on Tolmacheva," said Ana. "It's the house with a bird carved on the door."

As Calder had hoped, no one on the street recognized them as they made their way across town. Ana walked rather stiffly, holding hands with her brother, the empty eyeglasses making her face appear small and lost. The house was easily found, right where Ilya had described it to Ana, with that odd detail the other houses lacked—a carving of a wren in the center of the door. Calder left Ana and Alexis hiding in the narrow space between this house and the next, assuring them he would find out where Ilya was first so he could be brought to Ana in secrecy.

Calder tried to mount the front steps with self-assurance, but he was full of foreboding. His knees felt hollow and ready to buckle. He badly wanted for this to be easy, to find a nice young man with regret on his face and the Key around his neck. But his hand shook as he knocked on the door. He realized it might be too early to wake the house, but the door opened almost at once. A woman glared up at him, her white hair pressed down in waves by a tight black scarf.

"Who are you?" she demanded. "Who do you work for?"

"No one on earth," said Calder.

"What do you want?" So diminutive was she that her chin, thrust out in defiance, was hardly higher than his belt.

"Is this the home of Ilya Bogrov?"

"Why?"

"He's holding something for me." Calder thought that mentioning a Key would bring too many questions. "Is he here?"

"No."

"He might have left a message for . . ." Calder couldn't use Ana's name. "For one of our friends."

She gave one humorless laugh. "Friends? I've never seen you before."

"He wasn't at work."

"He's done with that house," she said.

Calder had no way to explain the urgency. "Please, where will I find him?"

"He's gone," she said, starting to close the door.

"Gone where?"

"Gone for good."

The way in which the door slammed convinced Calder she would give him no more answers, but the next moment Ana was pushing past him and had flung open the door again without knocking. Ilya's mother, or perhaps grandmother, screeched in protest, but Ana shoved her aside and began to hunt through the small house, room by room. The woman spewed a flurry of curses at Calder and hit him with tough little fists that would have hardly left bruises on a mortal man.

Calder ordered Ana to stop, but she ignored him.

Alexis came after his sister, but she had already searched the tiny sitting room and kitchen by the time Calder and the boy caught up with her on the second floor. She had startled an old man dressing in a bedroom, threw open a door to a small closet, and then burst into the last chamber—a tiny bedroom where two narrow beds stood only an arm's span apart.

"What are you doing?" Alexis asked.

In one of the beds a boy, younger than Alexis, woke from a deep sleep and gaped at them. Ana stared at the other bed. It was not only empty but the bedding had been removed and sat folded in a stack on the bare mattress. Pictures torn from magazines, actors and actresses, beaches and mansions, were pinned to the wall.

"I tell you, he's not here," the old woman barked at them. "Are you all mad?"

Ana dropped to her knees and felt the floor under the bed. Lifting one floorboard by its corner, she felt in the hole beneath and lifted out a cigar box. It was empty.

"So, you did know him, then." The woman folded her arms, still disgusted. "But I'm not lying to you. He's gone to America."

"So soon?" Ana's face was white with shock.

"You never should have given him the Key," said Alexis.

"Key to what?" the woman asked. The little boy, perhaps Ilya's younger brother, was sitting up, rubbing his eyes. The old man stood barefoot in the hallway, trying to see what was happening.

A sudden and irregular blush darkened Ana's cheeks. "He thought we were dead," she said. "And I know where he was going." She regarded the woman. "Where does his cousin Sasha live?" she asked. "I need the address."

"You *need?*" She waved a fist at the girl. "You need to get out of my house."

Seeing that Alexis was angered by this insulting tone, Calder herded brother and sister down the stairs before a fight could break out. He tried to console the old woman with apologies and a gold coin. As the three were scolded out the door, the old woman threw the coin down, though in her own entryway rather than into the street.

"Get away from here before I call the police," she yelled. But her husband retrieved the coin from the floor and called to them over his wife's shoulder.

"We don't have an address," he said. "Ilya was going to hunt him down in California."

The wife gave a snort of exasperation at this and slammed the door.

Several people on the street had shifted their attention to them, two soldiers among them. Calder took the brace from Alexis and hid it under his coat as he tried to hurry the two across the street without appearing as if they were running away.

"Didn't you tell him about the Key?" Alexis was asking.

"It's not easy to explain in a note," she said. "But he would never just leave me unless he thought I was dead."

Calder walked between them, holding Ana lightly by the elbow, guiding them past the church steps.

"He's one of them," said Alexis.

"He was nothing like the others," she snapped.

Brother and sister had stopped on the pavement.

"As soon as the family was liberated," Ana told them, "he wanted to marry me and for us to run away . . ." She hesitated. "His cousin would find us jobs in California."

"Why would Ilya go all the way to America for a job," the boy asked, "even if his cousin does live there?"

Ana seemed embarrassed to say. "It's not just a job. Sasha's an artist. He paints."

The shadow of a bird flew over their faces and drew Calder's eye up to the front of the church beside them and its domed arches. Although Fetches knew well that a church can be as corrupt as a gambling house and that a hill in the desert can be as holy as a cathedral, the idea that the church at hand might somehow hold a way into the Aisle made Calder's spirit rise.

Alexis was frowning at his sister. "You're lying," he said. "I can always tell."

"I'm not lying," said Ana.

They hardly seemed to notice as Calder led them up the church steps and through the open door.

"He paints scenery," Ana told her brother. "Beautiful landscapes.

They look so real on film, Ilya said. Like magic."

"Film?" said the boy. "What did you say?"

"Keep your voices down," Calder whispered as they entered the vestibule. The sanctuary was nearly deserted.

"Moving pictures," she whispered. "Sasha said he gave a photograph of Ilya to a director, who said he might use him as an actor—"

"You're not serious." The boy gave a disgusted groan. "You were going to leave the family and go with Ilya to make movies?"

"It's wonderful in California," said Ana. "You'll see." Then she told Calder, "We have to go to Ilya. He has the Key."

As Calder walked up the center aisle, his footsteps silent on the red carpeting, the walls, even the ceiling, every surface, seemed to be covered with doors: pillars formed doorways in the air, the altar was the great curved entrance to a cave, and along both walls of the sanctuary there were little arched and pinnacled inlets with paintings like portals into other worlds. And the worlds were like scenes from the Aisle: the Crucifixion, the Last Supper, the garden of Gethsemane.

The candles on the altar sputtered as Calder approached the front pews. He knew who had the Key and a general idea of where to search for him, but the time it took to travel over half the globe in a human body made him queasy. He hoped somehow in this holy place he might find a way to call on the Captain. He even had a secret hope that he would be shown how to open a Door directly to wherever the Key lay.

There were three parishioners seated near the front of the sanctuary, a young woman in mourning black and two old gentlemen—the rest of the church was empty except for a priest coming from a back room beside the altar. He wore dark robes that brushed the floor and a head cloth down his back. Calder had not been in many churches as a Fetch, but he remembered them as peaceful places. But not this one. Here the air jittered with discontent, making the candlewicks crackle. The shadows that danced on the ceiling vexed him by moving like thinking creatures at the corners of his vision.

And now the shadows came together as one and hung like an ominous stain on the ceiling above the first pew.

# Seventeen

The young woman, who had been quietly weeping as she prayed, stood suddenly, and the darkness above her seemed to rain a black mist over her head. Calder felt a chill between his ribs but kept himself from running away by gripping the pew next to him. Again the candles began to flare and flap; the glass lamps that hung from chains overhead creaked as they swung. The woman in black set her gaze on Calder, her expression both horrified and accusing.

"You are the Beast," she whispered.

Calder thought he'd heard wrong. But she pointed at him and said, "Don't come near me."

The two old gentlemen stared and the priest came to the young woman's side.

"Josef says he's the Devil." Her voice rang sharply in the hollow of the church. "Josef told me."

"Your husband." The priest took the hand that pointed to Calder and lowered it. "But he's been gone for two months. When did he tell you this?"

"Just now," she said, beginning to shake but never taking her eyes off Calder. "I heard his voice in my ear."

Calder felt this was all his doing, that his presence had drawn this young widow's husband from some corridor of the Land of Lost Souls to plague her.

"Show your true form," the woman hissed. Calder turned and walked straight from the church into the street, his hope of finding answers or comfort gone. Ana and Alexis followed him.

"What was wrong with that woman?" Alexis wanted to know.

Calder began to walk to the train station. "We have to go after the Key," he said. He slowed to let them catch up to him, surveying the street and the sky to see if a dark mist or unnatural shadow were following.

"Ilya talked about sailing from Vladivostok," said Ana. "He can't be more than a day ahead of us. Perhaps we'll find him before he leaves."

A man running past them, his arms full of newspapers, collided with Ana and called, "Watch it!"

Alexis shouted after him, "Do you know to whom you're speaking?"

But the man rushed on, taking no notice.

"Don't," Ana scolded her brother.

The boy scowled at her. "Why not tell them who we are? What are you afraid of?"

Calder saw a flash of fear in Ana's eyes instantly replaced with a firm resolve. "They already killed us once," she whispered. "Do you still believe you will be ruler of this land?"

Alexis stiffened.

"Father abdicated for you as well as for himself," she reminded him.

The boy stood stubbornly where he was. Now Ana's whole posture changed. She did not scold him like a mother, coo at him as a governess might, or nag at him like a sister. As she watched her brother, how the surprise and hurt of her harsh words hardened his face, she dropped her opposition to him.

"We'll be all right," she said.

Being neither alive nor dead, Ana and Alexis had been liberated from their traditional stations in life—she would never be one of his subjects, never again relegated to a lesser position because she had been born a girl. Instead of flaunting this new freedom, she spoke as one friend speaks to another. "I want to go to Mother and Father, don't you?"

Alexis shuffled his feet, frowning like a peevish child.

"We're not ourselves anymore," she told him. "We're the memories of us."

Calder stood over them, wanting to hurry them but not wanting to give Alexis another reason to rebel.

"What do you think?" Ana asked her brother. "Do you want to go with me?"

Alexis addressed Calder. "Is Heaven full of singing cherubs and saints and harp music?"

Calder had his personal ideas of great celebrations, games, feasts, but he hadn't yet been through the Gate. Still, one hears things. "I don't know." Calder knew his way around the Aisle, but most of what he knew of Heaven came to him through the oral tradition of

Fetchkind. Some stories sounded like myths, but others he had faith were true.

"Heaven sounds boring," said the boy.

"Shouldn't you try it and then judge?" said Calder. "Dismissing Heaven would be like getting a package in the post and never opening it because it might be empty."

"No, it's not," said Alexis, "because if I didn't like what was in the package I could throw it in the trash and go on with my day, but I can't try Heaven for a few days and come back, can I?"

Calder saw a snake of smoke from a passing gentleman's pipe curl unnaturally as it blew toward them. He wanted to throw Ana and Alexis over his shoulders and run, but he forced himself to stay calm. "Heaven is full of wonderful adventures we can't even imagine," he told the boy. "I would stake my soul on it."

Alexis sighed. "All right then."

Calder took brother and sister by the hand and began again to move to the depot, trying not to fixate on the dark ribbon of mist that floated alongside the boy's shoulder. It followed them until they entered the station, then it rose like a phantom crow and vanished.

The stationmaster had been pulled out of his booth to settle a dispute between some sailors and army men and was pushed down. A general cry went up all around. Calder rushed to the ticket window and, because he waved the larger bill and was taller than the others, the clerk gave him three tickets to Vladivostok.

As they waited to board, Calder felt Ana shiver beside him. The tremor ran from her hand to his.

"Are you cold?" he asked.

"I must be nervous," she told him.

Though it may have been the warmest day of the year in Ekaterinburg, he covered her hand in both of his. Without hesitation, she slipped their clasped hands into his coat pocket as if she had done this a hundred times, and perhaps on winter days gone by she had done just that with her father. It was a simple thing, but it made Calder's pulse quicken.

They were almost aboard, almost safe, Calder thought. No one cared who they were or would try to stop them.

"You, boy!" A soldier was struggling through the throng, calling to Alexis, pointing at the leg brace he still carried. "What've you got there?"

"It's nothing," said Calder, trying to hide the boy behind him.

The soldier threw his head to one side and cried, "Weapon!" Soldiers came running to see what kind of gun or knife had been spotted. The first soldier made a grab for the brace, but Alexis pulled back his arm and threw it over the heads of the people.

Calder dragged Ana and Alexis to the train step while the soldiers went after what they thought was a weapon. The three made it on board moments before the cars began to roll. There was a narrow aisle between the rows of seats in the first car they passed through, and an even narrower passage along the compartments in the next car. Alexis found them an empty compartment just as the walls around them gave a shudder and a rusty squeal rose from beneath the floor.

As the train began to grind and whine away from the depot, Ana sat and sighed at her brother. Alexis knelt on the other seat, hanging his head and shoulders out the window. Calder stood at the compartment door like a sentry.

The interior of the train was black, with empty racks above both seats for bags and packages. The window was large and square. Calder had an eerie feeling for a moment that they were peering out from a hearse.

He sat beside Alexis and watched people in the passageway shuffling past. A man carrying a jewelry box tied shut with rope; a woman carrying what might have been a vase wrapped in newspaper; a sailor with a bandaged arm; a little girl leading an old man by the hand. All different but the same—all burdened with sorrow.

Calder felt weary, but he knew he had to stay awake.

"You two sleep," he said. "I'll keep watch."

"Sleep?" said the boy, as if Calder were an idiot. "I don't want to sleep."

"Sometimes the spirit needs to rest," he explained. "But we can never all sleep at the same time."

"Why?" asked Ana.

"Because in this state, being . . . " Calder hesitated.

"What, you mean dead but not dead?" Alexis offered.

"Yes," said Calder. "In this state it's easy to sleep longer than you mean to." They stared at him. "Longer than it feels."

"What are you keeping watch for?" Ana asked.

He wouldn't tell them about the darkness he felt following them. At least, not yet. He wanted to say, "Nothing." But he knew Ana would not believe him. "Everything," he said. "I'm here to protect you until you're safe in Heaven."

The train was rocking and at first moved hardly faster than a cow might saunter. Alexis complained that they would get to the Sea of Japan faster if they walked. The day was bleak, and as they rattled toward the outskirts of the city, Ana slid to the window and watched the displaced people they passed. A young soldier with the buttons missing from his uniform ran alongside the tracks as if he meant to jump aboard, but gave up. Ana sat up on her knees for a better view.

Many people below searched the windows for something lost. Soldiers who walked among them pushed aside the poor as if they were filthy curs run wild in the streets. Two small children, dulled with confusion, were dragged after their parents. Old men, unable to protect or even keep up with their daughters or wives, seemed dead already, drained of understanding and worth. One old woman lay in the dry grass, sleeping or dead.

"Look at them," Ana whispered. "It's true, what they said." Her eyes followed one person and then another.

"It wasn't like this before," said Alexis. "It's because of the Germans. And the Bolsheviks."

"You've never seen the real Russia," said Ana. "Everywhere you went with Father, the way was always prepared for you. You only saw what was meant for you to see."

"And you stayed at home reciting French and painting pictures of bowls of fruit." The boy's face reddened. "What makes you think you know more about Russia than I?"

She stared at him sadly. "Look at them."

"They turned their backs on their tsar!"

Ana's voice was barely over a whisper again. "They warned him a war would bring only more suffering." She glanced at Calder, who had no idea how to help.

"There are always losses in wartime," said the boy.

"But it isn't just the war. They've been hungry and without schools since before you were born," she said.

"Did Ilya tell you that?" Alexis smirked.

"You've heard of Bloody Sunday."

The boy's face darkened. "That never happened."

"How would you know? You were only a baby."

"It's a lie."

Ana hit the window with her hand. "Look at their faces."

But Alexis wouldn't.

"Instead of receiving help, they were shot down like criminals," she said.

"So were we," said Alexis. He studied Ana now, the way she silently followed the faces of the people as the train picked up speed. The boy seemed to pause on the edge of affection, but then pushed himself the other way, lashing out at her.

"You don't know what you're talking about," he snapped. "Father was a great leader."

She sighed. "He wanted to be."

"Shut up!" Alexis stamped his foot. Calder jumped, ready to step between them.

"He was the best father we could have asked for," she said. "He tried to be a good leader."

"What do you know about it? Hiding in the library, acting out those idiotic plays." He sat down hard but was back on his feet at once. "Coddling babies on your knee isn't what makes a great man."

"I didn't say he wasn't a great man," said Ana. "But he should have seen what was happening—"

"That's treason!" Alexis glowered at her, his fists tight. "I command you to be silent."

"You don't rule me." Ana shook herself, throwing off her anger. "I love Father as much as you do," she said.

Calder expected Alexis to argue, but he seemed to have lost his passion for the fight.

"And I miss him as much as you do," said Ana.

Alexis stood before the glass, resting his head on the window frame.

"Let's go to him as fast as we can," she added.

Her brother sagged at these words, let himself be drawn toward her, and dropped onto the seat beside her.

"When we find the others in Heaven," she whispered, "I will hug Father first and then Mother." Ana curled her hand around Alexis's as he leaned against her. They gazed out the window, their faces side by side. The scenery now was filled with hills and fields. "I won't be able to hug Mother first because she'll rush to you and wrap you in her arms and hold you so tight, you'll grow a foot taller."

Calder watched them together, struck by how solitary his life as a Fetch had been. And his human life as well. As he observed Ana and Alexis, this attachment they had to each other, this burden of the heart, seemed familiar. It was what he had always felt the lack of in the Aisle. The bond between Ana and Alexis seemed to Calder more precious to humans than food or warmth, safety or wealth. More precious even than freedom or honor. But, like honor, it was probably hard to measure its value until lost.

His vision went dark, as if the train were passing through a tunnel, and Calder felt the shove of a hand against his shoulder, pushing him into an uneven step and making him laugh. He heard a boy's laughter, so close that he could have stretched out his arms and touched him. He saw the underside of a stone bridge and the bow and mast of a fishing boat up ahead. Water lapped to his right. He wanted to twist around and glimpse his friend, but in a blur the boy was running past him and he could see only his back. Perhaps ten years old, small with dark curls and a lame leg that slowed him down not one bit.

"And then I will kiss Olga and Tatiana and Maria," Ana was saying, "and they'll all be talking at once, telling us what Heaven is like and what we must see first."

When Calder's sight returned, he watched the world fly past the window and detected no black shadows trailing along with them. He hoped he had worn out the interest of the Land of Lost Souls. Ana and Alexis huddled together, gazing at the picture frame of the passing landscape as if nothing had happened. They stared through the glass as if it were a magic mirror into some other dimension. A life they had been sheltered from and imagined incorrectly. A world that had never understood them, either. But instead of feeling pity for them, Calder felt envy. Their closeness stirred him, hurt him, filled him with longing and discontent.

* * *

It was thirteen days before they reached Vladivostok. They rode past the huge grass plains of Mongolia, the dark blue waters of Lake Baikal, and the deserts of northern China. Their train was delayed countless times, not only at the little yellow stations along the way, but out in the middle of the wilderness. Soldiers would stop the train to search the compartments and passengers, sometimes to board, and often for no reason Calder could discern. The train would squeal and grind to a stop at the waving demand of a band of soldiers; it might be minutes or hours before they would chuff back into motion.

Ana was worried that the delays would mean they would not catch up to Ilya before he sailed. She would stand at the open window every time the train reached a new station, searching the faces of the men on the platform below for a familiar one. Even during the night, she'd lean to the window glass with the full moonlight shining on her hair.

One night as Calder watched the two sleep, he saw beside his hand on the windowsill another hand that was not his. He whipped around to see Rasputin clinging to the outside of the train car, grinning.

"You gave the Key to the boy and his sister," he said. "And now they are changed. It must be a very powerful charm. Where is it now?"

Calder didn't like the look in the man's eye. "It's safe. We're going to retrieve it now. And when we do, we need you nearby."

"Did someone steal the thing?" asked Rasputin. "You're on a very long journey."

Calder must have looked wary for next Rasputin laughed and said, "Never mind. I have another message for you." He leaned close to Calder and spoke quietly as if his words were confidential. "Your friends say you can't make Fetches of the children because you tricked them." He shrugged.

"Are they not the Squires I'm to guide to Heaven?" Calder asked.

"No, no," said Rasputin. "It's a Lost Soul you're meant to help."

"You?" asked Calder.

Rasputin scoffed. "I'm not a Lost Soul!" Then he sighed. "This Soul is one you knew while you were living."

Then with a wink, before Calder could get any more information from him, Rasputin let go of the train car, flying back away from the window like a dead leaf.

"Stay with us," Calder implored, but he was gone.

Calder would have willingly gone back to being a lowly Fetch if it healed the wound he had made in the world. And he wanted what was best for Ana and Alexis, for them to be safe in the arms of their family in Heaven. But he could not help feeling sorry that they would not be seated beside him as his Squires in the Afterlife.

And it worried him that he didn't know what Lost Soul he was to help or how to find him.

*  *  *

Travel began to wear on Alexis. One afternoon he sat kicking the wall. "I'm tired of this train," he groaned. "Why did you have to choose Ilya? We can't trust him."

"Of course we can," said Ana.

"What if he didn't believe the Key had any power?" the boy complained. "What if he threw the Key away?"

Ana seemed stricken for a moment but said, "You don't understand. If he gave me a memento, even if it were just a button on a piece of string, I would wear it and never take it off." She was passionate and absolutely sure. "He's got the Key next to his heart right now, I know it."

Alexis only sighed.

"You don't understand how we feel about each other," she said.

A crack rang out as a pebble hit the side of the train and bounced off. Ana gasped and jumped back from the glass, but Alexis flew to the window, ready to fight back if he'd had anything to throw. The train slowed but did not stop as it passed by a small station. Two score soldiers stood about in frustration.

"Bourgeois train!" one of them shouted. Several cheered at this, and another stone hit the side of the train. Calder closed the window and began to lower the shade, but before he did he saw a stone the size of a walnut fly off the ground and crack into the window in front of his face, leaving a spiderweb of fractures in the glass. As the train chugged away from the little depot, Calder could still hear a chorus of protests and rocks snapping at the cars like firecrackers.

# Eighteen

When finally they neared the eastern coast of Russia, makeshift hovels—tents made of old carpets, lean-tos formed from crates—filled with dirty soldiers began to appear on the hillsides, with hardly room to walk between them. The port city of Vladivostok looked like a place where everything had run aground. As they stepped off the train, they simply followed the crowds, for everyone seemed to want to get to America or Japan, or at least out of Russia. The freight yards were choked with boxes and piles of supplies that had never made it any farther. The bags of grain, tins of meat, and boxes of bandages were stacked in and all around the idle train cars patrolled by foot soldiers. On the waterfront, as they approached the docked ships, acres of provisions in half-opened crates, covered in Japanese and English labels, lay abandoned under flapping sailcloth—rolls of barbed wire, boxes of bullets.

Up one road they passed, Calder saw mansions that had perhaps once been beautiful but now stood open, windows broken, emptied of furniture and wall coverings. The landscape was barren and worn, the colors muted as if salts in the wind had bleached the place dry. And though the train yards and piers, with their undelivered goods, gave the place a stagnant appearance, the dock was bustling and crowded with Russian sailors in naval stripes, merchants waving cigarettes and trinkets at all who passed, Japanese soldiers in white puttee leggings and blue jackets guarding their ships and, of course, the hundreds of frantic travelers hoping to board the waiting ships out of Siberia.

With Ana and the boy in tow, Calder followed the throngs to the port offices, but he heard from the people in line before him that only those who had deposited their passports with the Bolshevik office could board. Dismayed and angry people moved out of line, not knowing where to go. But Calder was determined to sail with the waiting ship that was scheduled to leave within the hour.

"Calder!" Ana tugged on his sleeve. "They're going to kill him." Out in the road five sailors were just catching up with a Japanese boy who had apparently stolen a woman's purse. Alexis was shouting orders, furious that no one was obeying.

"Let go of him!" Alexis demanded. He tore the handbag from the little boy's hands and the child cowered on the pavement. Alexis threw the purse at the soldiers. "Can't you see he's only a child?"

But the soldiers began to kick the little boy in the back and legs. Calder felt as if he were in another place, standing beside some other body of water, watching another child being beaten. He didn't realize what he was doing until he found himself pulling soldiers away from the boys.

Two men grabbed Alexis by the arms. Ana flew to his aid. The Japanese boy lay still, limp and bleeding from the ear.

"He's not the one!" She tried to pry her brother free. And two men held Calder back. One was cursing but the other smiled.

"He'll be all right. We'll get him a doctor at police headquarters."

"There is no police anymore!" someone called from the crowd.

"I command you!" Alexis was snarling. "Take your hands off me!"

"He didn't steal anything," Ana told them. "My brother was trying to help."

These entreaties were ignored. What stopped the soldiers, what made them release Alexis and actually forget about him, was what happened next.

Calder noticed a familiar glow flickering over the little boy's body. A Death Door appeared, ebony carved with flowers, the handle and great dragon knocker made of shining brass. The Fetch who stepped through was a female, one Calder had seen before but whose name he did not know.

"Sister." Calder addressed the Fetch that no one else could see as the wind of the Aisle blew in his eyes. "I need the Captain. Please."

The soldiers released Calder. "Shut your mouth," one grumbled at him.

The Fetch was speaking to Calder as well, but her words were too far away, dissolving in the thick earthly air.

"I can't hear you," Calder told her. He knew the soldiers were asking him questions, making demands, but he didn't care.

With simple, fluid gestures, the Fetch told Calder all he needed to know. She motioned to the child's body, to herself, then to the Death Door. Next she motioned to the child, pointed to Calder, then swung her hand toward the ground and Calder understood. If the child chose to die and saw her when he came out of his flesh, he would pass into Heaven. If he fixated on Calder instead, he would fly off into the Land of Lost Souls.

Calder took a step back from the boy's body, but it was too late. The little boy climbed from his body, but instead of taking the hand of his Fetch, he stared at Calder and shrank back. Calder staggered backwards, holding up his hands, whispering in Japanese, "Don't be frightened. Go to the Door."

The child cried out as if Calder's words had been the roar of a dragon. He dashed into the invisible mouth of the Land of Lost Souls and his Fetch hurried after him. And Calder knew he had created a new Lost Soul. There was no doubt. For a few seconds the image of the Door remained.

Soldiers were shoving Calder, tugging at him, their words a meaningless buzz. He leapt for the handle of the dissolving Door and fell through the vision, causing the knocker to swing once. The sound of that single crack seemed to echo in Calder's bones. If the Captain heard it, Calder did not know. One of the soldiers struck Calder on the side of the head with his revolver. The pain blinded him for a moment, but as the Door was fading, Calder saw a pure light flash in the tiny eye of its keyhole.

Ana and Alexis were beside him then, jabbering to the soldiers.

"He's my father," the boy was telling them. "He's not right in the head. Leave him alone."

"Come along, Papa!" Ana helped him up. "He has spells," she explained.

The wind of the Aisle was gone. Apparently Calder was seen by the soldiers as more trouble than he was worth and they let all three of them go. Ana and Alexis led him back to the port office.

"They'll get a doctor now, won't they?" asked Alexis.

"Someone will take care of him," said Ana.

"What if there's no hospital?"

They didn't know the Japanese boy had already died and Calder didn't want to tell them. He was still stunned by the idea of the child running from him through the Land of Lost Souls. And the flash of white light that Calder had glimpsed from home, which had traveled all the way down the Aisle from a place beyond the Cell, all the way from the Captain's shore, made his heart ache.

"What were you doing?" Alexis demanded as they got in line for tickets.

"I saw one of my kind," he told them. "Didn't you see her? Or the Door?" Neither answered. He thought that since Ana had seen Alexis's Door when she was little, and because they had both remembered him the second time he'd visited the boy, and surely since they had been passed the Key, they would be able to see Fetches and Death Doors. But Alexis seemed baffled, and Ana shook her head. The flash of Heaven was beginning to seem like a dream.

"He's dead then?" asked Ana.

Alexis reddened. "They wouldn't listen to me!"

In the street a truck clattered past, full of shredded oil paintings in ornate frames and gilded music stands tossed together like trash. In the port offices an old couple huddled together reading a letter. In front of him Ana and Alexis stood speaking to each other, but Calder's vision and hearing were beginning to fade out, a sign that he was about to get another glimpse of his past.

He felt his hand resting on the port office table, heard himself explain that his identification papers and that of his children had been lost in a fire. He saw the clerk's wrinkled hands as he deftly pocketed the money Calder offered him as a bribe. He saw the ship towering over them as they came out of the office—not as elegant as the vessel that sank in 1912, but still massive, with four huge smokestacks stretching to the sky. He saw the planks under his feet as they boarded, but then he was seeing the Japanese boy again, how he had covered his ears as he was beaten. But it couldn't have been the Japanese boy. That boy was short, wearing a blue tunic and straw sandals. His hair had been straight and the fingers long and slender. The boy Calder was watching in his mind now had dark curls and his fingers were short and thick. This boy was kneeling in a puddle, weeping as two angry men struck him about the head. Calder tried to tell himself it was a Death Scene he had once visited, but he knew better.

Calder returned to the present long enough to see Ana at the edge of the railing toss her eyeglasses overboard. He both heard and felt the ship's horn pipe—a note so deep, it made his teeth tingle. But next he saw a puddle in the gutter of a dark street run red with blood. The boy was still crying. Calder knew Ana was speaking to him, but he couldn't see her until he was ducking his head, following her and Alexis into their tiny cabin.

It was a cramped space with a single porthole too dirty to see through. The narrow beds were so close together, one could hardly stand between them.

"Did they hit you in the head?" Ana asked him. "Are you hurt?"

"I thought you couldn't be hurt," said Alexis, flopping down onto one of the beds.

"I'm all right now," said Calder. He didn't want to tell them about the power his memories seemed to possess.

Alexis claimed he was not tired, but almost at once he was asleep. Ana said she would just sit with him for a while, but in minutes she was sleeping beside her brother. Calder sat straight up on the other bed, pressing his back to the wall in hopes of staying awake.

Calder used to have a trick for remembering the names of Fetches he'd forgotten. He'd go through the alphabet in his head, and when he came to the right letter, the name would come to him. Calder tried to recall the name of the blue-eyed boy by whispering the names of Fetches he knew starting with A: Arielle, Auben. Bails, Ben, Byrd. Cait, Chase, Conner, Cullers. Duncan, Dymar. He skipped ahead, one for each letter. Etta, Fannie, Gwyr, and Hannah. Ian, John, Kilmoira, and Liam, his own Master Fetch, Michaela, Noyce, Oma, Peter. And then he remembered: Pincher.

Pincher with the scar on his chin like a tiny arrow. With one leg shorter than the other. Who could whistle through his fingers. Pincher's family was Irish and had a sailing boat. He'd brag that his clan smuggled goods in coffins and that he himself had played the role of the "body" once when they'd used a child-size box. He said he'd lain atop hidden bottles of rare spices like a dead pharoah. Pincher, who had been beaten to death in the street and Calder had not saved him. Obviously Calder had been there. He had seen the blood. He should have tried to stop it.

But instead he had crawled through a hole in a stone wall and run away.

# Nineteen

Day and night came and went at the porthole. Calder didn't want to wake Ana and the boy, but neither would he leave them alone. So he stood guard by their cabin door or sat on his bunk and watched them. Ana's hand lay half open against her brown dress like a night-blooming lily. The narrow bed in which brother and sister lay close together resembled an open coffin, and for a brief time one afternoon, it became one in the belly of a small fishing boat.

Pincher, his black curls tied at the back of his neck with a piece of twine, was just lifting one of the coffin lids so that Calder could see the brass candlesticks wrapped in flour sacks that were packed within. Pincher reached into the foot of the coffin and pulled out a small bundle that stank of rotting flesh.

"See?" he said, unwrapping the desiccated body of a mouse. "If someone wants to know what's in the hold, we show them the coffins and when they take a sniff they never ask to see the dead men."

By the next day Pincher was dead.

※ ※ ※

The whistle that signaled their landing in Japan startled Calder back to the present, but it did not rouse Ana or her brother. Calder gave her shoulder a shake.

"What happened?" she asked.

"You slept."

She blinked at him curiously. "Did I?"

"Both of you, for quite a while," he added.

"I had strange dreams," said Alexis, sitting up.

"I did as well," said Ana.

"Tell me," said the boy.

"I can't remember."

Calder suspected they were not being truthful when Alexis said, "Neither can I."

"Were you watching over us all this time?" she asked Calder. "Was it tedious?"

"I'm not used to this kind of traveling," he admitted, "having to pass through air and over water and land to get from one place to another."

"How does an angel travel?" Alexis asked.

"A Fetch opens a Door and steps through."

"Is that what you are," asked Ana. "A Fetch?"

"Like a servant." Alexis smiled. "Fetch me my slippers!"

"He fetches spirits," Ana told her brother, watching Calder with new interest. "And he's not your servant." Then she asked, "Don't you miss a lot of beautiful scenery, jumping from one place to another?"

"To me," Calder said, "traveling in this manner is like not being able to flip to page one hundred in a book—it's like having to read ninety-nine pages to get there."

Ana folded her arms, and one of her eyebrows arched. She looked nearly as impish as she had at age three. "You're not one of those people who skips to the last sentence of a book to see how it ends, are you?"

Calder folded his arms, as well. "When you wish to bake a chocolate cake, do you read every recipe in a cookbook about preparing meat before you get to the dessert chapter?"

She smiled for the first time since she'd climbed from the mineshaft, and it bruised his heart.

❋ ❋ ❋

They disembarked in Japan in the city of Nagasaki. The land was low and thick with tall grasses. The bare masts of hundreds of small fishing boats looked themselves like tall, stiff shoreline reeds. The mountains beyond were muted in a sea salt haze. The passengers were herded down the ramp and along a fenced path to a room with a tin roof and tent walls that flapped in the wind. People's suitcases were opened and searched. There were both Japanese and Russian men milling about, but it was hard to tell who was in charge.

Calder kept some money folded and hidden in his hand, becoming nervous about offering another bribe but not wanting to be detained for lack of passports.

"What's the matter with you?" the boy asked his sister.

Ana's hand was pressed to her side, fingering the seam of her dress. "Nothing." But her face was drawn.

They were called to the front of the line. The man in charge was Russian and not in uniform. Calder repeated the story of their papers being destroyed and offered the money to pay for new ones, but the man scribbled some numbers on a slip of paper, slid it into Calder's hand, and waved them on.

As they came up a ramp past a mountain of crates and boxes, they were bombarded by the sounds and smells of Nagasaki: the tolls of brass bells, the whistles of dockworkers as ropes swung bales over-head, the voices of drunken men laughing and singing. The warm air hung heavy with the scent of fish and cigar smoke, wet grass mats and burning sesame oil.

The crowd was a strange mix of peoples and languages: Englishmen in monocles, Japanese women with babies strapped to their backs, Easterners with pointed beards and layers of colorful clothing, Chinese gentlemen with their hair in long braids, missionary ladies in prim black dresses. Soldiers of all sorts, Russian, Japanese, American, loitered near the merchant stalls. An American journalist squatted in a crowd of Japanese boys, showing them his camera.

Ana was still holding her side.

"Are you unwell?" Calder asked.

"Hide me," she whispered, pulling Calder by the sleeve and back-ing up to the trunk of a thick banyan tree. She yanked Alexis over as well and the two of them stood facing away from the tree, acting as a shelter behind which Ana fussed with her clothes for a few moments.

"It's all right now."

She showed them her opened hand, in which lay three small emeralds.

"They didn't find them all, then," said Alexis.

"We sewed jewels into the lining of our clothes in case we were rescued and had to live in exile," Ana explained.

*That's why her corset had been shredded,* thought Calder. *The guards had been hunting for treasure.*

She gave the gems to her brother and wiped her hands on her frock as if the stones were unclean. Alexis held one up to the sun, squinting through it, but Calder stopped him, afraid this was not the kind of place one should flaunt wealth. To his surprise Alexis was not offended.

"You keep them for us." He dropped the emeralds into Calder's hand. "We might need money later."

Calder slipped the tiny jewels into his trouser pocket. Then he noticed that Ana still did not look well. He feared she was blinded by memories, as he was so often—perhaps hearing screams, smelling gunpowder, feeling the burn of bullets and the hands of her sisters.

"It's finished," Calder whispered. "They're all right now."

Ana covered her face. Calder searched for a place where she could sit down, but the intense feeling that they were being watched caused him to search the crowds for staring eyes instead. An old Japanese woman slumbering in a canvas chair beside a market tent was gazing at Calder with one eye. She appeared perfectly asleep except for her left eye, which was open and fixed on them. Calder put his arm around Ana's shoulder to comfort her but kept his attention on the old woman.

He held his breath as the left side of this woman's mouth stretched up into a grin. The right side of her face remained slack.

"Where's Alexis?" asked Ana.

Calder was sure the boy could not be more than an arm's reach away, but he was nowhere in sight, and although Calder was taller than the crowd, he saw no sign of a white shirt and a head of dark blond hair. He followed Ana through the marketplace but was stopped by a small voice speaking Russian.

"Down here, escort." The old woman who had been watching him with half her face was standing beside him, grinning, a familiar twinkle in both her eyes. Calder felt a tightening in his stomach.

"You're not going mad," said the woman. "It's me, Grigori."

"You can't—" Calder was so stunned, he could hardly speak. "How did you—"

"I asked permission first," said Rasputin from inside the old woman's body.

It sickened Calder to think of Rasputin defiling an innocent old woman. "This isn't a game. Can't you see how disrespectful you're being?"

But Rasputin only laughed, a chilling sound from the throat of the tiny woman. "I thought you liked messages from me." He shrugged with narrow shoulders. "I don't need to visit you. I have plenty of other work."

"What kind of work?" asked Calder. He didn't like the sound of that.

"My comrades are learning all sorts of new tricks," said Rasputin. "They're learning to be heard and seen. They can move things. Still, they have a long way to go."

Calder tensed.

"All at once," said Rasputin. "It's remarkable. One learns a trick and soon they can all do it!"

"Do you have any messages for me from other Fetches?"

"I've forgotten," said Rasputin. "Now, you tell me, what are you playing at?" He regarded Calder with suspicion. "Where are you taking these children?" Then he added, "And you've lost one already."

Calder was at least glad to discover that Lost Souls were not omniscient. They could go where they wanted and see and hear all that was said and done one scene at a time, but they could not know what they had not observed. In days past, Calder might have confided in Rasputin and told him where they were going, who they wanted to see, and why, but now he wasn't sure he trusted the man. Rasputin had been in the Land of Lost Souls too long.

"Why do you do this when you could come to me and speak as you have before?" Calder asked.

The small shoulders lifted again in a shrug; the borrowed eyebrows rose. "This is more fun. Besides, sometimes we try to appear to you and you ignore us."

Calder heard the boy's voice now and ran toward the sound, leaving the little woman behind, pushing past merchants and sailors. He found Alexis standing between two angry men, talking fast and furious, in Russian to one and in broken English to the other.

# Twenty

CALDER SAW NOW THAT ONE OF THE MEN was the American with the camera, the other a Russian in a uniform so battered, only one button remained on the jacket.

Calder meant to pull Alexis away, but the boy's natural diplomacy was obvious.

Alexis spoke to the journalist. "He says you're making the Russian children into a . . ." He waved his hand in the air, trying to think of the right word in English. "A joke."

"Is he crazy?" asked the American, taking a step closer to the Russian, but Alexis put a hand to his chest, holding him back, and turned to the Russian with his creative translation.

"He says it's just an amusement for the little ones."

The Russian slipped his fingers around the handle of his gun. "Arrogant bastard."

Alexis told the American, "He wants to know if you'd mind putting the camera away."

"Tell him to back off or I'm gonna kick his ass," grumbled the man, but he put the camera back in its leather case.

Ana came across the scene and pushed past Calder, grabbing her brother out from between the two men. "What are you doing?"

"I wanted to see his camera." Alexis pulled free with irritation. "What's the matter with you?"

"Be more careful," she snapped. "What if you'd gotten lost?"

"Lost?" Alexis laughed. "You could see that ship for five miles!"

As Calder followed Ana and the boy back toward the ship, he noticed the old Japanese woman at his elbow. He hated to have Ana and Alexis see Rasputin uninvited in the body of an innocent, so he slowed and let the two walk ahead where they could not hear.

Calder looked down at the woman. "You should stay nearby us until we can summon a Door," he said. "But not hiding in a body."

"Going to California?" asked Rasputin.

Calder wanted to shake him. "Why would this woman agree to let you control her?" he asked him.

"She was dreaming at the time," Rasputin admitted. "When she wakes up, I suspect she'll kick me out."

Calder halted, caught one thin little arm in his hand, and pinched the stolen flesh. "Wake up!" he called.

The old woman's frame jerked. She scowled at Calder. "Don't touch me," she said in Japanese and marched away.

❊ ❊ ❊

They boarded their ship and stayed in the cabin until the next day when Japan vanished over the curve of the earth. Alexis wanted to walk the decks and Calder couldn't leave either of them alone, so all three promenaded together, Calder on the outside, Ana between them. Calder gave her his coat, though neither cold nor heat appeared to bother them. Ana linked arms with both her companions. This would have been sweet leisure for Calder, strolling with Ana's hand tucked at his elbow, but he couldn't help watching the shadows and strangers' faces, wondering when next they would be visited by the dead. And he couldn't help hoping that the Captain had heard of their plight and would soon send them aid.

Most of the passengers stayed in the seclusion of their cabins or sat wrapped in blankets, clumped together on deck chairs. The great planes of wooden flooring and yards of metal railings all painted white reminded Calder of a hospital. What must have once been a luxurious lounge was crammed with cots and folding chairs on which people sat huddled together or slept. What had been a gymnasium was lined with crates and boxes where passengers sat and watched a moving picture projected on a blank white wall at the far end. Calder walked with Ana and Alexis slowly past these rooms, looking in at the large windows.

In the film, a young man was stumbling through a blizzard. He collapsed only a few yards from a house he couldn't see. His eyes stared and snow began to bury him. Calder could remember his own death, the winter when he was nineteen, tripping and falling into the water. Having the strength to climb up on the dock but not to survive the night.

They began to stroll again, and after they rounded the stern and began to walk past the gymnasium on the other side, Ana spoke as if she could read his mind.

"Do souls forget how they died when they cross into Heaven?"

"In a way, they remember," said Calder, "but they don't feel bad about it any longer."

"So the moment Mother died, she wouldn't be frightened or sad?"

Calder covered her fingers with his hand. "That's right," he said.

"There would be a different Fetch for Father?" she asked.

"Yes. Everyone has his own Door and his own Fetch."

"What's the Door like?" asked the boy. "Not pearly gates."

When Calder explained about the Doors all appearing different, Alexis said, "I'd have mine made of fire."

Calder saw their reflections in the large window and was startled, thinking momentarily that Rasputin was following them, but it was himself, of course.

Ana wanted to know exactly what her parents and sisters had found at their death, and so Calder told them about the Theatre, Feast, Gallery, and the Garden.

"What do the other Fetches look like?" asked Alexis.

"They look like whatever you want them to look like."

"What if I want my Fetch to look like a frog?"

"At the moment that you died, if you wanted to be escorted by a frog, you would be," said Calder.

"Do I see you as I see you now because I want you to look that way?" asked Ana.

She was gazing up into his eyes in a way that made him unreasonably happy. "I believe you are seeing me in my human form," said Calder. "I was alive for nineteen years in London."

"Maybe one of our relatives saw you," said Alexis, intrigued by the idea.

"Not unless he's very old," said Calder. "I was born in 1555."

"Really?" A whole new line of questioning seemed to blossom in the boy's mind. "Why don't you talk like you were from the sixteenth century?"

For some reason Calder felt insulted. "Why don't you talk as you did when you were one year old?" He felt instantly sorry for his tone, but it made Alexis grin. "Language is not an obstacle," said Calder. "A Fetch can speak any language from any place or time on earth."

"You mean, if you came to get a dying thief in a saloon you'd speak to him in vulgarities?" Alexis laughed.

"No human language depends on vulgarities," said Calder. "And none depends on civility."

"Say something in Aramaic," said Alexis, his desire to command surfacing.

"To amuse you?" asked Calder in Aramaic. Then in Russian again, "I speak to a person in the language he will comprehend the most naturally. The language comes from the soul I'm escorting."

"That's interesting," said Alexis.

"Do I speak well enough?" asked Calder. "Do I fit in?"

A doubtful expression crossed the boy's face, but then he nodded. "You pass for human."

"We're immortal now, aren't we?" said Ana. "Why can't we speak Aramaic?"

"When you get to Heaven, you will speak any language you wish to speak," said Calder.

"You said the soul chooses whether to live or not," said Alexis. "So if someone's head was cut off could they choose not to die?" The boy's expression was one of both disgust and delight.

"No soul has ever chosen to stay in a body that is not life-worthy," said Calder.

"I would," said Alexis; then, seeing the anxiety in his sister's face, he added, "Maybe for just one night."

"It would be like a bird choosing to sit on the branch of a tree after it had been felled and cut into firewood," said Calder. "Difficult and pointless."

"Is the Garden the last room in the Aisle?" asked Ana.

The Aisle was a secret place. Only the dead who traveled it, the Fetches who worked in it, and God who created it knew about the Cell. But Ana and Alexis had been passed the Key and so Calder decided they could be told about the Cell without violating the secret.

They stopped next to a cramped staircase that led down to a closed hatch.

"Is it something dreadful?" asked Ana.

"Something to battle, like a dragon?" asked Alexis.

"It's a cell," said Calder. "Like a prison."

Ana looked appalled. "You put the soul in prison?"

"No." There was no way around explaining it. "The soul finds a Cell and a Prisoner and has to forgive the Prisoner and realize the Prisoner is himself before the Cell opens."

Ana and Alexis looked from him to the closed door at the foot of the stairs. For one fascinating moment Calder thought that there was a magic spell inherent in the Cell that made the telling of its secret impossible to hear.

"Dragons would be more interesting," said Alexis.

❊ ❊ ❊

The port of San Pedro, near Los Angeles, California, was a place of metal and concrete. Bland square structures stood close together as if the world had gathered its ugliest buildings and ships and stranded them on this beach.

As they came down the gangway, Calder could see that the passengers were being led through an inspection of their documents and then made to wait for their bags in a fenced yard. He had a feeling Russian rubles would not be enough. He meant to give a retelling of the story about the fire in which their passports had been lost, but he was so nervous by the time he approached the immigration desk that nothing came out when he opened his mouth.

"Our papers were stolen on board," said Ana.

"We have this," said Calder stupidly, handing the man the note scrawled with numbers that had gotten them back on the ship in Nagasaki. He was about to offer a bribe, but the man at the desk ordered them to step aside.

"Through that door and wait."

They came into a tiny yard surrounded by a tall wire fence and empty except for one narrow bench. It reminded Calder of a dog kennel. Two guards watched them, one at the entrance they had just come through and another beside a door that stood open to an office. Inside, an old man, slumped at a cluttered desk, almost hidden between two piles of ledgers and papers, listened at a telephone.

"They're not going to send us back to Russia, are they?" Ana asked Calder.

The old man hung up the phone and motioned for the guard to bring the next case forward. Ana and Alexis were made to stay behind on the bench while Calder was brought into the office. The old man was thin, wrinkled, and white haired as most old men would be by his age, but his eyes were two shades of green—forest green on the left, silver green on the right. And this made all the difference, for Calder had seen these eyes before.

# Twenty-one

It was perhaps one human year before Alexis was born that Calder had stood across a deathbed from this man. The old gentleman had been alone with his grown daughter, the doctors could do nothing for her, and the girl's mother had been in Heaven for years. Calder couldn't help remembering the old man's eyes; Calder had spent a long time gazing at them, for it had taken the daughter all night to make her choice.

Calder stood in front of the desk and spoke quietly so that the guard at the doorway would not hear. "I have been sent from Heaven," he told the old man. "Lilliana is there with your wife."

The old fellow might have laughed at this claim, but the sound of his daughter's name stopped him.

Calder recalled watching not only the mismatched green eyes but also the dying girl's closed eyes, the gray lids shifting with understanding as she listened to her father's stories about what Heaven would be like—the budding trees, the birds of every color.

"You told Lilliana there would be a brook of golden minnows and a mountain covered in stars," said Calder, trying to remember the images perfectly. "And you said that Saint Peter would wrap her in a cape of peacock feathers and she would dance in slippers of diamonds." Calder saw the old man's eyes, first staring wide with wonder, now flicker slightly at some mistake. "No, not diamonds," said Calder. Remembering, he corrected himself. "Slippers covered in sapphires."

"Yes," the old man whispered.

Calder nodded to the bench where Ana and Alexis waited. "I need to take these children safely away from here at once."

"Yes," said the old man. That was all he said as he passed them quietly through his office and out to freedom. "Yes."

✳ ✳ ✳

The day was hot and the air smelled of tar. The three walked for several blocks before they found a place that would exchange money; it was tucked between a tavern and bait shop. They passed fishermen, girls in tailored suits with USO armbands, naval officers, half-dressed women with paper fans lounging on stoops.

"Where do they make movies?" Ana asked one of these women. "We need to know which train to take." Ana's English was excellent, but she must have had an accent Calder did not notice, for the woman said, "Where you all from, honey?"

A wiry man came through a screen door behind her. "Hey!" He had tattoos on both arms. He snapped his fingers at Calder as if commanding a dog. "You're not one of those union people, are you?"

"No," said Calder.

"But you're Russian."

"The children are."

"Communists?" he asked.

Calder was startled by his vehemence and said only, "No."

The surrounding businesses—a bar called Leggy's, a smoke shop, a shoe repair shop—all began to come alive, with faces appearing at the windows and men in undershirts and women with bottles of beer coming into the doorways to hear what was wrong.

"I heard about that meeting last week," the man was shouting. "Right over there in Nick's junk shop, right?"

"Is this one of those guys?" asked the woman, who still sat on her stoop fanning herself. A man with a cigar stepped up behind Ana and Alexis. The whole neighborhood was buzzing with questions and grumbling. In seconds they were surrounded.

"Don't worry," said Calder. "We're just visiting."

"Step away from my sister," Alexis ordered. At the sound of warning in his tone, Ana swung around and called out, "Where is the closest hospital?"

Everyone stopped talking, but no one moved back.

"It's all right to step forward," she told them. "I don't believe that it's as contagious as they say."

The little crowd dispersed and Calder took Ana and Alexis each by a hand and marched them away.

After walking only a few blocks, they found the train station. When asked where they should go to find moving pictures being made, the clerk shook his head and sighed as if they were silly children but sold them tickets and told them which stop to take. After the struggles they had seen leaving Ekaterinburg, Los Angeles seemed oddly tranquil. Children laughed, a man with a tambourine sang and accepted coins in his hat, one elderly woman made her dog do tricks for a group of soldiers. When Calder took a deep breath, the warm air felt like the first day of spring after a long London winter.

Alexis knelt on the seat to get a better view out the train window, but Ana sat nervously checking her dress for wrinkles and trying to rub dirt off her hands. She took off her hat and smoothed her hair. Like Calder, Ana and Alexis no longer sweated or fed. Their clothes might become worn, their hands or feet dusty, but they did not have the human need for bathing. Still, Ana looked as if she wished she could find a mirror. When she caught Calder watching her, she blushed. Calder understood that she wished to make herself presentable, but he couldn't help thinking that if Ilya didn't find Ana desirable just the way she was, in an ill-fitting brown dress and covered in dust, the fellow deserved to be kicked down the stairs.

❖ ❖ ❖

"This can't be right," said Alexis as they stepped off the train.

It looked like the middle of nowhere. Orange and lemon groves surrounded them.

"Where's the city?" asked the boy.

They began to walk in the direction several cars were taking, along a dirt road toward a stand of oaks. Calder flagged down a truck that was stacked with alfalfa hay bales bound in twine.

"Do you know where they are making moving pictures?"

"Jump in back," said the old man.

Ana and Alexis sat on bales that rocked as they bumped along; Calder stood on the running board, holding on to the side and trying to see where they were headed through the dust other cars were kicking up. Soon the orchards receded and buildings appeared. Not fancy, they were like barns and sheds. Music came from somewhere nearby, and many cars and trucks were parked in rows by the longest structure. The truck stopped and the old man waved them on.

"End of the line," he called. Before Calder could give him a coin, the truck set off again with a grinding of gears and a cough of smoke. Alexis became instantly enthralled, but Ana was anxious, glancing from face to face, searching for Ilya's.

And there were plenty of faces. Red-faced men in dirty overalls, their bare arms tattooed with bulldogs or naked women; young women in slips and open kimonos wearing heavy makeup; boys with paint-spattered dungarees running with boxes and window frames and buckets of nails; girls with clipboards and straw hats; men carrying sections of walls with landscapes painted on them that seemed as light as paper, or pushing wheelbarrows stacked with mismatched items: a tuba, a bouquet of fake flowers, a baby bottle for a giant infant.

The strangers spoke so fast, Calder could hardly understand them. They rushed about or stood close together in the small amount of shade they could find. There seemed to be every nationality: two Italian boys were painting a statue of an eagle as they argued about a girl, a Japanese man and woman hung costumes up on a rack, a girl spoke Spanish to her friend as they carried horse saddles from one of the buildings. Although it seemed frantic and confusing, Calder recognized a kind of excitement in the frenzy, as if the making of movies were a new kind of gold to be dug out and sold as fast as possible.

Finally Calder stopped a young woman who was carrying a stack of thin manuscripts and a bottle of soda.

"Could you help us?" he asked.

"I don't know," she said. "What's your trouble?"

"We're trying to find . . ." Calder hesitated, having forgotten the name of Ilya's cousin.

"Sasha Bogrov," Ana said. She looked so nervous, Calder feared she might faint. Alexis held her hand, though he seemed embarrassed to have to stoop to that level of nurturing.

"We're here to see Sasha Bogrov," Calder told the girl. "He paints scenery."

"Benny!" the girl yelled. A bald man with an unlit cigarette behind his ear looked over from where he was inspecting a woman in a nurse's uniform. "You know a Sasha Borgov?"

The man shook his head no, but the nurse said, "The Russian guy? They call him Sam."

"Do you know where we can find Sam?" asked Calder.

The nurse shrugged. "I haven't seen him today, but he lives at Hank's Town."

The girl drew them a map on a piece of brown paper bag. Alexis watched two young men practicing rope tricks, spinning a noose in a circle just above the ground and stepping through it.

When the girl wished them luck and walked off, Ana held the paper and stared at it.

"Are you all right?" Calder asked.

"Scared," she said, and Calder could tell she was not well. He found her a place in the shade and took off his coat, laying it down for her. They sat side by side and Ana took many deep breaths.

"What's frightening you?" he asked.

She appeared painfully embarrassed.

"There's nothing you can't tell me," said Calder. "I've heard confessions at deathbeds for hundreds of years."

She kept her eyes down and her voice to a whisper. "With Ilya, when we touched, held each other . . . you know . . . kissed . . ." She hesitated and Calder wished he hadn't made himself out as a priest. He had actually heard very few intimate confessions from women during his Death Scenes, and for some reason when Ana spoke of Ilya he felt the acidic heat of jealousy burning in his chest.

"Well," she went on, "it was always in secret and rushed." She looked Calder in the eye, blushing deeply, but couldn't hold his gaze. "I'm afraid that for him the desire came from the danger."

Calder felt restless and irritated. He told her to stay in the shade and he would bring her some water. He knew that, being immortal, she was beyond the kind of thirst water could quench, but he thought it might comfort her better than he could. As he went in search of a well or faucet, a bright light stopped him, a warm wind lifted his hair, and he saw a Door open and a young woman in a white gown step through. At her feet a young man lay on his back in the shade, his eyes closed and arms spread. Calder held his breath, afraid of alarming the Fetch, but to his surprise, she did not lean over the body and wait for the soul to choose life or death. She smiled at Calder.

"I know you," she said. "Rasputin, right?"

# Twenty-two

THE DEAD BODY OPENED ITS EYES AND looked at Calder, too.

"It's Love, isn't it?" she asked. "Monty Love from *The Black Monk*?"

Calder realized then that she was not a Fetch and the man who now propped his head up on his hand and grinned at him was not dying. The door was a piece of scenery.

"No," said the man on the ground. "You're Ed Connelly from *The Fall of the Romanoffs*, right?"

"Oh, sorry," said the girl. She was dressed in a white ruffled gown and ballet slippers, but when she lifted her hand to her mouth, it held a lit cigarette. She sucked on it and blew the smoke away from him off to the side.

"Doing a Bible picture?" asked the girl. When he didn't answer she said, "Harem? Western?" Then she motioned to his beard.

Calder touched his whiskers and finally understood. They thought he was an actor they'd never met but recognized. "I'm not who you think I am," said Calder. If he understood now what was happening, these actors had seen moving pictures that told the story of the Romanov family being dethroned and Rasputin's hand in it. The idea nauseated him.

"Sorry, friend," said the man, lying back down with his hands behind his head.

Calder stared at the set door as it blew open a little farther, pushed by a hot, dry gust of air that smelled of baked straw and ripe oranges. Through the opening he saw a picture of a beach with sand and sea and a blue sky painted on an enormous canvas. The scene appeared so real, he thought he saw the surface of the water undulate. And just as the door swung shut again, he saw two gentlemen, one in a sea captain's hat, the other in a kilt, sitting on a trunk eating sandwiches. Both locked eyes with Calder for one peculiar moment.

Now the whole place seemed untrustworthy, as if around every corner there were people and things that were not what they seemed, and as if there were messages in everything that Calder could not comprehend. Constellations by which he was supposed to steer but that he did not recognize.

He had forgotten about the drink of water. Ana was not where he'd left her. He snatched up his coat and her hat that she had left on the ground. He started running between shacks and dodging strangers, searching for Ana and Alexis.

Calder passed an actress rehearsing a scene, a director coaching her, a woman sitting on a fruit crate painting the eyes back onto the face of a child's doll. He walked through a medieval castle made of thick wood and plaster and there found a young man reclining in the shade, sitting in a canvas chair with his feet propped up on a suitcase and a manuscript lying open across his chest.

Calder would've taken little notice of the man except that as he approached the chair, the man's arm rose. Not the way it would if he was waking from sleep. The arm lifted as if the wrist had been tied with invisible twine and pulled by some hidden puppeteer. The arm lifted and then the first finger pointed at Calder with intensity, though the rest of the man seemed to be still asleep. Calder was unnerved, worried that Rasputin had pirated away this lad's flesh as he had the old woman's in Nagasaki. It angered Calder that Rasputin would be so cavalier with the bodies and souls of mortals. As he passed the reclining man, the hand that pointed followed and then the fingers snapped at him as if commanding him to come. Next the hand gripped the wooden arm of the chair and the head lifted and pivoted toward Calder with the eyes still closed.

"Grigori," Calder whispered. "Stop this at once."

The eyes popped open and the lips parted in a most unnatural motion. "I am not Grigori," said the head, with a voice that Calder knew did not belong to the sleeping man. It spoke Spanish and rasped like the voice of an elderly man. "Come back here, child," it said to Calder. "Give me your hand, for I've lost my walking stick."

Calder stopped but would go no closer.

This did not please whatever Lost Soul was addressing him. The head and the left hand seemed to be the only parts of the unconscious man's flesh that the Soul could control. The left hand gripped the chair hard and the head tried to launch itself toward Calder like a viper. The young man's body tumbled from the chair and he woke, crying out in surprise and standing to dust himself off as if he had simply had a startling dream.

Calder wheeled away from the scene, but a voice in his ear stopped him.

"The others aren't very good at taking bodies," said Rasputin. "So far." He was standing halfway through a tree, his face and knees and the toes of his boots sticking out of the trunk.

Since no one seemed close enough to hear, Calder spoke to him. "Can't you be of help to us?"

Rasputin seemed taken aback for a moment. "Don't I help you?" he asked. "I bring news from the other side."

"What news?"

"How the Lost Souls are finding each other, organizing themselves . . . it's almost . . ." He thought a moment. "It's almost human."

"Stay with us. Don't dally with the Lost Souls. Help me protect the children," said Calder.

Rasputin seemed to ponder this request.

"Do you love your new company better than the boy whose life you claim to have saved?" asked Calder.

"You wound me," said Rasputin. This should have been a comfort to Calder, but Rasputin's tone betrayed his insincerity. "And after I've told so many charming stories about you."

"What kind of stories?" asked Calder. He hated to imagine who or what had listened to these tales.

"Of your walking backwards out of Heaven, of your wearing my shell, of your magical Key."

Before Calder could ask him more, Rasputin faded away like a puff of smoke.

\* \* \*

Calder found Ana and Alexis watching two men practicing a fistfight.

"Where have you been?" Calder asked them. Ana was pale and anxious.

"Where have *you* been?" Alexis wanted to know. Calder realized he was the one who'd gone after water for Ana and returned empty-handed.

"We have to find Ilya now," he told them.

They returned to the road again and followed the map that had been drawn for them. They passed a pub and a gas station, a pool hall, and finally came to a long one-story building with the words HANK'S TOWN painted across the slanted roof. In the office marked MANAGEMENT the woman behind the desk told them "the Russian boys" were in room nine.

The door that had the number nine stenciled on it in black paint was propped open with a folded newspaper jammed underneath. The room was spartan: a table and a single chair next to a rumpled bed, a cot standing upended and leaning on the wall, an open suitcase that was half unpacked. There was a stack of huge framed canvases, the top one painted like a garden wall with every detail, every crack in the brick and curl of morning glory vine, perfect and shadowed. Even one of the motel room walls was a mural. Someone had sketched a landscape in charcoal, a beautiful, sad expanse of hills and woods, meadows and ponds.

A young man in wrinkled trousers and an undershirt sat on the bed smoking a cigarette, with one foot on the floor and the other leg stretched out on top of the dingy sheets. Calder didn't recognize him until he swiveled toward the door. It was the young guard from the House of Special Purpose—the one who had staggered out into the courtyard and been sick while Fetch light still filled the air behind him. He had grown a short beard over his dimpled chin, and he was half undressed, but still it was those eyes, with sad sloped brows, that Calder remembered, and the curl that hung in the middle of his forehead. Ilya's body jerked with surprise and the lit cigarette dropped to the floor.

"Holy Mother," he whispered in Russian. His jaw tightened and he slipped a hand under his pillow. Before Ana had even spoken, he was aiming a small silver gun at her heart. Though Calder knew a bullet could not kill either Ana or Alexis, he stepped in front to protect them. Ana pushed past him, ran to the bed, and embraced Ilya.

"It's me," she laughed. "I'm not a ghost."

"What kind of witchcraft is this?" He pushed her away, his eyes wide and hard.

A flicker of hurt passed over Ana's face, but then she smiled and said, "The same magic I passed to you." When she saw how he leaned away from her, she took a step back. "Why did you leave home so suddenly?"

"I can't be awake," said Ilya, as if speaking to himself. He put the gun down on his pillow and swayed as if he might be sick. He blinked at Alexis. "I saw you die, both of you."

"I'm sorry I couldn't explain in the letter—" Ana stopped in mid-sentence, seeing the sheets beside him move.

Ilya was watching them, but his lips were moving in a silent prayer. A young woman, auburn hair falling in her eyes, sat up and squinted at Ana. She only wore a thin nightgown, and the smudges of makeup around her eyes made her look like a chimney sweep. Calder felt an irrational impulse to hit Ilya.

"Who is this?" Ana asked him.

"What's going on?" the girl asked Ilya in English.

Calder wanted to get Ana away from Ilya as fast as possible before he hurt her. "Ilya, do you have the Key?"

"And you," Ilya said, frightened, pointing to Calder. "You were shot as well."

"We are not going to hurt you," said Calder, "but we need the Key." He could see Ilya's exposed throat now. He was not wearing the Key on its chain.

The room seemed small and hot. *We have come halfway around the world. Where is the Key?*

The neckline of the young woman's nightgown fell from her shoulder.

"Who is this woman?" Ana demanded.

"I don't have your key," said Ilya.

Calder saw that although the girl in the bed had closed the neck of her gown, Ana was staring at the chain she wore around her neck. Whatever hung from it was hidden. *Please,* thought Calder. *Please be wearing the Key.*

"Who are these people?" the American girl asked. "Your family?"

"You see also?" Ilya whispered to her, his English awkward. "Three ghosts?"

"Did you give the Key to this woman?" Ana asked him.

Alexis's voice was forbidding. "Ana."

"I have prayed for forgiveness," Ilya said to Ana, then looked to Alexis and to Calder finally. "Don't torment me. I have no key."

"Listen to him," Alexis hissed.

"He's lying," said Ana.

Before Calder could stop her, Ana had snatched the gun from the pillow and aimed it at Ilya. "I'll prove it."

As simply as she might switch off a light, she pulled the trigger. Both Calder and Alexis lunged for her, Calder knocking her arm to one side. The room rang with a sharp sound and Ilya jumped, scrambling away from them. The girl screamed. Ilya grabbed his left arm.

"Go back to hell, in the name of Christ!" he shouted at them.

The girl stood up from the bed. "I'm calling the police!" She glanced at the door beyond them but was too scared to run out and find a telephone. She stood there, her nightgown hanging open. To Calder's despair, a small gold cross was swinging from the chain around her neck.

"No call police," said Ilya. Blood was running between the fingers he pressed to his arm.

Calder could tell that Ana had seen the cross, too. And the blood. "No," she whispered, letting the gun fall to the floor. "You can't bleed."

# Twenty-three

Muffled voices and the small sounds of footfalls, creaking floors, and rattling doorknobs began to grow. Ilya's neighbors and landlord were coming, if not to help, at least to see what had happened. From Ilya's eyes, bright with fear, Calder could see that he didn't care any longer whether or not Ana was a ghost. He wanted them gone. Wanted to forget he had ever been her sweetheart or her dungeon-keeper. Even as Calder was rushing Ana and Alexis from the room he could hear Ilya telling his lover that the intruders had mistaken him for someone else.

Calder hated himself for not anticipating what Ana had been think-ing. She thought Ilya would be like her when he put the Key around his neck. She didn't know that it only made her and Alexis immortal because they had been blessed with the gift of Fetch sight in Alexis's Death Scene. She thought she would find Ilya and bring him along with them to Heaven.

Several people watched from the doorways of their rooms, but, strangely, no one stopped them. Perhaps they had heard too many stage guns to believe there was any danger. Calder rushed Ana and Alexis in the opposite direction of the landlord's office.

*The Key could be anywhere,* Calder was thinking. The thought repeated in his head like a drumbeat. *It wasn't where Ana had left it. It wasn't with Ilya. Anyone at the Ekaterinburg house could have taken it. It could be anywhere by now.* He felt sick, but he swallowed back the fear. He kept his arm around Ana and walked straight ahead.

As they came onto the road, a car swerved around them and then stopped. The driver, a freckled woman wearing only a bathing dress, leaned out her window and frowned at Ana. "She all right?"

Calder held his arm about Ana's waist now. "She fainted," he said.

"Let me go," Ana told him, and he did.

"Can I give you a lift?" the woman offered.

Calder was worried that Ilya's girlfriend might have found a telephone by now.

"Thank you, yes." Calder and Alexis helped Ana into the back seat and sat on either side of her. The front seat was taken up by a pile of strange clothing, including what appeared to be a tiger's head and skin.

"Do you need a doctor?" asked the driver. "No, she's fine now."

But Calder knew she wasn't fine, and it wounded him that he couldn't stop her heart from breaking.

"Probably the heat. I'm Margie." The driver looked at Ana, who was weeping now into her hands, and Alexis, who glared back at her. "Where do you want to go?" asked Margie.

"A hotel," said Calder. "Not too close . . . " He wasn't sure how to explain that they wanted to get far away quickly without indicating that they'd done something to run from.

"I understand." Margie winked. "See what I can do."

"Stop crying," whispered Alexis. "You didn't kill him." The boy patted his sister on the back but gave Calder an angry glare.

"Where you folks from?" Margie asked, probably because Ana and Alexis spoke in Russian.

Ana began to speak through her tears. "I will never be a bride. I will never . . . " She skipped over some tender fantasy and went on. "I'll never have a child." When Alexis tried to put his arm around her, she shook him off. "Don't touch me." Then she looked at Calder. "You brought us to this," she said. "Couldn't you see that it was an abomination to keep us from crossing into Heaven with the others?"

"Wait until we're alone," Alexis whispered. He scowled back at Margie in the driver's mirror. She seemed curious but watched the road. They were passing from fields and shacks onto a wider road past a sea of orange trees and over a dried-up river. Calder glanced out the back window—no one was following them.

"Without the Key we're trapped here, aren't we?" asked Ana. "This appears to be life, but it's not. We can't be who we are. We can never make a home here because we'll never age. We'll never be able to die."

"I don't want any trouble." Margie was eyeing Calder in the mirror again. She may not have understood Russian, but she was unnerved by Ana's vehemence.

Calder knew Ana was right to be angry. It was his fault. She fell silent, would not look at Calder, but let Alexis take her hand. After many minutes they came into a town full of shops, cars, restaurants, and apartment buildings.

"This do?" Margie stopped the car in front of a battered building. The sign read GOOD KNIGHT INN. A thin façade around the door was decorated like a portcullis, and ivy vines in chipped paint encircled a small, round window.

"Too cheap?" asked Margie. "Want to keep trying?"

"No." Calder got out and offered her some money.

"Keep it, honey," she said, and winked at him as she drove off.

All the businesses around the little hotel seemed to be named after things much grander than they were. The tiny restaurant across the street was called the Silver Spoon. The hair salon with grimy curtains in the window was called Magic Touch. Even the service station where a truck covered in dust was being filled with gasoline was named Victory.

The man at the front desk of the inn wore a red smoking jacket over his dirty undershirt in an attempt, Calder realized, to appear courtly. They purchased a room for the night as a father and two children. As they walked down the dismal corridor, Ana spoke.

"It was my fault." Her voice was gentle now. "I should have given the Key to Father or Mother."

Calder wanted to tell her she was not to blame, but again words eluded him. Alexis walked ahead and stood in front of their room impatiently, his expression dark. Calder lifted the key. It was like a million other earthly keys—long, plain, heavy, and black. It did not hang from a chain but was tied to a cardboard tag that had the number seventeen written in pencil. Calder then had a most peculiar thought, one that made the hair rise on the back of his head.

*What if the power is not in the Key itself, but in the Fetch and the Squire?* Calder stopped. He held the hotel key out before him and whispered the words.

"Beyond this Door, Heaven waits."

Ana watched. No golden light or shimmering archway appeared.

"Over here," Alexis pointed out, as if Calder were senile.

Although he was still trapped inside a stolen body, Calder clung to a desperate hope as he unlocked the door marked seventeen, but beyond it lay a small dingy room with one bed and a folding cot.

As soon as they had their privacy, Alexis turned on Calder.

"We wouldn't have had to come all the way to America for nothing if you'd told us how it worked." The boy's face reddened. "You didn't ask us if we wanted to be Fetches. You tricked us."

"Alexis," said Ana, "you told me he was captured before he could explain about the Key. He didn't mean for this to happen."

"And that wasn't the first time he tricked me," Alexis said. "When I was eight and I wanted to die, you didn't offer to make me a Fetch then, did you?"

Calder's face stung as if the words were a striking hand.

"Now I'm this thing you've made me. I'll never even be fourteen. I'll never grow taller than I am right now." He opened the throat of his shirt as if the collar choked him. "I can't breathe in here." He rushed at the window. The panes were small and so dirty, they looked like milk glass. "They painted the windows here, too." Without trying to open the window he changed his mind, ran to the door, flung it wide and stormed into the hall.

"Don't leave me!" Ana started to follow him, but Calder caught her arm.

"Stay here," he told her. "I'll bring him back."

* * *

Calder had been only three steps behind Alexis, and already he'd lost the boy. He scanned the street, then spotted him on the other side of the road, standing in front of a brightly lit archway where, strangely, if all the electric light bulbs had been working, the huge sign overhead would have read PARADISE. Calder had an instinct to stop the boy from entering, but he wasn't sure why.

As he followed Alexis under the bright arc, he found a long, narrow room lined with games and toys—little metal horses that raced around a miniature track, a shooting gallery where play guns mounted on swiveling braces shot tiny pellets at flat wooden animals that sprang out of the painted scenery, peculiar slanted tables where ball bearings bounced from one little wooden wall to the next, and tiny iron figures that, if fed a coin, would do a mechanical trick by flipping the money into a dragon's jaws or down a wishing well. Alexis slowed in front of the first few games in awe. Calder followed him. Each game had its own whistle, rattle, and buzz.

"Ana's worried," said Calder. "We should go back."

"You go," said Alexis. His anger had subsided. He was pale but calm. "I don't need to be followed about, you know. I'm not a sickling anymore. And no one here wants to assassinate me."

Calder didn't have the energy to argue. "What do you want to do?" he asked.

Alexis shrugged. "I want to see things. I want to go wherever I feel like going." Then he smiled. "I want some of these coins. Do we have any?"

Calder found a twenty-five-cent piece in his pocket, and a woman in a tiny booth near the door changed it for pennies. Calder gave them all to the boy, but Alexis gave him half the coppers back.

"You have to play, too," he said.

As the boy made his way down the corridor of blinking lights and clanging bells, Calder followed. A half-dozen children played there and as many adults stood about, eating ice cream in sugared cones. It seemed safe not to crowd the boy. Calder stayed a few yards behind.

He jumped when what appeared to be an ordinary piano beside him began to play by itself. The other humans weren't frightened—they went on as if nothing had happened. Calder noticed the coin slot on the side of the instrument and realized it was another game—a magic piano with keys that depressed not by ghost fingers but by some mechanical tug from within. The child who had spent one of her pennies on the song frowned and skipped off after better winnings.

Calder stared down the long tunnel of the arcade, which seemed to go on forever, and watched Alexis stand before a glass box where a doll as big as a woman slowly waved plaster hands over three tarot cards. Calder had the feeling something was hiding nearby. He gazed in the reflection of every glass pane and into every shadowed place between machines. With each step he took toward Alexis, something that was real was shadowed by something that was not.

The memories came with each blink of his eyes. A plump bulldog lapped up a puddle of melted ice cream, and as Calder blinked, beside the bulldog sat the image of Calder's old scarred mutt. A woman reached into her husband's pocket and pulled out a handkerchief to wipe her neck and in a blink beside her came the image of the boy Pincher pulling the same handkerchief from a leather pouch on an old man's belt. A young man tossed an India rubber ball he had won high above his head, catching it with his hand behind his back, but as the ball rose Calder blinked and two doves flapped up toward the roof of the arcade, which was also the ceiling of an ancient church. With these flashes of recall came scents and sounds and sorrows.

When Calder's sight had cleared, he saw Alexis at the far end of the arcade in front of a row of black boxes. Two men near him were leaning their heads toward these mysterious machines, and soft lights flickered over their faces. The boy motioned Calder to join him. They were moving picture boxes, and the one Alexis was watching was, according to the sign, a famous family of acrobats performing a tumbling routine. The closest box to Calder said it would be a comedy with a stern bespectacled professor and a cherub-faced man in a dunce cap. But when Calder placed his face on the mask of the viewer and dropped his penny in, the coin clicked down into the enigmatic workings and a moving picture began to play of a boy and a girl being separated from their parents. They stood on a floating island of ice that was breaking into pieces. Their mother and father were stranded on a different slab of ice, gesturing frantically. The children fell to their knees, reaching for them, weeping, as the river took them away.

Calder jumped back as if the machine were a snapping viper.

"This would be fun if I could share it with Ana and the others."

Calder heard Alexis close beside him and lifted his face away from the box.

"Come away from there now," said the boy. "There's nothing else here we need to see."

They gave their leftover coppers to a boy and girl who lingered nearby.

As Calder followed Alexis back through the arcade out to the street and open air, a machine to his left chimed one minor chord and spit a prize at him. A tiny chute opened and a small toy dropped at Calder's feet. No human stood by who could have fed the game a coin. Alexis was far ahead, almost to the exit. Calder picked up the object—a key, so tiny it could have fit in a walnut shell, made of hollow tin and painted blue and yellow. Calder flipped it over in his hands, rubbed it with his thumb, and for good measure tried again.

"Beyond this Door, Heaven waits," he whispered.

A myriad of substitute heavens surrounded him—on the wall above the fortuneteller's booth was a poster for Story and Clark organs with cherubs tumbling in the grass, on the hand of a man standing nearby there was the tattooed image of a harp. As a truck passed in the street outside, Calder watched the framed picture in its open bed, a painting of an angel hovering over a dark river, glide languidly past.

Calder felt alone and foolish. The earthly world felt like one big house of tricks made to torture him. Instead of a Door, his incantation had summoned a little girl with brown curls and a dress two sizes too big.

She grinned up at Calder, bold and shy as only a small child can be. There was no use trying to resist her charm. He offered her the toy key. She put the key to her mouth and blew a shrill note. Calder jumped in surprise. He half expected police to run in from all directions and trounce him. But she simply skipped off tooting a tuneless song on the key that was apparently a whistle in disguise.

Alexis was waiting under the lit archway. "Why does the Key have to be a real Key?" he asked.

Calder was unable to comprehend his train of thought.

"Why can't it be a secret we have to uncover or a code we have to break to open Heaven's door?" said the boy. "Why does it have to be a little metal thing that can get lost?"

"It just is," said Calder. "I shouldn't have passed the Key to you without training you to be Fetchkind."

"Did you break the rules when you gave me the Key?"

"No," said Calder. "But I broke my Vows when I came into your world and used Rasputin as a disguise."

"What do you have to do to make amends?" Alexis asked him. Seeing that Calder did not understand, he explained, "In the fairy tales Olga used to read to us, the hero was always doing the one thing he was warned not to do. The witch or the hermit or the magic bird would say"—Alexis did the voice of a wizened mentor—"'Whatever you do, don't look at the princess after sunset,' or 'Don't ask the elf his name,' or 'Don't touch the king's rose.' But the hero always does it. Every time. And then the hero has to do something to make it right. Climb the seven mountains of midnight or find the banished prince or take the stone of glory to the hall of the ogre. See how it goes?"

"Yes," said Calder. "But this is not a story."

"It is," said the boy. "Everything's a story. The stories came from real life. The first time any story is told, it's true. When it gets retold, something always gets changed, and pretty soon it's a story."

Calder had been told to save a Lost Soul, but wasn't told how.

"You have to search for the signs," said Alexis.

This sounded easy, but Calder felt heavy with doubt. He was at the point of asking the boy what forms these signs took in the fairy tales when the street went dark. For one second every electric light went out, and then, as they surged back on, the light bulbs in the archway above them began to break, showering sparks with each pop. Calder pulled the boy out of the way as the metal frame of the letter *P* crashed down to the pavement. They stared as sparks continued to shoot from the arch. When the frame of the letter *S* also fell, Calder hurried Alexis around the corner and back in the direction of the hotel.

"If that was a sign," he said, "I don't understand it."

"Are you being haunted?" asked Alexis. "Like in the church in Ekaterinburg?"

The boy was right, but Calder didn't want him to worry. "It was just the electric storm," he said, for now there was a wind picking up and clouds overhead grumbling with flashes of light.

When they came to the door of room seventeen, it was unlocked.

Calder would have knocked, but Alexis opened it wide without hesitation, then froze at what he found. He went to the bed and sat down facing the wall. Calder saw then what had made him go pale. The door to the washroom was open and Ana stood before the mirror, leaning on the sink. A familiar sight was there: a bird's nest of hair filling the basin.

# Twenty-four

ANA HAD CROPPED HER GOLDEN-BROWN HAIR as close to her head as Calder had cut his, and not at all neater. She stared at her reflection, shivering and blanched. The sight of this made Calder dizzy for a moment, the idea of her struggling with despair the way a Lost Soul might. He took a chair from beside the little table, brought it to Ana, and gently lowered her into it. She let herself be seated, rested her hands in her lap, a rusty pair of shears still hooked in her fingers. Calder closed the washroom door most of the way, to keep the boy from hearing them, but not all the way, for the sake of propriety.

Sitting now, no longer able to see her reflection, Ana stared up at Calder with wide eyes.

"He never loved me."

Slowly, Calder took the scissors from her and set them in the sink.

"We caught the measles once," she said, "and had to shave off our hair. Ilya saw the photographs and told me that I was still beautiful." She felt the back of her head. "I wanted to believe everything he said, but he lied to me."

Calder lowered himself to one knee beside her. "If I speak plainly," he asked, "will you listen to me?" He saw fear flash behind her eyes, but she nodded consent. "I'm not going to lie to you," he warned. He could see Ana steel herself for whatever was coming next. She took a deep breath.

"You are beautiful," he said, "with or without hair, and you are worthy of the deepest love on Earth or in Heaven."

She shuddered and tears welled in her eyes. He retrieved the scissors from the bed of hair in the sink and gently tilted her head forward. He snipped at her ravaged locks, trying to smooth out the places where she had cut the most unevenly.

"Hopeless job," said Alexis. He stood in the washroom doorway, shaking his head.

"Can you do better?" asked Calder.

"Of course." The boy took over as his sister's barber, brushing the loose hairs from her shoulders and draping one of the hotel's threadbare towels around her neck. Calder slipped his fingers into the sink and stole a small lock of the golden-brown hair, hiding it in his pocket.

Somewhere in another hotel room two voices began to sing, then faltered, laughed, and began again in a rustic harmony—Italian perhaps, though the lyrics were too muffled to make out.

Ana's tears dried on her face, and by the time Alexis was finished and Calder had gathered the discarded tresses in the rubbish can, she was smiling. When she stood up and regarded herself in the mirror, she gave a start. "Oh, my . . . "

"It's . . . " Calder realized too late that he didn't know words to describe fashion.

"It's modern," said Alexis, and Ana laughed.

They sat down, all on the same bed, leaning back against the wall, Ana in the middle and Alexis on the side closest to the open window, outside of which distant thunder rolled but no rain fell. Calder had pulled a chair over, but Ana had him sit beside her on the mattress.

"What will we do now?" said Ana. "We don't—"

But Alexis interrupted. "Let's not think about it until the morning."

At first Ana and Alexis leaned against each other, holding hands. But when the singing voices from the next room were joined by a third and the song changed to a lullaby, the boy lay down flat on his back, his hands behind his head, and, because there was little room, Ana shifted herself closer to Calder.

He was acutely aware of her, the way her shoulder pressed against his, the way the top of her head, as downy as a duckling, rested below his chin. It wasn't long before Alexis rolled onto his side, facing away from them, and went to sleep. Moments later, Calder felt Ana's fingers slip into his hand. It was not a gesture full of adult meaning, but one of a simple habit. She linked her fingers into his as naturally as if he were one of her sisters. He wasn't even sure if she was awake. If she was asleep he didn't want to wake her, and if she was awake, he didn't want her to think that he was making overtures. For this reason Calder resisted the urge to lift her hand to his lips and kiss her fingers.

"River of Stones," Ana murmured.

He thought it might be her odd way of addressing him. "Yes?"

"That's a sad name."

"Why sad?"

"Because in a river the water flows fast and free above and the stones lie cold and still underneath, as if they're weighed down with some great trouble."

Her image was childlike, but some truth in it caught and tightened his chest.

"Do you know what my name means?" Ana kept her voice low.

"No."

"Resurrection," she said. "Anastasia means resurrection."

"That's beautiful," said Calder.

"Would have been a good name for a Fetch," she said.

Ana nestled even closer to him, as if she craved the breathing sounds and vibrations of loved ones. Calder's anxieties unraveled and an unexpected peace settled over him.

*But I will stay awake,* Calder told himself. *I will stay awake and keep watch over her.*

Which is probably why he fell asleep.

✸ ✸ ✸

It was so dark that the only way Calder could tell he was seeing the world through the eyes of a Lost Soul was because the dim light of lampposts along the street was visible in all directions right through the hotel's walls. He was not alone.

"Have you seen my boy?" The voice was low and hoarse; the face that appeared was lined with worry and seemed familiar. A sailor stood at Calder's side of the bed. His age was hard to determine. His eyes were passionate but filled with fear. "My boy," he repeated. "Have you seen him?"

"No," Calder answered. "But all will be well." He remembered that when Rasputin interrupted his sleep, he was able to adjust his sight by focusing on one object. He didn't want to see the skulls of Ana or Alexis showing through their faces, or their eyeballs jittering through invisible lids, so Calder stared at the wall beyond the sailor instead and concentrated on the color it should have been—a faded and grimy blue—and slowly everything became visible again.

"No, all is not well." The sailor was frightened and checked behind him and all around. "My boy needs me," the sailor whispered. And now he began to cry, but all the while his eyes scanned the room as if it were an imagined horizon. "He's this tall." The man held one hand at waist height. "He's wearing white."

Calder pitied this father, separated from his child, not understanding that he was dead. Whether his son had died as well or was living still, it mattered not. The man needed to let go of his search and find his Fetch.

"Is there someone searching for *you?*" Calder asked.

"I can hide from them."

"No, don't hide. They want to help you."

"No." The sailor glanced again over his shoulder and into the corners. "They say they're guardians, but they are his enemies."

The man's angst was beginning to make Calder feel nauseated. He sat up and checked the other two, but Ana and Alexis were still asleep.

"God will care for your boy now," Calder told him.

"I'm the one that knows how to keep him safe," he whispered.

"I follow just close enough to catch him, but not so close as to make him run. Do you understand?"

The man, his eyes soft but deep with desperation, reached into his pocket and stretched out his hand toward Calder. A silver crucifix dangled from a delicate chain between his fingers.

"They tried to take this from him," said the man, "but I stopped them. They mean to kill me."

"The one that calls for only you, that is the one you can trust." Calder was glad, at least, that this Lost Soul was thinking for himself, speaking as an individual, not merging into the other Lost Ones.

"They're in the yard, and in the house. They walk into the bedrooms without knocking." The man backed up into the wall so that only one shoulder and ear were in the room. "They've even blocked out the light," he whispered. "My boy needs air."

"God is protecting him," said Calder. "He's safe."

"They don't understand him." Then the man pulled all the way into the wall, silent, as if listening. "I can hear my boy breathing."

* * *

Calder opened his eyes. Although it was dark outside, a queer light hung in the room as if a pale fog floated around the bed. Calder switched the lamp on and the illusion was gone. He was awake and Ana and Alexis were still sleeping. The singers had presumably gone to bed, for it was perfectly quiet.

*If Lost Souls can break through into my dreams and speak to me,* thought Calder, *if they can speak through a sleeping mortal and break*

*light bulbs, why shouldn't I be able to break through in the other direction*
*and be heard by the Captain?*

Calder dropped from the bed and knelt on the hotel room floor. *My*
*Captain,* he prayed, *hear me.* He called for his Captain in his head a
dozen times and a dozen more. But no answer came. Calder sat back on
his heels, frantic with helplessness. He clasped his hands hard together
and squeezed his eyes shut tight so that odd flashes of light vexed his
prayers. He rocked on his knees, pleading silently for God to take pity
on him.

Instead of the Captain, in his mind's eye he saw the penny arcade
and the bits of memories that had come to him. But now they changed.
A thin mutt lay upon Calder's feet, pressing its bony spine against his
ankles. Pincher ran along the docks, turning back to grin at Calder
before he ducked under the tar-patched legs of a rotting pier. The high
ceiling of the arcade formed into the vaulted arches of a cathedral
clerestory, where the sound of the tin key whistle softened into the
pensive call of a flute.

A hardness swelled in Calder's throat and he was almost at the point
of weeping when he sensed that he was being watched. He stayed still,
his eyes closed, waiting for a vision or to hear a voice. When nothing
came, he opened his eyes and saw Ana sitting on the bed staring at him.
Calder felt his face heat with shame, but she did not appear disgusted
by his weakness. Her eyes were full of empathy.

"Mother always knew what to say or do when Father was feeling
lost," she said. "I don't have that talent."

Embarrassed, Calder stood quickly and tried to sound confident. "I was praying. Fetches pray every night. It's nothing to worry about."

"Was there an answer to your prayers?" she asked.

Dozens of replies flashed through his mind, every single one as inadequate as the others. "I'm afraid my Captain has forgotten me," he admitted.

"Because you cannot see or hear him?" she asked.

He regretted burdening her with his sorrows.

"Just because you can't see or hear someone doesn't mean they aren't thinking of you," said Ana. "When we were in confinement many people were praying for us. I'm sure the others are praying for us right now."

"Of course," said Calder. "I'm sure they are." Ana and Alexis had not sinned. Of course they were being prayed over. But he had deserted his sacred duties—he was an outcast.

"We're much alike," she said, which mystified Calder. He sat in the chair and Ana curled her legs under her as she sat on the bed beside her sleeping brother. "We both know what it's like to be foolish with our hearts."

To these words again there was no worthy response. She was right, that his infatuation with her mother, his mistaking her for a governess, was foolish, but that she could compare her own actions to his was absurd. She innocently believed a beautiful young man while she was under the duress of captivity. Calder, on the other hand, had broken the most sacred of Vows in Heaven to chase an illusion. There was no comparison, but it moved him that she should say such a thing.

"Why don't we make a pact to forgive ourselves?" she said. "It might clear our heads so we can think of a better plan."

Alexis woke with a cry. He blinked around the room and frowned. "I had a strange dream."

"I did, too," said Ana.

"What was yours about?" asked the boy.

"There were all these people around me, starving and sick, grabbing at me and all speaking at once."

Calder was certain that the creatures grabbing at her were Lost Souls.

"I dreamed someone was following me," said Alexis. "Trying to give me something."

Calder thought perhaps it was the Key, but as soon as he did he realized it made no sense. Wishful thinking. If only it was that easy to find. A dream away.

The room began to shake. A sound that was not thunder growled out of the walls, and Rasputin broke so suddenly into the room that the table and chair shot across the floor and crashed into the wall. Ana and Alexis cried out at this violent levitation, though they didn't seem to see Rasputin.

"They're coming!" Rasputin's eyes were blazing as he came up to Calder, his hair floating around his face like a lion's mane. "Take the children to a safe place before they find you! The spirits are angry."

"Why?"

"They think you are the jailer."

"Me? Why?"

"They see their own Fetches as enemies, but you're worse. They think you hold the key to their freedom. And they think they can destroy you and claim the Key, but they're fools."

Ana and Alexis were asking questions, but Calder's every nerve was focused on Rasputin's words. The man seemed, at least for the moment, genuinely intent on helping them.

"I'll try to lead them away from you. But they gossip faster than you can imagine." Here Rasputin flashed his old grin. "When the children are out of harm, call them out." He shook his head. "You can whip them, I'm sure of it."

"How?" Calder asked.

But Rasputin was sucked back into the wall and the room jumped again, making the window and bathroom door slam shut. The room began to shake again, but not just the wall. The earth was shaking.

"We're leaving," said Calder. "Now."

"Is it an earthquake?" asked Alexis.

"What did you see?" asked Ana.

Everything continued to tremble. A low sound like a thousand windows rattling at once grew to a roar. With the boy's shoes untied and Ana pulling her hat over her newly cut hair, Calder rushed them out into the dark street just as an electric pole fell across the road, the wires sparking and writhing at their heels as they ran. He couldn't take them to their family—their parents and siblings were already gone. The earthquake slowed, but Calder didn't.

"Do you have aunts and uncles?" Calder asked them urgently.

"Do you mean Uncle George?"

"Yes, Uncle George," said Calder. He hurried them down the street in what he hoped was the direction of the train station. People began to open windows and doors, finding cracked sidewalks, broken windows, toppled fences. "I need to take you to your family. Where is Uncle George?" asked Calder.

"Where?" Alexis gave a small laugh.

"England," said Ana.

Calder missed being a Fetch and stepping from America to England by going through a single Door. "That means east by land and then across the Atlantic," he sighed.

"What's chasing us?" asked Ana.

"Nothing," said Calder. "It's chasing me."

"What is?"

"Some Lost Souls," he told them.

"Ghosts?" asked Alexis.

"Maybe we shouldn't run," said Ana. "Maybe we should face them."

Calder admired her courage, but he believed Rasputin when he said the children needed to be taken to a place of safety. It was one of the tasks he needed to perform to rebalance the worlds: save the children.

He flagged down a passing car and asked where to board a train, and the driver took them to the depot. Calder had enough American dollars to purchase fares. As they waited for their departure in the huge and cavernous station, Calder stood in front of the bench where Ana and Alexis sat. He scanned in every direction for signs of darkness stalking them.

"Who was the person following you in your dream?" Ana asked her brother.

"I couldn't see him in the dark. And I was trying to get away."

"What was he trying to give you?" she asked. Then an idea made her start with excitement. "Was it the Key?"

"No," said her brother, "I think it was a cross on a chain."

Calder sat down on the bench, haunted by the realization. "Of course. Alexis is his boy!"

"What did you say?" Ana asked him.

It wasn't his son the sailor was searching for, it was the boy who was put in his keeping. He served in the royal navy, Alexis had said. Killed by the enemies of the tsar. Calder didn't want to tell Alexis—he was afraid it would hurt him to know his beloved companion was wandering in the Land of Lost Souls instead of safe in Heaven. Calder had seen this man *while living*. He had been with Alexis in the hallway at the Selo Palace. This was the Lost Soul he was meant to help toward Heaven, but he had failed to do so. Calder would remember the name, though, in case the same Soul visited him again. There was a better chance he could persuade the man to surrender to his Fetch if he could call him by name—Nagorny.

# Twenty-Five

Ana and Alexis stayed awake for a long while, watching the scenery change from palms and burnished hills to a colorful desert and distant mountains. They sat in seats facing each other beside a broad window. Their train car shook in such a constant rhythm, Calder was not surprised that it eventually rocked them to sleep. Calder stayed awake, watching over them, listening, and expecting the scent of burning hair.

For some reason he found himself thinking of Liam, his Master Fetch. *Don't shiver in the corner*, Liam told him at his first Death Scene. *No one wants to follow a coward. You have nothing to fear—you're already dead.* Liam had warned him that if a Fetch took too long to learn his duties, he would start to glow. It was called the Brightening and it was a message to the Captain that there was trouble afoot. This made Calder even more nervous—he wanted to learn quickly. With the big Scotsman by his side, Calder had stared down on the body of a man who had fallen off his roof. The man's soul made his decision quickly and had no qualms about taking Calder's hand. Calder had felt foolish afterward for having been anxious, and Liam understood. *Don't think about the last Door,* he advised, giving him a thump on the shoulder. *Just open the next one.*

At the moment of his own death, Calder had pictured his Fetch as a female angel with golden hair and a soft white robe, but when a soul accepts the Fetch Key and becomes a Squire, he sees his Master Fetch in his original form. Calder had been so startled by this transformation from the golden-haired angel in white to the barrel-chested Scotsman, Liam had laughed out loud at the expression on his face. And he was laughing still. Calder could hear him and see him clearly—his rough voice, his scarred hands, his tattered kilt and wool cloak, even his chipped front tooth. *Keep your eyes open*, he said, *and be bold about your duties. Demons can smell fear.*

"You're not really here, are you?" Calder asked him. "Am I dreaming?"

Liam nodded before he disappeared. "Smart lad."

When Calder realized he was asleep, he expected the surprise of it to wake him, but it didn't. He could tell he was trapped in a visitation, because he could see the train tracks through the floor of the car, the wood crossbeams a blur between them. The train had become a huge glass snake, its belly filled with a hundred skeletons and their bags of cobweb bundles. Some bones sat peacefully; others gestured good-naturedly and laughed in the curving, invisible body of compartments that rattled on. Knowing the way things appeared when he was dreaming in the presence of a Lost Soul, Calder glanced around for Rasputin or for another Soul—perhaps Nagorny—but as before he avoided looking directly at the transparent bodies of Ana and Alexis.

To make the train appear as solid as it felt, Calder stared at the floor, willing it to darken into brown wood. When he could no longer see the railway ties soaring by under him, Calder looked up. Instead of Rasputin's piercing eyes, or the sorrowful face of Nagorny, Calder found a creature he had never seen the likes of before, but he knew instantly what it was.

It held in its shape the idea of a man, but it swelled and shrank as if breathing through its skin. The eyes, like a hundred paintings or photographs of eyes laid atop one another, all seeing at once, were black and larger than any mortal's. The face was a mingling of splotches, as if the flesh were formed from many clays, the hair a burnt mix of coarse and curly, fine gray, and twisted black.

Calder's body jerked with the animal instinct of a deer bolting from a lion, but he pretended to be Liam and stood up, folding his arms over his chest. The creature that stood across from him had been newly made, was in fact still forming, still creating itself from many Lost Souls. The demon blinked and steamed as it spoke. But its first phrase was gibberish. It had not chosen a leader and was trying to speak from the minds of more than one spirit at once. This was a good sign—if it had not chosen one Lost Soul as its head, it would be easier to deconstruct.

Calder took one step to the side, standing between the creature and the seat where Ana and Alexis slept. He recalled from Liam, and from what he'd heard from other Fetches, that the way to bring a demon down was to break it into its many spirits. But he couldn't remember the first step.

The creature quaked like a great bear shaking water from its coat and glared at Calder with new focus. "You are the prison keep." It spoke in Latin, its voice a scouring sound, like a sword worrying against a sharpening stone. The lips moved in a squirming image of many mouths, thin and wide or thick and broken, a flutter of mismatched tongues behind the rows of uneven teeth. Calder remembered that Latin was often the first language of a new demon, when its lead spirit had yet to take control.

"You are wrong," said Calder, and he recalled just in time what Fetches agreed was the fastest way to whittle down a demoning. "Which of you has lost a child?" Calder addressed the creature as if it were not one thing but a room full of spirits. And it was the most vulnerable Lost Ones who were the easiest to remove from the merging Souls—the fathers and mothers whose wounds were the loss of a son or daughter.

"We want freedom," the creature told him. "Tell us the secret."

Calder played the part of the missing child "Papa?" he said softly. "Mama?"

One mortal voice answered, soft as a sigh. "Where are you?" it asked in Romanian. A pair of eyes drifted out of the creature and brought with it the shadow of a young woman. Lost Souls had trouble seeing their Fetches as benevolent—in their anger, fear, confusion, or sorrow they became deluded and saw their Fetches as wraiths, beasts, and monsters. Calder wanted to help this woman find her waiting Fetch, but before he could, she flew away, calling for her little girl. The creature barked at Calder furiously and coughed a cloud of gray stink.

"Give us the Key!"

This was good. The creature was new enough to be pulled apart. And it still said "we" rather than "I."

"All of you," said Calder, trying to sound as confident as Liam always had. "Be gone from here."

"We will hurt you," said the creature, "and anyone in your party. We can devour this entire caravan down our throat."

"You lie," said Calder. "You're not strong enough."

The creature grimaced, a distorted version of a smile that made Calder feel ill. "Almost strong enough," it said.

Calder remembered then another strategy. "So you are male, are you?"

Here was one of the most common grounds for disagreement in a demon-to-be that was formed from spirits, some of whom still felt very much like the sex they'd been as mortals. The creature tried to answer, but again the words were mangled together. Two other shadows drifted out of it and folded away into some unseen corridor.

"What is your name?" asked Calder.

The creature shook as if to rid itself of miscreant hangers-on and spoke again in Latin. "We have no name." Now it seemed to crumple in on itself. Calder hoped it was diminishing, but it flared back into life. "I know my name." This time it spoke in French and sounded almost human and frighteningly sure of itself.

Calder did not answer it in French but spoke again in Latin. The new leader had not yet gained power and Calder hoped to use this to his advantage. "The one that you have chosen to speak for you doesn't want to help you," said Calder. "He is weak and will fail."

The creature came at Calder as if to strike him, but its fists betrayed it. The face and chest lunged forward but the arms flew back and struggled in the air. Against his will Calder took a step back and, hitting the bench, dropped to sit beside Ana and Alexis. Curses spat from the creature's throat, in too many tongues to comprehend. It did not completely disband. It growled and fought itself for a moment first, then retreated into the dark of the Land of Lost Souls. Calder woke, sitting alone in the train compartment, for Ana and Alexis had gone.

❋ ❋ ❋

Calder wanted to believe that the creature he'd seen was a nightmare, but a patch of soot was visible on the ceiling over the place where it had stood and a trail of smoke led out of the compartment and through the train, hanging almost invisible above the heads of the passengers. *It isn't a strong demon yet,* Calder told himself, *but it could become one soon. And there may be others.*

Calder would have run through a hundred cars, down the aisle of a train ten miles long, to find them, but in the very next car, two rows from the door, Ana sat with three other young women, the four of them talking and laughing as if they were the best of friends. The girls wore navy blue uniforms and red lipstick and had combed Ana's short hair so that the front swept to one side. Their smiles were unpretentious and their eyes warm. Though in appearance they were nothing like Ana's sisters, Calder knew why she was drawn to them. When Ana saw him, she excused herself and the girls waved and called their farewells.

"I didn't want to wake you," she said. "I met some field translators. They're so nice. They're called Hello Girls. What happened? You smell like a chimney."

Calder was still trembling from his visitation. "Where's your brother?"

Ana seemed surprised. "He's not with you?"

"We have to stay together," Calder whispered. He tried to brush demonic smoke off his clothes and out of his hair. He could still see a vague shadow lingering in the air all the way down the aisle.

"Fanny was actually wounded, and the other two got sick, but they're going back to France now," said Ana. "They work at the front lines translating battle commands."

Calder walked ahead of her through the cars, thinking only of Alexis. In the third car he found the boy making friends with a young man in a plaid cap.

"We're on a moving train," Alexis pointed out. "I'm not going to get lost."

Ana and Calder sat across the aisle from them.

The young man had a pet mouse that would run across his shoulders and into his shirt pocket. He talked excitedly about his politics as his tiny pet walked around his dirty neck along the inside of his collar. "It's been like that all through history." He beamed at Alexis. "It's always been a class struggle."

The mouse stood up on his master's shoulder and sniffed the air.

"When one group is wielding power over another, you know, like serfs and lords," said the young man, "when the upper class is oppressing the working class, the little guy has to rise up eventually, you know, and take back what's his." He was wearing patched tweed trousers with a rope belt and a large shirt that may have once been white. He held a little book, so dog-eared the red cover had become brown and it could roll up in his hand like the handle of a hammer.

Calder watched and listened, afraid that eventually this relationship would go awry—this new friend was, after all, telling Alexis that the revolution that had forced his father to abdicate and eventually murdered his family was in the right. He wondered if Alexis was missing some of his friend's meaning because of the language.

"May I try?" asked Alexis. He held out the back of his hand and the little gray mouse crawled tentatively up his sleeve and back again, searching for crumbs.

"What's his name?" Alexis asked.

"Max."

"Max," said Alexis. "It means big?"

"You don't have to be big in size to be big in spirit." The young man smiled. "He likes you."

"I'm Alexis." He laughed as the mouse tried to run back up his arm under the sleeve. "What's your name?"

"David."

"David was a little guy," said Alexis. "And he brought down a giant."

"See?" said David. "Just like I said."

"Do you want to behead all the kings?" asked Alexis.

Calder stiffened at this, ready to call the boy back to his sister's side, but there was no need.

"Me?" A half smile played on David's face. "I want to take back their castles, dress them in work clothes, and teach them to fish."

Alexis laughed. "Fish?"

"Or to make chairs or write plays," said David. "Something useful." He grinned. "It's a great time to be young and alive in the world, don't you think?" He made a soft whistle between his teeth and the mouse leapt from Alexis's arm to David's cap. "When the power is changing from monarchies to the people."

To Calder's surprise, Alexis was not put off by this. And David ended up helping them sell one of the emeralds and buy fake passports. When they arrived in New York City, David led them from the station, which was even larger and more beautiful than the one in California, along the docks and into back streets, which were as decrepit as dungeons. The path David took was a maze of turns Calder couldn't have repeated.

Calder hoped that the darkness he'd spoken to on the train had somehow lost track of them, but he could still see shadows, like demonic minions, following them at the edges of his vision. Ana, Alexis, and Calder followed David, walking single-file between tall buildings so close together, no sunlight could find its way down. Lines of wash were strung from apartment to apartment, fire escapes were crowded with mattresses and half-clothed children with dirty faces, and in some alleys wooden planks, like tree houses, had been built from window to window. The narrow street sagged, too, dipping down into puddles in the center. Where a puddle was deep, someone had set an empty milk crate upside down as a steppingstone.

As they passed a pregnant woman napping on a broken bed frame, a black mist hovered over her and she woke with a start as the springs began to bounce. Calder stopped, horrified that what was chasing him would attack an innocent. But the darkness didn't stay with the woman—it slid along the wall and continued after them. Calder kept himself between this elusive shadow and Ana and Alexis, but the shadow kept disappearing and reappearing several yards away, sometimes as a cloud of gray mist, sometimes disguised as a common shadow cast by a cat or a trash can.

In what might be called the business district of those poor streets, every inch of wall was covered in advertising. All the tiny shops were either up a stoop or down a few steps in half-buried rooms underground. First David took one of the emeralds and had Calder, Ana, and Alexis wait on the street while he climbed up five steps to a little store with jewelry and watches in the window. Then he led them into the next street and had them wait while he went into an apartment building. He was gone only a few minutes, yet returned with three passports.

"They might not work if you get in trouble," said David. "But they'll get you on and off a ship to England."

Their temporary identities were Mary (fifteen), John (twelve), and William Smart (thirty-five) of Portland, Maine. Each document was a single sheet of parchment and appeared official enough, though Calder had never seen a real one.

To Calder's astonishment, David gave them back several American dollars. Calder tried to give him some of it, but he refused. Since they had no luggage and no change of clothes, David brought them down some steps into a cramped shop where plain clothes could be purchased cheap. They bought Alexis a shirt and trousers that actually fit and a vest that almost matched. Ana bought a blouse and skirt but kept her brown dress, the one that Calder had given her in Ekaterinburg. Alexis felt no such nostalgia for his old clothes. He was going to throw them in the trash, but David said he'd give them to someone who needed them. They also bought two battered suitcases so they would not look suspicious boarding an ocean liner without luggage.

Calder watched for the haunting darkness that had been following them, but by the time they were at the harbor, it seemed to have gone. He was able to buy passage on a ship to Portsmouth and still have ten American dollars left to change into British pounds. And there were two emeralds, as well. He tried again to give David a silver dollar.

"For Max," he said, but David shook his head.

"This is my home," he told them. "I can eat and sleep all over this city. I have lots of friends." He waited with them until they boarded the ship, waved his little rolled-up book, and called to Alexis, "Anarchy forever!"

※ ※ ※

The three stood on deck as the ship left New York. Ana's short hair curled around the brim of her hat in a way that made Calder stare at her when she wasn't looking.

Ships large and small bellowed their whistles at each other. On a tiny island in the harbor a colossus stood, a statue of a woman in Roman-style holding a torch out over the water. The buildings of the city receded, blending into one shape like a jagged mountain ridge. This ship was more luxurious than the ship from Vladivostok, but their cabin was not much larger. The porthole was fitted with a small curtain. The Atlantic was suspected of hiding German submarines and warships, and after dark ocean liners were required to hide their light. The three walked past the first-class dining hall. Wealthy men and women dressed for the evening meal, but the steerage passengers sat in deck chairs with blankets over their shoulders and ate apples and hard rolls.

Ana and Calder sat in wooden chairs along the lower decks watching Alexis make another new friend. He was an old fellow with skin so thin, his veins showed through. Perhaps the boy's accent had brought Russia to mind, for the old gentleman was telling Alexis all about how his grandparents on his mother's side had both been Russian. He bragged of the strength and heartiness of their ancestors. He told Alexis about Peter the Great.

"He was seven feet tall," said the old man. "Traveled all over the world, and when he came back to his homeland he cut the beards right off the nobles' faces. He changed the alphabet . . . he built cities."

"My father thought Peter got rid of too many of the Russian traditions," said Alexis, "and that he was too infatuated with Europe."

The old man let out a great laugh. "And who's your father?" The old man regarded Calder.

"My father's dead."

"I'm sorry," said the old man. "My father's dead, too."

Ana made friends as well, chatting with a wealthy couple who came out on deck that evening to stargaze. The woman gave Ana a magazine she had finished reading, filled with photographs of actors and actresses from the movies. Calder sat alone, keeping them both in his view, planning what to do after he got them tucked away with their relatives. He would go to a deserted place, away from mortals, and summon the Lost Souls. He had learned other tricks than the few he had tried on the train from Los Angeles. Other ways of disempowering a demon. If only he could remember them.

When they retired to their cramped quarters, Calder closed the curtain over the porthole to hide the light but kept the small lamp in their cabin burning all night. He had no intention of ever sleeping again. Ana and Alexis, as before, lay in one bed flipping through the magazine, and Calder sat on the other. Brother and sister drifted off, and the magazine slid from Ana's lap to the floor. It fell open to a page in the middle. An advertisement for soap. A woman with pale, cascading hair bent over a cherubic tot who was reaching up to her perfect face. And from this idyllic scene a memory rose in Calder's spirit from some place farther away than England or Russia or the moon. The light from the cabin was swallowed by his blindness and he was back beneath the cold underbelly of a bridge, waiting for his Golden Fairy.

# Twenty-six

THE BOY WHO HAD ONCE BEEN CALDER, A LAD OF not yet ten and as thin as a twig, sat alone on a frosty night. He quaked and hummed to himself under the bridge he called home and thought of Her. He knew there were no such things as fairies, but it didn't matter.

*She could come tomorrow,* he thought. *Why not? It could just as easily be tomorrow as the next day or next year. Every day that I have waited takes me one closer to the day my Golden Fairy will come for me.*

He pictured her dressed all in white, with smiling eyes and gold hair like a halo around her face. He imagined her riding up in a shining carriage, leaning out the window, knowing him at once. She would weep with joy and wrap him in a fur cloak, carry him into a large, warm house that smelled of fresh bread and roasted meat.

Calder remembered these thoughts clearly—as clearly as he now felt the needles of cold and the tinny pang of hunger. He had huddled behind a wooden crate as a shield against the wind, had pulled his arms in from his sleeves and hugged himself in the shelter of his tunic. Rags that by day were too filthy to touch he had wrapped around his throat by night. He would curl his knees up to his chin, hold himself tight, and sing, though there was no one close enough to hear.

Calder was ashamed now that he had clung to his belief in the Golden Fairy so hard that it had followed him into death, for surely this was why he had imagined Liam as a white-robed angel. And why Alexandra had seemed familiar. She was the perfect Golden Fairy and he had broken his Vows because of this folly. As a boy he was often so cold and hungry that he feared falling asleep at night; he might die before dawn, might wake up in hell for all the things he'd stolen. These dark thoughts would make it impossible to rest. But when he pictured the Golden Fairy, he would think, *Just one more night. You can keep breathing for a few more hours. That's all you will need, because tomorrow will be the day.*

Calder was saddened by guilt, realizing he had carried this dream with him through thousands of Death Doors and into the Land of the Living. But more painful was the pity he felt for the child he'd been. He felt sorry for his suffering, was astonished by his ability to hope, and wished that he could comfort the boy he used to be.

But the boy and the Fetch were centuries divided.

When Calder's vision returned, he closed the magazine and set it on the bunk at Ana's feet. Too heavy at heart to keep watch, Calder lay on his bunk and faced the wall but did not sleep.

❈ ❈ ❈

The next day as he stood on deck beside Ana and Alexis, Calder saw, a few yards away, a familiar face growing out of the back of a lady's hat. Rasputin pulled himself through the woman and waited, smiling, for Calder to leave Ana and Alexis and come over to the railing to speak with him.

"Still hunting down your Key?" Rasputin asked. "It's tedious tracking you across all these miles. It took me hours!"

Calder waited for the woman with the hat to move down the steps to the lower deck before he spoke. He faced the sea, hoping it would not look as if he were talking to himself.

"I thought you could fly anywhere instantly."

"If I know where I want to go," said Rasputin, as if Calder were an idiot.

Calder felt uneasy confiding in the man, but he had saved them once. "Thank you for holding back the Lost Ones and letting us escape."

"It wouldn't have been much of a fight," Rasputin said, smiling. "You needed a little head start to make it fair."

Calder couldn't tell if he was joking. "Bring me good news," he pleaded. "I'm doing what I was asked to do. I'm taking the boy and his sister to safety, but I could not turn the sailor toward his Fetch."

"The sailor?" said Rasputin. "What are you talking about?"

"You told me I must remember a Lost One that I knew while living and bring him to his Door."

"Who said anything about a sailor?" Rasputin wagged his head with pity. "Think, fool." He tapped Calder on the skull, or would have if his finger had been flesh and bone.

"Shall I call out a demon and try to pry the weakest spirit from it?" asked Calder.

Rasputin looked frightened for a moment. "Not wise, no." Then his cavalier attitude returned. "There is only one spirit in the Land of Lost Souls that can be turned toward Heaven by you. Only one that has a chance at all, at least until you save the children and enter the Aisle again," he said, as if this were the simplest of things. "But that will be all you will need. Even if ten thousand ghosts stood against you, if you can retrieve this one and send it home, the scales would tip."

"Which one?" Calder pleaded. "Where do I find him?"

Rasputin attempted to grasp Calder's head, but his hands passed through. "The answer's within you!" Rasputin sighed. "Try to remember."

Frustrated, Calder asked, "Are there any Fetches near you now?"

Rasputin looked pleased. "Oh, yes, let me just listen." He tilted his head to one side. "Oh, my! They say the Lost Souls have decided never to bother the Land of the Living again." He paused a second time. "They say the Souls worship you now and will do your bidding!"

Calder was stunned. "Truly?"

Rasputin laughed deeply. "Your face," he gasped. "You should have seen your expression!"

Since it seemed impossible to summon Rasputin at will, Calder needed him to stay close at hand, but when the man was in this unreliable mood, Calder wanted to shut him in a bottle like a genie and throw him out to sea.

"No, no," Rasputin confessed. "The demons don't worship you, but they do hunger for you."

"When the children are safe, I promise I will face them and break them apart," said Calder.

"Really?" Rasputin grinned. "I'm going to tell them you said so." And with that the man snapped out of view like the shutting off of an electric light.

*  *  *

Calder turned back to the place he had left Ana and Alexis, but they had gone. He found Ana on the far side of the upper deck standing with a flock of anxious passengers.

"Where's Alexis?" Calder asked.

Ana sheepishly pointed up. Alexis was scaling the side of one great smokestack, gripping the seams in the cowling and finding footholds on the rivets, making his way up to where a small boy was hanging, snagged by a wire. Calder could only imagine that the smaller boy had tried to climb the tower and been caught and stranded.

Below stood the child's mother with tears streaming down her face, a half-dozen spectators, and two ships' stewards arguing over where to find a net, a blanket, a ladder. But it was all over in seconds. Alexis caught the boy's jacket at the back just as the sleeve that had been suspending him tore free. Seeing no blanket ready to catch the child, Alexis swung him to his back, where the lad clung like a baby monkey. Then Alexis peered down, not at the crowd but at the deck, gauging whether anything would hinder his descent.

"Make way!" he called, and jumped. The child's mother screamed, but Alexis landed on his feet, stumbled one step forward, his face contorted with pain for the briefest moment, then swung the child into his mother's arms. The crowd gaped at Alexis, but before he could be congratulated, or questioned, Calder swept him and his sister down to the next deck and away.

"There are unseen spirits afoot," said Calder. "Dangerous spirits, and it's my duty to protect you."

"We're sorry," said Ana, but seeing that Calder still appeared anxious, she decided to explain. "It started out innocently enough. Alexis looked bored and I asked him what he would do if he knew he couldn't get hurt. And so we slid down a few railings and did a couple of somersaults, and then this lady dropped her sherry glass and this little girl—she could hardly walk, she was so young—started to reach for the glass, so Alexis and I scooped up the shards—"

"That hurt," said the boy, as if it were a fascinating observation.

"So, then"—Ana shrugged—"when we saw this boy . . ." She stopped. "I told him not to."

Alexis laughed. "You did not."

"I said we should call a steward," said Ana. "Did the fall hurt much?" she asked her brother.

"Some" was all he said.

Calder knew it was only natural for the boy to want to try things he would not have been permitted to do before because of his fragile health. And Ana had never been able to run and chase with him when he was human.

"Alexis, the defender." She grinned at her brother and then told Calder, "That's what his name means."

"It would've been a good name for a Fetch," said Calder.

"We'd be all the rage in a circus." Alexis looked at Calder. "You're like us, aren't you?" he asked. "You should test your body. It's so bracing."

Calder remembered the feeling of being shot, poisoned, beaten with a chain, and drowned. "I've had my fill of that," he said. "Let's just stay together and out of trouble."

"Why don't you tie us to you like mountain climbers?" said Alexis.

Ana swatted at his hair. "Don't be rude."

Calder wished there *were* something like a Fetch net. Catching Lost Souls would be much easier if they could be scooped up like fish.

Suddenly, Ana screamed and Alexis ducked as a chain from the lower deck flew up and over Calder's head. It hovered in the air just out of reach of Calder's fist as he jumped for it. Then it fell, rained down on his shoulders like rocks, every link mysteriously free from the others. The pile of iron loops lay silent on the deck around Calder's feet. Alexis and Ana gaped at him.

He rushed them to their cabin and stood against the locked door. Brother and sister sat on their bunk, shaken.

"Some spirits are not in Heaven," said Calder. "Some are not happy with me."

"The ghosts?" asked Ana.

"We call them Lost Souls."

"What do they want?" asked Alexis.

"Impossible things," said Calder. "I don't think they mean to hurt me," he lied. "They're like spoiled children. And they have no argument with you." He wanted to confide in them, tell them about the mysterious spirit he was meant to save, but he didn't have the heart.

Although he had hoped this explanation would calm them, and although they feigned understanding, Calder knew his thoughts were too evident on his face. Soon the spirits would have enough power to harm him and anyone else who got in the way. And although the Souls seemed to have no interest in Ana and Alexis, by proximity, they were in danger. But he couldn't send them off on a ship or train alone to find their family. He would have to get them somewhere safe before he distanced himself from them for their own good and called the evil out for a fight.

For the rest of the trip they stayed together, rarely left the cabin, and Calder did not sleep. He stood just inside the door with his hand in his right pocket, secretly holding the lock of Ana's hair that he had stolen. Ana took to entertaining herself by translating her favorite articles in the movie magazine out loud in rhyme. She also put her brown dress back on, having washed it and let it dry draped on a string clothesline in their cabin.

"That frock is awful," said her brother. "Throw it away." But she wouldn't.

* * *

On the day they would arrive in Portsmouth, they came out on deck where the sun was bright and the air was clear. But as they looked over the side of the ship, a dead whale floated on its side, its flesh burned and broken from tail to snout. As they stared in shock, a gull swooped between them, its wing striking Calder's shoulder, and smashed into the wall behind them, dropping to their feet, its neck broken.

None of them spoke of these horrors, but Calder couldn't help but remember Rasputin's description of Lost Souls flying through whales, past every rib.

They left their suitcases on board—Ana decided her brown dress was the only one she needed. As they began to disembark, Calder realized the dead animals must have frightened them both, for Ana and Alexis appeared as pale as statues.

As they moved down the gangway, Calder asked, "Where does your uncle live?"

"You're joking," said the boy.

"I don't think they're at the palace," Ana reminded Alexis. "I think they're in Norfolk."

"What do you mean by 'the palace'?" Calder asked.

"He's the king," she explained.

Calder stopped. "Of England?" His knees went hollow. "Your uncle is the king of England?"

"Not really," said the boy. "He's actually our cousin."

"And you didn't think to tell me this before?"

Ana shrugged. "Does it matter?"

Calder escorted them down the gangway and toward the train station, trying not to imagine the introductions with which he'd soon be faced. They boarded the train for Norfolk, where the royal cousins were staying.

In the seat in front of them sat a young mother with her baby daughter resting over her shoulder. In the seat across the aisle a soldier sat alone holding a rucksack. Ana sat by the window watching the platform below as the train whistled a wavering note. Alexis found a box of matches under the seat and picked it up. He shook it next to his ear. It rattled with several matchsticks.

The baby in front of Calder rested her head on her mother's shoulder and put the middle two fingers of her right hand in her mouth, soothing herself to sleep as the engine shifted and the train began to move. But the baby's eyes fixed on Calder's face and she didn't close them. Calder smiled at her and she smiled back, her baby teeth clamped around her fingers. Calder heard the sound of Alexis sliding open the matchbox and striking a match.

"Don't," said Ana.

Calder glanced over; as if it were a perfectly normal thing to do, the boy was holding his hand over the flame.

"Stop that!" Ana snapped at him.

Calder saw the pain in the boy's face and grabbed his wrist, shaking the flame out. Alexis showed them his blackened palm. Ana made a disgusted sound. The soot wiped off on the knee of his pants and Alexis showed his palm to them again, white and unharmed.

"Don't be grotesque," said Ana.

Calder took the box of matches and threw it out the window.

"I'm not blistered," said Alexis, "but it hurt like it was blistering."

Calder saw the mother of the baby shift in her seat. He doubted she could speak Russian, but he didn't want to keep the baby awake. He motioned for the boy to keep his voice down.

"Don't you see what this means?" whispered Alexis.

"You're scaring me," said his sister. "Stop trying to mutilate yourself."

"That's what makes it so dangerous," said Alexis. "I can't mutilate myself. If someone were to catch me, or any of us, and torture us, they could go on doing it as long as they liked and we'd keep suffering; we'd never weaken or die. They could torment us forever."

"Why would anyone want to do that?" Ana asked.

"I don't know," said Alexis. "If they'd lost their minds, or had an aversion to us."

Finally the train began to pick up speed, chugging out of the station, each car adding its weight to the one ahead. The baby was just beginning to drift off, her eyelids drooping when her mother began to weep quietly. The woman covered her mouth, but her trembling woke her daughter and the baby lay with open eyes, watching Calder again.

The soldier across the aisle began to fold up, it seemed, as the train gained speed. The rhythm of the tracks and the way the light flashed over his face as the shadows of buildings and poles and trees flickered over his eyes made him shake, curl into a ball on the seat, his knees pulled up, his arms wrapped around his head.

Calder had seen soldiers come home from war with torn spirits before, but now he worried that all sorts of things were made worse in the Land of the Living because of his breaking his Vows. What if the woman sitting in front of him was a new widow and her husband's Soul was clinging to her at that moment, like the woman in the church whose dead husband had thought Calder was the Devil? What if the soldier beside them was vexed by his fallen comrades because of the trouble Calder had started in the Land of Lost Souls?

He needed to do something. He waited for a brilliant idea to form in his mind, but the only one that came seemed silly.

Still, he started singing.

Calder began by humming the melody to the Children's Psalm, four train-track clicks to every note, using the rhythm of the train. And then he began to sing the lyrics.

The woman with the child took a long breath and listened. She sniffed; her tears stopped. Her daughter shifted and closed her eyes. The soldier began to unfold himself. One of his feet lowered to the floor. Then one hand floated down and rested on his knee. He leaned against the window and his face relaxed.

By the third time through the simple tune, Ana hummed along. Calder thought it was a pity that the woman and her child lacked a man, and that the soldier had no family to welcome him home. He wished he could somehow make them a gift of each other. He didn't realize they already were.

"Sophie?" the soldier said.

The woman with the baby stood slowly and came to sit down beside the soldier. The baby stayed asleep. They didn't say another word, but the soldier put his arm around the woman's shoulder and rested his fingers in the baby's hair.

※ ※ ※

At the first stop Sophie, the soldier, and their child got off the train. Alexis found a newspaper in an empty row and brought it back to read with Ana. The front page told of the mounting deaths from influenza and a street fight over food rationing. Ana and Alexis were each holding one side of the paper as the train pulled out of the station.

"What does this say?" asked Alexis, pointing to a column of print. "That can't be right. Russia was out of the war for months. We didn't lose that many men."

"One million seven hundred thousand killed," Ana read. "Six hundred thousand wounded—"

"They made a mistake," said Alexis.

Calder was shaken by the numbers. "How did a war on this scale begin?" he asked.

"Serbia murdered the heir to the Austrian throne," said the boy, "so Austria declared war on Serbia, and Russia had to come to defend them against Germany." The boy thought for a moment. "If we'd had more trains and supplies we would've wiped them out."

"Instead we had a revolution," Ana sighed. Then she stopped. "Alexis?"

She was as pale as snow, and her eyes were fixed on her brother's hand, which rested in the shadows. The skin of the boy's hand, Calder now observed, was glowing as white as a full moon.

"Your hand . . . " she began, but did not know how to go on.

The boy lifted his fingers into the light and they appeared normal, but when he let the newspaper drop and moved both hands out of the sunlight, they were indeed glowing. Not brightly yet, but they were emitting a pure white light.

Confused, Alexis turned his eyes on his sister. "Your face," he whispered.

# PART V

## THE BRIGHTENING OF THE FLESH

# Twenty-seven

It was true—Ana's face was also shining in an unnatural way, at least unnatural for earth.

"Calder!" Ana called, though he was close beside her. He knew what was happening to them and cursed himself that he had not given them warning.

"Don't be afraid," he said, hoping he sounded sure of himself.

"I—I'm shining," Ana stammered. "I'm . . . " She withdrew herself from the daylight that streamed in through the window to look at her fingers in the shadows. Alexis was hiding his hands under his arms.

"It's the Brightening." Calder took off his coat and draped it over them. "I'll be back in a moment." Thankfully no one was sitting near them.

Calder felt ashamed and nervous that he knew so little about the affliction. He had heard rumors, and it was spoken of briefly in the Ninth Psalm, but he didn't know enough. Did it hurt? Did its intensity increase with human time? What would it look like to the humans? Why should anyone in the Land of the Living see the Brightness if they couldn't see Fetches? On the other hand, Ana and Alexis weren't really Fetchkind. Still, Calder had to find them something with which to cover themselves, just in case. He couldn't have them gawked at as abominations.

He knew that what he was about to do was wrong and he was afraid of being caught and thrown off the train, leaving Ana and Alexis stranded, but he walked straight into the next car, where two dozen people sat, some chatting, some napping, one old man reading to his gray-haired wife. Calder stepped into an empty row behind a pair of napping men and a woman who had her head bent over a book. He stared out the window intently for one moment, and then matter-of-factly lifted the hats and gloves from the top of the coats that lay over the back of the woman's seat and walked away with them.

Ana peeked out from over the top of Calder's coat as he returned.

"Wear these." He gave Ana the woman's hat and Alexis the man's. Both were too big. Ana, who had a hat already, took the lace veil from the new hat and managed to fasten it to her own. Alexis's hat rode low on his ears. The glow of their hands was snuffed out like candle flame as they slipped on the gloves. The veil muted Ana's face, and she tucked it into the collar of her dress to hide her throat. But her brother's face still shone out from under the dark hat like a silver coin catching the light.

"Is this some kind of Fetch disease?" Alexis wanted to know.

"When a Squire Fetch clings to his Master Fetch too long, or if a Master Fetch is too slow in teaching," Calder told them, "the Squire goes Bright. It's a kind of hazard flag for the Captain, so he can see where the power isn't flowing." He didn't think he'd described it very well.

"Because we stayed too long. Because we don't have the Key," said Ana.

"Yes." Calder realized now that he had been given signs and ignored them—he thought they were merely pale from anxiety or fatigue. But he'd been blind and stupid.

"What about my face?" The boy touched his gloved fingers to his cheeks.

"Wait." Calder moved back through the train to the car behind theirs, the opposite direction he'd gone before.

When a young couple neared him going the other way, Calder pressed himself against the seats to make room. He smiled and nodded as they approached, but as they passed by he pinched the edge of the trailing scarf from the woman's back and it slipped off her unnoticed.

He returned so quickly with the purloined wrap, Ana asked, "Were you a pickpocket when you were human?"

"Yes," said Calder.

He suddenly went blind again. Calder could feel the scarf in his left hand, but now he could feel a small potato in his right. He saw a busy marketplace full of skirts and aprons and boots moving past his hiding place under a vegetable cart. Pincher was showing him that he should steal a little potato so he could close his fingers all the way over it and hide it better.

And now he was in the vestibule of a huge cathedral, loitering near the entrance, watching a crowd of parishioners file past. Pincher said

God meant them to have light and that He wouldn't mind if they took only one prayer candle each.

And now he was hiding under a bridge, weeping alone.

"Enough," Calder whispered.

"What's wrong?" asked Ana.

"I was remembering something from my life on earth." Calder held out the scarf toward where he thought Alexis was sitting. "Wear this." His vision returned as Alexis took the soft black fabric and frowned.

"It's for a lady," said the boy.

"Alexis." Ana's voice was edged with the reproach of a mother.

The boy wrapped the cloth loosely around his neck and chin, then pulled the brim of the hat down until it was low over his nose.

Calder felt relieved that Ana and Alexis were no longer emitting white light, but he knew he would have to find them better coverings when they arrived in Norfolk. Ana admired her brother's bundled appearance.

"The scarf smells nice," she said.

Alexis let out a growl of frustration and moved one row back, where he crammed himself against the window. Calder felt a surge of hope—the Brightening was meant to alert the Captain. If the Captain could see this light, surely he would send help.

"When we get to the Aisle, you'll be yourselves again," he said, sitting beside Ana.

"It's not fair!" Alexis kicked the back of their seat. "I was finally enjoying myself. But this hiding under a mess of other people's clothes . . . it's disgusting."

"What if we didn't cover ourselves?" Ana asked him. "What would people think?"

Ana was assuming that the living could see the Brightness. A natural assumption.

"Who cares what they'd think?" said Alexis.

"I wonder what they'd do," Ana said. "Maybe they'd admire us and make us the toast of the town."

"They'd probably be scared," said Alexis. "They'd probably run away."

"Maybe they'd lock us up."

"Let them try." But Alexis was losing some of his anger.

"Or maybe they'd just take us to hospital," she said. "Maybe they'd give us tests—do experiments."

Alexis sighed and folded his arms, staring out at the countryside. After a long moment he asked, "What if Aunt and Uncle want to take us to hospital?"

"They'll help us hide," said Ana. "We'll be safe."

"If they wanted to help us, they would have sent for all of us long ago."

Ana looked at Calder, her face dimmed by the veil. He didn't know how to help, had no idea of what had gone on while he was buried in Rasputin's grave. Had they asked their English relatives to take them in? Had they been refused?

"They were afraid," said Ana. "But now Uncle will risk nothing because no one will know we're here. Don't you want to see Cousin Johnnie again? He loves you so."

"They didn't write." Alexis flexed his hands in the awkward gloves. "How could they?"

Calder held perfectly still when he saw it—a darkness much heavier than any he'd yet seen was hanging in a wavering column at the far end of the train car.

Alexis sighed and came back to sit beside his sister. "Do you think they prayed for us?"

"I'm sure they did," she said. "Every night. And I thought I felt something curious every morning when Father read to us. That would be sunrise in Norfolk. I'd get this warm feeling, right here." She lay a hand under her right breast.

Alexis gave a little snort of superiority. "Your heart's on the other side," he pointed out.

"Not in my heart," she said. "Right where Johnnie would press his cheek to me when he wrapped his arms around my waist to say good morning."

Calder watched the dark shape without staring straight at it. He set his gaze out the window a few feet to the left. The shape didn't approach, but it didn't retreat, either. It pulsed and now the scent of burnt hair reached him.

"Our cousin . . . " Alexis explained to Calder. "There's something wrong with him."

"There is nothing wrong with him. He's the sweetest person I've ever met," Ana protested. She thought for a moment and added, "He's special."

"He's a good boy," said Alexis. "I'm not being cruel. He's got a big heart, but there is something different about him."

Ana still bristled, but kept quiet.

"Johnnie," said Alexis, as if recalling his face. "He's a funny one."

"We should go to Johnnie and Lalla," said Ana. "They would hide us. We wouldn't have to worry about politics or newspapers or crowds or hospitals."

When the train whistled for the Potters Bar station, the dark shape disappeared in every direction at once. Calder scanned the depot carefully before they disembarked, and he had Ana and Alexis wait on a bench as he went to buy them a few protections. He found them hiding behind a newspaper when he returned. They were using it as a way to cover the Brightening, but Ana was also reading.

"Germany is weakening." Her eyes scanned down the columns as she translated for Alexis. "The Americans have sent thirty thousand more men into Belgium, France, and Germany."

"Try this," said Calder. He'd bought a proper men's scarf for the boy and some face powder for them both.

Ana went to the ladies' room with the powder, returning in a much shorter time than Calder had anticipated, with her face and throat dusted in flesh-toned powder. And she must have covered her ankles and arms in powder as well, because she no longer wore the veil or gloves. She handed the powder over to Alexis, who hid it in his pocket with indignation.

"Think of it as theater makeup," she whispered. "All the great actors wear it."

Calder and Alexis went into the gentlemen's washroom. Since they were alone, they were able to stand at the sink instead of in a toilet stall. Calder helped Alexis cover his glowing face with powder. Though his skin radiated a heavenly light, his eyes, like those of his sister, shone with a more muted glow. Calder was relieved that darkened glasses would not be necessary.

Calder dusted the back of the boy's neck and Alexis powdered his own hands and wrists. Strangely, the heat of the Brightness seemed to sear the powder to the boy's skin like some fine coat of neutral color an artist might use to prime a canvas.

"Ridiculous." The boy shook his head in disbelief at his reflection and left the scarves and gloves inside the hat on the washroom counter for a needy soul who might pass through later.

"Just be glad you weren't born in the age of powdered wigs," said Ana as she stowed the powder in her pocket.

"All the great actors do not wear makeup," the boy complained. "Douglas Fairbanks doesn't wear face powder."

"Perhaps not," said Ana. "But I hear he wears a girdle."

The boy smiled in spite of himself. The stationmaster called for the boarding of the next train, and the wavering whistle gave its cry. As the three waited on queue, a man who stood in line in front of them boarded and walked through the car past the window. He was smartly dressed and carried a silver-topped walking stick, and even Calder couldn't help thinking he greatly resembled Nicholas. Ana glanced away at once, but Alexis watched the gentleman choose a row and seat himself.

"Do you remember your father?" Alexis asked Calder.

"I never had one," he answered.

"What is your Captain like?"

Calder was surprised how difficult this was to answer. "He's wise and strong." He watched the boy, who was no doubt missing his father. "He's patient."

"Do you miss him when you're away from him?"

"If I'm away a long time," said Calder, "as I am now." They climbed the train step and no one spoke as they passed the bearded gentleman. Ana chose them a row in the next car back.

"What do you do together," Alexis asked Calder, "you and your Captain?"

"He listens to my prayers at night, and when I bring him souls he takes them from me across the Great River."

Ana gazed out the window.

"What do you talk about?" Alexis asked.

This stumped Calder. "Talk about?"

"It's nice when you don't have to talk about anything," said Alexis.

"Most of the time," said Calder, "when the Captain is with me, he just stays with me. He's just there."

"I like that, too," said the boy.

Calder's stomach tightened as he caught the scent of smoke again, and there in the middle of the train platform below, just as the train began to roll away, a thick cloud of black moved back and forth as if pacing. A woman hurried toward the tracks, too late to catch their train, and screamed as the black cloud crashed against her. Calder stood up as the train pulled away, trying to see what would happen. The woman staggered backwards and the umbrella in her hand flew from her grip and smacked against a pillar. Calder hurried back through the car, staring out the windows. A station attendant came to the woman's aid and was thrown back by the darkness. Just as a stand of trees blocked the view, Calder saw the man land on his side, his eyeglasses cracked and his cheek bleeding.

"What's the matter?" asked Ana.

They hadn't seen. He had hoped for the Captain's help, but there was no sign of Heavenly intervention. Calder came and sat beside her. "We're almost there," he said.

When they had cleared the trees, daylight streamed into the train car and Alexis and Ana shielded their faces from the window, opened and closed their hands. Calder watched this, bewildered.

Alexis tried to explain. "It burns."

# Twenty-eight

"Is it the powder or is this part of the Brightening?" asked the boy.

Calder realized *he didn't know.*

"It's not the powder," said Ana. "I don't think it's the light, either. I think it's the air."

"Like a fever," said Alexis. Calder could see in the boy's eyes the watery pain of heat.

Ana got out the powder and covered their faces, necks, any exposed skin, with an extra layer of defense. To Calder's relief, this seemed to help. The idea that the Brightening would so soon become destructive to them drained the strength from him. He was taking them to safety, but that wouldn't stop it.

Ana and Alexis became quiet. The little stone walls and farm fences flittered by in a blur, and the green hilltops rolled past with the shadows of clouds making a patchwork of the fields—clouds Calder hoped were natural and not profane.

When they arrived at the King's Lynn depot, Ana and Alexis both seemed to know the way to their cousins' estate by back roads from the train station. After less than a mile, where hardly a bird or fox came, let alone a motorcar, they passed a beautiful mansion with gardens and hedges surrounded by tall loops of barbed wire that came almost to the edge of the paved road.

"Do you think Uncle George is being held captive like we were?" asked Alexis.

"Don't be silly," said Ana. "That's in case of some kind of attack. They're at war."

Soon they left the road and hiked through the woods. Alexis led the way into a forest of beech and oak. It was raining lightly, but the trees kept them from the worst of it.

"I'm nervous," said Ana.

Perhaps to keep her distracted, Alexis said, "What was that poem that Johnnie used to recite to everyone?"

"'The Death of Arthur,'" she recalled, smiling.

"Do you know it?" asked the boy.

"Not by memory."

"Do you know any poems?" Alexis asked Calder.

He thought a Fetch Psalm would be almost the same thing, and so he recited the Third Psalm as they moved between the trees.

> *Fear not, for you will never be alone;*
> *Each child of woman walks the earth a while*
> *And whether over cloverleaf or stone,*
> *Step by step, draws closer to the Aisle.*

*Now slip from shell and take the offered hand;*
*In disguise the holy gift is given.*
*Dust of His dust, stranger to this land,*
*Wake and hear the music of His heav'n.*
*Come and join the inescapable march.*
*Pass beneath the opalescent arch.*

"Beautiful," said Ana.

"Creepy," said Alexis. "I like it."

"Let's speak only to Johnnie at first," said Ana. "He'll accept us. He believes in magic."

"How will you find your cousin before his parents find you?" asked Calder.

"He lives in a separate cottage," said Alexis. "Away from the others."

"Why?"

"You know," said the boy, "because of how he is."

Calder slowed his pace as the silhouettes of the tree trunks up ahead melted together and the forest became black as pitch. He knew it was a blind memory when neither of the others cried out.

Calder was still treading unsteadily through the woods, but he was also cowering in a cellar, his nose suddenly full of the scent. Not the clean soil smell of a farmhouse cellar but the mildew and slime stench of a pit in the city. He was so small, he had to reach up to try the door latch, but it was fastened tight. Strangely, Calder could still hear Ana and Alexis talking.

"Mother never would've allowed such a thing," Ana was saying.

"When I was well, I looked and sounded normal," Alexis argued. "But if I'd been like Johnnie, who knows? I might have been sent away, too."

"Alexis!" Ana scolded. "You know Mother couldn't bear to be parted from you."

Calder stopped following Ana and Alexis since he could no longer see where to set his feet. He jumped at the sound of another voice.

"It's not like she left you on the steps of a church or on the door of some rich house." This voice was coming from the other side of the cellar door. "She dropped you in an alley without even a rag." The cellar door flew open and a red-faced woman reached in with her huge hand and dragged him out by the hair. "So I don't want to hear a word out of you. If Mister Grundy says slip your hand in a pocket, you do it. If he wraps a bandage over your eyes, you sit where he puts you and beg."

"What's the matter?" Calder could hear Alexis asking.

A man with a great, muddy cape tromped into the tiny kitchen and picked up the end of the rope that was tied around the boy Calder's waist and led him like a dog out into the frosted air, along a narrow walk, and into a bustling street.

"Here." The man paused, shoved a stick wrapped in rags at one end under Calder's arm, and said, "You won't move from where I put you, and you keep this foot off the ground, see?" He jerked Calder's right trouser leg up, showing him how to play lame. But the boy Calder saw something up ahead that made him throw down the crutch and run so hard that the end of his rope tore from his keeper's hand and flew after him along the ground like a writhing snake.

This had been the day Calder had broken away from the man and woman who had kept him alive for five years. And it was the simplest thing that gave him the courage to run and risk a beating worse than usual if he was caught. In the window of a passing carriage, Calder had seen a woman with rose-gold hair smiling at him. Not only had she seen Calder, but she had leaned forward before her carriage passed as if she meant to speak. And Calder had run after her, faster than he knew he could run, over cobblestone and bridge, right into the middle of the busy road, hopping up between the coaches, which all appeared the same to him, trying to find her. He followed one rattling carriage after another, turning down one street and then the next. It should have been a blessed day when he'd escaped that cellar, but Calder now felt a burdensome sorrow when he recalled the moment he had given up and stopped. He'd fallen down, winded, at the entrance to a cemetery miles from where he'd begun.

"I used to dream about trading places with Johnnie," Calder could hear Alexis saying.

"When you were in pain?" Ana was asking him. Their voices were not as close as before. They had walked on and left him standing in the woods, blind.

"No," said the boy. "When I was well but still not allowed to run, I used to picture myself with Johnnie, racing around, rolling down hills, never having to take lessons." The sound of their feet stopped crunching through the forest. "What's the matter with you?" Alexis called.

Calder was loath to admit his affliction. But before his eyes he still saw only the iron bars of the graveyard and the headstones beyond. He would be foolish to lie. "When I remember things from my mortal life," he told them, "I see it so well, I can't see the present." He heard them walking back to him and felt Ana take his hand.

"What are you seeing instead of us?" Alexis wanted to know.

"My childhood," said Calder.

"What does it look like?" Ana asked.

And then Calder saw Pincher's face peek out from behind a tombstone. It was the day he'd first met Calder. Next Ana's face appeared, then the boy, then the forest. "It's all right now," said Calder.

The rain grew heavier and was tapping and fidgeting the leaves of the trees and soaking the grass as they began again to walk. It was not cold, but Calder was trembling as they left the tree line and headed for a cottage with a fenced yard that stood alone a hundred yards down the hill.

"What if they don't want us?" Alexis asked his sister.

"Of course they'll want us," said Ana. "Johnnie loves us, and Lalla is so loyal to him." She still held Calder's hand. "You'll be welcome, too," she told him.

"He has to stay with us," said Alexis. "You will, won't you?"

"Of course he will," said Ana. "How else would we get to Heaven?"

Calder had told them that he needed to bring them to a safe place, but he hadn't yet told them the whole truth—that what would keep them the farthest from harm was his leaving them and drawing the Lost Souls as far away from them as possible before he fought them.

Alexis knocked at the cottage door, but when there was no answer Ana found it unlocked. It was a simple house, not at all the kind of place one would expect a prince to be brought up. Walking softly through the rooms, where fresh flowers wilted in vases and a book had been left out on the table, open and with a pair of reading glasses holding the page, it was hard to tell when the occupants had been there last.

"They must be out for a walk," said Ana.

"Or away on holiday," said Alexis.

"They would never leave the house unlocked."

Through the window Calder saw a black mist gathering near the edge of the wood. As it began to roll slowly down the hill toward the cottage, Calder turned to Ana. "Bolt the door after me," he told her. "Don't open it until your cousin comes back."

"Where are you going?" Alexis wanted to know.

Calder couldn't face them as he spoke. He started walking from window to window, locking them. "The Lost Souls are angry and they're following me. I need to lead them away from you to keep you safe."

They both followed him into the kitchen and bedroom. "Who will keep you safe?" asked Ana.

"I can't be killed," said Calder.

"Neither can we," she said.

"But we can be hurt," said the boy.

Calder latched the windows in both bedrooms and marched to the front door, but Ana caught him by the arm. "What will you do?"

Looking her in the eye, he was afraid he would tell her everything, the nature and unpredictable might of the giant he was about to battle. "I'll trick them and send them away," he said.

"And then you'll come back for us?" asked the boy.

"I'll come to you the moment it's safe," said Calder. This satisfied Alexis. But Ana could see through Calder's bravado. Not knowing how long they would be apart, he wanted to say goodbye, but he knew this was not a good idea. As he opened the door, Alexis was already stepping forward to lock it, but Ana stood and stared at him, her fists on her hips, her stubborn, impish chin set. She was on the verge, Calder feared, of calling him a liar.

Calder stepped out of the house and pulled the door tightly shut, and once he heard the boy lock the bolt, he turned toward the darkness and charged up the hill.

Up the slope, with the rain blowing in his face, Calder came at the black mist that lingered on the hillside, wishing he could scare it off the way he would a flock of crows. The cloud, stinking of smoke, swept around him as he rushed back into the woods. The shadows whispered and shifted around him. He spun to his right and there was only the black of a tree stump. To his left only the darkness of a berry bramble. But with each step away from the cottage, the shadows grew deeper and closer. It felt as if he were being not only watched but sniffed by every shrub and branch. He wanted to draw the Lost Souls even farther from the cottage, but he could feel them breathing on him like ice and knew it would be better to call them out than to be surprised by an attack.

"Show yourself, if you're so powerful," Calder said. The wind whipped leaves and dirt in his face, and the tops of the trees hissed. Lightning flashed nearby, bringing with it the stink of burning hair. "So, it's just as I thought—you can't break through into the Land of the Living." At this the tree beside Calder shook, swelled, and squealed like a green log on the fire before bursting open and dropping in two, the raw pulp boiling and bubbling, popping with hot sap. Calder stepped back, disturbed by the perversity of gutting a piece of God's work perhaps a hundred years old. It angered him.

"Is that the best of your might?" Calder shouted. Before he could think what next to say, he was flying through the bushes and striking another tree so hard, he rolled into a berry vine. And by the time he got to his feet, every scrap of wood and loosened leaf for ten paces around was rising off the ground and burning black, curling, crisping to ash in midair. Calder slapped a smoldering twig out of his face and yelled, "Are you afraid to speak to me?"

A sound hit his ear more frightening than any demonic howl he could have imagined. Down the hill he heard a girl screaming.

# Twenty-nine

CALDER TORE THROUGH THE FOREST, BACK toward the cottage. The rain and wind were heavy now, but he was out of the forest and down the hill before he even realized the voice was not Ana's. The front door of the little house stood open. As he slid and slipped down the grass to the yard fence, Ana and Alexis ran out and came to the side of the house. They peered in the windows until they found the one they wanted. They pressed against the glass and knocked. As Calder approached he saw what they were staring at through the small locked casement.

A servant girl had barricaded herself and a blond boy of twelve into one of the bedrooms. She gave little shrieks with each breath, but Johnnie was smiling at his cousins. He went to the window and put his hands to the pane, grinning. "My dead cousins came to see me!" he called. "I want to show you my garden!" But the servant girl yanked the boy away from the glass and forced him to kneel.

Alexis knocked at the window. "We're not ghosts!"

"We wouldn't hurt you," Ana called. "Don't be scared, Johnnie."

But the girl was crying and the boy, Johnnie, was beginning to worry at her hysterics. He grew pale when she forced his head down and he began to tremble.

"Please open the door!" Ana called. And to Alexis she said, "Who is that servant? Where's Lalla?"

Calder came to stand behind them at the window, rain running down his face. The girl was frantically holding Johnnie's hands together in prayer.

"Just let us in!" Alexis shouted. And when the girl saw the faces at the window, she screamed again and covered the boy's eyes.

"The rain," whispered Alexis. He showed his sister in the window's reflection that the shower had washed their powder away in rivulets. Their faces dripped white and glowed like ghostly orbs, their hands as well. Ana took a step back from the glass.

As the servant girl began to pray loudly, Cousin Johnnie fell onto his side, jerking and stiffening in convulsions.

"He's having one of his spells," said Ana. "We have to find Lalla."

"No." Alexis took his sister's hand. "We have to leave."

She pulled away. "He needs us."

"We have to leave and not come back," said Alexis. "We're hurting him."

Ana leaned on the windowpane, her forehead to the glass, watching Johnnie's quaking body. Then she whirled about and pushed past Calder, running up the hill into the woods. Calder went after her and Alexis followed. As she stumbled up the wet grass and began to tromp through the brush and trees, Calder looked around for signs of Lost Souls. For the moment they seemed to be alone.

Ana marched through the blackened leaves that still steamed from demonic fire. Calder took her elbow and guided her away from where the broken tree lay in pieces. He could see that it wasn't only the idea of being seen as a monster and frightening her cousin that was making Ana cry.

"I only wanted to sit by the fire, under a quilt, and tell them what happened to us," she said. "Why couldn't we hug him just once?" All these sweet things had been snatched from her and she was lost again.

They all were, hurrying away but toward nothing safe. And the unholy power pursuing him would again be following them all. Ana's sorrow hurt Calder, yet he was glad to be in their company. The three of them were alone in the world, but *they were together.*

The rain stopped, and so did Ana. In the dimness of a family of oaks she began to speak, trying to smile, but her eyes betrayed her every time she glanced at Calder.

"We can make a new life," she said. "We can choose new names for ourselves. I have the powder safe in my pocket. When we get out of this wet place we'll be all right." She took in a breath that was nearly a sob. "We'll stop tonight somewhere and hide in the back corner of a tavern where no one can hear us, and we'll create the new story of our lives. And then we'll find work. We can read books. Hear music. Even dance." She took in another breath and held it for a moment before she went on. "We'll rent a cottage in the country or an apartment in London," she said. "At night, when we're alone, we'll remember . . . "

That was as far as she got before the tears returned.

Alexis sighed and rubbed his chin. "I would've liked to grow whiskers one day."

Calder pictured the boy's father, the kind, bearded face of Nicholas as he had seen him at rest in the house at Ekaterinburg. Calder wished he were Liam and could give the kind of encouragement a fatherless boy needed. "When I bring souls to the Great River and they meet the Captain for the first time," Calder said, "to some of them he appears as a huge warrior and to others a babyfaced angel, but whether he is a giant or a cherub, he can strike fear into any heart with one look."

"How?" asked Alexis.

"Because his spirit is mighty."

The boy watched Calder for a moment and then smiled as if he appreciated the gesture even if he did not believe it. A warm wind swept through the woods. The breeze seemed to comfort Ana—her tears ceased and dried on her cheeks. She took the powder box from her pocket and dusted her brother and herself with makeup. The wind would have been a comfort to Calder, too, but it smelled of Lost Souls.

Eventually the three started back to the road in silence. Ana breathed in small gulps, holding her elbows, staring at nothing. Her head was bare, her hair sticking up in little spikes—she had left her hat in cousin Johnnie's cottage. Calder wanted to take her hand, but felt shy for some reason.

Ana walked in the middle with her brother at her side, but a fourth figure moved along with them on the other side of the boy. A chill ran over Calder's skin and rippled the hair at the back of his head.

Calder stopped and the others did as well, and so did the dim figure that stayed by Alexis's left shoulder.

"What's wrong?" asked the boy.

"Someone's here," Calder whispered. Ana slipped her fingers into his hand and held tight.

"Who?" asked the boy.

The figure was fully visible now, though much dimmer than Ana and Alexis, and the shapes of trees and vines could be seen faintly through his body. "Can't you see him?" Calder asked, staring at the soul, who at last stared back.

"No," Ana whispered.

The face was familiar, the eyes sad. He wore a white sailor's shirt. "Nagorny?" Calder asked. Though he kept his gaze on the Lost Soul, he saw the boy straighten with fear.

"Yes," said Nagorny. His voice was faint at first.

"You're back," said Calder.

The dead man seemed to relax now, happy to have someone to talk with. "I walked through the rooms where they kept the family," said Nagorny. "But there were only soldiers there, and the wall was down. They'd thrown away the key."

Ana and Alexis watched the air that Calder was addressing but apparently did not see or hear the man.

"And now you've found your boy," said Calder. Ana made a small sound, perhaps of fear, or perhaps empathy.

"I saw him," said Nagorny, "and his sister, too, far across the sea, shining like angels. Then they went dark, like candles that had blown out. I'm sorry it took me so long to find them."

"You saw them from Russia?" asked Calder. He wasn't sure if this was good news—could all the Lost Souls see the Brightening children halfway around the world before they covered themselves?

The man stood up straight. "It will not happen again, sir," said Nagorny. "I will never leave his side unless you command me to do so."

The shadows around them shivered, fluttered with unnatural excitement. "Are there still others here with us now," Calder whispered, "that wish to do us harm?"

"Yes," said Nagorny. Again the shadows shifted in closer.

With tentative fingers, the boy reached out and touched the air where the dead man stood. And without looking at him, Nagorny put a hand on the boy's back.

"Can you protect us?" Calder asked the man.

"We've always taken care of Alexis."

"We?" Calder asked him.

"Father Grigori is here, too," said Nagorny.

Calder felt Rasputin before he saw him, felt the odd weight of the man's eyes on him. Rasputin was standing behind a tree ten paces away, grinning, watching them with large black eyes.

"You know, escort," he said, "face powder can't mask their light from the eyes of the Lost Ones for long."

Calder's skin went cold at the expression on Rasputin's face.

"Father Grigori," he said, and both Ana and Alexis gasped and twisted around in search of the spirit. "You need to protect the children," Calder told him. "Be a friend to them."

"You took my body," said Rasputin. "Take my duties, why don't you."

"Why are you hiding?" Calder asked.

"I came to watch." Rasputin folded his arms, leaned on the tree. "The young ones are attracting a great crowd."

Calder's stomach tightened into a knot.

"I want to carry the boy on my shoulder as I used to," said Nagorny. "But I can't seem to. I tried to bring the boy's chair, but they cleared everything out and burned it. Only ashes left," he said. "Except for what would not burn."

"In Ekaterinburg?" Calder asked. "What would not burn?"

Nagorny shrugged. "Metal," he said. "Forks and spoons, wheels from the boy's chair."

Calder wanted to slap his hand over Nagorny's mouth to keep him from speaking, but he could not. He took Ana and Alexis each by a hand and started to hurry them toward the road. *They'd thrown away the key*, Nagorny had said. The Fetch Key was there, swept into a burn pile outside the House of Special Purpose.

Nagorny's spirit floated along at the boy's side, but unfortunately Rasputin's spirit followed, as well.

"Metal things?" Rasputin asked the sailor. "What about a key on a chain?"

"Don't speak to him, Nagorny," said Calder, but he was already answering.

"I thought it was a crucifix," said Nagorny. "But it was only a key. The doors are open now. No need for keys."

As Calder caught a glance of Rasputin, he grinned and darted away like a fly, heading, no doubt, back to Ekaterinburg to try to snatch the Key from a pile of char and cinders. Calder started running, pulling the two along, though it was no use. Rasputin could fly to Russia in a heartbeat—they would have to take the high road over land and sea.

"Nagorny," said Calder. "Can you get to the Key before Father Grigori?"

"It's no use," said the sailor. "I can't touch anything in your world."

Calder hoped Rasputin would have this same difficulty, but what would happen if Rasputin had gained enough power to somehow use the Key? Would it bring a Door for him and with it that momentary portal between worlds? And if he did break out of the Land of Lost Souls, who or what would he bring with him? And what horrors might they leave in their paths if they were able to swarm into the Land of the Living?

# Thirty

ALTHOUGH NAGORNY FLOATED AT THE BOY'S side as his protector,
Calder knew Ana and Alexis were not safe. The dark mist that had
hung in the air around Rasputin had not left with him—it flowed
along at their backs instead, stinking of burnt bone and fur and
drawing with it earthly storm clouds that rumbled and churned.
And at their backs, in the depths of the forest, Calder could hear
trees sizzling and the cry of a wounded bird.

Calder led them back to the road and, as they headed south to the
train station, he caught Nagorny's attention. When the man came to
float at Calder's shoulder instead of the boy's, Calder whispered,
"We need help."

Nagorny neither agreed nor offered ideas, but when Calder
asked, "Do you think you could confuse the others that follow us?"
Nagorny nodded slowly. "If you could lure them off our scent for
a while, to give us a chance to lose them, I would be grateful."

"I will lead them away," Nagorny whispered, "but you must
watch over the boy and his sister for me."

"I will." And with not a flicker of hesitation, Nagorny's spirit lifted like a paper kite in a pocket of warm air and vanished. The stink of smoke cleared from the air. The sky quieted. Calder did not know what kind of lie Nagorny had offered the Lost Souls to change their path, but he was so relieved, he felt light in the head. Alexis lengthened his stride, and Ana ran to keep up with Calder.

✵ ✵ ✵

As they stood at the ticket window in the King's Lynn station, an old woman in a straw hat overheard Calder's plan to travel to Russia by way of France.

"Not likely." She was sitting on a bench knitting a black shawl. "We're at war with Germany, you know."

Calder felt foolish not to have thought of this.

"We could go back the way we came," said Alexis. "The Atlantic, New York, California, Japan . . ."

The idea of having to go all that way was unfathomable.

The woman spoke again. "You could sail up." She shrugged. "North. Though any captain would have to be crazy to agree." She grinned and, with her weathered skin and missing tooth, reminded Calder of a pirate.

Which might have been why Calder remembered then that for the right price one could secure a boat in London and sail the Thames out to the English Channel and into the North Sea. So they boarded a train for London rather than Portsmouth. It wasn't until they were nearing the Surrey docks that Calder began to suspect that the boat he was thinking of belonged to Pincher's family. That boat would have been gone for centuries. But they had no better plan.

\* \* \*

Calder had been to Death Scenes in London many times since his own death, so it wasn't that this was his first trip back, but it was his first time walking along the waterfront since he was a human. Much had changed, but he could feel the old London hiding just under the skin of this new one. Crooked stones in the pavement, the slight curve of a narrow street, the hiding places beneath piers where the barnacles made the underside of the planking look like a crab's shell. These things had changed little. But the new melted into the ghost of the old with each blink of his eyes. There was Pincher sitting on the curb, and then he was gone. There was an apple core with enough sweet fruit around the stem to snatch up out of the gutter, but as Calder saw his hand dip down to pluck it from the stones, it would be gone and only a scrap of newspaper in its place.

Certainly the streets were busy with modern humans—nurses in white dresses pushed soldiers in wheelchairs and boys on dusty bicycles wove between passersby. Women walked about smoking cigarettes, with their hair cut short; one even wore trousers. But as he blinked, Calder would see the image of a woman in a long gown and cape stepping from an open carriage. His eyes would open again and she would become a girl in a tailored suit stepping out of a motorcar. His ears deceived him as well. The music coming from some nearby tavern shifted to the instruments and melodies of his childhood.

Victrolas playing piano music and the jazzy lines of trombones would fade and be replaced by harps and flutes until Calder would tilt his head to catch the strains more clearly—then they would fade. Only the smells were constant, as if they'd remained the same for three hundred years: burning butter and onions, salted fish, ale, coal smoke, and pipe tobacco.

Calder stopped in his tracks and closed his eyes, kept them closed, until Pincher appeared in his mind's eye, skipping along the slums of the London docks. He watched the boy leap over the bow of his family's boat and disappear into the glowing warmth within. As a child Calder had envied Pincher's life: his floating house and his loud and smiling clan. If he hadn't been ashamed of being homeless, he might have found shelter with them, but that was long ago.

Calder knew where to turn now and led the two down along the far end of the waterfront where the ships got smaller and were crowded closer together.

"There used to be this family of Irish sea merchants."

"Pirates?" asked Alexis.

"They were fishermen, traders, storytellers." He saw a familiar bridge between two piers. It was dark and echoed with a sound Calder knew well, the way the water lapped.

As Calder brought Ana and Alexis around a certain haunting corner of stone wall and rotting fence post, he remembered the boat with blazing recall—ten paces long, three across, the kind of dark wood that would be easy to hide at night along a shady cove, two masts, glass box lanterns hanging from chains. He could see the ghost of the vessel before his open eyes, and the vision did not disappear like the earlier images when he blinked—this memory rocked gently at its mooring and a blue-eyed man stepped out of the cabin.

"Do you see it?" Calder asked the others.

"A little sailboat that looks like it might sink at any moment?" said Alexis. "Yes, I see it."

"You lost?" The young man had black hair, pale skin, rosy cheeks.

"You've never met anyone so lost," said Alexis.

"I used to know someone whose family had a boat out this way," said Calder. It wasn't until after he'd spoken that he realized it would be hard to explain. The three came up and stood beside the small vessel. Up close Calder could see that the dark wood of the cabin was carved with long interlocking chains, braiding into each other and forming animals—birds, running horses, leaping dogs, and hiding rabbits.

"I've heard that a clan of Irish merchants docked here three hundred years ago. They were storytellers and musicians," said Calder. "They traded in the marketplace." *And they looked very much like you,* he wanted to add.

"Our family has had boats right here for more than four hundred years," the man bragged. Another man came up from the cabin and a third came strolling from behind them. "What family were you trying to find?" he asked.

"I can't remember the family name," said Calder. "But we need to hire a boat."

The three men came to stand together on the deck of the vessel, smiling at them. They were all of the same beauty: black curls, blue eyes. They wore tattered shirts, trousers cropped below the knee, and no shoes.

"What do you need a boat for?"

"To get to Russia," said Calder.

The three men laughed but smiled kindly at them.

"You can't take us to Russia, then?" asked Ana.

The first man seemed to get a certain lift from being spoken to by a woman. "We can do anything," he said. "We find treasures, sneak through battlefronts, steal hearts . . . everything."

"So you could take us to Russia," said Ana.

"Why would you want to go there?" said one of the others. "It's so nice here."

Calder stepped forward and pulled out one of the emeralds, offering it to the first man.

The three passed the gem around and admired it. "Beautiful," he said, returning it to Calder. "There must be a story behind that one."

"You wouldn't believe it if we told you," said Alexis.

"Are these your children?" one of the men asked Calder.

"We're friends," Ana told him. It pleased Calder to think that she didn't want to play his daughter.

"It's not that we don't want to help you," said the first man. "You seem like good people. And it's not the money."

"You're afraid?" asked Alexis.

"Alexis!" Ana scolded.

All three men pretended to be offended; one pulled up his sleeve and showed off his muscled arm. "No, lad," said the first man. "We're no cowards. But for this request, which our family might call"—he thought for a moment—"dodgy, we would agree only if we were shown that it was *our* adventure. Know what I mean?" He shrugged. "It would have to be fate that gave it to us."

"For you to take us where we ask," said Ana, "what would fate have to do?"

"It would take a bloody miracle," said one of the other men.

"I'll do it," said Calder. "What kind of a miracle do you want?"

The three men laughed again, but the first said, "Hang on, let me think."

Calder prayed they would want something easy to deliver, such as him surviving a knife in the heart or a bullet in the head.

"Have him find the Holy Grail," said one, but another said, "Or that knife Finn dropped overboard last month."

The first man brightened at this. "Now that would be useful," he said. "If you find the pocketknife Finn dropped right here"—he motioned in the water beside the boat—"we'll know we were meant to take you wherever you want to go. Agreed?"

"Don't do it," Ana whispered to Calder, as if she thought it was a trap.

"I'll do it!" Alexis chimed in.

"No," said Calder. "I'll go."

"And you can't take a week to do it," said one of the others. "Find it in three breaths."

"I'll only need one breath," said Calder, taking off his boots. The men laughed again. "So, what does it look like?" he asked them. When none of them answered, Calder asked the first one, "What's your name?"

"Tomas," he said. "And yours, friend?"

"Calder."

Not wanting to lose the emeralds or pound coins he carried, Calder turned out his trouser pockets and put the contents into Ana's waiting hands. The lock of her hair, which he had forgotten about, rested on her palm for a moment, then whisked away in the breeze and was scattered over the water. Calder hoped she hadn't understood the stolen memento, but as she looked up at him curiously, she touched the fringe of her hair.

Calder blushed and turned back toward the men.

"So, Tomas, what does this knife look like?" said Calder. "There might be a lot of weapons down there."

This delighted the men, and Tomas described the lost pocketknife. "This long." He held his fingers three inches apart. "Silver and mother-of-pearl."

"When you dropped it, was it opened or closed?" asked Calder.

The one that must have been Finn answered, "Closed."

"All right, then," said Calder.

"Be careful," said Ana. Calder had a strong instinct to kiss her goodbye. It was tempting. He could throw her over his arm like a hero going forth to slay a dragon. He knew the men would be amused, but he wasn't sure if Alexis would approve. He was only half certain Ana wouldn't slap him.

Instead, he motioned for Ana and Alexis to step back; he didn't want to splash them and risk washing off their protective powder. He gave Ana a reassuring smile and dropped down into the brackish water beside the boat.

It was deeper than he expected, with the river floor some forty feet down. The water was quite a bit warmer than the Russian river where he had been dumped with his hands and feet tied. He kicked his way down after his initial descent slowed. The bottom was much more confusing than he'd expected. The water was murky, everything covered in barnacles. Long sea grasses grew on the dock legs and waved with the currents. A few centuries' worth of junk that had fallen overboard coming in or out of London lay strewn about in varying stages of decay. Lumps, some as small as cats and some as large as pianos, hid under the carpet of silt that spanned as far as the eye could see. Tin cups, old boots, broom handles, ropes, broken china, and half-buried wine bottles were scattered about. Fish as small as his hand darted about, sucking in and spitting out mouthfuls of muck.

Calder wished he could conjure a Lost Soul dream so that everything would become transparent. It would be so much easier to find a three-inch pocketknife if he could see through the vegetation and crustaceans. He saw a rusting tin of sardines, an ivory button, a broken pipe, a woman's slipper, an ear horn.

At first the sensation of not breathing hurt his chest, but soon he'd forgotten about it. He began to see objects from his own days in London: a snuff box, an ivory fan fallen apart like a pile of fish bones, the silver tip from a dagger's scabbard.

A door, pale wood with the blue paint peeling off it in curling slivers, stood nearly straight up on the bottom of the river floor, wedged between some rocks. The brass knob and hinges were missing; a tiny silver fish swam into the keyhole and disappeared. Calder knew it had nothing to do with the Aisle, but he couldn't stop himself. He went to the door and slid his fingers around the side where it had once opened when it was on land. It fell aside with a cloud of silt billowing upward.

Among the stones and shells beyond its threshold, he thought he saw the curved arrangement of the bones of a human hand and the ominous yellowed brow and hollow eyes of a skull, but it was only a row of ivory beads and a china vase half covered in mud with two holes broken in its side. Calder wanted to bring the bead necklace back for Ana, but the string that had bound it had rotted away. He took a single bead, the centerpiece of the necklace in the shape of a bird in flight.

Although the corpse had been nothing more than an illusion, one of the hand's fingers pointed toward him with a glint of mother-of-pearl.

When the men helped Calder out of the water, they seemed frightened. Even Ana, who knew he had no need of air, looked scared, but Alexis was sitting on the dock as if bored. Calder tossed his catch to Tomas, who snatched it from the air. After an astonished moment, Finn picked up the little pocketknife from Tomas's palm and all three men cheered and embraced Calder.

"Friend," said Tomas, "you are going to Russia."

Calder took back the gems and coins from Ana and put the ivory bead in her hand. She admired it for a moment, then slipped it into her pocket with a smile. Calder paid the men with one of the emeralds.

"That's fair," said Tomas. "And we'll keep the knife."

"How long was I under water?" Calder asked Ana as he put his boots back on.

"Forever," she said.

"Fifteen minutes," said Alexis. "What took you so long?"

❋ ❋ ❋

Tomas and Finn's cousin was named Luke. The men agreed to take the three across the North Sea and the Baltic, through the Gulf of Finland, and to the Russian port of Kronstadt.

"Tell me about this Irish family you knew," said Tomas as they prepared the boat. "We're sure to have met them."

"It was years ago," said Calder. "They had a boy my age. They all sang together. They used a coffin to hide things they didn't want people to find."

"That was us," said Luke. "Our family did that."

# Thirty-one

As they boarded the tiny boat, it was like going back in time. Calder had to make note of the new things he saw so that he wouldn't feel he was going mad. A fishing pole fitted with a metal reel hung along the roof of the cabin, a deck of playing cards with modern dancing girls on the backs lay on a barrel, and a wristwatch buckled in a loop dangled from a nail beside the cabin door. If he didn't check for these proofs that they were still in 1918, he would think they had stepped onto the same boat that had docked there three centuries before. The boards from which the cabin was made seemed ancient and their carvings familiar.

"Did your ancestors teach you how to carve these patterns?" Calder asked, fingering the engravings of knotted ivy vines and animals.

"Every generation, we use the same wood when we rebuild," explained Tomas. "There's probably a bit of wood from our first boat here somewhere."

"Probably a piece of Noah's ark, too," said Luke. "And the Holy Cross."

Calder was haunted by the idea that these young men were truly Pincher's family descendants, from a dozen generations later. He ducked under the cabin doorway and gave Ana his hand as she followed him into the hold. Alexis was still above deck, asking the men about the name of the ship.

The area below was so small, Calder could touch both side walls with his hands outstretched. On either side of the steps leading down hung two hammocks. In front of them, nestled in the narrow bow, sat two plain wood coffins.

"Did you hear that?" Alexis was laughing. He stumbled down the step behind them. "The name of this boat." He saw the coffins and said, "How fitting for a Fetch."

"There are only two beds," said Ana. "Are we to sleep in the coffins? I suppose *we're* what they're smuggling now."

"But listen," said Alexis. "*Comhartha Ó Dia.* You'll never believe what they said it means."

"'Sign from God,'" said Calder. He felt unsteady and sat on the cabin step.

"I told Calder he should keep his eyes open," Alexis told Ana. "I said he had to search for signs so he could follow his quest, you know, and lift the curse."

"That's good, then," said Ana.

Alexis examined the coffins.

"When you take us to Heaven," Ana asked, sitting beside Calder, "what will happen to you?"

She wouldn't look away from him. Calder would have kissed her then if Alexis hadn't pulled her up on deck.

Calder stayed where he was, his clothes still damp from his miracle-working. He gave a prayer of thanks and a prayer for help. The Key had to be where he thought it was. And it had to wait for them to come back.

※ ※ ※

Tomas, Luke, and Finn buttoned suspenders to their pants, pulled thick woolen jumpers over their heads, and tied back their dark curls with pieces of string. Their wives and children came to the dock with provisions. The clan was introduced to the three travelers and politely shook hands. Calder expected them to be unhappy with him for taking their men on such a treacherous voyage, but instead they congratulated Calder on his miraculous underwater discovery. They all looked like Tomas: light-skinned and blue-eyed, with black hair and bright smiles. When one of the small boys turned his back to Calder, he so resembled Pincher, it made his heart jump.

Calder expected to wait until morning to set sail, but they set off that evening as the sun was setting.

"Doesn't matter to us," said Tomas. "In clear weather the stars are easier to follow than the sun."

The first night, Calder lay awake in one coffin, watching Ana and Alexis sleep in the other. The boy wanted to sleep on deck, but the spray off the ocean threatened to wash off the protective powder. As Calder sat up with them, he heard the small sounds of distress in their dreams. The faintest moan or an intake of breath would make him sit up and watch their faces. Though the powder kept them from shining, the Brightening seemed to be wearing on them from the inside. After only an hour of sleep they woke with alarm.

"I dreamt about mermaids, but they were horrible-looking," said Alexis.

"I dreamt there was a boat full of people sailing beside us," said Ana. "They kept calling for me to swim over to them."

Calder would have spent all night beating Souls away from them if he only had a weapon that worked on the Lost.

"I don't want to dream anymore," said Alexis. "But I'm so tired."

Ana patted her brother with extra powder and Calder sat in the other coffin as they lay down again, on their sides, close together and facing him. He wished he had an incantation that would ward off nightmares, but the best he could think of was the Children's Psalm. He sang it quietly over and over until he was sure they were asleep.

> *Behold, dear soul, beyond the moon*
> *The bright and opening gates*
> *And there, upon your windowsill,*
> *The golden ship that waits.*
> *The hour now is late; to earth say your goodbye.*
> *"Sleep safe and dream sweet," the stars sing around you.*
> *Spread wings and take the sky.*

\* \* \*

When on the first morning both brother and sister claimed to have slept peacefully, Alexis asked Calder if he would sing them to sleep with that same psalm every night. Although the boy wanted to stay on deck and help the crew, the fever of the Brightening was taking its toll. Alexis spent most of the trip asleep, which was a relief to Ana, Calder could tell. He suspected the Brightening was also wearing on her, but she took to sitting up with Calder as he sang the boy to sleep and coming up on deck with him when the seas were calm.

"If you're awake," she told him, "I want to be awake."

Calder worried that she was suffering by not resting, but she wouldn't stay in Alexis's coffin after the first night. So Calder lay down beside her in the other coffin. She reclined on her side and he lay behind her with his arm around her, hoping she would relax and sleep. But long after he thought she had drifted off, she spoke.

"Alexis never really liked Ilya," she told him. "But he likes you." His heart went from the burn of envy to the rush of pleasure in one all-too-human pulse. He was a Fetch. He should be strong and want only those things for Ana that would be best for her.

She softly hummed a hymn and Calder lay behind her, secretly grateful that she resisted sleep; he loved her company even when they didn't speak at all.

※ ※ ※

To appear mortal, the three pretended to eat. Calder hated to waste any of the food that the men might have needed, and so he claimed no appetite. Their hosts were no fools—they could see there was something different about the three, and the men had their superstitions, like all sailors did: they poured a few drops of wine on the deck for good luck before starting the journey, they kept a silver coin in a leather pouch tied to the top of the mast to ward off a shipwreck, and each man kept a wren's feather in his pocket to protect him from drowning. But the men were also by nature comfortable with the arcane and did not see their passengers as a threat. They treated them more like charms against evil and soon stopped offering them bread and wine, teasing them instead about being saints in disguise.

Calder kept a careful watch the first day, expecting a cloud of Lost Souls to catch up to them at any moment, but the clouds all appeared natural and the smoke smelled of Luke's pipe, sweet like burning apples and pinecones. For the first time Calder began to feel the pleasure of comaraderie with Tomas and his cousins that he'd enjoyed in the company of other Fetches. Earth almost felt like home.

The *Comhartha* stayed close to land in case they were stopped and boarded. If they were discovered by the enemy, Tomas had reassured them, they would claim they had gotten lost finding a place to bury the dead at sea.

The scenery was always changing; every hour brought them past a new land: storybook hills of long blowing grasses, cliffs with round castle towers, stark black hills with silhouette windmills, mountains as pointed as Egyptian pyramids.

Ana and Calder took to sitting together on an extra coil of rope that had been covered in a blanket below the wheel. It made a kind of chair just wide enough for them both. Calder put his arm across her shoulder and with his body screened her from the spray when a wave hit the boat. He didn't want her powder to wash away and leave her burning.

One evening, a strange formation of clouds lay over the land—a giant funnel of gray above the hilltops with sunlight streaming out from behind it in a huge fan. Calder watched Luke and Finn working the sail and rudder, saw the way their dark hair curled at the backs of their necks, and thought of Pincher and wondered what his real name was.

And then, as quiet as a lock of hair shifting in the wind across his ear, Calder heard a name whispered.

"Were any of your relatives named Duggan?" he asked the men.

"No doubt," said Tomas. "Like the dancing boy."

"Was that the name of your little friend?" Finn asked.

Calder was going to say, "I think so." But instead he answered, "Yes."

"Remember that dancing boy song?" Tomas asked Finn, and Finn began to sing a wordless melody so familiar to Calder that the hair rose on his arms.

Ana woke and listened to the tune.

"I've forgotten the words," said Finn.

"Something about Duggan with a hop in his step," said Tomas. "He danced to the mermaids' song and stole the boots off the Devil's feet. Something like that."

Calder shivered and Ana asked, "What is it?"

Although it seemed impossible, he said, "I think I wrote that song."

A wind whipped up, flapping the sail, frosting the waves with foam. When an iron ring bucked free from its mounting on the mast, Tomas cried for Calder to help him catch the line before the sailcloth could tear. As Calder stepped up on the edge of the bow and reached for the fluttering rope, he thought he saw a small figure standing at the stern, a barefoot boy, his dark curls blowing.

Then Calder's sight left him in one black wave. He could still hear the men yelling and feel the spray of salt water, though he saw nothing but his childhood. All the glimpses he had recalled since coming to the Land of the Living, of his days in London with Pincher, flooded his heart and took his breath away. He and Pincher had been companions for only a few short seasons, but every adventure now seemed to play in his mind, one after the next, then overlapping, bringing with them fears and joys so sudden, Calder felt paralyzed.

Laughing with Pincher in their hideaway under the bridge with stolen carrots in their fists, teaching Dog to bite the cuffs of merchants when the two needed a diversion, throwing pebbles at the gulls on the pier. Then all at once the images slowed. Pincher was weeping and bleeding as two huge men kicked and beat him. Calder could hear Dog barking and howling. He could smell the blood. And he felt the terror strangling him as he turned and crawled through a nearby wall.

This was the way they always got to safety, but until that day, Pincher was always ahead of Calder. Through the hole in the barricade near the marketplace, along a low wall and across the traders' road, under the cemetery gate, and up ahead he'd duck through the gap in the ruins of the old churchyard wall, but Pincher was not in front of him. He turned and looked back as he crossed the cemetery. He thought he heard Pincher breathing at his back, but his friend was not following. When he got to the underside of the bridge where they always met, he was alone. He stayed there, shaking and sick, and hoped that Pincher would come back, but soon Dog trotted around the corner, with blood on his coat and a torn ear. The pitiful creature climbed into Calder's lap, never left him again. Calder knew his friend was dead—Dog never would have left him otherwise. Calder pleaded with Pincher.

"Come back to me," he wept. "You can't leave me here alone."

The memories raced forward again through Calder's childhood, flying in painful disorder until the moment of his own death. Then everything slowed down a second time and he was lying on his side on the midnight dock, drenched and freezing, alone. Or perhaps not alone. He felt someone nearby, but he could see no one. He hadn't the strength to look around.

Calder heard Tomas shouting at him. Something struck him in the chest and he was in the sea. Something cold and rough was sliding through his hand so fast, it burned. He clutched his fingers shut, clamping down on the rope before it could slither all the way out of his grip. The sea spun Calder like a child's toy, thrashed him against the hull of the boat, where his head hit with a crack.

Suddenly Calder was seeing all the same scenes from his childhood, only he was seeing himself. He was watching it all from Pincher's eyes. Stealing carrots, playing with Dog, and then he was on the ground, being kicked by two men, watching the boy Calder duck through a hole in a wall. Pincher leapt from his body and followed Calder, through the hole, along a low wall, across the road where a cart came so close to hitting him it seemed to pass right through his shoulder. As Pincher ducked under the cemetery gate after his friend, a Door opened to his right and a figure stepped through, but Pincher darted away between the headstones, through the gap in the churchyard wall, and flew to the bridge where he found Calder.

"Come back to me," Calder was sobbing.

"I did," Pincher answered. Dog looked up at him, but Calder didn't raise his head.

"You can't leave me here alone," Calder told him, and Pincher promised, "I won't."

❖ ❖ ❖

When Calder opened his eyes he was sitting on the *Comhartha Ó Dia* where he always sat, but Ana was not beside him. No one was on board. And seeing the clear ocean through the transparent ship made Calder's stomach lurch. He focused his eyes on the deck until it was solid brown wood. He lifted his head and found a dark-haired boy, his hands on his hips, standing barefoot on the edge of the bow.

# Thirty-two

Pincher had a coil of rope over one shoulder, and his blue eyes smiled.

*Here was the Lost Soul that Calder had known while living.*

"You were gone a long time," said Pincher.

"Yes." Calder stayed very still, afraid of scaring him off.

The sky and sea were the same deep iron blue. The wind was slow, the waves even slower, as if the ocean were a slumbering beast whose great body swelled and sighed with each silent breath. Calder was struck with the horror of the length of Pincher's wanderings—Calder had spent the last three hundred years in the Aisle with the Captain, while Pincher had spent the same number of years among the Lost Ones.

"Do you remember when I told you never to leave me?" Calder asked. He knew no mortal had the power to force a dying spirit into the Land of the Lost Souls, but all the same he felt guilty now that he had begged Pincher not to abandon him.

"Yes," said Pincher. "But you were the one who left me behind."

Calder remembered the feeling of being watched at his own death. "When I died?" asked Calder.

"After that I went and found my boat," said Pincher.

"Remember the day you promised not to leave me?" asked Calder. Pincher nodded.

"Did you see a Door open? One that had never been there before?"

"You mean in the graveyard?" he asked. "Did you see it, too?"

"Why did you run from it?" asked Calder.

"A devil came out," said the boy. "He wanted to catch us."

Calder wanted to run and embrace him, but he smiled instead.

Pincher jumped down and limped toward Calder. "I got lost," he admitted. "This is my boat. I can tell. But I can't find my da. And those devils never stop chasing me."

"We're still friends, aren't we?" Calder asked the boy.

Pincher nodded.

"I'm going to tell you a secret," Calder whispered.

Pincher smiled then.

"There really is a Golden Fairy—remember the Golden Fairy?"

"But you made that up," he said.

"I thought I made her up, but she was real. I'll show you."

Pincher shook his head, took a step away.

"It's all right. Call her. She'll bring a magic door and take you to your father."

Pincher began to tremble.

"It's not a trick," said Calder. "I promise."

"What if I don't like it on the other side of the door?" asked the child.

Calder knew this was impossible, but he made an offer. "Tie your rope around your waist, and if you don't like what you find you can yank on the rope and I'll pull you back to me, all right?"

Pincher smiled, but his fingers were shaking as he knotted the rope around his middle and handed Calder the loose end, which Calder was surprised he could feel in his fist.

"Do you remember what she looks like?" asked Calder.

"A white dress and gold hair," said Pincher.

"Call her."

Pincher held still, searching the air around him.

"Ask her to take you to your family," Calder whispered.

"Please, miss." Pincher's voice was small. "Come take me to my da."

A pale light opened up in the air above the boy's head, followed by three shimmering steps, and a Fetch descended, in a gown as white as snow, with hair as yellow as honey, smiling eyes, and a hand held out to the child. Calder longed to speak to the Fetch—to ask for help or to beg her to send a message to the Captain, but he was afraid of scaring Pincher away from his Door. For a moment Calder thought the boy would be too terrified to accept her, but he took her hand, leaned forward, and pressed his face into her dress, then let her guide him up and into the Aisle.

"Goodbye," Calder whispered.

He held the end of the rope but knew Pincher would not need to be dragged back out of the Aisle. He was surprised then when he felt the rope jerk nearly out of his grasp. The Door was gone and the sea swung up and knocked him over the side. The rope tied to Pincher became the rope that tethered Calder to the ship. He held it with both hands, opened his eyes at the dark confusion of the underside of the waves. He thought he heard shouts from far away, somewhere above.

Dark hands splashed about at the surface of the water above him. Far above him, too far to reach. And below, he thought he saw pale faces, giant fish with the features of men and women slowly undulating toward him. He tightened his fist on the rope and tried to climb the slick hull of the *Comhartha*.

Like a beacon, an arm thrust down into the sea, as white and brilliant as an angel's. A small bright hand with the palm open wide, the fingers splayed. Calder was frightened by the idea that as Ana reached into the waves for him she was washing herself clean and would start to burn. He dragged himself up the rope, staring at her hand but not touching it for fear of hurting her. Four dark hands grabbed the rope, his arm, his shirt. In a mighty struggle, Tomas and Luke dragged Calder up over the side of the *Comhartha* and onto the deck. They sat heavily beside him, dripping and gasping for breath. Ana leaned against the stern, staring at Calder, shaking. She must have been splashed with seawater, for not only her arms but her face and throat were wet and Bright. Tomas, Luke, and Finn gazed at the glowing girl but did not ask questions or show fear.

Calder got to his feet and caught her as she swayed. They held each other for a moment. "You shouldn't be frightened for me," he whispered. "You know I can't drown."

As if Finn had sensed the essence of Pincher's story still hanging on the air like sea spray, he took in a deep breath and said, "I remember now." And Finn began to sing.

> *He danced a jig on the palace wall,*
> *On the top of London's Tower,*
> *But when he stole the boots from the Devil's hoofs,*
> *That was Duggan's finest hour.*

The ballad had changed very little since Calder had sung it on the waterfront streets, accepting ha'pennies on a handkerchief spread out on the pavement.

Now as he helped Ana down the steps into the hold, Tomas found them two blankets and then left them alone. Alexis still slept in his open coffin. Above, Finn's voice still sang.

> *There was a fine hop in his step;*
> *He danced for bread and water.*
> *Then one night, by the full moon's light,*
> *He danced for Neptune's daughter.*

Calder helped Ana dry her arms, face, throat, patting the skin gently. She didn't make a sound; neither did she relax until he had dusted her skin with powder. He wrapped the dry blanket around her shoulders. Calder could look nowhere else but in her eyes, where some gravity, as strong and natural as the spin of the earth, drew him closer. Because he was still dripping with the sea, he didn't touch her. She took the damp blanket and was drying his hair when Alexis spoke. Still dreaming, the boy gasped and whispered, "They know. They're coming now."

"We've got company!" Luke yelled.

Tomas jumped down the steps and said, "In you go."

Alexis never woke up as the lid over his bed was nailed down. Ana and Calder climbed into the other coffin. Calder was afraid his wet clothes would wash the powder from her skin, but she pulled him close and they lay in each other's arms while Tomas hammered nails at the corners of the lid. They listened as the *Comhartha* was boarded. Whatever kind of boat had found them, whether military or civilian, enemy or ally, Calder was glad the crew were living human men.

Ana shifted against him, hiding her face under his chin. He expected to feel anxious about them being discovered, but a great peace settled over his heart. What a sweet and eerie refuge, he thought, hiding in the dark, holding Ana. It was a coffin, not a bridal bed, but for a few minutes at least, it was theirs alone.

"How would I have ever found you again," she whispered, "if you were lost at sea?"

He didn't answer her with words because he heard voices and the bump of another hull. But he lay his hand on her cheek, his thumb resting on her lips, and listened for danger. Tomas or one of the others was using the old trick and had brought out some small, dead creature. The hold stunk of corruption as someone thumped down the cabin steps and up again without prying off either coffin lid.

Foolishly Calder wanted to whisper in Ana's ear, "Thank you for caring if you lost me." But he didn't speak. And too soon Tomas began to rip the nails from the coffins. Neither he nor the others would tell Calder whether it had been Germans or allies.

As he helped them out of the box, Tomas shook his head. "Bad luck to repeat the story," he said. "Good luck not to ask."

Once on deck, Calder looked back the way they'd come and saw no other boat, but on the horizon a brooding cloud hung black and roiling over the sea.

"Think we'll outrun it?" he asked Tomas. All three men scanned the horizon.

"Outrun what?" asked Luke.

"The bad weather."

Calder knew as they regarded the sky in bewilderment that it was not a storm of water and wind that gathered at their backs. It was a tempest of dark spirits. He'd known that Nagorny would not be able to keep the Lost Souls away forever, but he had hoped to get to Ekaterinburg before they were overtaken. Calder had performed his first task: he had helped a Lost Soul to cross to Heaven. But he still needed to save the children.

❋ ❋ ❋

They stopped once in a small port of tall rose-brick buildings with white wooden shutters and black stone chimneys—all the boats were as small as the *Comhartha*. The boy woke briefly and wanted to go into the town, but Calder knew they were being followed again and made Ana and Alexis stay hidden while Tomas and Finn went ashore to buy food and drink.

Calder stood over the coffins where brother and sister sat, pale and tired. As he heard the men returning, he came on deck. The horizon to the east was clear and blue, but the whole western sky was filled with darkness. A black cloud, as high as a mountain, was disturbing enough, but what it brought with it was even more terrifying. Upon the face of the water walked two score Lost Souls, stepping along the surface of the sea as if it were a grassy meadow. And just under the ocean's skin swam a hundred more, glowing pale and greenish through the dark water.

# Thirty-three

"Trouble?" asked Tomas.

Calder didn't want to lie to him. The men had done so much for them already.

"Yes," said Calder. "We are being followed."

"We can outrun most boats, and those we can't outrun we can outsmart." Tomas's smile faded at Calder's expression.

"What hunts us is not natural," Calder whispered.

Tomas put a hand on his shoulder. "You're blessed by God, that's easy to tell," he said. "Anything that wishes you harm must be wicked. Your enemy is my enemy. Should we stand and fight?"

Calder wished he could use the heart and strength of the men against the Lost Souls.

"Thank you, but that won't work," said Calder. "What you can do for us is to get us to Russia as soon as possible."

Tomas thumped him on the back. "Like the wind."

As they again set sail, the black cloud at their backs was drawing closer and the figures of Lost Souls walking the water were near enough to distinguish one from another—this one an old woman with an angry frown, that one a man so thin, his skull was nearly visible through his veined skin, the next a young man swinging a lantern. All of them stared with large black eyes, even the swimmers that dipped up and down as they came, smooth as the coils of a sea serpent.

Calder remembered then that Rasputin could only fly instantly to a place in the world if he knew the location: his home in Siberia, Alexandra at Selo, the pyramids at Giza. It seemed to take him hours or days when he wasn't sure where he was going, as when he caught up with Calder and the others on their journey. The creatures pursuing them might be likewise hindered. As moths that fly to a lamplight but are confounded when the flame is blown out, the Lost Souls hunting them, Calder hoped, would lose the trail and be unable to see the Brightening now that Ana was covered again.

Calder tried to watch the eastern horizon instead, but fear gnawed at his stomach.

"Don't do that," said Ana. "You take all the trouble of the world and try to lift it on one shoulder."

Much more of the world's troubles than she could imagine truly were his fault. The Land of Lost Souls, the Aisle of Unearthing, and the Land of the Living were all suffering from his mistakes. Calder felt ill every time he faced west, but to the east the morning sun shone under a white cloud—it lit the faces of Tomas, Finn, and Luke with a hopeful glow. Any one of them would have been a stronger leader, Calder thought.

"Why would Liam think I would be a good Fetch?" he wondered aloud.

"Who is Liam?" asked Ana.

"He was my Master Fetch," he told her. "I wasn't a fine musician. I was a beggar and a thief."

"Being poor is nothing to be ashamed of," said Ana. "Why shouldn't a beggar have as beautiful a voice as a king?"

"The only thing I was good at was surviving," said Calder. "I don't know why he chose me."

But Ana said, "I do."

He was embarrassed that this, like so many things she said and did lately, filled him with joy. They were sailing near the shore, just coming around a small outcropping of land.

"You never had your walk down the Aisle," said Ana. "Fetches don't get a Theatre or a Feast or any of that, do they?"

"That's true."

"You know you died, so perhaps you don't need a Theatre or a Feast," she said, "And you carry your Gallery around with you. But what you need is your Garden."

He knew what she was saying—the words made sense to him—but his heart did not stir at the idea.

"I lived a sheltered life," said Ana. "I didn't really have time to accomplish anything. I might have been a doctor or an actress or a poet, but I didn't have a chance. But you," she said. "Think of all the souls you helped to find Heaven."

At that moment, as the *Comhartha* rounded a tiny peninsula thick with trees, the sun hit a hillside covered in flowers as it blazed into view. It glistened with a multitude of red and purple tulips with brilliant green stalks. Just as suddenly, it disappeared behind another hill of trees.

"What is it?" Ana cried, as if Calder had been struck by lightning.

She hadn't seen the flowers. He could only laugh, which annoyed her. But not only had the flowers given him a momentary shock of joy; they had brought back a forgotten conversation, too. Calder remembered now what Liam had said when he'd offered him the Key. When Calder had asked if there had been a mistake, Liam had laughed.

"Why, lad?" He'd folded his thick arms and looked him up and down. "You done something bad?"

"Yes," Calder had said, thinking how he had run when Pincher was caught instead of throwing himself at the men who were beating the boy.

"You didn't do the right thing?" asked Liam. "That it?"

"Yes."

"Everyone's done wrong," said Liam. "Be grateful you feel it. Some souls don't notice the tip of that scale at all."

"Why me?" asked Calder. "You do know I'm not a gentleman, don't you?"

Liam gave a stomp this time when he laughed. "Better to be good than gentle. A good soul gives his dog half his food and loves his friends even when they're far away and forgives the ones who hate him." Liam smiled. "A good soul sings in the face of sorrow and stands up and lives every morning he's given." Liam clapped a hand on Calder's shoulder. "You're a good boy."

Calder could remember the exact weight of Liam's hand. Now as he gazed down into Ana's face, the slanted light giving her pale cheeks a touch of rose, the pain of being left to die when he was born and the pain of not dying, of surviving as a motherless thing, homeless nights and days of hunger, the solitude of Fetching, all seemed, in a peculiar way, to be redeemed by the peace he now felt with Ana. If all his dark years had brought him to this day, then he blessed those years. For the memory of sitting with Ana on the deck of the *Comhartha Ó Dia* would sustain him through ten thousand miles of shadow.

❋ ❋ ❋

When Ana fell asleep against his shoulder, Calder thought he caught glimpses of the Captain in Finn's face as he stood beside the foremast and something of Liam in Luke's eyes as he glanced over at Calder from where he crouched at the bow dipping gracefully over the sea. Tomas stood at the wheel and Calder felt them pulling ahead and away from the Lost Souls.

When they eventually came to shore in a rough alcove, a rocky and wooded bit of bay short of the true port of Kronstadt, Calder could see only white clouds to the west. Tomas floated the three of them over to the beach on a raft that had spent the trip lashed to the roof of the cabin.

"The train station is just through these trees, to the north," Tomas told them.

Calder helped Ana and Alexis onto the rocks and then gave Tomas the two English pounds. "Bring your wife some wine," he said.

Tomas took the coins and thanked him. "You know," he said confidentially, "people who travel with us are always falling in love. There's nothing to be done about it."

Calder meant to deny it but found himself smiling. Tomas laughed at the way he blushed. And now Calder found himself reluctant to say goodbye. This sea voyage was the happiest he'd been since he came to earth, and he suspected it was for Ana and Alexis their most peaceful hours since they'd been separated from their family. Calder thought now how foolish he'd been as a child not to come to Pincher's family instead of living alone in the street. They probably would have been as kind to him then as their descendants were now. Tomas must have seen some hesitation in Calder's aspect, because he thumped him on the back.

"We won't forget you, friend. Maybe we'll write a song about Calder the Miracle Man and your descendants will come to London four hundred years from now and hear us singing it."

"I'm not sure what's going to happen next," said Calder. He spoke quietly, not wanting Ana or Alexis to hear this. "I would do anything to keep them safe."

Tomas shrugged. "No one ever knows what's going to happen next. But don't worry—you've been aboard the *Comhartha*. Everyone who sails with her is blessed forever."

Calder climbed up the bank to where Ana and Alexis waited, and then the three walked up through a stand of pines and onto a road that led into Kronstadt.

Alexis still seemed only half awake. "I'm just getting my land legs," said the boy. This made Calder remember how hard it was, when he first came into the Land of the Living, to get his earth legs. Ana held Calder's hand as they walked, and Alexis, if he noticed at all, did not comment.

Kronstadt looked like a city that had weathered a great storm. Buildings were left with fences and roofs dilapidated and stained. Walls once covered with frescoes were slashed and broken. As they neared what Calder hoped was the train depot, they passed a deserted building. Its windows and doors were missing, but it was strung with a hand-painted sheet that read THE COMMITTEE OF SOLDIERS AND SAILORS MEETING HOUSE, and under this MUNICIPAL QUESTIONS AND DISPUTES ADDRESSED.

Ragged civilians looked underfed and numb; soldiers, most of them hardly older than Alexis, loitered with cigarettes hanging from their lips and their bayonets ready. The railway lines had apparently been neglected, for the depot was strewn with so many bent and dented rods and pistons, Calder was surprised that the train waiting to leave still had enough engine parts to run at all.

A small man he took to be the stationmaster stood in the center of the platform surrounded by civilians. Calder tried to buy tickets with the last emerald they had, but the man snatched up the gem, pocketed it in a flash, and then told them what he had been telling everyone—he was not in charge. Calder smelled smoke. The mob rushed toward the train as the whistle screamed.

"Go!" the man behind Calder was yelling. His brow was furrowed and there were dark shadows under his eyes. Calder couldn't tell if it was human nature or a haunting that was frightening the crowd. He took Ana and the boy each by a hand and guided them to the nearest car. They squeezed into the train, standing in the aisle shoulder to shoulder. The engine puffed and growled like a dying dragon. Finally they began to move and the people began to shuffle into other cars until there was room to breathe. Soon there was even a seat for them.

Though Calder didn't see any black clouds or Lost Souls through the windows, it appeared as if something biblical had befallen the country. Broken glass glittered along the tracks, and they passed the wreck of a motorcar abandoned beside the rails as if it had been pushed there by the train for miles. Shops were not only closed; many stood open with doors hanging on one hinge. Mines and farmhouses stood charred and deserted.

Alexis, who sat closest to the window, watched all this and said nothing, but Calder knew it must've been hard to see—this fallen land his bloodline had helped destroy and that he would not get the chance to rebuild. Ana sat between her brother and Calder, holding Calder's hand hidden between them on the seat. But soon she fell asleep and rested against his shoulder.

"Will you come with us into Heaven?" the boy asked Calder.

"To be honest," said Calder, "I'm not sure how far I'll be allowed to go with you, but don't worry. Once we cross into the Aisle you'll be taken safely to your family."

"The thing is," said Alexis, "I never really had friends, except Nagorny. I wasn't allowed to play like most boys, and no one was allowed to get too close because my illness was a secret." He paused then, as if to explain his meaning. "You're not so bad now that I'm used to you."

If Calder was not mistaken, Alexis was telling him that he would be missed.

"Not to mention," said Alexis, "Ana is not altogether indifferent to you, in case you haven't noticed."

❊ ❊ ❊

Like his sister, eventually Alexis slumbered as hard as he had at sea. And he was difficult to wake. When they arrived in Ekaterinburg in the twilight before dawn, Calder shook him, but the boy did not move. He woke Ana, who immediately scolded him.

"I wanted to sit up with you. Why didn't you wake me?"

"I slept, too," Calder told her.

She smiled. "So, Fetches can lie after all, I see."

She shook her brother gently and called his name, and finally his eyes opened. Like his sister, Alexis seemed profoundly weary, but neither of them complained. While still in the station, Ana stopped and powdered Alexis's face and hands, as well as her own. Her brown dress was dusted with white around the collar and cuffs now. It was a plain and unremarkable frock, but Calder had watched Ana wearing it for so long, she had given it a certain life. If someone else were to ever put it on, or even if it were to hang empty on a clothesline, he imagined it would still move with her unintentional grace.

The depot was in a shambles. A poster had been nailed to the wall, with two illustrations side by side: Nicholas on one side with the words GOD SLEEPS and two men that must have been leaders of the revolution on the other with the words GOD WAKES.

Ana and Alexis studied the image of their father for a moment. When Ana sighed and moved away, the boy turned to Calder, but all he said was "I thought they didn't believe in God."

There was hardly a soul up at that hour as they began to walk toward the House of Special Purpose. Ana asked, "Do you think anyone will recognize us?"

"With your hair cut and the pound of makeup I'm wearing," said Alexis, "Mother wouldn't recognize us."

As they neared the dreaded place, Ana and Alexis slowed as if the Brightening were draining their strength. Calder was also feeling the weight of Rasputin's flesh. Each step seemed a task in itself.

"You've done it," said Alexis, out of breath. "We've traveled all the way around the world." He smiled at Calder. "Like the knights in the stories."

Ana held tight to Calder's hand with the same conflicted thoughts that pulled at his heart, he could sense it. In only a short while they hoped to find Heaven, but soon they might be parted.

He hardly recognized the house. The fence, which had seemed so high before, was torn down and lay in stacks a few yards from the west wall. It was a very ordinary building now that it was being used for something else. It was dark but for one dim light on the upper floor.

Calder doubted it was a family dwelling, for outside the front door a soldier's jacket lay across a wooden chair. Perhaps it was a military office of some kind. Both Ana and Alexis stared as they approached.

"We won't need to go inside," Calder assured them. "And none of the soldiers in there would be the same guards," he whispered, though he wasn't certain of this.

He walked them along the west and north sides of the property, staying well away from the house itself. Alexis watched the lit window, which had once been his room.

"Don't look," Ana told him.

Calder kept himself closest to the house and tried to block their view. As they neared the trees at the corner of the property, a pile of charred debris lying uncovered in the grass came into view. Mostly ashes, but some pieces of the Romanov's lives had survived: the handle of a hairbrush, a wheel from Alexis's wheelchair, even the photograph of Calder that looked like Rasputin, with the bottom part of the face burned away.

And at the edge of the pile, its chain curled like a blackened fern, lay Calder's Fetch Key half buried in ash. He bent to touch it.

"Careful," said Alexis. "It's still hot."

"He's right," said Ana. "Can't you smell it burning?"

The ashes around the chain puffed. Calder stepped back. Again the ashes stirred and the chain of the Key squirmed as if alive. The shape of a man, the spectral figure of Rasputin, appeared, slow as a sunrise. Kneeling above the Key, he swiped at it angrily, unable to lift it from the spot in which it had rested since the night Ana and Alexis had been parted from their family.

A growl churned in Rasputin's throat and he turned his face sharply to Calder, the eyes black and hollow, not his own.

# THIRTY-FOUR

RASPUTIN SAT BACK ON HIS HEELS AND A DARK mist rose over his head like a halo, leaving his eyes clear. "I have picked at this wretched pile of char for days," he said. "If I could just get the thing into my hand—"

"No," Calder interrupted. "It's not for you."

"Who?" asked Alexis, but Ana hushed him. The two could not see or hear Rasputin, only smell the demonic smoke, a warning of his impure state.

"I tried to borrow a body," Rasputin sighed. "But no one would let me in." Then an unpleasant smile distorted his face. "Now you are here and I will have my old flesh back."

"No." Calder's tone was forceful. "You're not alone. How many souls are hiding in you?"

Rasputin floated to his feet, up into the shadows, and his eyes became a dark and huge family of eyes, his voice the inharmonious grate of a rasping chorus. "We are legion. Let us in or we will hurt the children."

Though this startled Calder, it also shot him through with fury. "Liar," he said. "You don't have the power."

Rasputin fell to his knees, momentarily out of the swarm of black mist surrounding him.

Calder saw that his eyes were his own again, at least for a moment. "Grigori," he whispered. "You used to be Alexis's savior."

Rasputin's voice was small and strained. "Don't tell them I am powerless," he said. "They will turn on me."

"You're not powerless," said Calder. "They listen to you."

"They're angry," Rasputin whispered.

"Because you invaded their world?" asked Calder.

Rasputin smiled. "Me, they like. I brought them passion. And we were gaining in number every day you walked the earth." Then an invisible weight seemed to force him closer to the ground. "But after what you did, they fear the tide is shifting."

"What I did?" asked Calder.

Rasputin's eyes blazed, but his face was drawn in pain. "You stole a child from them."

"Pincher?" Calder asked.

A dark and stinking wind swept over the burn pile. Ana and Alexis stepped back. Leaves, twigs, dust, and grass circled the nearby trees in tiny twisters. Ashes rose and hovered in the air.

"I helped a Lost Soul find the Aisle," said Calder. "Isn't that what I was supposed to do?"

"He was the only one to be taken from our number since I arrived," said Rasputin.

Calder was sorry that Rasputin was suffering at the hands of his companions, but he was relieved to know Pincher was safely away from them. Calder tried to reach out and embrace Rasputin as he was lifted back into the dark cloud, but his fingers passed through. "Throw off the ones that cling to you," said Calder. "I will steal you away as well."

Rasputin bent forward and dropped his hands to his knees, his eyes pulsing between their former brightness and the hollow depths of demonic possession. "Too many," he whispered. "They don't answer to me."

A black mist swept through the field, bringing with it sick smells, fear, and sorrow, and the buzz of insects where there were none. Calder was racked again with anger. "Stand up to them," he ordered. "Who do they think they are? *You* are Rasputin!"

The tree branches danced as the wind became a tempest; the air pricked at Calder's face with unseen needles.

Rasputin's voice rang like thunder. "Enough!" He shot up tall and stomped his foot, breaking the earth under him in ten-foot cracks. The wind lashed out fiercer and snapped a limb from the closest aspen. Ana and Alexis jumped from its spinning path. "Yield to me," Rasputin ordered the storm. "I carry you. And I command you." Then a darkness stretched out of Rasputin like a serpent and came at Calder, swung out as if to strike him across the face. The ghostly tentacle swept through him, but Calder was struck by something unseen and mighty. He was thrown onto his back and before he could rise Ana stood between him and Rasputin.

She didn't know where to look, but she shouted at the air. "Go back to hell!" The wind ebbed away from her for a moment, dropping debris and ash as it slowed. But as Calder got to his feet, he felt the madness of the storm drawing its strength together to strike again like the sucking of water from a beach before a great wave. Shadows swam in the air not only around Rasputin, but through him.

"I have the power," Rasputin proclaimed. "Where I command you to go, we will go." Calder expected to see his eyes black and haunted, but they were a man's eyes, twinkling through the pain. "They'll follow me," Rasputin whispered.

"But I need to take you with me back into the Aisle," said Calder.

"No," said Rasputin. "I am unclean." He smiled sadly and as the storm of shadows rushed back over them in a roar, he opened his great arms, embraced the wind, and was gone. Twigs and leaves dropped from the air. The field was quiet and still.

Calder touched his cheekbone, surprised to feel the sting of a wound, but it was not Rasputin's flesh that was cut. Somehow it was his own face. His fingers showed no blood, but Ana could see it. She took his face in her hands and tilted it toward the sunrise.

"How did they hurt you?" Alexis asked.

"I'm not hurt," said Calder. He knelt and sifted through the leaves that had been scattered over the burn pile until he found the chain and slid his Key out of the ashes.

Calder wondered if Rasputin could be right. Did they not need to take him to Heaven after all? Could they summon a Door without him?

As he stood and was about to put the chain over his head, Calder felt a ponderous sorrow. Home might only be moments away. Many of the souls he had escorted hardly noticed Calder as they passed through the Aisle with him. He worried now, when Ana and Alexis stepped through the Death Door, would they recall this journey? He held the Key in his hand but did not put it around his neck yet.

"Alexis," he said. "You have a mighty spirit."

The boy seemed stricken. "You're coming with us," he said.

But Calder could see that Ana knew the truth—nothing was for certain. He wanted to tell Ana how he felt, to say out loud that he loved her, but he couldn't.

"You said you wouldn't leave us," she reminded him.

*I would do anything,* he thought, *to stay beside you forever.* Aloud he said, "Don't worry."

Calder took a deep breath, tried to still his heart, and placed the chain around his neck. He straightened his back and spoke the summoning. "Beyond this Door, Heaven waits."

The sun was lightening the eastern sky, and a pale mist hung over the ground in the empty field to the west—there was not a bird or cricket, not even a breeze. Calder turned very slowly in a circle, searching for the Door, not knowing how close or far from them it would appear. Not knowing if it would be a curtain, an iron gate, or a coffin lid. But there was nothing. No Door.

Calder trembled at the idea that perhaps he wouldn't be able to fulfill his second task by saving the children. The trembling began to move into his legs and arms.

"I'll be your Squire," said Alexis. "Give it to me."

Calder put the chain around Alexis's neck and the boy held the Key in his hand, walking in a circle. "Beyond this Door, Heaven waits."

"You try," Alexis told Ana. He whipped the chain off his neck and gave the Key to his sister.

She glanced at Calder uncertainly but put the chain around her neck and did as her brother had done. She kissed the Key first. "Beyond this Door," she said, moving slowly around, "Heaven waits."

No Door.

"I know," said Alexis. "Pass it back to the Master Fetch."

Ana stepped up to Calder, took the chain from over her head, and paused. Calder bowed his head and she placed the chain gently around his throat. Then she took his hand, opened it, and placed the Key in his palm, closing his hand around it with both of hers. "I pass this Key to you," she said, "my chosen one."

Like a groom anxious to kiss his bride, Calder leaned toward her, but Alexis interrupted.

"Say the words!"

Calder could not look away from Ana. Even after she had released his hands and stepped back, all he could do was look at her.

"Summon the Door," said Alexis. The sound of his voice, as if he were on the last hour of his strength, woke Calder from his trance.

"Beyond this Door," said Calder, staring at the Key, "Heaven waits."

Alexis searched frantically, whispering the summoning charm, and finally stopped, staring at Calder. Ana's lips were parted as if she wanted to speak but was at a loss.

He blinked at the Key. He felt the metal shape of it between thumb and finger, saw that there were ashes caked on the stem. He had lost Rasputin to the demons and now he couldn't take Ana and Alexis home.

Calder was sick with dread. When he looked at Ana, he could see clearly, but whenever he looked away from her and the boy, anywhere he might see a Door, the world seemed warped and unfocused. He had come to the end of things—he had no answers, no strength, no power to protect the two people he wanted to protect above all others.

He could think of no kinder way to tell them, so Calder was blunt. "I've failed," he said, "and now we're barred from Heaven."

"You paid your price," Alexis protested. "You found the *Comhartha*, your sign from God, and you came all the way around the world!"

Calder felt the weight hit him like a lance. He tried to hold himself still.

"What is it?" Ana's voice was full of fear for him. "Are you in pain?"

He would have done anything to be strong for her at that moment. He wanted to be their guardian, and champion, but instead he dropped to his knees. He could hear Ana and Alexis speaking, feel their hands on his back and head. He struck at the ground with his fist, hoping to shock his body back into control, but it was no use. Openly, helplessly, he was weeping before them.

"Do something!" Alexis told Ana.

He knew it was the worst thing he could do, but he was mourning at their feet—all the pain of their journey, and of his first brief walk on earth as a human, of running them aground at the very edge of the Aisle. They had only enough strength left to get this far, no farther, and he had failed them.

Ana knelt beside him, put her arms around him, and said, "We're still here for some reason."

He stopped crying. "I don't know what else I can do to protect you."

"We don't need Keys and Signs," said Ana.

"What do we need, then?" said Alexis.

She answered her brother but held Calder's gaze. "We need each other, and we have that," she said. "All we can do is help the ones we can reach." She offered her hand to Calder. When he took it, she held on tight. "All we can hope for is the good we can do right here, right now." The rising sun lit her short and unruly hair as if from the inside of each strand.

"Look!" Alexis was on his feet before Calder saw the smoke or heard the cries. The boy was bounding up the road faster than Calder thought him capable, away from the House of Special Purpose, toward a towering column of black.

"Wait!" He ran after the boy with Ana following. *They have done it,* Calder was thinking. *The Lost Souls have broken a hole from their world to this, and Alexis is flying into their jaws.*

# PART VI

## THE RECKONING

by the humans. The farmhouse was like a storybook picture of Purgatory—angry, wild eyes, bloody hands, gnashing teeth, and the red and black dance of hellfire.

The dog stopped barking. Calder saw the animal, ears up, staring toward the open end of the house.

"Stop!"

Calder's heart jumped to his throat. It was Alexis's voice.

A light that was not dawn, and not the glow from the burning walls, came from the broken wall. Framed in the great opening, Alexis, sitting bareback on the gray mare, held one hand aloft. Shirtless and blazing as bright as the sun, he shouted at the crowd.

"If you hear my voice, obey me! Stay your hands!"

Calder was frightened to see Alexis uncovered and burning in his Brightness, but it was a glorious vision—imposing and wondrous. Heads came up, but the cries of amazement were drowned by the thunder of gunfire. Every man that held a gun turned, both soldiers and civilians, and fired. Alexis's body arched back and the mare reared. The boy made one gasp of pain, but he kept his fist in the horse's mane and would not fall. The animal wheeled back around. Ana wanted to run to her brother, but Calder held her. Now the crowd cried out in fear, for the shining boy on horseback sat up straight and raised his hand toward the sky. The bullets had left not one wound.

The men who had fired on Alexis lowered their guns.

"I am a sign sent to you!" the boy yelled at them. "Lay down your weapons!"

First came a silence. Then the crowd went mad. Some ran away

# THIRTY-FIVE

AT FIRST THE SOUND, A SHARP CRACK, made Calder think of an ax hitting a chopping block, but the second shot was clearly gunfire. It came from a farmhouse a hundred yards up a hill. The house, which had once been a fine building in the old style—rough log beams and slant-shingle roof—was left with only three full walls. Where the front door should have been, it stood open to the world like a barn. The roof was burning. He tore past a gray mare whose lead was lashed to a supporting beam. The beast whinnied and jumped, her eyes rolling with terror.

His boots slid on the packed dirt floor as he stopped. It wasn't a demonic attack but one from mortal men, two soldiers standing over a body, kicking it and cursing. Calder threw himself over the prostrate figure, a small man hiding his face from the blows. One of the soldiers standing over them kicked Calder in the chest, but he caught the boot under his arm and knocked the man to the ground.

The place was full of civilians, both men and women holding tools as weapons, and soldiers with revolvers and rifles ready. The soldiers were outnumbered, but they had the only guns. It seemed as slow as a dream, but one of the soldiers swung his rifle toward Calder and fired. The bullet cracked through his chest. The impact threw him back and the pain confused him for a moment; he didn't realize at first that the man on the ground behind him had been struck in the shoulder by the same bullet that had passed through his ribs.

As if the soldier were one of the same brutes who had beaten the life out of Pincher, Calder flew at the soldier, tore the rifle from him, and threw it to the ground.

What happened next was an agonizing implosion. Some things Calder could see clearly: the way one of the civilians picked up the gun and another grabbed an iron woodcutter's froe from the floor, flipped it in the air, and caught it in his rough hand with the blade ready, how a soldier shot the loft ladder into splinters when he saw one of the women starting to climb it. But many things ran together in a riot of noise and a flurry of movement.

Calder lunged at another soldier, grabbed his rifle, and struggled to keep its muzzle above the heads of the humans as it fired. He thought he heard a child scream, but he could see no children. He didn't know where Ana and Alexis were, or if they were safe. Soldiers tore blankets off crates and boxes under the loft, and a fight erupted over the bags of grain, tins of meat, and sacks of vegetables hoarded there. The loft above, which was filling with smoke, was also filled with boxes. It stunned Calder that this fierce battle had been caused by a store of wheat and potatoes, provisions that could have been divided among them all without shedding a drop of blood.

The soldiers used their guns to hit the others and Calder wonde if they were conserving ammunition. He could hear a dog barkin the distance. Calder shouted for everyone to stop and kept grabb weapons, trying to wrest them away from the hands that meant ha But his attempts to make peace only seemed to fuel the chaos. A sm mutt ran into the farmhouse, yapping wildly. He was followed by mc peasants, who dropped the bags of vegetables they carried and thre themselves into the battle.

Calder knew his interference was not helping; still, he couldn't sto himself. They had to throw down their weapons. He fell on the nea est revolver, struggling to wrench it from a soldier's grasp, but as the twisted to one side, the gun fired and a man fell, wounded in the hip Calder stepped back, shocked by what he had done. It seemed as i there would be no stopping them until they had all killed each other.

A lantern was thrown from its hook on the wall and smashed on the floor below the loft, where the barking mutt dashed back and fort Calder saw Ana now—she was pulling a blanket from one of the crat and trying to tamp out the spreading flames. Calder flew to her, duc ing a swinging rifle. Before he could reach her, the blanket and l sleeves caught fire. She cried out in pain but still would not stop tryi to snuff out the flaming boxes. Calder pulled her into his arms : smothered the burning dress in his coat. She was shaking, her slee charred and her arms black with soot. Calder rubbed the mark off of her wrists to make sure that her flesh was not blistered. Of cou the skin was white and unharmed.

They backed away from the flames that seemed to go unnot

from the shining boy to the far end of the house with fearful cries, some fell to their knees in cowering prayer, some went as still as pillars of salt.

"Listen," Ana whispered.

Somewhere children were crying. Coughing and weeping. Calder looked toward the roof. On the side of the loft farthest from the fire, back in the corner, tiny pieces of bark floated down and the pink of small fingers poked through a hole in the gap between two beams. The woman who had tried to climb to the loft when the ladder was shot to pieces had not been going there to take cover or to save boxes of food. She was trying to get to the children.

Calder saw that the ladder was not only in splintered halves but now on fire. The dog jumped and barked under the corner of the loft where the children were trapped.

"We need help!" Calder yelled. But the ones who cowered against the wall did not look at him, those kneeling did not hear him, the few who stood as if paralyzed regarded him but appeared unable to comprehend.

"I'll find the well," said Ana. She ran out the open wall. Alexis was nowhere in sight.

"Wake up!" Calder yelled. *They're acting like a pack of demons*, he thought.

Calder looked around him at the closest human. The woman who had tried to climb into the loft stood near him, her arm bleeding. She seemed in a trance, but Calder moved in front of her. "What's your name?"

She shuddered once and blinked at him.

"What's your name?" he asked again.

"Irina," she said.

"Irina," said Calder. "Help me with the children."

Irina woke from her dream and ran to the corner under the loft, calling to the children by name to see if all were there.

Calder knelt by one of the praying men. "What is your name?"

The man cried out in surprise but then answered, "Victor."

"Victor, help us with the children," said Calder, and he saw Irina dragging a plank over to the loft as a bridge.

Ana was tugging at a cowering soldier, asking his name, dragging him outside. Within less than a minute, every person had awakened another. Ana ran with soldiers and villagers to and from the well and threw small buckets and tins of water at the flames. The loft was on fire and not strong enough to hold the plank as a walkway when Calder stepped onto it—the board fell and the front of the loft cracked, sending two burning boxes down onto the floor. Wheat sprayed out and potatoes rolled underfoot.

The front of the loft was aflame and the children wouldn't run through the fire. They coughed and screamed but would not come out of the far corner. Since there was no furniture to stack and the crates were already on fire, Calder and a soldier ran outside and, standing one on the other's shoulders, tried to reach the shuttered vents just under the roof where smoke was beginning to flow. The dog leapt around their ankles, howling like a wolf.

It took three men standing—Calder and Victor on the bottom with another on their shoulders—and two others to help a soldier climb the tower of bodies. Calder could hear the ax striking, see the chips of wood falling past his shoulder. He was afraid, but it gave him hope that no Death Doors were lighting the area. Irina stood beneath as the children, seven in all, were handed down, dangling from the top man's arm to the hands of the man below, into Calder's hands and into Irina's arms. One of them still clutched a sock doll. They were frightened, and their faces were sooty, but they were all alive. Three boys and four girls.

Ana was waiting for Calder when the tower of men was released like a troop of circus tumblers. Everyone moved away from the house, for it was too late to save it or the food. Guns were left on the floor of the burning building. Even the wounded watched the fire as if they no longer remembered how it had begun.

The children sat far back from the house, their mothers wiping their faces and hands with wet rags. Two of the children sat together with the dog across their laps.

"Where's Alexis?" Ana asked.

She and Calder circled the house, hunting in every direction for him. Calder found the boy's discarded shirt a few paces from the house, soaking wet in a puddle milky with face powder.

"He washed here," he told Ana, picking up the shirt and wringing it out.

Ana started running up the hillside toward a small forest. He ran after and then saw the gray horse, without a rider, trotting down from the trees.

# Thirty-six

ANA RAN, STRUGGLING IN HER WEAKNESS, driving her body on. The mare walked past them, bobbing its head. Calder caught up to Ana and they entered the dimness of the wood together. They called Alexis's name again and again but heard no answer.

Finally Calder sensed there was light coming from the west, not the east where the sun was rising. He ran toward the glow to the spot where Alexis had fallen and lay on his side. His skin was lighting every leaf around him with a pure white glow, but it seemed to Calder that there was also a shadow hovering above him.

Ana and Calder stumbled through the brush to his side. Calder started to pick him up. Alexis was limp but cried out in pain. Calder carefully sat down beside him, letting the boy lean against him as he and Ana gently dressed him in his shirt to protect him from the air. His eyes were glazed and his breathing labored, but he smiled at Ana.

"Did it work?" he asked.

"Yes," said Ana. "You saved the day."

"Did you see their faces?" said Calder.

The boy laughed, but the sound was cut short as he cringed.

Once most of his skin was covered, Alexis breathed a little easier. He saw that Ana was close to tears. "Don't be so dramatic," he said. "I've had worse."

As serious as a nurse, she took the box of powder from her pocket and began to dust his face. Alexis closed his eyes and coughed as if he'd inhaled the powder. His hand bumped Ana's and the box of face powder dropped. She gave a cry as it flipped over before it landed upside down. A pale cloud hung in the air, and the grass and bushes were sprinkled with white.

"No!" Ana grabbed at the grass to try to collect whatever tiny amount of powder she could retrieve.

"It's all right," Alexis told her.

But Ana took the powder from her fingertips and patted it tenderly on his cheeks and eyelids. She took the empty box, her hands shaking, and scooped out every speck she could, carefully dusting along his jaw.

"Ana," said Alexis.

She saw that his skin still glowed white and her eyes filled with tears. She put her hands on the collar of his wet shirt and squeezed a little moisture onto her palms, then rubbed them across her cheeks.

"Don't," Alexis ordered her, but she took the white smears from her palms and used her fingers to paint him with the powder from her own face. She painted his nose and his temples.

"It's all right," said Alexis, trying to lift a hand to stop her. She tried to rub powder from her wrists, but her fingers were dry.

"Stop, Ana." Her brother's voice was stern now.

A tear began to run down her cheek. She caught it on her fingers, brushed her eyelids with the moisture, then painted his throat with the milky film.

Alexis was leaning against Calder's chest and so couldn't look him in the eye, but he whispered to him, "Stop her."

Calder had been watching this helplessly, but at the boy's request he intervened. All he had to do was touch Ana's elbow and she stopped. Calder knew what she was thinking. They were safe from Death, but not from suffering. It was clear that the Brightening was weakening Ana and Alexis both. There seemed no end to the fever. It worsened by the hour and Alexis's appearance as a blazing angel was taking its toll. It was just as the boy had observed when he'd held a match to his flesh: *They could go on tormenting us forever.*

Ana's eyes were still wet and frightened.

"Look at you," said Alexis, tugging at Ana's sleeves, which had been burned away at both cuffs. Apparently she had not noticed this yet, for she gasped and pulled at the blackened cloth, her eyes brimming with tears.

"Oh, I see," the boy teased her. "You cry more for that ugly dress than for your own wounded brother."

She gave him a reproving look, but smiled a little. "I love this dress," she said.

"It's hideous," said Alexis.

Ana spoke to her brother, but she looked at Calder. "It was a present."

"Just let me rest a minute," said Alexis, but his eyes stared at nothing, his breath was strained, and he rested the weight of his head against Calder.

"I'm sorry." The voice was not the boy's or his sister's. Calder stayed very still, listening. Nagorny crouched on one knee at Alexis's shoulder. "I'm sorry that the darkness found you across the sea," he said. "They stopped listening to me."

"You did well, Nagorny," Calder whispered. Ana gasped but said nothing. "Thank you," Calder told him.

"The boy needs Father Grigori." Nagorny stood. "He could calm his pain, every time. How I envied that gift."

Calder hated to tell him, but he felt he had to. "Rasputin has gone back to the demons."

"Yes." Nagorny smiled. "For you he keeps the angry ones at bay."

Calder's heart rose at this. "He's helping us?"

"But I will go and take his place," said Nagorny. "I'll send him to the boy." Nagorny bent and cupped Alexis's head in his invisible hand for a moment. "I'll be waiting for you," he whispered.

Calder said, "I'm afraid Alexis won't be going to where you are."

Nagorny held Calder with his gentle gaze. "It's you I will be waiting for," he said. "When you come to this dark place to face the angry ones, I will fight beside you."

Calder wanted to speak, to rise and take his hand, but he was still cradling the boy in his arms and Nagorny was gone.

Ana took Calder's free hand and held it tight.

\* \* \*

It took Calder by surprise when Rasputin's large fingers appeared, pressed to the boy's brow and chest. He did not bring the scent of burning hair or a black mist with him. "My little one," he whispered to

Alexis. "Listen to my voice." The boy did not stir.

Calder was nervous, afraid to trust Rasputin's gentleness. "I don't think he can hear you," said Calder.

Rasputin's eyes were sad and clear. "You be my voice, then." He patted the boy's head but could not stir his hair. "Close your eyes, my love."

Calder spoke to Alexis, though he was not sure the boy was aware of his surroundings. "Alexis, Father Grigori wants you to close your eyes."

Calder felt Ana jump at the name, but she kept quiet.

"Breathe in and God heals you," said Rasputin, his voice deep and soothing.

"Breathe in and God heals you," Calder repeated. The boy took a slow deep breath.

"Breathe out and the pain leaves you," said Rasputin.

"Breathe out—" Calder began.

"And the pain leaves me," Alexis whispered.

Rasputin hovered and waited. The boy took three long and careful breaths before sitting up and searching the air for his old friend.

At once Rasputin leaned close to Calder. "Be quick, before they find us," he whispered, as if demons prowling nearby might overhear him. "Steal me back from this place."

"Are you alone?" Calder knew Rasputin would understand what he was asking: *Are you shackled to any other Lost Souls?*

"There is only me, but hurry."

Calder told Ana, "Don't be afraid. I need to return this body."

But Ana was horrified. "Don't leave us alone here."

"I won't." Calder knew he was taking a risk—Rasputin had tricked him before, but he stood and removed the Key's chain from his throat, held the Key tight in his hand, and held it out to Rasputin.

"What're you doing?" asked the boy.

Rasputin stood facing Calder and rested his hand over the fist that held the Key. A chill prickled up Calder's arm and into his chest. He closed his eyes and fell freely backwards to the forest floor. He heard Ana cry out. With a tug that ran from his hand up his spine and down through his legs, Calder felt Rasputin's spiritual weight—his soul's heft and energy—making a bond between them. Calder landed lightly on the ground and seemed to bounce upright again, with only his hand anchoring him to the flesh he had lived in for so many weeks. There lay the body of Rasputin with the soul of Rasputin within it again, staring up at Calder in amazement. And Calder was standing over him, no longer taking up space in the earthly realm, but still present and, thankfully, still holding his Key.

Ana gaped at the body in confusion, for to her eyes the flesh she had seen as Calder had again become Father Grigori. Calder let go of Rasputin's hand and immediately the body twisted as Rasputin struggled to breathe. The old body no longer worked. They were past saving it. So Calder offered his spectral hand to Rasputin's soul.

"Don't try to use the flesh. Come out," Calder told him.

Rasputin's soul lurched out of the body and clasped Calder's hand in both of his own. As Calder pulled him free, the body below lay still—the eyes of flesh were neither demonic nor Rasputin's nor Calder's. They were finally dead.

To his relief, when Calder looked up at Ana, he found she could see him—perhaps not as clearly as she had, but at least as well as she had seen him when he'd come into her brother's Death Scenes. She jumped up and tried to take his hand. When her fingers passed through his, she gasped.

"I'm still here," Calder told her, but she took a step back, sat down in the leaves, and wept. Alexis pulled himself to her and put an arm around her shoulder. The boy must have been able to see Calder as well.

"It's not like he's dead," he told her, "or that we're alive. We're all still here." Calder felt wretched and helpless, unable to hold her or dry her tears. And he wished he had kissed her while they still both had a physical form.

"Where is Rasputin's spirit?" asked Alexis.

"Here with us," said Calder.

"He needs a grave." Alexis got to his knees. Ana seemed doubtful. "We are not leaving him here without a burial," said the boy.

Again Calder felt like a fool—he should have foreseen this and dug a grave before he'd given up the body.

"We have no shovel," said Ana. "And I don't think either of us could walk far enough to find one or carry the body more than ten paces."

"We can use what we have here," said her brother.

Rasputin's soul hovered near Alexis while Calder walked beside Ana as she brought armloads of twigs and leaves and two branches as thick as her wrists for digging. Calder stayed close to her side, aching to help. Alexis and Ana worked on their knees, scraping at the forest floor with their sticks until they had dug a shallow grave. They pulled the body into the hole and pushed the dirt and twigs over it, the best they could do. Finally they lay the leaves over the mound like rose petals. With Rasputin close by his elbow, Alexis ground a deep little well in which to stand up the two branches tied with a vine in a cross as the grave marker. Calder spoke the Seventh Psalm, "The Gentle Crossing," gazing down at Ana and Alexis, their folded hands brown with earth.

Something about this sight made him weak. Calder knelt at the foot of the plot, gazing down past the grave toward the heart of the wooded darkness.

A thought came to him then for the first time. "We saved the children," he said aloud.

"What children?" asked the boy.

"Yes," said Ana. "We saved them from the fire."

Looking past the grave, Calder saw a strange thing. The stick cross and the gap between the curved trees beyond it made the shape of an arched door frame. It seemed so much like a real door that Calder thought he saw a tiny silvery spot, halfway down one side, the size and nearly the shape of a keyhole. The wind ruffled his hair and stirred the Key on its chain about his neck. The Fetch Key was not only stirring, but had risen off his chest and was quivering in the air, pointing to the illusion of a door.

"It's beautiful," said Rasputin, who stood close beside Calder now. "Why does it look different from the last time we passed through?"

*I'm not the only one who is seeing this vision*, thought Calder. Ana and Alexis were looking past the grave as well.

"Calder?" Ana's voice was balanced between fear and joy. She held a hand out to him, though he did not have solid fingers to grasp.

"Wait." Calder walked toward the end of the grave, past the makeshift marker, but still he saw a cross before him as it formed into the pewter edging between four panes of clear glass in a tall cherry-wood doorway.

Without a doubt, he could see that it was not a mirage but a true Death Door. As he took the hovering Key, he felt it being drawn toward the Door, and as he stepped up to the threshold, the Key slipped into the tiny stationary light the size and shape of a keyhole.

"Hurry!" He did not have to call twice. They were all at his side at once and Ana again tried to embrace him, her hands passing through him with a flicker of longing.

"Stay close," said Calder. Ana's eyes asked him wordlessly if this was their last moment. "Stay close," he whispered again. He turned the Key and felt the Door open.

Ana's hand miraculously materialized in his as she crossed out of the Land of the Living. And she was no longer burning with fever, for which Calder gave a silent prayer of thanks.

He looked his last upon the scene they had just left—a simple grave with a tenant no one would ever guess. But unlike Rasputin, Ana and Alexis had crossed into the Aisle as Star Fetches would—ascending body and soul, leaving no bones and no graves.

Just as it had done when he had stepped into the Land of the Living, the universe rumbled with a pounding, thunderous blow as Calder stepped back into the Aisle. The woods they left behind shook and hissed, the leaves rippled, the trees swayed. The Door creaked and the darkness beyond the threshold groaned. In a sudden fury, the surrounding trees split open, bubbling with sap, and a swarm of shadows rushed at the Death Door, faces forming out of the darkness, opened mouths biting and eyes black and throbbing.

Calder slammed the Door, relieved to be back in the Aisle, but frightened by how he had left the Land of the Living infested with hauntings. He knew then that after he took his companions to safety, he'd have to go back to earth.

Calder turned to see if the others were well. Rasputin wore his long black coat. Alexis was wearing a white tunic and black trousers, with high black boots. He could have been thirteen or twenty-three; it was impossible to tell. He was tall and straight. Rasputin took the boy in his arms and held him hard, murmuring to him.

Ana, to Calder's surprise, was not wearing a fine gown but the plain brown dress he had given her. Even her hair was the short clipped style Alexis had tried to repair. Ana and Alexis were now glowing with a natural heavenly light, no longer stricken with

Brightness as they had been on earth. There was no pain in their faces. No weakness. Only the life that comes after life.

Calder wanted to ask if she remembered him and all that they had been through together, but the Death Door was still unlocked. He twisted the Key quickly. When he tried to withdraw it, there was a dry, snapping sound and the Key slipped loosely on its chain, lighter than before.

# Part VII

## The Great River

# Thirty-seven

THE STEM OF HIS KEY HAD BROKEN and the half with the teeth was trapped inside the keyhole. Fear rose in Calder's chest like a flood.

"We don't need the Key anymore," Ana whispered. "We're home."

He wasn't sure that Ana was right, but when he looked down at her, he forgot everything else.

She lifted herself on her toes and kissed him on the mouth, as simply as that. Calder found that she held in her hair and breath and skin the scents of their journey—the fresh wind skimming the North Sea, the sweetness of oranges in summer air, the sad steam of a train. And she tasted like a freshet after a year of desert sand. She was open and relaxed, probably believing that they would be together forever from that moment on. Before her heels could touch the floor again, Calder caught her up in his arms, but his kiss was driven with desperation, knowing their time together was short.

Now that he was finally kissing her, he was shocked by the power of it. He heard her hoarse, childlike laugh as she caught a breath, and he became aware that they were being watched.

Gingerly Ana touched his cheekbone and found blood on her fingers—inexplicably his true form had been cut by the rage of the Lost Souls that had besieged them. An odd unloosing, a kind of detachment from time and gravity and all that the Land of the Living prescribed made Calder lightheaded. And when he gazed at Ana, a confidence filled him from the soles of his feet up to the crown of his head. Past any embarrassment and all logic, they clung to each other, knowing without a doubt, as only lovers in Heaven can, precisely how the other felt.

Alexis and Rasputin were smiling at them without judgment, but obviously waiting.

* * *

The dimness of the Aisle was only an arm's span long and opened immediately into the light of the Great River's shore.

"Magnificent," Rasputin whispered.

"Is this your Captain?" Alexis asked Calder.

In the lapping shallows stood the Captain, his blue robes billowing. He smiled as if nothing out of the ordinary had happened. Calder did not know whose vision of a ship had been granted, but behind the Captain the *Comhartha Ó Dia* sat in the sand, her sails already full.

"Yes, that's my Captain." Calder forced himself to lead the others forward as slowly as he would have at the end of any other Aisle. The Captain looked from Rasputin to the boy to Ana and finally to Calder, who trembled so he could hardly speak.

"I pass these souls to your care."

"I will take them the rest of the way," said the Captain. "God be with you."

"And also with you."

But he couldn't bear the weight of it. Calder dropped to his knees at the Captain's feet. "I have broken my Vows."

"What are your sins?" the Captain asked him.

He was sure the Captain could see easily into his heart, but he recited them. "I neglected my duties, refused to take this boy's soul when he asked to die. I stole this man's body and sent his spirit into the Land of Lost Souls." Calder indicated Rasputin. "Because of me the Lost Souls grew in number and became restless. I led this boy and his sister astray, giving them the Key without teaching them the way of the Fetch. I lost my Key . . ." And here he had to admit to what felt like the worst sin, though he knew least what it meant. "And now my Key is broken."

The Captain's face was grave. "Your sins are forgiven." He then placed a hand on Calder's head and leaned down to whisper in his ear. "You'll know what to do to make things right again."

Calder wondered if he had heard wrong. He was forgiven? He had no trouble believing that the direst of human sinners was forgiven the moment he crossed into the Aisle, but as a Fetch, Calder was certain his transgressions were vastly darker. And, almost incomprehensible to him, his punishment was in his own hands.

The Captain touched Calder's cheek where he had been wounded and the pain vanished. Then he straightened up, speaking loud enough so that the others could hear. "You'll cross over with those you have brought to me."

As if overjoyed at being gifted with her beloved, Ana took

Calder's hand again and the four were led to the boat. The Captain stood at the wheel while the wind pushed the *Comhartha* away from the shore.

Rasputin and Alexis sat on either side of the bow, enjoying the curiosities of the Great River—the way it swelled and rolled like a huge serpent and its ever-changing reflections, like cerulean scales—while Ana and Calder sat pressed together and speechless, on a blanket in a great coil of rope below the wheel. She ran her finger along the thin scar that had replaced the cut on his cheekbone.

It was hard for Calder to hold Ana close and see her so happy while he knew he would still have to pay for his transgressions. He watched her being charmed by the sky where auroras rolled and birds, never seen on earth, in shades of emerald and rose, floated on the currents of wind, where clouds in magnificent mountains of lavender and gold pointed toward their destination. Ana joined Rasputin and Alexis at the side of the boat to watch graceful fish shimmering like precious metals, their schools moving in and out of each other in a sparkling dance. The ivory spires of huge and intricate underwater cities made them gasp with wonder.

Ana was happy to leave Calder's arms and gaze over the side of the ship because she believed she and Calder would have an infinite number of kisses in their afterlife together. Calder could only watch her and remember that one kiss where heat and tenderness had merged. It had opened for him a vast world that he would never have again.

It had been so important to Calder that Ana remember him when they passed out of the Land of the Living, but now he realized she would be happier if she forgot him when she crossed through the Gate. She could revel in the pleasures of Heaven, and love and be loved by her family, without pining for him. If she forgot him, he could be the only one that suffered. Nothing would have color or meaning without her, but that would be part of his punishment.

A frosted light stole over the horizon; they were nearly to the other side. Ana smiled at him, came and sat with him again, holding his arm around her. She reached into her pocket and with a delighted smile showed him what she'd found: on the palm of her hand she held the tiny ivory bead in the shape of a bird that he had brought her from the bottom of the Thames. Calder rested his chin on the top of her head, as a blissful and devastating chiming rippled out over the waters. It shimmered the waves and glittered in Ana's eyes. Despite his torment, he was amazed by the approaching shore, for he had never been to the far side of the Great River, the bank that sloped up to Heaven's Gate. It pulsed with a glorious light. Whatever lay beyond the glow was impossible to discern: a moving, busy brightness of rhythm and vibration too fast to comprehend, no more readable than a letter written on the wings of a hummingbird in flight.

"Beautiful," said Ana.

As the boat slid into the bosom of the shore, Rasputin and Alexis leapt over the side at once. Calder waited for Ana to be overwhelmed by the ecstasy of Heaven and succumb to the amnesia that would cure her of loving him. But she was still holding Calder's hand as tightly as she had before. Tighter still. His troubled eyes confused her.

"Don't be afraid," she told him. It charmed him that she thought he was afraid of Heaven.

Calder helped Ana step out onto the sand but stayed in the boat himself. She would not let go his hand. When she saw the pain in his face, she tried to climb back aboard, but Alexis was standing behind her, only half visible in the flooding light.

Ana held her ground and would not look away from Calder. "Come with me," she commanded, pulling at his hand.

"I can't," he said.

"But you are my chosen one," she said.

His voice was crumbling. "And you are my chosen one, as well."

Calder felt his heart beating through every chamber of his being, into his fingers, into Ana's hand. He had to grip the side of the boat to keep himself from leaping out and into her arms.

"You said you would never leave us!" she cried.

"I'm sorry." He pulled his fingers from hers as the boat began to move again.

If Alexis had not stepped forward and put his arm around his sister's waist, holding her steady as she began to weep, Calder was not sure what he would have done. Ana watched the boat slip back into the waters and off from the shore. Behind Ana, behind Alexis and Rasputin, who all stood watching the *Comhartha* drift out to sea, Calder caught sight of other figures: Nicholas, Alexandra, and their girls. Just to the left of Alexis stood Liam. He waved to Calder and put a large hand on the boy's shoulder.

Ana did not fall into the waves or fight or yell, as Calder wanted to do. She simply watched him float away from her. Her eyes never left his face.

Calder kept his grip tight on the boat's side to make sure he would not try to swim back. He watched her until the light had enveloped her in a pale cloud of gold.

※　※　※

"Can you take me to the Land of the Living?" asked Calder.

"As you wish," said the Captain.

They sailed in silence. Calder stood where he was, still gripping the side of the boat. The water now was dark; the ivory of undersea cities loomed like white bones under the surface. The fish and birds had gone. The clouds were edged with black and rumbled softly.

Calder thought how Ana had been right—his name was sad and the sorrow of it fit him. A river of stones . . . of course he was not able to hold on to her; she was the light and bright water that flowed freely above and he was the stone that lay below, heavy with guilt and sin. The joy of her had touched him for only one precious moment and then was gone.

Calder thought the mourning would overwhelm him. Yet he was still there, still standing. "What damage did I cause?" Calder asked the Captain.

"More souls were lost while you were stranded on earth," said the Captain, "than in a hundred years before."

Calder had suspected something like this, but still the blow felled him. He slid to the deck, too weak with anguish to stop himself. But the Captain's voice was calming.

"Come here," the Captain ordered.

Calder pulled himself to his feet and came to stand at the wheel beside the Captain.

"I prayed for you," said the Captain. "We all did."

*All?* A queer shiver ran through Calder. Had all the Fetches been praying for him? All heavenly beings?

The shore of the Fetch beach was drawing near, the place where trips through the Aisle of Unearthing ended—Calder had never seen it from this side. Different souls saw it in different forms, but to Calder it was a sloped bank of smooth sand, with a grassy hill, and a cliff beyond crowded with cedars that reached toward the sky. The Captain turned to regard Calder at the same moment, and he was struck by the sensation of looking into a mirror.

"Give me your Key," said the Captain.

Calder felt flushed with shame as he showed the Captain what was at the end of the chain about his neck. The Captain took the broken Key from over Calder's head and sighed. "You are not like other Fetches, Calder."

The Captain rarely used his human name. A foreboding ache gnawed at Calder's heart. *He's known the truth all along,* Calder thought, *that I have always been unfit to be a Fetch.*

"You," said the Captain with grave intensity, "have been scarred. And yet . . ." The Captain placed the chain over his own head and wore the broken Key himself. "Which of your fellow Fetches has felt the impact of breaking a holy Vow? You alone have walked among earthlings in the disguise of a mortal and climbed your way back to Heaven. You are the only one to have faced a forming demon."

These words, together with the Captain's sweet tone, sounded like a dream, bewildering and too good to trust as real. The ship pushed up onto the beach and stopped.

"You are a Fetch of true mettle," the Captain told him.

"You make my foolish acts sound like great feats," said Calder, "but they were not."

"And that is the only way to turn a mistake into a badge of survival," the Captain added. "Humility." The Captain drew something from his robes, something small enough to fit hidden in his closed hand. "Like you, this is the only one of its kind." In his palm lay a fine chain with a small Key attached. It was not like any Fetch Key Calder had ever seen. It shone with a deep copper luster, it was short and slender, its grip was carved like a rounded gate, and the stem appeared to have no teeth at all.

The Captain spoke seriously as he led Calder out of the boat and onto the sand. "I pass this Master Key to you." The Captain lowered the chain over Calder's head. "Our Chosen One."

Calder felt the weight of the Key, rubbed its cool surface with his fingers.

"Will you vow to go wherever you are commanded?" the Captain asked him. "To open every Door you are presented, and to do whatever is asked of you, for the sake of Heaven and Earth?"

Calder stared at the Captain, still stunned by the gift. "I will."

"Then in the name of God, I bless you to this task."

"Does this open Death Doors?" Calder asked.

"It opens all Doors," said the Captain.

*And will Ana ever be on the other side of a Door I might open?* he wanted to ask.

"Not to worry," said the Captain. "You'll see her again."

*At the end of time*, thought Calder, *when she has been in Heaven for a thousand years and has forgotten me?*

"Soon," the Captain added.

Calder could feel the Captain was about to leave him. "Will I have a Prayer Room? How will I find you?"

The Captain took Calder in his arms and gave him one strong embrace. "We'll find ways of sending messages," said the Captain, who seemed unshaken by their parting.

"How do I get back to the Land of the Living?" he called, but the ship was already moving away even before the Captain had taken the wheel.

"Look for your Doors," the Captain called. "And at least give your friends a wave."

Calder had no idea what the Captain meant until he turned toward the cliffs, where hundreds of Fetches stood on the crest among the cedars. Calder wasn't sure of the mood of his comrades. The ones who had glimpsed him when he was hiding in Rasputin's flesh had seemed angered by him, but as he raised a hand to them in greeting, a cheer rose through the trees and flowed down from the cliffs at him. Almost at once hundreds of Doors appeared behind these Fetches and they passed through them and were gone.

Calder was alone but filled with a surge of joy. *Not to worry*, the Captain had said. *You will see her again. Soon.*

When he thought about it, the cryptic nature of this statement left it open to the most hopeful of interpretations. Ana might be only an hour, or a minute, away, waiting in some corridor of Heaven, and he had the Master Key. She might be behind any door, even *this one*.

A Door had appeared, nestled snug in the sand, made of heavy, rustic wood, weatherworn and scratched, with a twisted iron handle. Its long hinges stretched across the bottom and top, dark hammered metal like ancient spears. Between the hinges the wood had been hewn inward with four triangles, forming a cross in what was called a witch door, one designed to keep out evil spirits.

Beneath the iron door handle there was no keyhole. This didn't seem to matter. As Calder approached, holding his new Key, the door handle rattled and the hinges began to grind. He didn't know what corner of the world lay beyond.

*But*, he thought, *not to worry*.

Calder touched the Door and it swung open.

The Imperial family, July 1918, a few days before the executions (left to right) Olga, Alexis, Tatiana, Tsar Nicholas, Ana, and Maria.

One of the last photos of Alexis.

One of the last photos of Ana.

# Where the Jackals Howl
and Other Stories

# Other books by Amos Oz

Translated from the Hebrew
by Nicholas de Lange
and Philip Simpson

# Amos Oz

# Where
# the Jackals
# Howl
## and Other Stories

A Helen and Kurt Wolff Book

Harcourt Brace Jovanovich

New York and London

Library of Congress Cataloging in Publication Data

Oz, Amos.
Where the jackals howl, and other stories.

"A Helen and Kurt Wolff book."
Revised translation of Artsot ha-tan.
CONTENTS: Where the jackals howl.—Nomad and
viper.—The way of the wind.—[etc.]
I. Title.
PJ5054.O9A8713    1981        892.4'36        80-8754

ISBN 0-15-196038-0

Printed in the United States of America

B C D E

To Nily

"Nomad and Viper," "The Way of the Wind,"
"A Hollow Stone," and "Upon This Evil Earth"
were translated by Nicholas de Lange.
The other stories were translated by Philip Simpson.

The translations are based on a revised edition
published 1976 in Hebrew.
The dates given at the end of each story
refer to the year when they were first written.
The author revised them extensively for this volume.

# Contents

# Where the Jackals Howl
and Other Stories

# Where the Jackals Howl

## 1

At last the heat wave abated.

A blast of wind from the sea pierced the massive density of the *khamsin*, opening up cracks to let in the cold. First came light, hesitant breezes, and the tops of the cypresses shuddered lasciviously, as if a current had passed through them, rising from the roots and shaking the trunk.

Toward evening the wind freshened from the west. The *khamsin* fled eastward, from the coastal plain to the Judean hills and from the Judean hills to the rift of Jericho, from there to the deserts of the scorpion that lie to the east of Jordan. It seemed that we had seen the last *khamsin*. Autumn was drawing near.

Yelling stridently, the children of the kibbutz came streaming out onto the lawns. Their parents carried deck chairs from the verandas to the gardens. "It is the exception that proves the rule," Sashka is fond of saying. This time it was Sashka who made himself the exception, sitting alone in his room and adding a new chapter to his book about problems facing the kibbutz in times of change.

Sashka is one of the founders of our kibbutz and an active, prominent member. Squarely built, florid and bespectacled, with a handsome and sensitive face and an expression of fatherly assurance. A man of bustling energy. So fresh was the evening breeze passing through the room that he was obliged to lay a heavy ashtray on a pile of rebellious papers. A spirited straightforwardness animated him, giving a trim edge to his sentences. Changing times, said Sashka to himself, changing times require changing ideas. Above all, let us not mark time, let us not turn back upon ourselves, let us be vigorous and alert.

The walls of the houses, the tin roofs of the huts, the stack of steel pipes beside the smithy, all began to exhale the heat accumulated in them during the days of the *khamsin*.

Galila, daughter of Sashka and Tanya, stood under the cold shower, her hands clasped behind her neck, her elbows pushed back. It was dark in the shower room. Even the blond hair lying wet and heavy on her shoulders looked dark. If there was a big mirror here, I could stand in front of it and look myself over. Slowly, calmly. Like watching the sea wind that's blowing outside.

But the cubicle was small, like a square cell, and there was no big mirror, nor could there have been. So her movements were hasty and irritable. Impatiently she dried herself and put on clean clothes. What does Matityahu Damkov want of me? He asked me to go to his room after supper. When we were children we used to love watching him and his horses. But to waste the evening in some sweaty bachelor's room, that's asking too much. True, he did promise to give me some paints from abroad. On the other hand, the evening is short and we don't have any other free time. We are working girls.

How awkward and confused Matityahu Damkov looked when he stopped me on the path and told me I should come to his room after supper. And that hand in the air, waving, gesticulating, trying to pluck words out of the hot wind, gasping like a fish out of water, not finding the words he was looking for. "This evening. Worth your while to drop in for a few minutes," he said. "Just wait and see, it will be interesting. Just for a while. And quite ... er ... important. You won't regret it. Real canvases and the kind of paints professional artists use, as well. Actually, I got all these things from my cousin Leon who lives in South America. I don't need paints or canvases. I ... er ... and there's a pattern as well. It's all for you, just make sure that you come."

As she remembered these words, Galila was filled with nausea and amusement. She thought of the fascinating ugliness of Matityahu Damkov, who had chosen to order canvases and paints for her. Well, I suppose I should go along and see what happens and discover why I am the one. But I won't stay in his room more than five minutes.

# 2

In the mountains the sunset is sudden and decisive. Our kibbutz lies on the plain, and the plain reduces the sunset, lessens its impact. Slowly, like a tired bird of passage, darkness descends on the land surface. First to grow dark are the barns and the windowless storerooms. The coming of the darkness does not hurt them, for it has never really left them. Next it is the turn of the houses. A timer sets the generator in motion. Its throbbing echoes down the slope like a beating heart, a distant drum. Veins of electricity awake into life and a hidden current passes through our thin walls. At that moment the lights spring up in all the windows of the veterans' quarters. The metal fittings on the top of the water tower catch the fading rays of daylight, hold them for a long moment. Last to be hidden in the darkness is the iron rod of the lightning conductor on the summit of the tower.

The old people of the kibbutz are still at rest in their deck chairs. They are like lifeless objects, allowing the darkness to cover them and offering no resistance.

Shortly before seven o'clock the kibbutz begins to stir, a slow movement toward the dining hall. Some are discussing what has happened today, others discuss what is to be done tomorrow, and there are a few who are silent. It is time for Matityahu Damkov to emerge from his lair and become a part of society. He locks the door of his room, leaving behind him the sterile silence, and goes to join the bustling life of the dining hall.

# 3

Matityahu Damkov is a small man, thin and dark, all bone and sinew. His eyes are narrow and sunken, his cheekbones slightly curved, an expression of "I told you so" is fixed upon his face. He joined our kibbutz immediately after World War II. Originally he was from Bulgaria. Where he has been and what he has done, Damkov does not tell. And we do not demand chapter and verse. However, we know that he has spent some time in South America. He has a mustache as well.

Matityahu Damkov's body is a cunning piece of craftsmanship. His torso is lean, boyish, strong, almost unnaturally agile. What impression does such a body make on women? In men it arouses a sense of nervous discomfort.

His left hand shows a thumb and a little finger. Between them is an empty space. "In time of war," says Matityahu Damkov, "men have suffered greater losses than three fingers."

In the daytime he works in the smithy, stripped to the waist and gleaming with sweat, muscles dancing beneath the taut skin like steel springs. He solders together metal fittings, welds pipes, hammers out bent tools, beats worn-out implements into scrap metal. His right hand or his left, each by itself is strong enough to lift the heavy sledgehammer and bring it down with controlled ferocity on the face of the unprotesting metal.

Many years ago Matityahu Damkov used to shoe the kibbutz horses, with fascinating skill. When he lived in Bulgaria it seems that his business was horsebreeding. Sometimes he would speak solemnly of some hazy distinction between stud horses and work horses, and tell the children gathered around him that he and his partner or his cousin Leon used to raise the most valuable horses between the Danube and the Aegean.

Once the kibbutz stopped using horses, Matityahu Damkov's craftsmanship was forgotten. Some of the girls collected redundant horseshoes and used them to decorate their rooms. Only the children who used to watch the shoeing, only they remember sometimes. The skill. The pain. The intoxicating smell. The agility. Galila used to chew a lock of blond hair and stare at him from a distance with gray, wide-open eyes, her mother's eyes, not her father's.

She won't come.

I don't believe her promises.

She's afraid of me. She's as wary as her father and as clever as her mother. She won't come. And if she does come, I won't tell her. If I tell her, she won't believe me. She'll go and tell Sashka everything. Words achieve nothing. But here there are people and light: supper time.

On every table gleamed cutlery, steel jugs and trays of bread.

"This knife needs sharpening," Matityahu Damkov said to his neighbors at the table. He cut his onions and tomatoes into thin slices and sprinkled them with salt, vinegar and olive oil. "In the winter, when there's not so much work to be done, I shall sharpen all the dining-room knives and repair the gutter as well. In fact, the winter isn't so far away. This *khamsin* was the last, I think. So there it is. The winter will catch us this year before we're ready for it."

At the end of the dining room, next to the boiler room and the kitchen, a group of bony veterans, some bald, some white-haired, are gathered around an evening paper. The paper is taken apart and the sections passed around in turn to the readers who have "reserved" them. Meanwhile there are some who offer interpretations of their own and there are others who stare at the pundits with the eyes of weary, good-humored old age. And there are those who listen in silence, with quiet sadness on their faces. These, according to Sashka, are the truest of the true. It is they who have endured the true suffering of the labor movement.

While the men are gathered around the paper discussing politics, the women are besieging the work organizer's table. Tanya is raising her voice in protest. Her face is wrinkled, her eyes harassed and weary. She is clutching a tin ashtray, beating it against the table to the rhythm of her complaints. She leans over the work sheets as if bending beneath the burden of injustice that has been laid or is about to be laid on her. Her hair is gray. Matityahu Damkov hears her voice but misses her words. Apparently the work organizer is trying to retreat with dignity in the face of Tanya's anger. And now she casually picks up the fruits of victory, straightens up and makes her way to Matityahu Damkov's table.

"Now it's your turn. You know I've got a lot of patience, but there are limits to everything. And if that lock isn't welded by ten o'clock tomorrow morning, I shall raise the roof. There is a limit, Matityahu Damkov. Well?"

The man contorted the muscles of his face so that his ugliness intensified and became repulsive beyond bearing, like a clown's mask, a nightmare figure.

"Really," he said mildly, "there's no need to get so excited. Your lock has been welded for days now, and you haven't come to collect it. Come tomorrow. Come whenever you like. There's no need to hurry me along."

"Hurry you? Me? Never in my life have I dared harass a working man. Forgive me. I'm sure you're not offended."

"I'm not offended," said Matityahu. "On the contrary. I'm an easygoing type. Good night to you."

With these words the business of the dining room is concluded. Time to go back to the room, to put on the light, to sit on the bed and wait quietly. And what else do I need? Yes. Cigarettes. Matches. Ashtray.

# 4

The electric current pulses in twining veins and sheds a weary light upon everything: our little red-roofed houses, our gardens, the pitted concrete paths, the fences and the scrap iron, the silence. Dim, weak puddles of light. An elderly light.

Searchlights are mounted on wooden posts set out at regular intervals along the perimeter fence. These beacons strive to light up the fields and the valleys that stretch away to the foothills of the mountains. A small circle of plowed land is swamped by the lights on the fence. Beyond this circle lies the night and the silence. Autumn nights are not black. Not here. Our nights are gray. A gray radiance rising over the fields, the plantations, and the orchards. The orchards have already begun to turn yellow. The soft gray light embraces the treetops with great tenderness, blurring their sharp edges, bridging the gap between lifeless and living. It is the way of the night light to distort the appearance of inanimate things and to infuse them with life, cold and sinister, vibrant with venom. At the same time it slows down the living things of the night, softening their movements, disguising their elusive presence. Thus it is that we cannot see the jackals as they spring out from their hiding places. Inevitably we miss the sight of their soft noses sniffing the air, their paws gliding over the turf, scarcely touching the ground.

The dogs of the kibbutz, they alone understand this enchanted motion. That is why they howl at night in jealousy, menace, and rage. That is why they paw at the ground, straining at their chains till their necks are on the point of breaking.

An adult jackal would have kept clear of the trap. This one was a cub, sleek, soft, and bristling, and he was drawn to the smell of blood and flesh. True, it was not outright folly that led him into the trap. He simply followed the scent and glided to his destruction with careful, mincing steps. At times he stopped, feeling some obscure warning signal in his veins. Beside the snare he paused, froze where he stood, silent, as gray as the earth and as patient. He pricked up his ears in vague apprehension and heard not a sound. The smells got the better of him.

Was it really a matter of chance? It is commonly said that chance is blind; we say that chance peers out at us with a thousand eyes. The jackal was young, and if he felt the thousand eyes fixed upon him, he could not understand their meaning.

A wall of old, dusty cypresses surrounds the plantation. What is it, the hidden thread that joins the lifeless to the living? In despair, rage, and contortion we search for the end of this thread, biting lips till we draw blood, eyes contorted in frenzy. The jackals know this thread. Sensuous, pulsating currents are alive in it, flowing from body to body, being to being, vibration to vibration. And rest and peace are there.

At last the creature bowed his head and brought his nose close to the flesh of the bait. There was the smell of blood and the smell of sap. The tip of his muzzle was moist and twitching, his saliva was running, his hide bristling, his delicate sinews throbbed. Soft as a vapor, his paw approached the forbidden fruit.

Then came the moment of cold steel. With a metallic click, light and precise, the trap snapped shut.

The animal froze like stone. Perhaps he thought he could outwit the trap, pretending to be lifeless. No sound, no movement. For a long moment jackal and trap lay still, testing each other's strength. Slowly, painfully, the living awoke and came back to life.

And silently the cypresses swayed, bowing and rising, bending and floating. He opened his muzzle wide, baring little teeth that dripped foam.

Suddenly despair seized him.

With a frantic leap he tried to tear himself free, to cheat the hangman.

Pain ripped through his body.

He lay flat upon the earth and panted.

Then the child opened his mouth and began to cry. The sound of his wailing rose and filled the night.

# 5

At this twilight hour our world is made up of circles within circles. On the outside is the circle of the autumn darkness, far from here, in the mountains and the great deserts. Sealed and enclosed within it is the circle of our night landscape, vineyards and orchards and plantations. A dim lake astir with whispering voices. Our lands betray us in the night. Now they are no longer familiar and submissive, crisscrossed with irrigation pipes and dirt tracks. Now our fields have gone over to the enemy's camp. They send out to us waves of alien scents. At night we see them bristling in a miasma of threat and hostility and returning to their former state, as they were before we came to this place.

The inner circle, the circle of lights, keeps guard over our houses and over us, against the accumulated menace outside. But it is an ineffective wall, it cannot keep out the smells of the foe and his voices. At night the voices and the smells touch our skin like tooth and claw.

And inside, in the innermost circle of all, in the heart of our illuminated world, stands Sashka's writing desk. The table lamp sheds a calm circle of brightness and banishes the shadows from the stacks of papers. The pen in his hand darts to and fro and the words take shape. "There is no stand more noble than that of the few against the many," Sashka is fond of saying. His daughter stares wide-eyed and curious at the face of Matityahu Damkov. You're ugly and you're not one of us. It's good that you have no children and one day those dull mongoloid eyes will close and you'll be dead. And you won't leave behind anyone like you. I wish I wasn't here, but before I go I want to know what it is you want of me and why you told me to come. It's so stuffy in your room and there's an old bachelor smell that's like the smell of oil used for frying too many times.

"You may sit down," said Matityahu from the shadows. The shabby stillness that filled the room deepened his voice and made it sound remote.

"I'm in a bit of a hurry."

"There'll be coffee as well. The real thing. From Brazil. My cousin Leon sends me coffee too, he seems to think a kibbutz is a kind of kolkhoz. A kolkhoz labor camp. A collective farm in Russia, that's what a kolkhoz is."

"Black without sugar for me, please," said Galila, and these words surprised even her.

What is this ugly man doing to me? What does he want of me?

"You said you were going to show me some canvases, and some paints, didn't you?"

"All in good time."

"I didn't expect you to go to the trouble of getting coffee and cakes, I thought I'd only be here for a moment."

"You are fair," the man said, breathing heavily, "you are

fair-haired, but I'm not mistaken. There is doubt. There has to be. But it is so. What I mean is, you'll drink your coffee, nice and slow, and I'll give you a cigarette too, an American one, from Virginia. In the meantime, have a look at this box. The brushes. The special oil too. And the canvases. And all the tubes. It's all for you. First of all drink. Take your time."

"But I still don't understand," said Galila.

A man pacing about his room in an undershirt on a summer night is not a strange sight. But the monkeylike body of Matityahu Damkov set something stirring inside her. Panic seized her. She put down the coffee cup on the brass tray, jumped up from the chair and stood behind it, clutching the chair as if it were a barricade.

The transparent, frightened gesture delighted her host. He spoke patiently, almost mockingly:

"Just like your mother. I have something to tell you when the moment's right, something that I'm positive you don't know, about your mother's wickedness."

Now, at the scent of danger, Galila was filled with cold malice:

"You're mad, Matityahu Damkov. Everybody says that you're mad."

There was tender austerity in her face, an expression both secretive and passionate.

"You're mad, and get out of my way and let me pass. I want to get out of here. Yes. Now. Out of my way."

The man retreated a little, still staring at her intently. Suddenly he sprang onto his bed and sat there, his back to the wall, and laughed a long, happy laugh.

"Steady, daughter, why all the haste? Steady. We've only just begun. Patience. Don't get so excited. Don't waste your energy."

Galila hastily weighed up the two possibilities, the safe and the fascinating, and said:

"Please tell me what you want of me."

"Actually," said Matityahu Damkov, "actually, the kettle's boiling again. Let's take a short break and have some more coffee. You won't deny, I'm sure, that you've never drunk coffee like this."

"Without milk or sugar for me. I told you before."

# 6

The smell of coffee drove away all other smells: a strong, sharp, pleasant smell, almost piercing. Galila watched Matityahu Damkov closely, observing his manners, the docile muscles beneath his string shirt, his sterile ugliness. When he spoke again, she clutched the cup tightly between her fingers and a momentary peace descended on her.

"If you like, I can tell you something in the meantime. About horses. About the farm that we used to have in Bulgaria, maybe fifty-seven kilometers from the port of Varna, a stud farm. It belonged to me and my cousin Leon. There were two branches that we specialized in: work horses and stud horses, in other words, castration and covering. Which would you like to hear about first?"

Galila relaxed, leaning back in the chair and crossing her legs, ready to hear a story. In her childhood she had always loved the moments before the start of a bedtime story.

"I remember," she said, "how when we were children we used to come and watch you shoeing the horses. It was beautiful and strange and so ... were you."

"Preparing for successful mating," said Matityahu, passing her a plate of crackers, "is a job for professionals. It takes expertise and intuition as well. First, the stallion must be kept in confinement for a long time. To drive him mad. It improves his seed. He's kept apart from the mares for several months, from the stallions too. In his frustration he may even attack another male. Not every stallion is suitable for stud, perhaps one in a hundred. One stud horse to a hundred work horses. You need a lot of experience and keen observation to pick out the right horse. A stupid, unruly horse is the best. But it isn't all that easy to find the most stupid horse."

"Why must he be stupid?" asked Galila, swallowing spittle.

"It's a question of madness. It isn't always the biggest, most handsome stallion that produces the best foals. In fact a mediocre horse can be full of energy and have the right kind of nervous temperament. After the candidate had been kept in confinement for a few months, we used to put wine in his trough, half a bottle. That was my cousin Leon's idea. To get the horse a bit drunk. Then we'd fix it so he could take a look at the mares through the bars and get a whiff of their smell. Then he starts going mad. Butting like a bull. Rolling on his back and kicking his legs in the air. Scratching himself, rubbing himself, trying desperately to ejaculate. He screams and starts biting in all directions. When the stallion starts to bite, then we know that the time has come. We open the gate. The mare is waiting for him. And just for a moment, the stallion hesitates. Trembling and panting. Like a coiled spring."

Galila winced, staring entranced at Matityahu Damkov's lips.

"Yes," she said.

"And then it happens. As if the law of gravity had suddenly been revoked. The stallion doesn't run, he flies through the air. Like a cannon ball. Like a spring suddenly released. The mare bows and lowers her head and he thrusts into her, blow after blow. His eyes are full of blood. There's not enough air for him to breathe and he gasps and chokes as if he's dying. His mouth hangs open and he pours saliva and foam on her head. Suddenly he starts to roar and howl. Like a dog. Like a wolf. Writhing and screaming. In that moment there is no telling pleasure from pain. And mating is very much like castration."

"Enough, Matityahu, for God's sake, enough."

"Now let's relax. Or perhaps you'd like to hear how a horse is castrated?"

"Please, enough, no more," Galila pleaded.

Slowly Matityahu raised his maimed hand. The compassion in his voice was strange, almost fatherly:

"Just like your mother. About that," he said, "about the fingers and about castration as well, we'll talk some other time. Enough now. Don't be afraid now. Now we can rest and relax. I've got a drop of cognac somewhere. No? No. Vermouth then. There's vermouth too. Here's to my cousin Leon. Drink. Relax. Enough."

# 7

The cold light of the distant stars spreads a reddish crust upon the fields. In the last weeks of the summer the land has all been turned over. Now it stands ready for the winter sowing. Twisting dirt tracks cross the plain, here and there are the dark masses of plantations. fenced in by walls of cypress trees.

For the first time in many months our lands feel the first tentative fingers of the cold. The irrigation pipes, the taps, the metal fittings, they are the first to capitulate to any conqueror, summer's heat or autumn's chill. And now they are the first to surrender to the cool moisture.

In the past, forty years ago, the founders of the kibbutz entrenched themselves in this land, digging their pale fingernails into the earth. Some were fair-haired, like Sashka, others, like Tanya, were brazen and scowling. In the long, burning hours of the day they used to curse the earth scorched by the fires of the sun, curse it in despair, in anger, in longing for rivers and forests. But in the darkness, when night fell, they composed sweet love songs to the earth, forgetful of time and place. At night forgetfulness gave taste to life. In the angry darkness oblivion enfolded them in a mother's embrace. "There," they used to sing, not "Here."

> There in the land our fathers loved,
> There all our hopes shall be fulfilled.
> There we shall live and there a life
> Of health and freedom we shall build. . . .

People like Sashka were forged in fury, in longing and in dedication. Matityahu Damkov, and the latter-day fugitives like him, know nothing of the longing that burns and the dedication that draws blood from the lips. That is why they seek to break into the inner circle. They make advances to the women. They use words similar to ours. But theirs is a different sorrow, they do not belong to us, they are extras, on the outside, and so they shall be until the day they die.

The captive jackal cub was seized by weariness. The tip

of his right paw was held fast in the teeth of the trap. He sprawled flat on the turf as if reconciled to his fate.

First he licked his fur, slowly, like a cat. Then he stretched out his neck and began licking the smooth, shining metal. As if lavishing warmth and love upon the silent foe. Love and hate, they both breed surrender. He threaded his free paw beneath the trap, groped slowly for the meat of the bait, withdrew the paw carefully and licked off the savor that had clung to it.

Finally, the others appeared.

Jackals, huge, emaciated, filthy and swollen-bellied. Some with running sores, others stinking of putrid carrion. One by one they came together from all their distant hiding places, summoned to the gruesome ritual. They formed themselves into a circle and fixed pitying eyes upon the captive innocent. Malicious joy striving hard to disguise itself as compassion, triumphant evil breaking through the mask of mourning. The unseen signal was given, the marauders of the night began slowly moving in a circle as in a dance, with mincing, gliding steps. When the excitement exploded into mirth the rhythm was shattered, the ritual broken, and the jackals cavorted madly like rabid dogs. Then the despairing voices rose into the night, sorrow and rage and envy and triumph, bestial laughter and a choking wail of supplication, angry, threatening, rising to a scream of terror and fading again into submission, lament, and silence.

After midnight they ceased. Perhaps the jackals despaired of their helpless child. Quietly they dispersed to their own sorrows. Night, the patient gatherer, took them up in his arms and wiped away all the traces.

# 8

Matityahu Damkov was enjoying the interlude. Nor did Galila try to hasten the course of events. It was night. The girl unfolded the canvases that Matityahu Damkov had received from his cousin Leon and examined the tubes of paint. It was good quality material, the type used by professionals. Until now she had painted on oiled sackcloth or cheap mass-produced canvases with paints borrowed from the kindergarten. She's so young, thought Matityahu Damkov, she's a little girl, slender and spoiled. I'm going to smash her to pieces. Slowly. For a moment he was tempted to tell her the truth outright, like a bolt from the blue, but he thought better of it. The night was slow.

In oblivion and delight, compulsively, Galila fingered the fine brush, lightly touching the orange paint, lightly stroking the canvas with the hairs of the brush, an unconscious caress, like fingertips on the hairs of the neck. Innocence flowed from her body to his, his body responded with waves of desire.

Afterward Galila lay without moving, as if asleep, on the oily, paint-splashed tiles, canvases and tubes of paint scattered about her. Matityahu lay back on his single bed, closed his eyes and summoned a dream.

At his bidding they come to him, quiet dreams and wild dreams. They come and play before him. This time he chose to summon the dream of the flood, one of the severest in his repertoire.

First to appear is a mass of ravines descending the mountain slopes, scores of teeming watercourses, crisscrossing and zigzagging.

In a flash the throngs of tiny people appear in the gullies. Like little black ants they swarm and trickle from their hiding places in the crevices of the mountain, sweeping down like a cataract. Hordes of thin dark people streaming down the slopes, rolling like an avalanche of stone and plunging in a headlong torrent to the levels of the plain. Here they split into a thousand columns, racing westward in furious spate. Now they are so close that their shapes can be seen: a dark, disgusting, emaciated mass, crawling with lice and fleas, stinking. Hunger and hatred distort their faces. Their eyes blaze with madness. In full flood they swoop upon the fertile valleys, racing over the ruins of deserted villages without a moment's check. In their rush toward the sea they drag with them all that lies in their path, uprooting posts, ravaging fields, mowing down fences, trampling the gardens and stripping the orchards, pillaging homesteads, crawling through huts and stables, clambering over walls like demented apes, onward, westward, to the sands of the sea.

And suddenly you too are surrounded, besieged, paralyzed with fear. You see their eyes ablaze with primeval hatred, mouths hanging open, teeth yellow and rotten, curved daggers gleaming in their hands. They curse you in clipped tones, voices choking with rage or with dark desire. Now their hands are groping at your flesh. A knife and a scream. With the last spark of your life you extinguish the vision and almost breathe freely again.

"Come on," said Matityahu Damkov, shaking the girl with his right hand, while the maimed hand, his left, caressed her neck. "Come on. Let's get away from here. Tonight. In the morning. I shall save you. We'll run away together to South America, to my cousin Leon. I'll take care of you. I'll always take care of you."

"Leave me alone, don't touch me," she said.

He clasped her in a powerful and silent embrace.

"My father will kill you tomorrow. I told you to leave me alone."

"Your father will take care of you now and he'll always take care of you," Matityahu Damkov replied softly. He let her go. The girl stood up, buttoning her skirt, smoothing back her blond hair.

"That isn't what I want. I didn't want to come here at all. You're taking advantage of me and doing things to me that I don't want and saying all kinds of things because you're mad and everyone knows you're mad, ask anyone you like."

Matityahu Damkov's lips broadened into a smile.

"I won't come to you again, not ever, And I don't want your paints. You're dangerous. You're as ugly as a monkey. And you're mad."

"I can tell you about your mother, if you want to hear. And if you want to hate and curse, then it's her you should hate, not me."

The girl turned hurriedly to the window, flung it open with a desperate movement and leaned out into the empty night. Now she's going to scream, thought Matityahu Damkov in alarm, she'll scream and the opportunity won't come again. Blood filled his eyes. He swooped upon her, clapped his hand over her mouth, dragged her back inside the room, buried his lips in her hair, probed with his lips for her ear, found it, and told her.

# 9

Sharp waves of chill autumn air clung to the outer walls of the houses, seeking entry. From the yard on the slope of the hill came the sounds of cattle lowing and herdsmen cursing. A cow having difficulty giving birth perhaps, the big torch throwing light on the blood and the mire. Matityahu Damkov knelt on the floor and gathered up the paints and the brushes that his guest had left scattered there. Galila still stood beside the open window, her back to the room and her face to the darkness. Then she spoke, still with her back to the man.

"It's doubtful," she said. "It's almost impossible, it isn't even logical, it can't be proved, and it's crazy. Absolutely."

Matityahu Damkov stared at her back with his mongoloid eyes. Now his ugliness was complete, a concentrated, penetrating ugliness.

"I won't force you. Please. I shall say nothing. Perhaps just laugh to myself quietly. For all I care you can be Sashka's daughter or even Ben-Gurion's daughter. I shall say nothing. Like my cousin Leon I shall say nothing. He loved his Christian son and never said I love you, only when this son of his had killed eleven policemen and himself did he remember to tell him in his grave, I love you. Please."

Suddenly, without warning, Galila burst into laughter: "You fool, you little fool, look at me, I'm blond, look!"

Matityahu said nothing.

"I'm not yours, I'm sure of it because I'm blond, I'm not yours or Leon's either, I'm blond and it's all right! Come on!"

The man leaped at her, panting, groaning, groping his way blindly. In his rush he overturned the coffee table, he shuddered violently and the girl shuddered with him.

And then she recoiled from him, fled to the far wall. He

pushed aside the coffee table. He kicked it. His eyes were shot with blood, and a sound like gargling came from his lips. She suddenly remembered her mother's face and the trembling of her lips and her tears, and she pushed the man from her with a dreamy hand. As if struck, they both retreated, staring at each other, eyes wide open.

"Father," said Galila in surprise, as if waking on the first morning of winter at the end of a long summer, looking outside and saying, rain.

# 10

The sun rises without dignity in our part of the world. With a cheap sentimentality it appears over the peaks of the eastern mountains and touches our lands with tentative rays. No glory, no complicated tricks of light. A purely conventional beauty, more like a picture postcard than a real landscape.

But this will be one of the last sunrises. Autumn will soon be here. A few more days and we shall wake in the morning to the sound of rain. There may be hail too. The sun will rise behind a screen of dirty gray clouds. Early risers will wrap themselves in overcoats and emerge from their houses fortified against the daggers of the wind.

The path of the seasons is well trodden. Autumn, winter, spring, summer, autumn. Things are as they have always been. Whoever seeks a fixed point in the current of time and the seasons would do well to listen to the sounds of the night that never change. They come to us from out there.

1963

# Nomad and Viper

## 1

The famine brought them.

They fled north from the horrors of famine, together with their dusty flocks. From September to April the desert had not known a moment's relief from drought. The loess was pounded to dust. Famine had spread through the nomads' encampments and wrought havoc among their flocks.

The military authorities gave the situation their urgent attention. Despite certain hesitations, they decided to open the roads leading north to the Bedouins. A whole population—men, women, and children—could not simply be abandoned to the horrors of starvation.

Dark, sinuous, and wiry, the desert tribesmen trickled along the dirt paths, and with them came their emaciated flocks. They meandered along gullies hidden from town dwellers' eyes. A persistent stream pressed northward, circling the scattered settlements, staring wide-eyed at the sights of the settled land. The dark flocks spread into the fields of golden stubble, tearing and chewing with strong, vengeful teeth. The nomads' bearing was stealthy and subdued; they shrank from watchful eyes. They took pains to avoid encounters. Tried to conceal their presence.

If you passed them on a noisy tractor and set billows of dust loose on them, they would courteously gather their scattered flocks and give you a wide passage, wider by far than was necessary. They stared at you from a distance, frozen like statues. The scorching atmosphere blurred their appearance and gave a uniform look to their features: a shepherd with his staff, a woman with her babes, an old man with his eyes sunk deep in their sockets. Some were half-blind, or perhaps feigned half-blindness from some vague alms-gathering motive. Inscrutable to the likes of you.

How unlike our well-tended sheep were their miserable specimens: knots of small, skinny beasts huddling into a dark, seething mass, silent and subdued, humble as their dumb keepers.

The camels alone spurn meekness. From atop tall necks they fix you with tired eyes brimming with scornful sorrow. The wisdom of age seems to lurk in their eyes, and a nameless tremor runs often through their skin.

Sometimes you manage to catch them unawares. Crossing a field on foot, you may suddenly happen on an indolent flock standing motionless, noon-struck, their feet apparently rooted in the parched soil. Among them lies the shepherd, fast asleep, dark as a block of basalt. You approach and cover him with a harsh shadow. You are startled to find his eyes wide open. He bares most of his teeth in a placatory smile. Some of them are gleaming, others decayed. His smell hits you. You grimace. Your grimace hits him like a punch in the face. Daintily he picks himself up, trunk erect, shoulders hunched. You fix him with a cold blue eye. He broadens his smile and utters a guttural syllable. His garb is a compromise: a short, patched European jacket over a white desert robe. He cocks his head to one side. An appeased gleam crosses his face. If you do not upbraid him, he suddenly extends his left hand and asks for a cigarette in rapid Hebrew. His voice has a silken quality, like that of a shy woman. If your mood is generous, you put a cigarette to your lips and toss another into his wrinkled palm. To your surprise, he snatches a gilt lighter from the recesses of his robe and offers a furtive flame. The smile never leaves his lips. His smile lasts too long, is unconvincing. A flash of sunlight darts off the thick gold ring adorning his finger and pierces your squinting eyes.

Eventually you turn your back on the nomad and continue on your way. After a hundred, two hundred paces, you may turn your head and see him standing just as he was, his gaze stabbing your back. You could swear that he is still smiling, that he will go on smiling for a long while to come.

And then, their singing in the night. A long-drawn-out, dolorous wail drifts on the night air from sunset until the early hours. The voices penetrate to the gardens and pathways of the kibbutz and charge our nights with an uneasy heaviness. No sooner have you settled down to sleep than a distant drumbeat sets the rhythm of your slumber like the pounding of an obdurate heart. Hot are the nights, and vapor-laden. Stray clouds caress the moon like a train of gentle camels, camels without any bells.

The nomads' tents are made up of dark drapes. Stray women drift around at night, barefoot and noiseless. Lean, vicious nomad hounds dart out of the camp to challenge the moon all night long. Their barking drives our kibbutz dogs insane. Our finest dog went mad one night, broke into the henhouse, and massacred the young chicks. It was not out of savagery that the watchmen shot him. There was no alternative. Any reasonable man would justify their action.

# 2

You might imagine that the nomad incursion enriched our heat-prostrated nights with a dimension of poetry. This may have been the case for some of our unattached girls. But we cannot refrain from mentioning a whole string of prosaic, indeed unaesthetic disturbances, such as foot-and-mouth disease, crop damage, and an epidemic of petty thefts.

The foot-and-mouth disease came out of the desert, carried by their livestock, which had never been subjected to any proper medical inspection. Although we took various early precautions, the virus infected our sheep and cattle, severely reducing the milk yield and killing off a number of animals.

As for the damage to the crops, we had to admit that we

had never managed to catch one of the nomads in the act. All we ever found were the tracks of men and animals among the rows of vegetables, in the hayfields, and deep inside the carefully fenced orchards. And wrecked irrigation pipes, plot markers, farming implements left out in the fields, and other objects.

We are not the kind to take such things lying down. We are no believers in forbearance or vegetarianism. This is especially true of our younger men. Among the veteran founders there are a few adherents of Tolstoyan ideas and such like. Decency constrains me not to dwell in detail on certain isolated and exceptional acts of reprisal conducted by some of the youngsters whose patience had expired, such as cattle rustling, stoning a nomad boy, or beating one of the shepherds senseless. In defense of the perpetrators of the last-mentioned act of retaliation I must state clearly that the shepherd in question had an infuriatingly sly face. He was blind in one eye, broken-nosed, drooling; and his mouth—on this the men responsible were unanimous—was set with long, curved fangs like a fox's. A man with such an appearance was capable of anything. And the Bedouins would certainly not forget this lesson.

The pilfering was the most worrisome aspect of all. They laid hands on the unripe fruit in our orchards, pocketed the faucets, whittled away piles of empty sacks in the fields, stole into the henhouses, and even made away with the modest valuables from our little houses.

The very darkness was their accomplice. Elusive as the wind, they passed through the settlement, evading both the guards we had posted and the extra guards we had added. Sometimes you would set out on a tractor or a battered jeep toward midnight to turn off the irrigation faucets in an outlying field and your headlights would trap fleeting shadows, a man or a night beast. An irritable guard decided one night to open fire, and in the dark he managed to kill a stray jackal.

Needless to say, the kibbutz secretariat did not remain silent. Several times Etkin, the secretary, called in the police, but their tracking dogs betrayed or failed them. Having led their handlers a few paces outside the kibbutz fence, they raised their black noses, uttered a savage howl, and stared foolishly ahead:

Spot raids on the tattered tents revealed nothing. It was as if the very earth had decided to cover up the plunder and brazenly outstare the victims. Eventually the elder of the tribe was brought to the kibbutz office, flanked by a pair of inscrutable nomads. The short-tempered policemen pushed them forward with repeated cries of "Yallah, yallah."

We, the members of the secretariat, received the elder and his men politely and respectfully. We invited them to sit down on the bench, smiled at them, and offered them steaming coffee prepared by Geula at Etkin's special request. The old man responded with elaborate courtesies, favoring us with a smile which he kept up from the beginning of the interview till its conclusion. He phrased his remarks in careful, formal Hebrew.

It was true that some of the youngsters of his tribe had laid hands on our property. Why should he deny it. Boys would be boys, and the world was getting steadily worse. He had the honor of begging our pardon and restoring the stolen property. Stolen property fastens its teeth in the flesh of the thief, as the proverb says. That was the way of it. What could one do about the hotheadedness of youth? He deeply regretted the trouble and distress we had been caused.

So saying, he put his hand into the folds of his robe and drew out a few screws, some gleaming, some rusty, a pair of pruning hooks, a stray knife-blade, a pocket flashlight, a broken hammer, and three grubby bank notes, as a recompense for our loss and worry.

Etkin spread his hands in embarrassment. For reasons best known to himself, he chose to ignore our guest's Hebrew and to reply in broken Arabic, the residue of his studies during the time of the riots and the siege. He opened his remarks with a frank and clear statement about the brotherhood of nations—the cornerstone of our ideology—and about the quality of neighborliness of which the peoples of the East had long been justly proud, and never more so than in these days of bloodshed and groundless hatred.

To Etkin's credit, let it be said that he did not shrink in the slightest from reciting a full and detailed list of the acts of theft, damage, and sabotage that our guest—as the result of oversight, no doubt—had refrained from mentioning in his apology. If all the stolen property were returned and the vandalism stopped once and for all, we would be whole-heartedly willing to open a new page in the relations of our two neighboring communities. Our children would doubtless enjoy and profit from an educational courtesy visit to the Bedouin encampment, the kind of visit that broadens horizons. And it went without saying that the tribe's children would pay a return visit to our kibbutz home, in the interest of deepening mutual understanding.

The old man neither relaxed nor broadened his smile, but kept it sternly at its former level as he remarked with an abundance of polite phrases that the gentlemen of the kibbutz would be able to prove no further thefts beyond those he had already admitted and for which he had sought our forgiveness.

He concluded with elaborate benedictions, wished us health and long life, posterity and plenty, then took his leave and departed, accompanied by his two barefooted companions wrapped in their dark robes. They were soon swallowed up by the wadi that lay outside the kibbutz fence.

Since the police had proved ineffectual—and had indeed abandoned the investigation—some of our young men suggested making an excursion one night to teach the savages a lesson in a language they would really understand.

Etkin rejected their suggestion with disgust and with reasonable arguments. The young men, in turn, applied to Etkin a number of epithets that decency obliges me to pass over in silence. Strangely enough, Etkin ignored their insults and reluctantly agreed to put their suggestion before the kibbutz secretariat. Perhaps he was afraid that they might take matters into their own hands.

Toward evening, Etkin went around from room to room and invited the committee to an urgent meeting at eight-thirty. When he came to Geula, he told her about the young men's ideas and the undemocratic pressure to which he was being subjected, and asked her to bring along to the meeting a pot of black coffee and a lot of good will. Geula responded with an acid smile. Her eyes were bleary because Etkin had awakened her from a troubled sleep. As she changed her clothes, the night fell, damp and hot and close.

# 3

Damp and close and hot the night fell on the kibbutz, tangled in the dust-laden cypresses, oppressed the lawns and ornamental shrubs. Sprinklers scattered water onto the thirsty lawn, but it was swallowed up at once: perhaps it evaporated even before it touched the grass. An irritable phone rang vainly in the locked office. The walls of the houses gave out a damp vapor. From the kitchen chimney a stiff column of smoke rose like an arrow into the heart of the sky, because there was no breeze. From the greasy sinks came a shout. A dish had been broken and somebody was bleeding. A fat house-cat had killed a lizard or a snake and dragged its prey onto the baking concrete path to toy with it lazily in the dense evening sunlight. An ancient tractor started to rumble in one of the sheds, choked, belched a stench of oil, roared, spluttered, and finally managed to set out to deliver an evening meal to the second shift, who were toiling in an outlying field. Near the Persian lilac Geula saw a bottle dirty with the remains of a greasy liquid. She kicked at it repeatedly, but instead of shattering, the bottle rolled heavily among the rosebushes. She picked up a big stone. She tried to hit the bottle. She longed to smash it. The stone missed. The girl began to whistle a vague tune.

Geula was a short, energetic girl of twenty-nine or so. Although she had not yet found a husband, none of us would deny her good qualities, such as the dedication she lavished on local social and cultural activities. Her face was pale and thin. No one could rival her in brewing strong coffee—coffee to raise the dead, we called it. A pair of bitter lines were etched at the corners of her mouth.

On summer evenings, when the rest of us would lounge in a group on a rug spread on one of the lawns and launch jokes and bursts of cheerful song heavenward, accompanied by clouds of cigarette smoke, Geula would shut herself up in her room and not join us until she had prepared the pot of scalding, strong coffee. She it was, too, who always took pains to ensure that there was no shortage of biscuits.

What had passed between Geula and me is not relevant here, and I shall make do with a hint or two. Long ago we used to stroll together to the orchards in the evening and talk. It was all a long time ago, and it is a long time since it ended. We would exchange unconventional political ideas or argue about the latest books. Geula was a stern and sometimes merciless critic: I was covered in confusion. She did not like my stories, because of the extreme polarity of situations, scenery, and characters, with no intermediate shades between black and white. I would utter an apology or a denial, but Geula always had ready proofs and she was a very methodical thinker. Sometimes I would dare to rest a conciliatory hand on her neck, and wait for her to calm down. But she never relaxed completely. If once or twice she leaned against me, she always blamed her broken sandal or her aching head. And so we drifted apart. To this day she still cuts my stories out of the periodicals, and arranges them in a cardboard box kept in a special drawer devoted to them alone.

I always buy her a new book of poems for her birthday. I creep into her room when she is out and leave the book on her table, without any inscription or dedication. Sometimes we happen to sit together in the dining hall. I avoid her glance, so as not to have to face her mocking sadness. On hot days, when faces are covered in sweat, the acne on her cheeks reddens and she seems to have no hope. When the cool of autumn comes, I sometimes find her pretty and attractive from a distance. On such days Geula likes to walk to the orchards in the early evening. She goes alone and comes back alone. Some of the youngsters come and ask me what she is looking for there, and they have a malicious snicker on their faces. I tell them that I don't know. And I really don't.

# 4

Viciously Geula picked up another stone to hurl at the bottle. This time she did not miss, but she still failed to hear the shattering sound she craved. The stone grazed the bottle, which tinkled faintly and disappeared under one of the bushes. A third stone, bigger and heavier than the other two, was launched from ridiculously close range: the girl trampled on the loose soil of the flower bed and stood right over the bottle. This time there was a harsh, dry explosion, which brought no relief. Must get out.

Damp and close and hot the night fell, its heat pricking the skin like broken glass. Geula retraced her steps, passed the balcony of her room, tossed her sandals inside, and walked down barefoot onto the dirt path.

The clods of earth tickled the soles of her feet. There was a rough friction, and her nerve endings quivered with flickers of vague excitement. Beyond the rocky hill the shadows were waiting for her: the orchard in the last of the light. With determined hands she widened the gap in the fence and slipped through. At that moment a slight evening breeze began to stir. It was a warmish summer breeze with no definite direction. An old sun rolled westward, trying to be sucked up by the dusty horizon. A last tractor climbed back to the depot, panting along the dirt road from the outlying plots. No doubt it was the tractor that had taken the second-shift workers their supper. It seemed shrouded in smoke or summer haze.

Geula bent down and picked some pebbles out of the dust. Absently she began to throw them back again, one by one. There were lines of poetry on her lips, some by the young poets she was fond of, others her own. By the irrigation pipe she paused, bent down, and drank as though kissing the faucet. But the faucet was rusty, the pipe was still hot, and the water was tepid and foul. Nevertheless she bent her head and let the water pour over her face and neck and into her shirt. A sharp taste of rust and wet dust filled her throat. She closed her eyes and stood in silence. No relief. Perhaps a cup of coffee. But only after the orchard. Must go now.

# 5

The orchards were heavily laden and fragrant. The branches intertwined, converging above the rows of trunks to form a shadowy dome. Underfoot the irrigated soil retained a hidden dampness. Shadows upon shadows at the foot of those gnarled trunks. Geula picked a plum, sniffed and crushed it. Sticky juice dripped from it. The sight made her feel dizzy. And the smell. She crushed a second plum. She picked another and rubbed it on her cheek till she was spattered with juice. Then, on her knees, she picked up a dry stick and scratched shapes in the dust. Aimless lines and curves. Sharp angles. Domes. A distant bleating invaded the orchard. Dimly she became aware of a sound of bells. She was far away. The nomad stopped behind Geula's back, as silent as a phantom. He dug at the dust with his big toe, and his shadow fell in front of him. But the girl was blinded by a flood of sounds. She saw and heard nothing. For a long time she continued to kneel on the ground and draw shapes in the dust with her twig. The nomad waited patiently in total silence. From time to time he closed his good eye and stared ahead of him with the other, the blind one. Finally he reached out and bestowed a long caress on the air. His obedient shadow moved in the dust. Geula stared, leapt to her feet, and leaned against the nearest tree, letting out a low sound. The nomad let his shoulders drop and put on a faint smile. Geula raised her arm and stabbed the air with her twig. The nomad continued to smile. His gaze dropped to her bare feet. His voice was hushed, and the Hebrew he spoke exuded a rare gentleness:

"What time is it?"

Geula inhaled to her lungs' full capacity. Her features grew sharp, her glance cold. Clearly and dryly she replied:

"It is half past six. Precisely."

The Arab broadened his smile and bowed slightly, as if to acknowledge a great kindness.

"Thank you very much, miss."

His bare toe had dug deep into the damp soil, and the

clods of earth crawled at his feet as if there were a startled mole burrowing underneath them.

Geula fastened the top button of her blouse. There were large perspiration stains on her shirt, drawing attention to her armpits. She could smell the sweat on her body, and her nostrils widened. The nomad closed his blind eye and looked up. His good eye blinked. His skin was very dark; it was alive and warm. Creases were etched in his cheeks. He was unlike any man Geula had ever known, and his smell and color and breathing were also strange. His nose was long and narrow, and a shadow of a mustache showed beneath it. His cheeks seemed to be sunk into his mouth cavity. His lips were thin and fine, much finer than her own. But the chin was strong, almost expressing contempt or rebellion.

The man was repulsively handsome, Geula decided to herself. Unconsciously she responded with a mocking half-smile to the nomad's persistent grin. The Bedouin drew two crumpled cigarettes from a hidden pocket in his belt, laid them on his dark, outstretched palm, and held them out to her as though proffering crumbs to a sparrow. Geula dropped her smile, nodded twice, and accepted one. She ran the cigarette through her fingers, slowly, dreamily, ironing out the creases, straightening it, and only then did she put it to her lips. Quick as lightning, before she realized the purpose of the man's sudden movement, a tiny flame was dancing in front of her. Geula shielded the lighter with her hand even though there was no breeze in the orchard, sucked in the flame, closed her eyes. The nomad lit his own cigarette and bowed politely.

"Thank you very much," he said in his velvety voice.

"Thanks," Geula replied. "Thank you."

"You from the kibbutz?"

Geula nodded.

"Goo-d." An elongated syllable escaped from between his gleaming teeth. "That's goo-d."

The girl eyed his desert robe.

"Aren't you hot in that thing?"

The man gave an embarrassed, guilty smile, as if he had been caught red-handed. He took a slight step backward.

"Heaven forbid, it's not hot. Really not. Why? There's air, there's water...." And he fell silent.

The treetops were already growing darker. A first jackal sniffed the oncoming night and let out a tired howl. The orchard filled with a scurry of small, busy feet. All of a sudden Geula became aware of the throngs of black goats intruding in search of their master. They swirled silently in and out of the fruit trees. Geula pursed her lips and let out a short whistle of surprise.

"What are you doing here, anyway? Stealing?"

The nomad cowered as though a stone had been thrown at him. His hand beat a hollow tattoo on his chest.

"No, not stealing, heaven forbid, really not." He added a lengthy oath in his own language and resumed his silent smile. His blind eye winked nervously. Meanwhile an emaciated goat darted forward and rubbed against his leg. He kicked it away and continued to swear with passion:

"Not steal, truly, by Allah not steal. Forbidden to steal."

"Forbidden in the Bible," Geula replied with a dry, cruel smile. "Forbidden to steal, forbidden to kill, forbidden to covet, and forbidden to commit adultery. The righteous are above suspicion."

The Arab cowered before the onslaught of words and looked down at the ground. Shamefaced. Guilty. His foot continued to kick restlessly at the loose earth. He was trying to ingratiate himself. His blind eye narrowed. Geula was momentarily alarmed: surely it was a wink. The smile left his lips. He spoke in a soft, drawn-out whisper, as though uttering a prayer.

"Beautiful girl, truly very beautiful girl. Me, I got no girl yet. Me still young. No girl yet. Yaaa," he concluded with a guttural yell directed at an impudent goat that had rested its forelegs against a tree trunk and was munching hungrily at the foliage. The animal cast a pensive, skeptical glance at its master, shook its beard, and solemnly resumed its munching.

Without warning, and with amazing agility, the shepherd leapt through the air and seized the beast by the hindquarters, lifted it above his head, let out a terrifying, savage screech, and flung it ruthlessly to the ground. Then he spat and turned to the girl.

"Beast," he apologized. "Beast. What to do. No brains. No manners."

The girl let go of the tree trunk against which she had been resting and leaned toward the nomad. A sweet shudder ran down her back. Her voice was still firm and cool.

"Another cigarette?" she asked. "Have you got another cigarette?"

The Bedouin replied with a look of anguish, almost of despair. He apologized. He explained at length that he had no more cigarettes, not even one, not even a little one. No more. All gone. What a pity. He would gladly, very gladly, have given her one. None left. All gone.

The beaten goat was getting shakily to its feet. Treading circumspectly, it returned to the tree trunk, disingenuously observing its master out of the corner of its eye. The shepherd watched it without moving. The goat reached up, rested its front hoofs on the tree, and calmly continued munching. The Arab picked up a heavy stone and swung his arm wildly. Geula seized his arm and restrained him.

"Leave it. Why. Let it be. It doesn't understand. It's only a beast. No brains, no manners."

The nomad obeyed. In total submission he let the stone drop. Then Geula let go of his arm. Once again the man drew the lighter out of his belt. With thin, pensive fingers he toyed with it. He accidentally lit a small flame, and hastily blew at it. The flame widened slightly, slanted, and died. Nearby a jackal broke into a loud, piercing wail. The rest of the goats, meanwhile, had followed the example of the first and were absorbed in rapid, almost angry munching.

A vague wail came from the nomad encampment away to the south, the dim drum beating time to its languorous call. The dusky men were sitting around their campfires, sending skyward their single-noted song. The night took up the strain and answered with dismal cricket-chirp. Last glimmers of light were dying away in the far west. The orchard stood in darkness. Sounds gathered all around, the wind's whispering, the goats' sniffing, the rustle of ravished leaves. Geula pursed her lips and whistled an old tune. The nomad listened to her with rapt attention, his head cocked to one side in surprise, his mouth hanging slightly open. She glanced at her watch. The hands winked back at her with a malign, phosphorescent glint, but said nothing. Night.

The Arab turned his back on Geula, dropped to his knees, touched his forehead on the ground, and began mumbling fervently.

"You've got no girl yet," Geula broke into his prayer. "You're still too young." Her voice was loud and strange. Her hands were on her hips, her breathing still even. The man stopped praying, turned his dark face toward her, and muttered a phrase in Arabic. He was still crouched on all fours, but his pose suggested a certain suppressed joy.

"You're still young," Geula repeated, "very young. Perhaps twenty. Perhaps thirty. Young. No girl for you. Too young."

The man replied with a very long and solemn remark in his own language. She laughed nervously, her hands embracing her hips.

"What's the matter with you?" she inquired, laughing still. "Why are you talking to me in Arabic all of a sudden? What do you think I am? What do you want here, anyway?"

Again the nomad replied in his own language. Now a note of terror filled his voice. With soft, silent steps he recoiled and withdrew as though from a dying creature. She was breathing heavily now, panting, trembling. A single wild syllable escaped from the shepherd's mouth: a sign between him and his goats. The goats responded and thronged around him, their feet pattering on the carpet of dead leaves like cloth ripping. The crickets fell silent. The goats huddled in the dark, a terrified, quivering mass, and disappeared into the darkness, the shepherd vanishing in their midst.

Afterward, alone and trembling, she watched an airplane passing in the dark sky above the treetops, rumbling dully, its lights blinking alternately with a rhythm as precise as that of the drums: red, green, red, green, red. The night covered over the traces. There was a smell of bonfires on the air and a smell of dust borne on the breeze. Only a slight breeze among the fruit trees. Then panic struck her and her blood froze. Her mouth opened to scream but she did not scream, she started to run and she ran barefoot with all her strength for home and stumbled and rose and ran as though pursued, but only the sawing of the crickets chased after her.

# 6

She returned to her room and made coffee for all the members of the secretariat, because she remembered her promise to Etkin. Outside the cool of evening had set in, but inside her room the walls were hot and her body was also on fire. Her clothes stuck to her body because she had been running, and her armpits disgusted her. The spots on her face were glowing. She stood and counted the number of times the coffee boiled—seven successive boilings, as she had learned to do it from her brother Ehud before he was killed in a reprisal raid in the desert. With pursed lips she counted as the black liquid rose and subsided, rose and subsided, bubbling fiercely as it reached its climax.

That's enough, now. Take clean clothes for the evening. Go to the showers.

What can that Etkin understand about savages. A great socialist. What does he know about Bedouins. A nomad sniffs out weakness from a distance. Give him a kind word, or a smile, and he pounces on you like a wild beast and tries to rape you. It was just as well I ran away from him.

In the showers the drain was clogged and the bench was greasy. Geula put her clean clothes on the stone ledge. I'm not shivering because the water's cold. I'm shivering with disgust. Those black fingers, and how he went straight for my throat. And his teeth. And the goats. Small and skinny like a child, but so strong. It was only by biting and kicking that I managed to escape. Soap my belly and everything, soap it again and again. Yes, let the boys go right away tonight to their camp and smash their black bones because of what they did to me. Now I must get outside.

# 7

She left the shower and started back toward her room, to pick up the coffee and take it to the secretariat. But on the way she heard crickets and laughter, and she remembered him bent down on all fours, and she was alarmed and stood still in the dark. Suddenly she vomited among the flowering shrubs. And she began to cry. Then her knees gave way. She sat down to rest on the dark earth. She stopped crying. But her teeth continued to chatter, from the cold or from pity. Suddenly she was not in a hurry any more, even the coffee no longer seemed important, and she thought to herself: There's still time. There's still time.

Those planes sweeping the sky tonight were probably on a night-bombing exercise. Repeatedly they roared among the stars, keeping up a constant flashing, red, green, red, green, red. In counterpoint came the singing of the nomads and their drums, a persistent heartbeat in the distance: One, one, two, One, one, two. And silence.

# 8

From eight-thirty until nearly nine o'clock we waited for Geula. At five to nine Etkin said that he could not imagine what had happened; he could not recall her ever having missed a meeting or been late before; at all events, we must now begin the meeting and turn to the business on the agenda.

He began with a summary of the facts. He gave details of the damage that had apparently been caused by the Bedouins, although there was no formal proof, and enumerated the steps that had been taken on the committee's initiative. The appeal to good will. Calling in the police. Strengthening the guard around the settlement. Tracking dogs. The meeting with the elder of the tribe. He had to admit, Etkin said, that we had now reached an impasse. Nevertheless, he believed that we had to maintain a sense of balance and not give way to extremism, because hatred always gave rise to further hatred. It was essential to break the vicious circle of hostility. He therefore opposed with all the moral force at his disposal the approach—and particularly the intentions—of certain of the younger members. He wished to remind us, by way of conclusion, that the conflict between herdsmen and tillers of the soil was as old as human civilization, as seemed to be evidenced by the story of Cain, who rose up against Abel, his brother. It was fitting, in view of the social gospel we had adopted, that we should put an end to this ancient feud, too, just as we had put an end to other ugly phenomena. It was up to us, and everything depended on our moral strength.

The room was full of tension, even unpleasantness. Rami twice interrupted Etkin and on one occasion went so far as to use the ugly word "rubbish." Etkin took offense, accused the younger members of planning terrorist activities, and said in conclusion, "We're not going to have that sort of thing here."

Geula had not arrived, and that was why there was no one to cool down the temper of the meeting. And no coffee. A heated exchange broke out between me and Rami. Although in age I belonged with the younger men, I did not agree with their proposals. Like Etkin, I was absolutely opposed to answering the nomads with violence—for two reasons, and when I was given permission to speak I mentioned them both. In the first place, nothing really serious had happened so far. A little stealing perhaps, but even that was not certain: every faucet or pair of pliers that a tractor driver left in a field or lost in the garage or took home with him was immediately blamed on the Bedouins. Secondly, there had been no rape or murder. Hereupon Rami broke in excitedly and asked what I was waiting for. Was I perhaps waiting for some small incident of rape that Geula could write poems about and I could make into a short story? I flushed and cast around in my mind for a telling retort.

But Etkin, upset by our rudeness, immediately deprived us both of the right to speak and began to explain his position all over again. He asked us how it would look if the papers reported that a kibbutz had sent out a lynch mob to settle scores with its Arab neighbors. As Etkin uttered the phrase "lynch mob," Rami made a gesture to his young friends that is commonly used by basketball players. At this signal they rose in a body and walked out in disgust, leaving Etkin to lecture to his heart's content to three elderly women and a long-retired member of Parliament.

After a moment's hesitation I rose and followed them. True, I did not share their views, but I, too, had been deprived of the right to speak in an arbitrary and insulting manner.

# 9

If only Geula had come to the meeting and brought her famous coffee with her, it is possible that tempers might have been soothed. Perhaps, too, her understanding might have achieved some sort of compromise between the conflicting points of view. But the coffee was standing, cold by now, on the table in her room. And Geula herself was lying among the bushes behind the Memorial Hall, watching the lights of the planes and listening to the sounds of the night. How she longed to make her peace and to forgive. Not to hate him and wish him dead. Perhaps to get up and go to him, to find him among the wadis and forgive him and never come back. Even to sing to him. The sharp slivers piercing her skin and drawing blood were the fragments of the bottle she had smashed here with a big stone at the beginning of the evening. And the living thing slithering among the slivers of glass among the clods of earth was a snake, perhaps a venomous snake, perhaps a viper. It stuck out a forked tongue, and its triangular head was cold and erect. Its eyes were dark glass. It could never close them, because it had no eyelids. A thorn in her flesh, perhaps a sliver of glass. She was very tired. And the pain was vague, almost pleasant. A distant ringing in her ears. To sleep now. Wearily, through the thickening film, she watched the gang of youngsters crossing the lawn on their way to the fields and the wadi to even the score with the nomads. We were carrying short, thick sticks. Excitement was dilating our pupils. And the blood was drumming in our temples.

Far away in the darkened orchards stood somber, dust-laden cypresses, swaying to and fro with a gentle, religious fervor. She felt tired, and that was why she did not come to see us off. But her fingers caressed the dust, and her face was very calm and almost beautiful.

1963

# The Way of the Wind*

## 1

Gideon Shenhav's last day began with a brilliant sunrise.

The dawn was gentle, almost autumnal. Faint flashes of light flickered through the wall of cloud that sealed off the eastern horizon. Slyly the new day concealed its purpose, betraying no hint of the heat wave that lay enfolded in its bosom.

Purple glowed on the eastern heights, fanned by the morning breeze. Then the rays pierced through the wall of cloud. It was day. Dark loopholes blinked awake at daylight's touch. Finally the incandescent sphere rose, assaulted the mountains of cloud, and broke their ranks. The eastern horizon was adazzle. And the soft purple yielded and fled before the terrible crimson blaze.

The camp was shaken by reveille a few minutes before sunrise. Gideon rose, padded barefoot out of his hut, and, still asleep, looked at the gathering light. With one thin hand he shaded his eyes, still yearning for sleep, while the other automatically buttoned up his battle dress. He could already hear voices and metallic sounds; a few eager boys were

*[The Hebrew word *ruah* has multiple meanings: wind, spirit, intellect, ghost, to mention only a few. In this story it also refers to the ideological convictions of the old man. The title is borrowed from Ecclesiastes 11:5. —TRANS.]

cleaning their guns for morning inspection. But Gideon was slow. The sunrise had stirred a weary restlessness inside him, perhaps a vague longing. The sunrise was over, but still he stood there drowsily, until he was pushed from behind and told to get cracking.

He went back into the hut, straightened his camp bed, cleaned his submachine gun, and picked up his shaving kit. On his way, among whitewashed eucalyptus trees and clustering notices commending tidiness and discipline, he suddenly remembered that today was Independence Day, the Fifth of Iyar. And today the platoon was to mount a celebratory parachute display in the Valley of Jezreel. He entered the washroom and, while he waited for a free mirror, brushed his teeth and thought of pretty girls. In an hour and a half the preparations would be complete and the platoon would be airborne, on its way to its destination. Throngs of excited civilians would be waiting for them to jump, and the girls would be there, too. The drop would take place just outside Nof Harish, the kibbutz that was Gideon's home, where he had been born and brought up until the day he joined the army. The moment his feet touched the ground, the children of the kibbutz would close around him and jump all over him and shout, "Gideon, look, here's our Gideon!"

He pushed in between two much bigger soldiers and began to lather his face and try to shave.

"Hot day," he said.

One of the soldiers answered, "Not yet. But it soon will be."

And another soldier behind him grumbled, "Hurry it up. Don't spend all day jawing."

Gideon did not take offense. On the contrary, the words filled him with a surge of joy for some reason. He dried his face and went out onto the parade ground. The blue light had changed meanwhile to gray-white, the grubby glare of a *khamsin*.

# 2

Shimshon Sheinbaum had confidently predicted the previous night that a *khamsin* was on its way. As soon as he got up he hurried over to the window and confirmed with calm satisfaction that he had been right yet again. He closed the shutters, to protect the room from the hot wind, then washed his face and his shaggy shoulders and chest, shaved, and prepared his breakfast, coffee with a roll brought last night from the dining hall. Shimshon Sheinbaum loathed wasting time, especially in the productive morning hours: you go out, walk to the dining hall, have a chat, read the paper, discuss the news, and that's half the morning gone. So he always made do with a cup of coffee and a roll, and by ten past six, after the early news summary, Gideon Shenhav's father was sitting at his desk. Summer and winter alike, with no concessions.

He sat at his desk and stared for a few minutes at the map of the country that hung on the opposite wall. He was straining to recapture a nagging dream which had taken hold of him in the early hours, just before he had awakened. But it eluded him. Shimshon decided to get on with his work and not waste another minute. True, today was a holiday, but the best way to celebrate was to work, not to slack off. Before it was time to go out and watch the parachutists—and Gideon, who might actually be among them and not drop out at the last minute—he still had several hours of working time. A man of seventy-five cannot afford to squander his hours, especially if there are many, painfully many, things he must set down in writing. So little time.

The name of Shimshon Sheinbaum needs no introduction. The Hebrew Labor Movement knows how to honor its founding fathers, and for decades now Shimshon Sheinbaum's name has been invested with a halo of enduring fame. For decades he has fought body and soul to realize the vision of his youth. Setbacks and disappointments have not shattered or weakened his faith but, rather, have enriched it with a vein of wise sadness. The better he has come to understand the weakness of others and their ideological deviations, the more ferociously he has fought against his own weaknesses. He has sternly eliminated them, and lived according to his principles, with a ruthless self-discipline and not without a certain secret joy.

At this moment, between six and seven o'clock on this Independence Day morning, Shimshon Sheinbaum is not yet a bereaved father. But his features are extraordinarily well suited to the role. A solemn, sagacious expression, of one who sees all but betrays no reaction, occupies his furrowed face. And his blue eyes express an ironic melancholy.

He sits erect at his desk, his head bent over the pages. His elbows are relaxed. The desk is made of plain wood, like the rest of the furniture, which is all functional and unembellished. More like a monastic cell than a bungalow in a long-established kibbutz.

This morning will not be particularly productive. Time and again his thoughts wander to the dream that flickered and died at the end of the night. He must recapture the dream, and then he will be able to forget it and concentrate on his work. There was a hose, yes, and some sort of goldfish or something. An argument with someone. No connection. Now to work. The Poalei Zion Movement appears to have been built from the start on an ideological contradiction that could never be bridged, and which it only succeeded in disguising by means of verbal acrobatics. But the contradiction is only apparent, and anyone who hopes to exploit it to undermine or attack the movement does not know what he is talking about. And here is the simple proof.

Shimshon Sheinbaum's rich experience of life has taught him how arbitrary, how senseless is the hand that guides the vagaries of our fate, that of the individual and that of the community alike. His sobriety has not robbed him of the straightforwardness which has animated him since his youth. His most remarkable and admirable characteristic is his stubborn innocence, like that of our pure, pious forebears, whose sagacity never injured their faith. Sheinbaum has never allowed his actions to be cut loose from his words. Even though some of the leaders of our movement have drifted into political careers and cut themselves off completely from manual labor, Sheinbaum has never abandoned the kibbutz. He has turned down all outside jobs and assignments, and it was only with extreme reluctance that he accepted nomination to the General Workers' Congress. Until a few years ago his days were divided equally between physical and intellectual work: three days gardening, three days theorizing. The beautiful gardens of Nof Harish are largely his handiwork. We can remember how he used to plant and prune and lop, water and hoe, manure, transplant, weed, and dig up. He did not permit his status as the leading thinker of the movement to exempt him from the duties to which every rank-and-file member is liable: he served as night watchman, took his turn in the kitchens, helped with the harvest. No shadow of a double standard has ever clouded the path of Shimshon Sheinbaum's life; he is a single complex of vision and execution, he has known no slackness or weakness of will—so the secretary of the movement wrote about him in a magazine a few years ago, on the occasion of his seventieth birthday.

True, there have been moments of stabbing despair. There have been moments of deep disgust. But Shimshon Sheinbaum knows how to transform such moments into secret sources of furious energy. Like the words of the marching song he loves, which always inspires him to a frenzy of action: *Up into the mountains we are climbing, Climbing up toward the dawning day; We have left all our yesterdays behind us, But tomorrow is a long long way away.* If only that stupid dream would emerge from the shadows and show itself clearly, he could kick it out of his mind and concentrate at last on his work. Time is slipping by. A rubber hose, a chess gambit, some goldfish, a great argument, but what is the connection?

For many years Shimshon Sheinbaum has lived alone. He has channeled all his vigor into his ideological productions. To this life's work he has sacrificed the warmth of a family home. He has managed, in exchange, to retain into old age a youthful clarity and cordiality. Only when he was fifty-six did he suddenly marry Raya Greenspan and father Gideon, and after that he left her and returned to his ideological work. It would be sanctimonious to pretend, however, that before his marriage Shimshon Sheinbaum maintained a monastic existence. His personality attracted women just as it attracted disciples. He was still young when his thick mop of hair turned white, and his sunbeaten face was etched with an appealing pattern of lines and wrinkles. His square back, his strong shoulders, the timbre of his voice—always warm, skeptical, and rather ruminative—and also his solitude, all attracted women to him like fluttering birds. Gossip attributes to his loins at least one of the urchins of the kibbutz, and elsewhere, too, stories are current. But we shall not dwell on this.

At the age of fifty-six Shimshon Sheinbaum decided that it befitted him to beget a son and heir to bear his stamp and his name into the coming generation. And so he conquered Raya Greenspan, a diminutive girl with a stammer who was thirty-three years his junior. Three months after the wedding, which was solemnized before a restricted company, Gideon was born. And before the kibbutz had recovered from its amazement, Shimshon sent Raya back to her former room and rededicated himself to his ideological work. This episode caused various ripples, and, indeed, it was preceded by painful heart-searchings in Shimshon Sheinbaum himself.

Now let's concentrate and think logically. Yes, it's coming back. She came to my room and called me to go there quickly to put a stop to that scandal. I didn't ask any questions, but hurried after her. Someone had had the nerve to dig a pond in the lawn in front of the dining hall, and I was seething because no one had authorized such an innovation, an ornamental pond in front of the dining hall, like some Polish squire's château. I shouted. Who at, there is no clear picture. There were goldfish in the pond. And a boy was filling it with water from a black rubber hose. So I decided to put a stop to the whole performance there and then, but the boy wouldn't listen to me. I started walking along the hose to find the faucet and cut off the water before anybody managed to establish the pond as a *fait accompli*. I walked and walked until I suddenly discovered that I was walking in a circle, and the hose was not connected to a faucet but simply came back to the pond and sucked up water from it. Stuff and nonsense. That's the end of it. The original platform of the Poalei Zion Movement must be understood without any recourse to dialectics, it must be taken literally, word for word.

# 3

After his separation from Raya Greenspan, Shimshon Sheinbaum did not neglect his duties as his son's mentor, nor did he disclaim responsibility. He lavished on him, from the time the boy was six or seven, the full warmth of his personality. Gideon, however, turned out to be something of a disappointment, not the stuff of which dynasties are founded. As a child he was always sniveling. He was a slow, bewildered child, mopping up blows and insults without retaliating, a strange child, always playing with candy wrappers, dried leaves, silkworms. And from the age of twelve he was constantly having his heart broken by girls of all ages. He was always lovesick, and he published sad poems and cruel parodies in the children's newsletter. A dark, gentle youth, with an almost feminine beauty, who walked the paths of the kibbutz in obstinate silence. He did not shine at work; he did not shine in communal life. He was slow of speech and no doubt also of thought. His poems seemed to Shimshon incorrigibly sentimental, and his parodies venomous, without a trace of inspiration. The nickname Pinocchio suited him, there is no denying it. And the infuriating smiles he was perpetually spreading on his face seemed to Shimshon a depressingly exact replica of the smiles of Raya Greenspan.

And then, eighteen months before, Gideon had amazed his father. He suddenly appeared and asked for his written permission to enlist in the paratroopers—as an only son this required the written consent of both parents. Only when Shimshon Sheinbaum was convinced that this was not one of his son's outrageous jokes did he agree to give his consent. And then he gave it gladly: this was surely an encouraging turn in the boy's development. They'd make a man of him there. Let him go. Why not.

But Raya Greenspan's stubborn opposition raised an unexpected obstacle to Gideon's plan. No, she wouldn't sign the paper. On no account. Never.

Shimshon himself went to her room one evening, pleaded with her, reasoned with her, shouted at her. All in vain. She wouldn't sign. No reason, she just wouldn't. So Shimshon Sheinbaum had to resort to devious means to enable the boy to enlist. He wrote a private letter to Yolek himself, asking a personal favor. He wished his son to be allowed to volunteer. The mother was emotionally unstable. The boy would make a first-rate paratrooper. Shimshon himself accepted full responsibility. And incidentally, he had never before asked a personal favor. And he never would again. This was the one and only time in his whole life. He begged Yolek to see what he could do.

At the end of September, when the first signs of autumn were appearing in the orchards, Gideon Shenhav was enrolled in a parachute unit.

From that time on, Shimshon Sheinbaum immersed himself more deeply than ever in ideological work, which is the only real mark a man can leave on the world. Shimshon Sheinbaum has made a mark on the Hebrew Labor Movement that can never be erased. Old age is still far off. At seventy-five he still has hair as thick as ever, and his muscles are firm and powerful. His eyes are alert, his mind attentive. His strong, dry, slightly cracked voice still works wonders on women of all ages. His bearing is restrained, his manner modest. Needless to say, he is deeply rooted in the soil of Nof Harish. He loathes assemblies and formal ceremonies, not to mention commissions and official appointments. With his pen alone he has inscribed his name on the roll of honor of our movement and our nation.

# 4

Gideon Shenhav's last day began with a brilliant sunrise. He felt he could even see the beads of dew evaporating in the heat. Omens blazed on the mountain peaks far away to the east. This was a day of celebration, a celebration of independence and a celebration of parachuting over the familiar fields of home. All that night he had nestled in a half-dream of dark autumnal forests under northern skies, a rich smell of autumn, huge trees he could not name. All night long pale leaves had been dropping on the huts of the camp. Even after he had awakened in the morning, the northern forest with its nameless trees still continued to whisper in his ears.

Gideon adored the delicious moment of free fall between the jump from the aircraft and the unfolding of the parachute. The void rushes up toward you at lightning speed, fierce drafts of air lick at your body, making you dizzy with pleasure. The speed is drunken, reckless, it whistles and roars and your whole body trembles to it, red-hot needles work at your nerve ends, and your heart pounds. Suddenly, when you are lightning in the wind, the chute opens. The straps check your fall, like a firm, masculine arm bringing you calmly under control. You can feel its supporting strength under your armpits. The reckless thrill gives way to a more sedate pleasure. Slowly your body swings through the air, floats, hesitates, drifts a little way on the slight breeze, you can never guess precisely where your feet will touch ground, on the slope of that hill or next to the orange groves over there, and like an exhausted migrating bird you slowly descend, seeing roofs, roads, cows in the meadow, slowly as if you have a choice, as if the decision is entirely yours.

And then the ground is under your feet, and you launch into the practiced somersault which will soften the impact of landing. Within seconds you must sober up. The coursing blood slows down. Dimensions return to normal. Only a weary pride survives in your heart until you rejoin your commanding officer and your comrades and you're caught up in the rhythm of frenzied reorganization.

This time it is all going to happen over Nof Harish.

The older folk will raise their clammy hands, push back their caps, and try to spot Gideon among the gray dots dangling in the sky. The kids will rush around in the fields, also waiting excitedly for their hero to touch down. Mother will come out of the dining hall and stand peering upward, muttering to herself. Shimshon will leave his desk for a while, perhaps take a chair out onto his little porch and watch the whole performance with pensive pride.

Then the kibbutz will entertain the unit. Pitchers of lemonade glistening with chilly perspiration will be set out in the dining hall, there will be crates of apples, or perhaps cakes baked by the older women, iced with congratulatory phrases.

By six-thirty the sun had grown out of its colorful caprice and risen ruthlessly over the eastern mountain heights. A thick heat weighed heavily on the whole scene. The tin roofs of the camp huts reflected a dazzling glare. The walls began to radiate a dense, oppressive warmth into the huts. On the main road, which passed close to the perimeter fence, a lively procession of buses and trucks was already in motion: the residents of the villages and small towns were streaming to the big city to watch the military parade. Their white shirts could be discerned dimly through the clouds of dust, and snatches of exuberant song could be caught in the distance.

The paratroopers had completed their morning inspection. The orders of the day, signed by the Chief of Staff, had been read out and posted on the bulletin boards. A festive breakfast had been served, including a hard-boiled egg reposing on a lettuce leaf ringed with olives.

Gideon, his dark hair flopping forward onto his forehead, broke into a quiet song. The others joined him. Here and there someone altered the words, making them comical or even obscene. Soon the Hebrew songs gave way to a guttural, almost desperate Arabic wail. The platoon commander, a blond, good-looking officer whose exploits were feted around the campfires at night, stood up and said: That's enough. The paratroopers stopped singing, hastily downed the last of their greasy coffee, and moved toward the runways. Here there was another inspection; the commanding officer spoke a few words of endearment to his men, calling them "the salt of the earth," and then ordered them into the waiting aircraft.

The squadron commanders stood at the doors of the planes and checked each belt and harness. The CO himself circulated among the men, patting a shoulder, joking, predicting, enthusing, for all the world as though they were going into battle and facing real danger. Gideon responded to the pat on his shoulder with a hasty smile. He was lean, almost ascetic-looking, but very suntanned. A sharp eye, that of the legendary blond commander, could spot the blue vein throbbing in his neck.

Then the heat broke into the shady storage sheds, mercilessly flushing out the last strongholds of coolness, roasting everything with a gray glow. The sign was given. The engines gave a throaty roar. Birds fled from the runway. The planes shuddered, moved forward heavily, and began to gather the momentum without which takeoff cannot be achieved.

# 5

I must get out and be there to shake his hand.

Having made up his mind, Sheinbaum closed his notebook. The months of military training have certainly toughened the boy. It is hard to believe, but it certainly looks as though he is beginning to mature at last. He still has to learn how to handle women. He has to free himself once and for all from his shyness and his sentimentality: he should leave such traits to women and cultivate toughness in himself. And how he has improved at chess. Soon he'll be a serious challenge to his old father. May even beat me one of these days. Not just yet, though. As long as he doesn't up and marry the first girl who gives herself to him. He ought to break one or two of them in before he gets spliced. In a few years he'll have to give me some grandchildren. Lots of them. Gideon's children will have two fathers: my son can take care of them, and I'll take care of their ideas. The second generation grew up in the shadow of our achievements; that's why they're so confused. It's a matter of dialectics. But the third generation will be a wonderful synthesis, a successful outcome: they will inherit the spontaneity of their parents and the spirit of their grandparents. It will be a glorious heritage distilled from a twisted pedigree. I'd better jot that phrase down, it will come in handy one of these days. I feel so sad when I think of Gideon and his friends: they exude such an air of shallow despair, of nihilism, of cynical mockery. They can't love wholeheartedly, and they can't hate wholeheart-edly, either. No enthusiasm, and no loathing. I'm not one to deprecate despair per se. Despair is the eternal twin of faith, but that's real despair, virile and passionate, not this senti-mental, poetic melancholy. Sit still, Gideon, stop scratching yourself, stop biting your nails. I want to read you a marvel-ous passage from Brenner. All right, make a face. So I won't read. Go outside and grow up to be a Bedouin, if that's what you want. But if you don't get to know Brenner, you'll never understand the first thing about despair or about faith. You won't find any soppy poems here about jackals caught in traps or flowers in the autumn. In Brenner, everything is on fire. Love, and hatred as well. Maybe you yourselves won't see light and darkness face to face, but your children will. A glorious heritage will be distilled from a twisted pedigree. And we won't let the third generation be pampered and corrupted by sentimental verses by decadent poetesses. Here come the planes now. We'll put Brenner back on the shelf and get ready to be proud of you for a change, Gideon Sheinbaum.

# 6

Sheinbaum strode purposefully across the lawn, stepped up onto the concrete path, and turned toward the plowed field in the southwest corner of the kibbutz, which had been se-lected for the landing. On his way he paused now and again at a flower bed to pull up a stray weed skulking furtively beneath a flowering shrub. His small blue eyes had always been amazingly skillful at detecting weeds. Admittedly, because of his age he had retired a few years previously from his work in the gardens, but until his dying day he would not cease to scan the flower beds mercilessly in search of undesirable intruders. At such moments he thought of the boy, forty years his junior, who had succeeded him as gardener and who fancied himself as the local water-colorist. He had inherited beautifully tended gardens, and now they were all going to seed before our very eyes.

A gang of excited children ran across his path. They were fiercely absorbed in a detailed argument about the types of aircraft that were circling above the valley. Because they were running, the argument was being carried out in loud shouts and gasps. Shimshon seized one of them by the shirttail, forcibly brought him to a halt, put his face close to the child's, and said:

"You are Zaki."

"Leave me alone," the child replied.

Sheinbaum said: "What's all this shouting? Airplanes, is that all you've got in your heads? And running across the flower beds like that where it says Keep Off, is that right? Do you think you can do whatever you like? Are there no rules any more? Look at me when I'm speaking to you. And give me a proper answer, or ..."

But Zaki had taken advantage of the flood of words to wriggle out of the man's grasp and tear himself free. He slipped in among the bushes, made a monkey face, and stuck out his tongue.

Sheinbaum pursed his lips. He thought for an instant about old age, but instantly thrust it out of his mind and said to himself: All right. We'll see about that later. Zaki, otherwise Azariah. Rapid calculation showed that he must be at least eleven, perhaps twelve already. A hooligan. A wild beast.

Meanwhile the young trainees had occupied a vantage point high up on top of the water tower, from which they could survey the length and breadth of the valley. The whole scene reminded Sheinbaum of a Russian painting. For a moment he was tempted to climb up and join the youngsters on top of the tower, to watch the display comfortably from a distance. But the thought of the manly handshake to come kept him striding steadily on, till he reached the edge of the field. Here he stood, his legs planted well apart, his arms folded on his chest, his thick white hair falling impressively over his forehead. He craned his neck and followed the two transport planes with steady gray eyes. The mosaic of wrin-

kles on his face enriched his expression with a rare blend of
pride, thoughtfulness, and a trace of well-controlled irony.
And his bushy white eyebrows suggested a saint in a Russian icon. Meanwhile the planes had completed their first
circuit, and the leading one was approaching the field again.

Shimshon Sheinbaum's lips parted and made way for a
low hum. An old Russian tune was throbbing in his chest.
The first batch of men emerged from the opening in the
plane's side. Small dark shapes were dotted in space, like
seeds scattered by a farmer in an old pioneering print.

Then Raya Greenspan stuck her head out of the window
of the kitchen and gesticulated with the ladle she was holding as though admonishing the treetops. Her face was hot
and flushed. Perspiration stuck her plain dress to her strong,
hairy legs. She panted, scratched at her disheveled hair with
the fingernails of her free hand, and suddenly turned and
shouted to the other women working in the kitchens:

"Quick! Come to the window! It's Gidi up there! Gidi in
the sky!"

And just as suddenly she was struck dumb.

While the first soldiers were still floating gently, like a
handful of feathers, between heaven and earth, the second
plane came in and dropped Gideon Shenhav's group. The
men stood pressed close together inside the hatch, chest
against back, their bodies fused into a single tense, sweating
mass. When Gideon's turn came he gritted his teeth, braced
his knees, and leapt out as though from the womb into the
bright hot air. A long wild scream of joy burst from his
throat as he fell. He could see his childhood haunts rushing
up toward him as he fell he could see the roofs and treetops
and he smiled a frantic smile of greeting as he fell toward
the vineyards and concrete paths and sheds and gleaming
pipes with joy in his heart as he fell. Never in his whole life
had he known such overwhelming, spine-tingling love. All
his muscles were tensed, and gushing thrills burst in his
stomach and up his spine to the roots of his hair. He
screamed for love like a madman, his fingernails almost
drawing blood from his clenched palms. Then the straps
drew taut and caught him under the armpits. His waist was
clasped in a tight embrace. For a moment he felt as though

an invisible hand were pulling him back up toward the plane into the heart of the sky. The delicious falling sensation was replaced by a slow, gentle swaying, like rocking in a cradle or floating in warm water. Suddenly a wild panic hit him. How will they recognize me down there. How will they manage to identify their only son in this forest of white parachutes. How will they be able to fix me and me alone with their anxious, loving gaze. Mother and Dad and the pretty girls and the little kids and everyone. I mustn't just get lost in the crowd. After all, this is me, and I'm the one they love.

That moment an idea flashed through Gideon's mind. He put his hand up to his shoulder and pulled the cord to release the spare chute, the one intended for emergencies. As the second canopy opened overhead he slowed down as though the force of gravity had lost its hold on him. He seemed to be floating alone in the void, like a gull or a lonely cloud. The last of his comrades had landed in the soft earth and were folding up their parachutes. Gideon Shenhav alone continued to hover as though under a spell with two large canopies spread out above him. Happy, intoxicated, he drank in the hundreds of eyes fixed on him. On him alone. In his glorious isolation.

As though to lend further splendor to the spectacle, a strong, almost cool breeze burst from the west, plowing through the hot air, playing with the spectators' hair, and carrying slightly eastward the last of the parachutists.

# 7

Far away in the big city, the massed crowds waiting for the military parade greeted the sudden sea breeze with a sigh of relief. Perhaps it marked the end of the heat wave. A cool, salty smell caressed the baking streets. The breeze freshened. It whistled fiercely in the treetops, bent the stiff spines of the cypresses, ruffled the hair of the pines, raised eddies of dust, and blurred the scene for the spectators at the parachute display. Regally, like a huge solitary bird, Gideon Shenhav was carried eastward toward the main road.

The terrified shout that broke simultaneously from a hundred throats could not reach the boy. Singing aloud in an ecstatic trance, he continued to sway slowly toward the main electric cables, stretched between their enormous pylons. The watchers stared in horror at the suspended soldier and the powerlines that crossed the valley with unfaltering straightness from west to east. The five parallel cables, sagging with their own weight between the pylons, hummed softly in the gusty breeze.

Gideon's two parachutes tangled in the upper cable. A moment later his feet landed on the lower one. His body hung backward in a slanting pose. The straps held his waist and shoulders fast, preventing him from falling into the soft plowland. Had he not been insulated by the thick soles of his boots, the boy would have been struck dead at the moment of impact. As it was, the cable was already protesting its unwonted burden by scorching his soles. Tiny sparks flashed and crackled under Gideon's feet. He held tight with both hands to the buckles on the straps. His eyes were open wide and his mouth was agape.

Immediately a short officer, perspiring heavily, leapt out of the petrified crowd and shouted:

"Don't touch the cables, Gidi. Stretch your body backward and keep as clear as you can!"

The whole tightly packed, panic-stricken crowd began to edge slowly in an easterly direction. There were shouts. There was a wail. Sheinbaum silenced them with his metallic voice and ordered everyone to keep calm. He broke into a fast run, his feet pounding on the soft earth, reached the spot, pushed aside the officers and curious bystanders, and instructed his son:

"Quickly, Gideon, release the straps and drop. The ground is soft here. It's perfectly safe. Jump."

"I can't."

"Don't argue. Do as I tell you. Jump."

"I can't, Dad, I can't do it."

"No such thing as can't. Release the straps and jump before you electrocute yourself."

"I can't, the straps are tangled. Tell them to switch off the current quickly, Dad, my boots are burning."

Some of the soldiers were trying to hold back the crowd,

discourage well-meaning suggestions, and make more room under the powerlines. They kept repeating, as if it were an incantation, "Don't panic please don't panic."

The youngsters of the kibbutz were rushing all around, adding to the confusion. Reprimands and warnings had no effect. Two angry paratroopers managed to catch Zaki, who was idiotically climbing the nearest pylon, snorting and whistling and making faces to attract the attention of the crowd.

The short officer suddenly shouted: "Your knife. You've got a knife in your belt. Get it out and cut the straps!"

But Gideon either could not or would not hear. He began to sob aloud.

"Get me down, Dad, I'll be electrocuted, tell them to get me down from here, I can't get down on my own."

"Stop sniveling," his father said curtly. "You've been told to use your knife to cut the straps. Now, do as you've been told. And stop sniveling."

The boy obeyed. He was still sobbing audibly, but he groped for the knife, located it, and cut the straps one by one. The silence was total. Only Gideon's sobbing, a strange, piercing sound, was to be heard intermittently. Finally one last strap was left holding him, which he did not dare to cut.

"Cut it," the children shrilled, "cut it and jump. Let's see you do it."

And Shimshon added in a level voice, "Now what are you waiting for?"

"I can't do it," Gideon pleaded.

"Of course you can," said his father.

"The current," the boy wept. "I can feel the current. Get me down quickly."

His father's eyes filled with blood as he roared:

"You coward! You ought to be ashamed of yourself!"

"But I can't do it, I'll break my neck, it's too high."

"You can do it and you must do it. You're a fool, that's what you are, a fool and a coward."

A group of jet planes passed overhead on their way to the aerial display over the city. They were flying in precise formation, thundering westward like a pack of wild dogs. As the planes disappeared, the silence seemed twice as intense. Even the boy had stopped crying. He let the knife fall to the ground. The blade pierced the earth at Shimshon Sheinbaum's feet.

"What did you do that for?" the short officer shouted.

"I didn't mean it," Gideon whined. "It just slipped out of my hand."

Shimshon Sheinbaum bent down, picked up a small stone, straightened up, and threw it furiously at his son's back.

"Pinocchio, you're a wet rag, you're a miserable coward!"

At this point the sea breeze also dropped.

The heat wave returned with renewed vigor to oppress both men and inanimate objects. A red-haired, freckled soldier muttered to himself, "He's scared to jump, the idiot, he'll kill himself if he stays up there." And a skinny, plain-faced girl, hearing this, rushed into the middle of the circle and spread her arms wide:

"Jump into my arms, Gidi, you'll be all right."

"It would be interesting," remarked a veteran pioneer in working clothes, "to know whether anyone has had the sense to phone the electric company to ask them to switch off the current." He turned and started off toward the kibbutz buildings. He was striding quickly, angrily, up the slight slope when he was suddenly alarmed by a prolonged burst of firing close at hand. For a moment he imagined he was being shot at from behind. But at once he realized what was happening: the squadron commander, the good-looking blond hero, was trying to sever the electric cables with his machine gun.

Without success.

Meanwhile, a beaten-up truck arrived from the farmyard. Ladders were unloaded from it, followed by the elderly doctor, and finally a stretcher.

At that moment it was evident that Gideon had been struck by a sudden decision. Kicking out strongly, he pushed himself off the lower cable, which was emitting blue sparks, turned a somersault, and remained suspended by the single strap with his head pointing downward and his scorched boots beating the air a foot or so from the cable.

It was hard to be certain, but it looked as though so far he had not sustained any serious injury. He swung limply upside down in space, like a dead lamb suspended from a butcher's hook.

This spectacle provoked hysterical glee in the watching children. They barked with laughter. Zaki slapped his knees, choking and heaving convulsively. He leapt up and down screeching like a mischievous monkey.

What had Gideon Shenhav seen that made him suddenly stretch his neck and join in the children's laughter? Perhaps his peculiar posture had unbalanced his mind. His face was blood-red, his tongue protruded, his thick hair hung down, and only his feet kicked up at the sky.

# 8

A second group of jets plowed through the sky overhead. A dozen metallic birds, sculpted with cruel beauty, flashing dazzlingly in the bright sunlight. They flew in a narrow spearhead formation. Their fury shook the earth. On they flew to the west, and a deep silence followed.

Meanwhile, the elderly doctor sat down on the stretcher, lit a cigarette, blinked vaguely at the people, the soldiers, the scampering children, and said to himself: We'll see how things turn out. Whatever has to happen will happen. How hot it is today.

Every now and again Gideon let out another senseless laugh. His legs were flailing, describing clumsy circles in the dusty air. The blood had drained from his inverted limbs and was gathering in his head. His eyes were beginning to bulge. The world was turning dark. Instead of the crimson glow, purple spots were dancing before his eyes. He stuck his tongue out. The children interpreted this as a gesture of derision. "Upside-down Pinocchio," Zaki shrilled, "why don't you stop squinting at us, and try walking on your hands instead?"

Sheinbaum moved to hit the brat, but the blow landed on thin air because the child had leapt aside. The old man beckoned to the blond commander, and they held a brief consultation. The boy was in no immediate danger, because he was not in direct contact with the cable, but he must be rescued soon. This comedy could not go on forever. A ladder would not help much: he was too high up. Perhaps the knife could be got up to him again somehow, and he could be persuaded to cut the last strap and jump into a sheet of canvas. After all, it was a perfectly routine exercise in parachute training. The main thing was to act quickly, because the situation was humiliating. Not to mention the children. So the short officer removed his shirt and wrapped a knife in it. Gideon stretched his hands downward and tried to catch the bundle. It slipped between his outstretched arms and plummeted uselessly to the ground. The children snickered. Only after two more unsuccessful attempts did Gideon manage to grasp the shirt and remove the knife. His fingers were numb and heavy with blood. Suddenly he pressed the blade to his burning cheek, enjoying the cool touch of the steel. It was a delicious moment. He opened his eyes and saw an inverted world. Everything looked comical: the truck, the field, his father, the army, the kids, and even the knife in his hand. He made a twisted face at the gang of children, gave a deep laugh, and waved at them with the knife. He tried to say something. If only they could see themselves from up here, upside down, rushing around like startled ants, they would surely laugh with him. But the laugh turned into a heavy cough; Gideon choked and his eyes filled.

# 9

Gideon's upside-down antics filled Zaki with demonic glee.

"He's crying," he shouted cruelly, "Gideon's crying, look, you can see the tears. Pinocchio the hero, he's sniveling with fear-o. We can see you, we can."

Once again Shimshon Sheinbaum's fist fell ineffectually on thin air.

"Zaki," Gideon managed to shout in a dull, pain-racked voice, "I'll kill you, I'll choke you, you little bastard." Suddenly he chuckled and stopped.

It was no good. He wouldn't cut the last strap by himself, and the doctor was afraid that if he stayed as he was much longer he was likely to lose consciousness. Some other solution would have to be found. This performance could not be allowed to go on all day.

And so the kibbutz truck rumbled across the plowland and braked at the point indicated by Shimshon Sheinbaum. Two ladders were hastily lashed together to reach the required height, and then supported on the back of the truck by five strong pairs of hands. The legendary blond officer started to climb. But when he reached the place where the two ladders overlapped, there was an ominous creak, and the wood began to bend with the weight and the height. The officer, a largish man, hesitated for a moment. He decided to retreat and fasten the ladders together more securely. He climbed down to the floor of the truck, wiped the sweat from his forehead, and said, "Wait, I'm thinking." Just then, in the twinkling of an eye, before he could be stopped, before he could even be spotted, the child Zaki had climbed high up the ladder, past the join, and leapt like a frantic monkey up onto the topmost rungs; suddenly he was clutching a knife—where on earth had he got it from? He wrestled with the taut strap. The spectators held their breath: he seemed to be defying gravity, not holding on, not caring, hopping on the top rung, nimble, lithe, amazingly efficient.

# 10

The heat beat down violently on the hanging youth. His eyes were growing dimmer. His breathing had almost stopped. With his last glimmer of lucidity he saw his ugly brother in front of him and felt his breath on his face. He could smell him. He could see the pointed teeth protruding from Zaki's mouth. A terrible fear closed in on him, as though he were looking in a mirror and seeing a monster. The nightmare roused Gideon's last reserves of strength. He kicked into space, flailed, managed to turn over, seized the strap, and pulled himself up. With outstretched arms he threw himself onto the cable and saw the flash. The hot wind continued to tyrannize the whole valley. And a third cluster of jets drowned the scene with its roaring.

# 11

The status of a bereaved father invests a man with a saintly aura of suffering. But Sheinbaum gave no thought to this aura. A stunned, silent company escorted him toward the dining hall. He knew, with utter certainty, that his place now was beside Raya.

On the way he saw the child Zaki, glowing, breathless, a hero. Surrounded by other youngsters: he had almost rescued Gideon. Shimshon laid a trembling hand on his child's head, and tried to tell him. His voice abandoned him and his lips quivered. Clumsily he stroked the tousled, dusty mop of hair. It was the first time he had ever stroked the child. A few steps later, everything went dark and the old man collapsed in a flower bed.

As Independence Day drew to a close the *khamsin* abated. A fresh sea breeze soothed the steaming walls. There was a heavy fall of dew on the lawns in the night.

What does the pale ring around the moon portend? Usually it heralds a *khamsin*. Tomorrow, no doubt, the heat will return. It is May, and June will follow. A wind drifts among the cypresses in the night, trying to comfort them between one heat wave and the next. It is the way of the wind to come and to go and to come again. There is nothing new.

1962

# Before His Time

## 1

The bull was warm and strong on the night of his death.

In the night, Samson the bull was slaughtered. Early in the morning, before the five o'clock milking, a meat trader from Nazareth came and took him away in a gray tender. Portions of his carcass were hung on rusty hooks in the butcher shops of Nazareth. The ringing of the church bells roused droves of flies to attack the bull's flesh, swarming upon it and exacting a green revenge.

Later, at eight o'clock in the morning, an old effendi arrived, carrying a transistor radio. He had come to buy Samson's hide. And all the while Radio Ramallah piped American music into the palm of his hand. It was the wildest of tunes, some unbearably mournful piece of jazz. The church bells accompanied the wailing melody. As the tune came to an end, the transaction was concluded. The bull's hide was sold. What will you do, O Rashid Effendi, with the hide of Samson the mighty bull? I will make ornaments from it, objects of value, souvenirs for rich tourists, pictures in many colors on a screen of hide: here is the alleyway where Jesus lived, here is the carpenter's workshop with Joseph himself inside, here little angels are striking a bell to proclaim the birth of the Saviour, here the kings are coming to bow down before the cradle, and here is the Babe with light on His forehead, parchment work, real bullskin, all hand-made with an artist's vision.

Rashid Effendi went to Zaim's café to spend the morning at the backgammon table. In his hand the radio with its cheerful music, and at his feet, in a sack, the hide of the dead bull.

And a Nazareth breeze, heavy with smells, plucked at the bells and the treetops, stirring the hooks in the butcher shops, and the flesh of the bull gave out a crimson groan.

# 2

Samson the bull was at the height of his powers, the pride of the kibbutz herdsman, the finest bull in the valley. Had it not been that his potency failed, Yosh would not have come to him suddenly in the night to slit his throat.

Samson was asleep on his feet, his head bowed. The steam of his breath mingled with the smell of sticky cattle sweat. The beam of the pocket flashlight caressed his chest and lingered on his neck. The bull sensed nothing.

Poisoned bait, thought Yosh. The howl of the jackals rose from the darkness. In late autumn a stray jackal had broken into the cattle shed, rabid or crazed with hunger, and had bitten Samson in the leg. Samson killed him with a kick, but the poison in the bite killed the bull's potency. Thus was sealed the fate of the most ferocious bull in the Valley of Jezreel.

With a gentle, quiet hand Yosh gripped the bull's jaw and raised the dark head. The bull breathed deeply. His eyes quivered, almost winked. Yosh pressed the point of the knife to Samson's gullet. The bull's nostrils flared suddenly and his foreleg kicked at the balls of dung beneath him. Still he did not open his eyes. Nor did he open them for a long while—not until the blade had pierced his hide and flesh and jugular vein.

First to appear were a few thin, tentative drops. The bull let out a muffled groan of unease and swung his head from side to side as if shaking off an obstinate fly, or expressing violent disagreement on a conversational point. Then came a weak, hesitant trickle, as if from a trivial scratch.

"Well," said Yosh.

Samson lashed his muddy hindquarters with his tail and exhaled nervously, warmly.

"Well, get on with it," said Yosh, and he thrust his hand into his pocket. The cigarette that appeared between his lips was moist and somehow unclean. What possessed Yosh to stub out the match on the forehead of the dying bull? The flame died and darkness returned. The bull was groaning in pain now, but his groaning was restrained, and he fell silent, took two clumsy paces backward, raised his head, and stared at the man.

And as he lifted his wonderful head the blood burst out from the wound and streamed down in black torrents, bubbling in the flashlight beam. Yosh felt disgust and impatience.

"Well, really," he said.

The sight of the spurting blood tickled his bladder. Something prevented him from urinating in the presence of the dying bull. But his patience was ready to snap, and he smoked nervously and angrily. Samson was dying very slowly. His blood was warm and sticky. The bull fell on his knees, his forelegs first, then unhurriedly he lay down. His drooping horns tried to butt, searching in vain for a target.

The bull's eyes died first, while his hide still quivered. Then his hide was still, and there was just one foreleg poking at the straw like a blind man's stick. The leg stopped moving, and all was quiet. The tail flicked weakly once, and once again, like a hand waving good-bye. And when his blood had all drained away, Samson curled up as if he chose to die in the fetal position.

"Well, well," said Yosh.

Then the herdsman finished his cigarette and emptied his bladder and turned and went to the little kitchen where Zeshka kept watch at night.

Zeshka, the estranged wife of Dov Sirkin, gave Yosh a drink of warm, sweet milk in an earthenware cup. She was an old, wrinkled woman with sunken eyes like an owl's. The earthenware cup was large and thick. There was something sharp and nervous in Zeshka's movements. Her body was stunted, shriveled. Steam rose from the cup, and a film of grease floated on the surface of the milk.

# 3

Every night, until daybreak, Zeshka sits in the little kitchen where special food is prepared for the babies and the sick children. Her angular face rests on her knees. Her knees are gripped in her arms, like a closed penknife. Every hour she wraps herself up in a long, rough overcoat and goes out to patrol the nursery buildings. She straightens a blanket here, closes a window there, but she does not like this new breed of children, and she feels that there is now no need for children or parents or anything but total quiet.

In between she sits on her bench, not moving, not thinking, as if in the no man's land on the frontiers of sleep. But she is not asleep. If a child cries in the night or coughs in the distance, she sniffs her way to him and touches him and says:

"Shh. That's enough, now."

Or: "That's enough, now. Quiet."

And to herself she says:

"So be it."

Ever since that day, long ago, when Dov Sirkin left his family and his kibbutz, Zeshka has been growing bitter. She speaks ill of the kibbutz and of certain individuals in particular. We do our best to be patient. When her eldest son, Ehud, was killed in a ferocious reprisal raid, we stood by her and guarded her against the threat of insanity. We would come in turns to sit with her in the evening hours. We sent her to a craft training course. And when it occurred to her to demand without shame that we allow her to serve as a regular night watchman, relieving her of all other duties, we did not insist on our principles but said: All right. By all means. You are a special case, and we have decided to grant your request. But please bear in mind . . . and so on.

If Samson had chosen to die with a wild shriek rather than a groan of resignation, Zeshka would certainly have nodded her head and said, "Right," or "That's it." But Samson chose to die quietly, and Yosh sipped the drink that she prepared for him and left without saying more, without telling one of his stories from the old days. Sometimes he would stay for a while and even tell jokes. Tonight he came, drank, and went out into the darkness.

And then, until the light of morning, the jackals.

Outbursts of weeping, outbursts of laughter, sometimes you would think a child was being burned alive next door. And sometimes it sounds as if lustful men are clinging to a loose woman, pushing her this way and that and scratching and tickling her until she shrieks and laughs and they groan and then even Zeshka smiles and says to herself:

"Yes, that's right."

At five or at five-fifteen, when the sky grows pale and a ghostly luster appears on the mountains in the east, long before sunrise, Zeshka goes to her room to sleep. On the way she pauses in the younger members' quarters, knocks loudly on Geula's door, and shouts:

"Time to get up. It's well after five. Good morning. Get up!"

Geula Sirkin, the surviving child of Zeshka and Dov, wakes up in hatred and rises to wash her face under the cold-water faucet. She runs to the dining hall, and if anyone says, "Good morning, Geula," she may reply wearily, drowsily, "Fine. All right." When she gets to the kitchen she switches on the big urns and makes coffee for the workers. Her nails are cracked, her hands rough and scabby, and there are two bitter creases at the corners of her mouth. Her legs are thin and pale and covered with a down of black hairs. That is why she always wears trousers, never a skirt or a dress. And although she is now more than twenty years old, there are still adolescent pimples on her cheeks. She is also in the habit of reading modern poetry.

Coffee in big urns, thinks Geula, is revolting stuff. You make proper coffee in an Arabic coffeepot. Ehud did not come home on leave often, but every visit had been a delight to the unmarried girls. And sometimes to the married girls as well. He used to prepare coffee like a primeval wizard, with spells and whispered incantations. And he would laugh suddenly as if to say: What do you know, and what could you know, about the terrors of bazooka fire at close range? But he was a man of few words. He just burst out laughing and asked why they were all hanging around him, as if they had no homes to go to, as if they had nothing to do. And long before he died, his eyes were full of death. He did not leave the kibbutz, but he did not live there, either: his army service was extended from year to year, and he became a legendary figure in the army and in the border settlements; he was twenty-three years old and they gave him command of a battalion. He roamed the land in a tattered uniform and sandals, with a submachine gun plundered from the corpse of a Syrian. He took part in all the reprisal raids—he did not miss a single one. Once he set out, while suffering from a severe case of pneumonia, and blew up the police station in Bet Ajar. It was he who caught, singlehanded, in a night expedition to Mount Hebron, Isa Tubasi, the murderer of the Yaniv family from the *moshav* of Bet Hadas. When he returned from his solitary mission to Mount Hebron he said to his sister, Geula, "I killed him and six others as well. I had to."

As the coffee urns begin to steam and Geula smokes her first cigarette of the day on an empty stomach, the jackals of the valley disperse to their hiding places. The smell of Samson's blood has disturbed their night. The jackals of the valley are feeble creatures, dripping saliva, mad-eyed. They have diffident paws and quivering tails. Sometimes one of them goes mad with hunger or jubilation and breaks into the farmyard and starts biting until the watchmen shoot him. And his comrades laugh maliciously amid their bitter whining.

At one time, many years ago, Dov Sirkin would lay poisoned bait for these jackals, also little gin traps that he himself had designed and constructed. He laughs longest who laughs last, Dov Sirkin used to say. Later he got up and left the kibbutz and his family and went out to roam the land.

To his wife he said, "A man must try to leave some finger-prints that will remain after he is dead; otherwise there is no point in being born at all."

According to the orders of the general staff, our soldiers are forbidden to withdraw from enemy territory until all the wounded and the dead have been evacuated. How was it that Ehud's corpse was left in no man's land? Two commis-sions of inquiry had investigated this disgraceful episode and lessons had been learned. For three nights Ehud lay in no man's land. The enemy soldiers tried to retrieve the body so they could display it in one of their cities and thus soften the humiliation of their defeat in this and other battles. Crazed with anger and shame, Ehud's comrades thwarted the enemy's purpose with a heavy, continuous stream of fire from our frontier. The enemy forces also covered the dead man and would not let his comrades retrieve him. Night after night Ehud's comrades risked their lives, crawling into that godforsaken patch of ground, riddled with bushes and mines, but they were driven back again and again. The en-emy set up powerful searchlights and scattered the dark-ness. On the fourth night, and at the cost of six casualties, Ehud's comrades succeeded in recovering him—in spite of all the dangers, and although they had been ordered to abandon the attempt. They brought him to the camp, and from there to his home, and they said to him: Ehud, our friend, you would not have deserted us even to save your life, and we have not deserted you. Rest in peace.

But the jackals had torn his face and ruined his beau-tiful square chin. Dov Sirkin appeared at his son's funeral looking mortally ill. Zeshka did not talk to him and he did not talk to her. He tried to speak to Geula, but she did not answer.

Jet-black and frothy, the coffee bubbles in the steaming urns. Let it boil seven times, Geula Sirkin decides, a full sev-en times. Her lips are clenched. Her teeth are clenched. Her mouth is like a curved dagger.

# 4

At six in the morning the sound of engines is heard from the direction of the tractor sheds, and the kibbutz members start moving down toward the dew-drenched fields. By eight o'clock the sky is already ablaze, its color changing from blue to a dirty white. Tractors, irrigation pipes, farming implements, all metal objects become inflamed. Put out your hand to touch or to take, and the response is white-hot hatred. The rusty faucets gurgle and emit splinters of iron.

At one time, many years ago, Dov Sirkin was in charge of all the orchards. He used to sing happily, ecstatically, as, stripped to the waist, he flitted like a knife among the rows of trees, appearing at one end of the orchard, shouting to scold and encourage the pickers, then disappearing and springing up at the other end. He had powerful shoulders and a chest and trunk like a bear's: dark and dense.

Toward evening on summer days, he would wander around the orchards carrying on his shoulders a fair-haired little boy with slender, finely molded limbs, as pretty as a girl. Dov taught this boy to be ready to be tossed suddenly into the air without any warning, as high as the treetops, and to fall into his strong father's arms without a cry of fear, without a sound.

"A man needs to be strong and self-assured," he used to say, although he knew that these words were as yet beyond the child's understanding. "To murder an innocent victim is the most repulsive crime in the world. To be the innocent victim yourself is almost as bad. And you, Ehud, you're going to be a terribly strong man. So strong that nobody will be able to harm you, and you won't need to harm other people, because they won't dare start a fight. Now it's getting dark and we're going home. No, not together. You're going on your own through the wadi and I'm going a different way. You must learn not to be afraid of the dark. Yes, there are all kinds of creatures in the wadi, but they will be afraid of you if you're not afraid of them. Off you go."

The orchard is laid out in blocks, each variety divided from the next by a neat furrow. Alexander the Great apples, coarse and lacking flavor. Gallia apples. Juicy Golden Delicious. Then come the peach trees, whose fruit is furry and smells intoxicating. And dark plums, and melancholy guavas, and then another block of apple trees of the variety called Incomparable. It was Dov Sirkin who laid out the plots and planted the saplings in the early days. This orchard would never have existed had it not been for Dov Sirkin and his persistence. He argued and threatened and bullied the founders of the kibbutz into accepting his schemes, and on two occasions he made mistakes and they told him he was mad, he should give up, and twice he uprooted and replanted. Twenty years ago he left his orchard and his family and the kibbutz and went out to roam the land. He did not even take the trouble to leave a letter behind.

Generations of jackals have passed away since then, but the young ones follow the lead of their fathers, and nothing is changed. In every generation the gray open spaces are filled night after night with sounds of wailing and jubilation, with cries of impiety, malice, and despair.

After the departure of Dov Sirkin the kibbutz was filled with noisy indignation: in those days, anybody who left the kibbutz was sure to be one of the weaklings, not a central pillar. And if one of the central pillars left, before going he would address a meeting and beat the table with his fist and call a spade a spade and expose once and for all the corruption that lay hidden behind the façade, and then sit back and listen to the speeches of reply in which they told him once and for all exactly what they thought of him and his motives. But Dov slipped away without any argument, without accusations or excuses: he disappeared early one morning and did not return in the evening, or the following day. Gone.

As time passed our anger subsided. There was perplexity. There was a shrugging of shoulders: He's gone, let him go. We've known him a long time. We always knew.

Later a rumor sprung up concerning a girl from Mexico, an itinerant artist, and everything became clear. The kibbutz assumed responsibility for Zeshka and her children. It was Ehud whó, at the age of fourteen and a half, constructed with his own hands the revolving milking-drum that transformed our dairy. When he was sixteen years old, he left school and began wandering about the mountains, and at that time he may already have been in the habit of slipping across the cease-fire line and returning unscathed. He made love behind the barn to girls from the Training Corps who were four or five years older than he. When he was drafted into the army he became more settled. At the age of twenty-three he was a major, and his name was known throughout the land. Only Geula caused us concern. Zeshka, too.

Dov went first to Haifa, where he worked on the docks to save a little money—he had sixty-two piasters in his pocket when he left the kibbutz. From Haifa he went to the Novomeisky mineral works on the shores of the Dead Sea. And from there he traveled to places both in Israel and abroad, and we lost track of him. In recent years—and this we know from a first-hand source—Dov Sirkin has settled in Jerusalem and become a geography teacher in the lower classes of a secondary school. His first heart attack forced him to slow down. After the second he gave up teaching and stayed at home. His face has turned very gray.

# 5

Dov Sirkin was sitting in his home. It was night. He sat in his chair motionless and erect, not blinking, not yawning. He sketched with firm lines.

Two o'clock in the morning. An unshaded yellow electric light burned overhead. A flake of plaster drifted down from the ceiling and landed on an old wooden chair. Dov's room was meticulously tidy. Every object lay in the exact spot where Dov had decided to place it, two years before the Declaration of Independence. Despite its precise order, the room seemed to be filled with a strident and unruly herd of piebald furniture. There was chaos in the combination of incongruous objects: the contrast between light, transparent curtains and an antique chest of drawers, an oval table dating from the years of Jerusalem's Sephardic aristocracy and a dark wardrobe with legs carved in the shape of weird prehistoric creatures. In the middle of all this was a garish, flowery bedspread, colored red and blue and made of lingerie silk. A heavy chandelier hovered above the chaos. In the corner of the room a large flowerpot sent out twisted snakes of cactus in all directions, and in the center, at an ornate desk with gold and silver fittings, Dov Sirkin sat and sketched.

He laid down the compass and picked up a ruler. He put the ruler back in its place and began sharpening his pencil. He pressed too hard, breaking the point twice. Dov decided some compromise was necessary. From a heap of colored pencils he picked out a red and a black.

Many years before Dov had been a laborer in the port of Haifa, then a factory foreman, a trooper in His Majesty's Bedouin Cavalry, an arms dealer in Latin America on behalf of the Jewish underground, a staff officer in the War of Independence, a development consultant in the Negev, and finally a teacher of geography, which in those days still retained its literal meaning of "drawing the Earth."

He sat leaning forward with bowed head. His face cold, as if sparingly made, each detail for a purpose. There was a parsimonious look on his features, a pure, concentrated parsimony, without any element of avarice or enjoyment. Only his eyebrows were on a lavish scale, as if mocking the square forehead in whose folds they grew. His pencil squeaked on a page torn from a mathematics notebook.

And silence, the silence of a desolate suburb of Jerusalem at a desolate hour of the early morning, roaming the streets outside and plucking needles from the tops of the pine trees in the gardens. The plucked needles rustled softly, the sound penetrating the sealed shutters, penetrating bones. Cats bristled with fear on the balcony rails in the darkness. Dov turned his head to look at the door:

All right. Closed. Locked.

Then a faraway jackal let out a short bark, like the leader of an orchestra who is the first to tune his strings. Many years had passed since Ehud's one and only visit to this place: there was some youth congress in Jerusalem, or it may have been a camp for archeology enthusiasts, and the young man found out the address for himself and came and stayed for two days. That is, he appeared after midnight with a girl, smiled at his father wearily, and said that he would explain everything in the morning; then they both immediately fell asleep in their clothes. When Dov woke up at six o'clock the next morning, they had gone, and there was just a note saying, "Thanks a lot. Be seeing you. P.S.: everything's OK." The next night he arrived with two girls. He also brought some ancient pieces of pottery. Until three o'clock in the morning he worked at repairing a leaking hot-water pipe in the bathroom, and then he went out to join the girls, who were in their sleeping bags on the balcony. In the morning he was gone, leaving no trace besides the pipe that he had repaired.

Four years later they met briefly and by chance in Beersheba, and Ehud half-promised to come again to visit him. "Some night in the summer," he said. "I'm taking these miserable clods out for training in the Adullam hills, trying to turn alley cats into tigers. And I'm sure you'll be surprised if I turn up some time in the middle of the night to visit you and take a shower." Dov did not believe this promise and hardly expected to hear footsteps at night during the next summer. At the end of that summer Dov Sirkin received a personal letter of condolence from the commander of the paratroopers, and among other expressions of eulogy appeared the words "Happy is the father." He shook his head and decided to concentrate on his drawing and dispel these random thoughts. He was tired, but steeped in self-discipline. The churches behind the walls of the Old City, across the border in the Kingdom of Jordan, began to converse, in the language of bells, with the churches of Bethlehem, also on the alien side of the truce line. The bells of Bethlehem chimed in reply: Yes, here, yes, here He was born. And the bells of East Jerusalem sang: And here He died and here He arose.

# 6

Dov put down the black and red pencils. With the aid of his compass he drew a neat semicircle. Then he picked up the blue pencil and sketched for about a quarter of an hour without a break.

On the paper a gigantic port took shape. Its blue water flowed from his gray eyes to his fingers and through them to the pencil, which swallowed up the squares on the paper until almost the whole of the page was covered with blue. The jetties of Dov's harbor were broader than the broadest jetties, the piers longer than any ever built by human hands, and the cranes more massive than the greatest cranes in the world. And the warehouses were as tall as the silence poking its dark fingers through the cracks in Dov Sirkin's shutters. A complex of highways, connecting roads, bridges, tunnels, and approach routes writhed like a nest of snakes. Yellow machines spewed out giant sparks. Steel platforms and rubber conveyor belts were sketched in, capable of unloading whole mountains of merchandise from colossal ships. All in meticulous architectural perspective, in matching scale, lunatic fire trapped in the amber crystals of mathematics. If the greatest ship in the world were enticed to lay anchor between Dov's quays in his harbor of the Jerusalem night, this ship would look like a beetle crawling on an elephant's tusk.

The blue pencil shaded in the whole of the bay and then delicately scattered water into a network of canals. A stranger's footsteps sounded on the stairs outside. Somebody leaned heavily on the banister. There was a creak. And silence.

Dov leapt up from his seat, rushed to the window, and checked the bolts of the shutters. They were screwed down. In the cracks the empty street appeared. Beam upon beam of desolate starlight stretched across the street, from rooftops to balcony rails, from garbage cans to the crowns of cypress trees, from the Municipal Information Bureau to the telephone booth, from the top of the stone steps to the cracks in the sidewalk. A silent crust covered the earth, and a blue vapor came down. Or dew.

Another fragment of plaster fell from the ceiling, larger than the first. Tiny flakes of whitewash were scattered over the bedspread that resembled the intimate clothing of a loose woman. The footsteps on the staircase ceased. Perhaps the stranger was now on the first floor. There was silence, no sound of a key turning in a lock, or of a bell ringing.

He must be standing motionless, examining the peeling doors and perhaps taking in the names of the residents on the mailboxes. Dov clenched his teeth. His jaws tensed like a fist. He stood up, hid his plan of the port of Jerusalem in the antique chest of drawers, and returned to the writing desk. He ripped out a fresh sheet of graph paper, sat down, and started to draw a picture-map of a mountainous land.

# 7

He was a gray man: gray eyes, face, and hair. But he almost invariably chose to wear a blue shirt of the kind favored by young athletes, and sandals of biblical style. Hidden beneath his shirt was a strong and hairy torso, crisscrossed with sinews. At first sight he seemed still in his prime, and he had the build of a stevedore. Only his heart was weak, but this was not evident to the eye. In the autumn he would be sixty years old.

He sketched the map of a mountainous land. A green police patrol car raced down the street, ripping the silence apart, and then silence returned and sewed up the breach with a cool, dreamy hand. The patrol car receded southward, toward the steep alleyways at the approaches to the railway station. On three sides the truce line encircled the city of Jerusalem. To the north and east of this line a different Jerusalem brooded. And to the south lay Bethlehem and, farther still, the godforsaken hills of Hebron, and at their feet, forever, the desert.

Dov drew a land of black basalt hills. To these hills he gave sharp snow-capped peaks tall enough to pierce the embroidered-silk screen of the stars. He drew monsters of rock, sharp daggers of stone, summits like drawn swords. And wild ravines cleaving the vaulted ranges. Here and there were ominous overhangs, threatening at any moment to hurl primeval cataracts of smashed rock down into the abyss. Canyons and gorges carved out in drunkenness. Brooding labyrinths and volcanic caves, the menace of a different silence.

At last he stopped drawing and stared at the page. His

jaws were gray. He took a red crayon and began to write in the altitudes of his peaks. The foothills of these mountains could have laughed the summits of the Alps to scorn.

# 8

Driven by hunger and cold, perhaps by regret, one of the jackals of Bethlehem began to weep bitterly. At once he was answered by jackal packs from the heights of Bet Zafafa, from Zur Bahar, from the hill of Mar Elias, in an outburst of perverted laughter and malice. The wind stopped blowing, as if listening with rapt attention.

The stairs creaked again. A thrill passed through his body. His fingers turned pale. Heavily the stranger climbed another step, then another, and a third, coughed, and then paused. And again the stillness of death descended on the house, on the street, and on the city. This time Dov ran into the kitchen. Close the window. Seal the lattice. Keep the light on.

Until a few years before he had been teaching geography to a junior class of the national secondary school. Hundreds of pupils had passed through his hands over the years. They used to respect his grayness and obey his gray voice. Rumors proliferated among them and passed from generation to generation, rumors concerning the elderly schoolmaster who was once a leading figure in the underground and one of the founding fathers of the kibbutz movement. As they gripped the chalk his fingers looked strong and decisive. With one firm sweep of his hand he was capable of drawing a thin, straight line that no ruler in the world could have improved upon. Sometimes he would try to entertain his class: his jokes were thin, gray. Occasionally he would suddenly become animated by a sort of restrained pathos, and something would come alive in his eyes. This would be interpreted by his pupils as anger; it would fade and disappear as suddenly as it had arisen.

Two or three times a year he used to put on khaki clothes, take a bundle of maps and a smart army knapsack that always aroused envy in the hearts of his pupils, and lead a party of schoolchildren on a hiking tour. He cut a strange and almost eccentric figure in his hiking gear: tattered windbreaker with many pockets and buckles, tall walking boots, a rather antiquated firearm that he called a Tommy gun. With his pupils from the intermediate classes he would often climb to the heights of the hills of Naphtali, and with his senior students he used to cross over Little Crater to the Scorpion's Path and beyond, to the Meshar.

Once, during one of these trips, Dov's party was held up in Beersheba. A representative of the Military Authority told them to change their route and not to pass through the Desert of Paran. For security reasons. In a general sense; he did not go into details. The officer was thin and tall, curly-haired, barefoot and taciturn, his uniform disgracefully casual. It was four years since Dov had seen this young man. Four years before the young man had come to Jerusalem for some congress or other and had spent two nights in Dov's apartment. The first night he arrived with a girl whom he did not even bother to introduce to his father, and the second night there were two girls with him. Dov remembered the beauty of these girls, the softness of their voices, the muffled laughter from the sleeping bags in the early morning. Now he did not know what words he could use, or if the proper words even existed. His pupils pressed around him and the thin officer, and he found nothing to say.

"Anyway," said Ehud casually, drawling as if too lethargic to move his lips and speak intelligibly, "anyway, as far as I'm concerned the best thing you can do is turn around and go home. We've got enough problems as it is. We don't need schoolkids and teachers here. Still, seeing as you've got this far, you may as well go on a little farther. Head straight for Eilat, sing your "Southward Ho!" songs there, and go home. Don't waste any time on the way."

The teacher let his shoulders droop. He was taller and more powerfully built than the arrogant officer. In the days of the War of Independence he had been a staff officer in the Negev, with the rank of lieutenant colonel. But at that moment he could not speak of these things to his pupils or to the drowsy youth who stood before him chewing something, perhaps gum, perhaps his tongue.

"I know," he murmured, "you don't need to tell me. I

know." The Beersheba sun drew sweat from every pore of his body. "I know this terrain much better than you do. I was fighting here in the Negev when you were so high."

"OK," said the curly-haired officer, "fine, OK, just don't start giving me your memoirs now. If you know the terrain, you can stop wasting my time. I've got too many tourists making nuisances of themselves. Good-bye."

"Just a moment," said Dov angrily, "one moment, please. Listen. In my day they would have cleared the area of terrorists within twenty-four hours. What's the matter with you people? You let infiltrators stroll around the Negev as if it were the Baghdad bazaar. What have you got to be so arrogant about? Why don't you do something, instead of chasing girls?"

The schoolchildren were stunned. Even Ehud was taken aback. He turned. The ghost of a smile passed over his lips and disappeared.

"Pardon?"

"It's just ... what I meant was, perhaps we could talk about this, just the two of us. Not now. Why don't you drop in some time? Why not, really?"

"Why not? Some night in the summer," he said. "I'm taking these miserable clods of mine out for some training in the Adullam hills. Making tigers out of alley cats. That would be a real shock for you, wouldn't it, if I turned up some time in the middle of the night to take a shower at your place and sleep for a couple of hours."

Later, when the summer was over, Dov's request was granted, and he was allowed to take a last look at the lean and tousled officer. Something about him had changed. The pride of those casual lips had disappeared. Little night predators had eaten half his face.

In the course of every one of these trips Dov Sirkin would raise his voice—only slightly—and give a brief and fluent lecture on terrace cultivation in Galilee, or on the export of minerals and merchandise to Africa and Asia through the Red Sea Straits. His eyes were as sharp as the needle of a compass. At times he would suddenly halt the bored and weary party, point to a silent ruin, and tell a story. Or he would show the hikers an innocent-looking mound

and say: There is a mystery hidden here. Sometimes in the
desert he would sniff out the skeleton of a camel, a hyena,
or a jackal. Or a spring that an inexperienced traveler would
be unable to find even if he was dying of thirst twenty paces
from it.

After such trips Dov Sirkin used to ask the Hebrew
teacher to lend him the notebooks in which the pupils had
described their expedition—a thousand versions of a thousand trifling details. Even in the most mundane account Dov
would find something of interest. Sometimes he even took
the trouble to copy items from his pupils' essays into his
own journal, before returning the notebooks to the Hebrew
teacher and the journal to the bottom drawer of the brown
Berlin-style chest of drawers.

Geula used to come once a year, on the eve of Independence Day. After the festival she would always return to the
kibbutz. Throughout the night and the morning after, she
would sit by herself on Dov's little balcony, watching with
trembling lips the fireworks erupting in the Jerusalem sky
and in the sky above the mountains and the desert, listening
to the loudspeakers blasting out their message far away in
the main thoroughfares of the city, chain-smoking as she
watched the young people singing their festive songs. She
called her father Dov. She never talked to him about herself,
or about her mother and brother. She spoke sometimes
about Ben-Gurion, about the politics of moderation and restraint as opposed to the politics of revenge and summary
retaliation. Altermann she considered a very Polish poet, incorrigibly in love with the tools of power, in love with death.
Dov tried hard to engage her in conversation, to understand,
to influence, but Geula asked him not to disturb her as she
listened to the dance music from Terra Sancta Square and
imagined the distant revelry. At the funeral Dov said to her,
"You must, you must believe me when I say that I had no
idea. How could I have known?"

She did not answer but moved away from him. Her eyes
were dry. Her teeth were clenched. And her mouth was like
a curved Arabian sword.

After that she stopped visiting him and never again appeared in Dov's apartment in Jerusalem.

# 9

Dov completed his sketch of the mountainous country and began to draw a raging river unlike any other river on the face of the earth. He carved out a huge canal, added a series of tributary waterways, and laid out a complicated network of gradients, slopes, dams, reservoirs, and lakes, complete with measurements. He also drew up an intricate scheme for calculating angles of incline, tolerance of road surfaces, pressure of water against the stress capacity of the dam, strength of rock, stability of the subsoil beneath lakewater, pressure of currents and winds, accumulations of eroded sand. About an hour earlier the sound of footsteps on the staircase had stopped. Now it returned. Somebody was treading the stairs, slowly, very heavily, leaning on the creaking old banister. The heart attack had come near the end of the school year. Between the first attack and the second there had been solid months of extreme discomfort and horrific nightmares: he was alone in the desert, alone on a raft in the middle of the ocean, alone in an airplane without any idea of how to handle the controls or how to land or avoid crashing into the mountains that drew closer by the second. Dov decided to give in. He retired from teaching and shut himself away in his room. There was nobody to interfere with his daily and nightly routine: light meals, a slow and pensive walk, the evening paper, music, working at his desk until daybreak, morning sleep, and at midday, yogurt, bread, and a cup of lemon tea.

He lived on a pension. In addition to this, he sometimes took original and perhaps artistic landscape photographs, which he would send to one of the weekly magazines. But these pictures were almost invariably printed on inferior paper and appeared at the bottom of page sixteen, between the recipes and crossword solutions. All that was left of their beauty was a smudgelike stain and a caption such as, "Monastery in the village of Ein-Kerem at evening, photographed by Sirkin."

All these photographs find their way eventually into

Zeshka's massive old album. Week by week, one by one, she cuts the smudged pictures out of the magazine, sticking them with thick homemade paste to the black pages of her album. As she works her eyes sparkle with a kind of delight. And wrinkles of cold cunning converge around her sunken eyes. Behind her back we call her by the unkind nickname Owl.

Every morning, after finishing his night's work and before going to bed, Dov Sirkin would stand at the window and gaze out eastward, watching the sun climb up from beyond the mountains of Moab, casting white flames on the surface of the Dead Sea, thrusting its rays like spears into the flanks of the bare mountains, striking down without mercy on the walls of shaded monasteries, heavy with bells. The day would begin.

At midday, after waking up, after tea, bread, yogurt, and olives, he would sit on his little balcony among potted cacti and dead houseplants, watching the street. The street was curved, with stone walls, gardens, rusty iron latticework at every window. And a long line of garbage cans along the sidewalk. Toward evening he used to go out for a walk, and in the course of his stroll he would sometimes photograph some unexpected scene. The charm of the approaching night, the distant cries of children, a radio blaring in a neighboring house, all of these contributed to a sense of peace. He ate supper at a small cooperative café: eggplant salad, fried egg with pickled cucumber, yogurt, and café au lait.

At night he sketched. All the drawers of his cupboard were crammed with drawings and photographs, plaster models, detailed arithmetical calculations regarding the properties of raw materials, development costs, building techniques, mechanical equipment, manpower, synchronized schedules for construction and communication projects, integrated systems, geometrical and architectonic principles expressed numerically and in diagrams. There were also timetables for trains faster than the fastest trains in existence, winding railways plunging into giant tunnels, carved out of the bedrock of imaginary lands. Avenues of a thousand fountains bathed in dazzling light, crossroads of dream cities that never were and could never be. Exquisite

spires of tall cities rising beyond the line of the mountain
peaks and looking down on the bays of the sea, blue rollers
breaking on the threshold of silence.

# 10

At four o'clock in the morning the wind began to walk the
streets. It plucked the lid from a rusty garbage can and
tossed it against the asphalt road and the stone steps.

Light, brisk footsteps approached the door of the apartment. For two hours the stranger had been loitering between
the ground floor and Dov's apartment. Now he suddenly began to hurry. He was running, racing up the stairs two at a
time. He had no time to spare. What's the matter, where's
the fire, Dov grumbled.

He stood up and stumbled to the door, his shoulders
drooping.

Many years before, Dov used to seal the shutters of his
little room on the edge of the kibbutz, closing the window
and the curtain, shutting the stillness into the room and the
night with its darkness outside. He would sit on the carpet
and build a tower of bricks for his children: raising it higher
and higher, laughing, making jokes, laying brick upon brick
until it reached his waist, reached his shoulders, with the
children watching in disbelief and starting to gasp and giggle
in anticipation, and sure enough, in the end there was always an avalanche. From the sofa came the sound of Zeshka's knitting needles, calmly going about their business. And
the smell of coffee and the smell of children washed spot-
lessly clean. Outside, beyond the walls, the shutters and the
curtain, the jackals were crying piteously. Geula laughed
and Ehud laughed and Dov, too, would smile a neat smile to
himself as if saying: Good.

The jackals are pathetic creatures, dripping saliva and
mad-eyed. Their footsteps are soft and their tails quiver.
Their eyes shoot out sparks of cunning or despair, their ears
prick up, their mouths hang open and their white teeth flash,
spittle and foam drip from their jaws.

The jackals circle on tiptoe. Their snouts are soft and moist. They dare not approach the lights of the perimeter fence. Around and around they shuffle, mustering as if in readiness for some obscure ritual. A ring of jackals prowls every night about the circle of shadows that encloses the island of light. Till daybreak they fill the darkness with their weeping, and their hunger breaks in waves against the illuminated island and its fences. But sometimes one of them goes insane and with bared teeth invades the enemy's fortress, snatching up chickens, biting horses or cattle, until the watchmen kill him with an accurate volley from medium range. Then his brothers break into mourning, a howl of terror and impotence and rage and anticipation of the coming day.

Day will come. Or night.

Slowly, like black-robed priests in a ceremony of mourning, they will approach the young man's corpse in no man's land. With agile steps, as if caressing, not treading, the dust of the earth. With dripping muzzles. First they will form a circle, at a distance, and sniff softly. Then one of them will approach the body and bend down, probing with the tip of his snout. A lick, or a final sniff. Another will advance and rip open the tunic with razor-sharp teeth. A third and a fourth and a fifth will come to lap his blood. Then the first will give a low chuckle. The oldest jackal will cut himself a portion with his gleaming curved teeth. And then the whole pack will roar with laughter.

An everlasting curse stands between house dwellers and those who live in mountains and ravines. It happens sometimes in the middle of the night that a plump house-dog hears the voice of his accursed brother. It is not from the dark fields that this voice comes; the dog's detested foe dwells in his own heart. "Ehud," said Dov, and he gripped the doorknob.

First there was a light cough. Then a shudder. Great weariness. A shivering fit. A shuffling of feet. Sit down. Lie down. Fall. The pain was sharp and persistent, like a Latin monk repeating and repeating a thousand times the same obscure verse.

The jackal pack of the Bethlehem hills gave a laugh. Their laughter ran through the empty streets of the night, Ramat Rachel, Talpiot, Bakah, the German Colony and the Greek Colony, Talbiah, and like a monkey the laughter climbed the gutters of the house and penetrated inward in a thousand jagged splinters. When the kibbutz was founded we believed that we really could turn over a new leaf, but there are things that cannot be set right and should be left as they have been since the beginning of time. I said, There are things that man can do if he wants them with all his heart. But I did not know that there is no point in leaving a fingerprint on the face of the water. I am the last, my child, and I am not laughing.

# 11

The first cracks appeared in the east, above the Mount of Olives and between the two towers. A light-shunning bird let out a shriek of hatred. Stealthily some pale-red force arrived and slipped through the chinks in the eastern shutter. Flocks of birds began frantically ripping the silence.

And then it was day. Kerosene sellers began to sing. Children with satchels appeared on their way to school. Yellow smells arose from vegetable stands. Newspaper vendors proclaimed the great tidings. A minister's car appeared in the street, its tires squealing on the asphalt. Shop after shop opened up, folding iron shutters like winking eyes.

Around a stall laden with antiques stood a crowd of rosy-cheeked tourists. There was excitement. Among the knickknacks on the stall were sacred pictures on parchment screens, all of fine craftsmanship, genuine leather, strong and ancient, declared Rashid Effendi.

How sublime are the distant bells of the monasteries. How contemptible, how savage and irreverent are these jackals, answering the pure message of the bells with their twisted laughter. Malice inspires them, incorrigible malice, malice and sacrilege.

1962

# The Trappist Monastery

## 1

In the autumn the provocations intensified. There was no longer any reason for restraint. Our unit was ordered to cross the border at night and raid Dar an-Nashef.

"Tonight a nest of murderers will be wiped off the face of the earth," our commander declared in his deep, calm voice, "and the whole Coastal Plain can breathe freely." The men replied with a great cheer. Itcheh shouted loudest of all.

The whitewashed huts of the base camp looked clean and cheerful. Already the busy supply men were grappling with the steel doors of the armory. Mortars and heavy machine guns were brought out from the darkness into the light and laid in neat rectangles on the edge of the parade ground.

The last rays of the sun were fading in the west. Soon there was no dividing line between the peaks of the mountains to the east and the cloud banks that stooped over them. A small group of staff officers, wrapped in windbreakers, were conferring around a map that was spread out on the ground and held down by a stone at each corner. They were studying the map by the light of a pocket flashlight, and their voices were muffled. One man suddenly left the group and went bounding off toward the operations room: Rosenthal, thin and always immaculate; rumor had it that he was the son of a well-known candy manufacturer. Then a voice was heard calling out in the darkness, "Itamar, come on, it's getting late." And another voice replied, "Go to hell. Leave me alone."

The battalion paraded in readiness for the sortie. On the edge of the square, facing the combatants who meandered sleepily into position in ragged ranks of three, stood a noisy group of general-duty men. They did not look sleepy; on the contrary, they were feverishly excited, talking in whispers, pointing with their fingers, giggling in shame or malice. Among them was a medical orderly named Nahum Hirsch who was forever scratching his cheeks; he had shaved in a hurry and his skin smarted with irritating little wounds. He took off his glasses and, staring at the combat troops, made a joke that was lost on his fellow orderlies. Nahum Hirsch rephrased the joke. They still did not find it funny, perhaps it was too subtle for them to understand. They told him to shut up. So he kept quiet. But the night would not keep quiet; it began to resound with all kinds of different noises. From a distant orchard we heard the sound of an irrigation pump, throbbing as if dividing time itself into equal symmetrical squares. Next the generator began its dull persistent hum, and along the perimeter fences of the camp the searchlights were switched on. The parade ground, too, was suddenly floodlit, so that the soldiers and their weapons suddenly appeared pure white.

Far away, on the foothills of the eastern mountains, rose the beam of the enemy searchlight. It began wandering nervously, aimlessly, across the sky. Once or twice the trails of falling stars were caught in this beam and their light was swallowed by its glare. The combat troops huddled over their final cigarettes. Some had already taken a last deep gulp of smoke and were stubbing out the butts on the rubber soles of their heavy boots. Others tried hard to smoke slowly. A convoy of trucks with dimmed lights moved to the edge of the square and stopped there, engines still running. The commander said: "Tonight we shall obliterate Dar an-Nashef and bring a bit of peace to the Coastal Plain. We shall operate in two columns and with two rear-guard parties. We shall try to cause a minimum of civilian casualties, but we won't leave a stone standing in that nest of murderers. Every man is to act precisely in accordance with his instructions. In the event of any unforeseen development, or if any man gets cut off from the rest, then use the brains that God gave you and I've sharpened for you. That is all. Take care. And I don't want anyone drinking cold water when he's sweating. I promised your mothers I'd take care of you. Now, let's get going."

The squad answered him with a clicking of buckles on shoulder straps. Without any further signal, all began jumping lightly up and down in place, listening for any tinkling of metal or splashing of water in a canteen that had not been properly filled. Then a group of general-duty men walked between the lines, carrying tin pots full of soot. They passed from soldier to soldier, and each dipped his finger in the soot and smeared it on his cheeks, forehead, and chin: if the light of the enemy's searchlights should catch their faces as they crawled on their stomachs toward the objective, the soot would prevent their sweating skin from giving them away. To Nahum Hirsch, the medical orderly, the procedure looked like some primeval initiation ritual, and the men carrying soot were like priests.

The battalion began trudging toward the trucks. The girls swooped upon them: clerks, typists, and nurses, all handing out candy and chewing gum. Itcheh flung his bearlike arms around the waist of Bruria, the adjutant, swung her through the air in a wide circle, and roared, "Make sure our cognac's ready, girls, or you won't get any pretty souvenirs!"

There was laughter. And silence again.

Nahum Hirsch wanted to boil over with anger or disgust, but laughter got the better of him and he laughed with the rest of them and he was still laughing to himself as the soldiers began climbing aboard the trucks that waited for them with lights dimmed.

# 2

And then the enemy threw up into the sky three nervous flares, red, green, and purple. Dar an-Nashef crouched there at the foot of the eastern mountains, chewing its fingernails in fear. All its lights were extinguished. The darkness of guilt or of terror brooded over its cottages. Only the beam of the searchlight rose from it, probing the sky as if the danger lay there. At that very moment our reconnaissance party was making its way through the dense orchards toward the crossroads that were to be blocked against enemy reinforcements.

The general-duty men, those who never took part in any raid and for that reason were dubbed by Itcheh Les Misérables, began crowding around the trucks, staring awkwardly at the combat troops. They tried to cheer them up with jokes. Nahum Hirsch put his arm around little Yonich, then clapped him twice on the shoulder and whispered, "A sheep in wolf's clothing, eh?" It was supposed to sound ironical, but his voice betrayed him, and the words rang with venom.

Yonich was not one of the combat troops but a general-duty man. He was a refugee from Yugoslavia, a gloomy little survivor who served the men of our unit from behind the canteen counter. Sometimes they called him the Biscuit Brigadier. His face was deformed, set in a permanent grimace. The right side of his mouth was always smiling as if he found everything endlessly funny; the left was as grim as death. Some said that the Germans had twisted his face once and for all in some labor camp or in the selection process. Or perhaps it was the Yugoslav partisans who had broken his chin or his jaw with a punch, telling him to stop getting on their nerves with his Jewish misery.

Why had they decided this time to put little Yonich, of all people, into the task force, and authorize him to join in the raid against Dar an-Nashef? Perhaps they saw him as a sort of mascot. His little body looked ludicrous, almost pathetic, in the straps of the tattered harness. Evidently one of the officers had seen some kind of subtle humor in putting Yonich in the task force. He was to serve as personal runner to the unit commander, keeping close to him throughout the progress of the battle and ready to leap up when necessary and run to the commanders of the back-up troops, keeping communications going. He had been told: "You're going to have to run like hell, pal. Imagine that the biscuits are here and the customer's over there, and at the same time there's somebody waiting for soda and somebody else who wants cigarettes and matches."

Nahum Hirsch said: "Yonich, you're going into battle like Samson's little brother, and you don't understand that they're just treating you as a joke. Lucky that the Arabs can't see who's coming to beat the shit out of them."

Yonich turned around, and Nahum saw the twisted half-smile and then the front teeth protruding from the cleft lips. And he stepped back.

At that moment the tank engines suddenly started up beside the pine grove, and the earth shook. These tanks would not participate directly in the raid against Dar an-Nashef but were to be deployed in the mountain passes to anticipate any possible development, however remote. The roar of the mighty engines set all hearts pounding. The signal was given and the convoy set out toward the mouth of the wadi. There the troops would be ordered down from the transports and would set out on foot to cross the dense orchards, then march over the frontier and to the outskirts of Dar an-Nashef from the northwest and the southwest. The girls waved their hands, bidding them good-bye and good luck.

Nahum left the parade ground. He sat down at the foot of a whitewashed eucalyptus tree. Little fragments of whitewash fell from the tree trunk, and some of them stung his sweating brow. As always, his thoughts turned to men and women, and not to the other creatures of which the night is full. The sounds of the night came and dispersed his thoughts.

# 3

Our unit could boast of a distinguished commander and many daring officers, but Itcheh was our pride. He was a king. It was not only Bruria who loved him and bore everything in silence. We all did. He loved to pinch everybody, the soldiers, the girls, Bruria herself. She would say, "You're disgusting, stop that," but these words always came from her lips warm and moist, as if she were really saying, "More, more!" And he loved to insult her and even to humiliate her in the presence of the entire battalion, from our commanding officer to the last of the general-duty men, Yonich or Nahum Hirsch or somebody of that sort. He used to scold Bruria, telling her to leave him alone, stop running after him all day, and come to him only at night, stop clinging to him as if she were his mother or he were her father: he'd had enough, he was sick of her.

When his insults were more than she could bear, she would sometimes go to the operations room to seek consolation from Rosenthal, the operations officer. Let them tell Itcheh, let him be jealous, she didn't care, he deserved it. Rosenthal did not treat her as Itcheh did. He was not the type to fling up her skirt or thrust his hand inside her blouse when there were drivers and supply men standing around. His courting manners were like something out of a film, and he often tried to impress her by speaking English with a slight American accent. He was slim and athletic, he dressed immaculately, and his compliments were as deft as his tennis shots. Often, when he sat with Bruria in the operations room, he would translate for her into Hebrew the contents of the pornographic magazines that his brother had brought from Europe. But he did not dare touch her, or perhaps he did not want to; if ever he did touch her, it was gently and courteously. In the end she always came back to Itcheh, chastened, moaning and servile, almost begging for punishment, and everything was as before. The whole battalion was waiting for the day when Itcheh's jealousy would explode and there would be a showdown with the soft-spoken operations officer. In fact, Itcheh surprised us and showed not the slightest hint of jealousy; he only laughed and told Bruria to go to blazes, to leave him alone, he was sick of her and he was sick of them all and why did she hang around him all day.

After every reprisal operation Itcheh's name was heard in high military circles. Twice he was seen in newsreels, and once his picture appeared on the cover of the army magazine. It was he who discovered the Viper's Path, leading from the south of Jerusalem across the desert of Judea and through enemy territory to Ein Gedi on the shores of the Dead Sea in one night's march. It was he who settled a long-standing account with the Bedouins of the tribe of Arab al-Attata. The Divisional Commander himself once described him as the spiritual brother of the warriors of King David in Adullam or of the Gideonites and Jephthahites. In the course of one raid he leapt, alone, into a cave where dozens of enemy soldiers were entrenched. He so terrified them with his ferocious, blood-curdling yells that they melted away before him as he darted among the murky rifle pits throwing in hand grenades. Petrified by astonishment or horror, the enemy troops gave themselves up, as if mesmerized, to the bursts of fire from his machine gun. Alone he entered the cave and alone he emerged from it, panting and disheveled, roaring and waving his gun above his head.

Itcheh let his beard grow wild. The hair on his head was thick and matted and seemed always to be full of dust. His beard began at his temples and almost met his thick eyebrows, flowing down over his cheeks and neck and merging without a break into the bear's fur that covered his chest and arms and perhaps the whole of his body.

Sometimes Itcheh surprised Nahum Hirsch in the tin shower hut. The medical orderly would dry himself in a hurry and leave without bothering about the soap bubbles left in his armpits. For it was well known that Itcheh always made a point of humiliating the supply men and the drivers and the orderlies, his greatest admirers, those whom he called Les Misérables. Yet he would sometimes astonish them with an act of unexpected generosity. He would give one of them a pistol taken from a dead Syrian officer, or he would take one of the supply men aside and talk to him as an equal, chatting about politics and girls and striking the poor fellow dumb with his frankness.

Between the men's and the women's shower there was a thin partition of patched tin. The general-duty men had punched peepholes here and there, and they used to spend hours in the shower hut, especially on weekends. Itcheh loved to press his huge naked body against the partition until the tin began to creak and groan. On the other side of the partition the girls responded with squeals of fright or anticipation. Then Itcheh would roar with laughter and all those present on both sides of the wall would join in his laughter. Once it happened that Itcheh sprained his ankle on the camp soccer field. He limped to the clinic and surprised Nahum Hirsch as the young man was cutting nude pictures out of a foreign magazine. Nahum probed the twisted ankle to make quite sure that it was a sprain and not a fracture. Itcheh was his usual carefree self. Even when the young man's fingers groped higher up the leg and his whole body shook, still Itcheh continued to joke and he noticed nothing. Then Nahum fitted an elastic bandage on the ankle joint and stretched it mercilessly. Itcheh let out a low moan of pain but still he seemed not to suspect anything. Finally Itcheh smiled, thanked the orderly for the treatment, and held out his hand. Nahum put his fingers into the huge hand. Itcheh began to squeeze his fingers with fearful pressure. Wave upon wave of pain, pride, and pleasure flowed around the base of the young orderly's spine. Itcheh intensified his grip still further. Nahum abandoned himself to the sweet ripples of pain, but on his face there was only a polite smile as if to say: I only bandaged your ankle because it was my duty. Then Itcheh relaxed his hold and released Nahum's hand. He said, "Perhaps we'll decide to take you on the next raid. The time has come to make you a combat orderly. Eh?"

The sweet smell of chewing gum was wafted over Nahum's face, and he found nothing to say.

Of course Itcheh had forgotten this promise, and perhaps he was in the habit of throwing similar promises around among the general-duty men. They had chosen little Yonich, of all people. Now, at this very moment, he was running around bent double in the clinging darkness, or perhaps crawling on the ground, half of his face grinning foolishly and the other half like a stone carving. Still complete silence, not a sound to be heard. Only crickets and jackals and faint music from a radio in the living quarters. There is still time.

# 4

A dense night breeze came and stirred the treetops. The shower of whitewash fragments grew. Nahum was overcome by the kind of weariness that follows despair. Suddenly he noticed that unconsciously he had been snapping small twigs between his fingers.

The enemy searchlight was still raking the sky. Even the conquered earth kept sending out waves of clinging warmth, heavy with fragrance.

Light footsteps approached. Nahum knew those footsteps. He stood up and pressed himself against the trunk of the eucalyptus. He lay in wait in the darkness, allowing a crazy hallucination to take control of him. When she passed in front of him, he leapt out from his hiding place and blocked her path. She let out a low cry of fear. But at the same moment she recognized him.

"Hey," said the orderly in a low voice.

"Out of my way, cut it out," she said. "Don't be childish."

"He's going to be wounded," said Nahum sadly and patiently.

"Idiot," said Bruria.

"He's going to be wounded tonight. Seriously wounded."

"Let me pass. I don't want to see you or listen to you. You're mad."

"He's going to be wounded seriously, but he won't die. I promise you that he won't die."

"Go away. Go to hell."

"Are you angry? I'm going to save him myself; you shouldn't be angry with me—this very night I'm going to save his life."

"You're a joke. Stop running after me. Don't say things

like that to me. I didn't tell you to follow me. Get out. I didn't
give you permission to enter this room. Get out, go away, or
I'll call the sergeant major. Get out of here or you'll be in
trouble."

Nahum followed her movements with a look of longing.
She switched on the light, nervous and distracted, began
sorting out some papers that were scattered on the chair and
the table, pushed something away under the cupboard, and
sat down on the unmade camp bed, her face to the wall
and her back to him.

"Are you still here? What do you want from me? Tell
me, what have I done that makes people like you come here
and cause trouble? Get out. Leave me alone. You men make
me sick."

"You've insulted me twice in less than ten minutes,"
said Nahum Hirsch, "but I won't hold that against you, not
tonight. I'm going to save his life."

Bruria said: "Any minute now, Jacqueline will be back.
If she comes in and finds you here you'll regret it. I don't
even know who you are. You're Nahum the orderly. OK, Nahum the orderly, get out of here, now."

Suddenly Nahum ripped off all the buttons of his khaki
shirt with a wild, hysterical movement, and the girl pressed
herself against the wall, her hand over her mouth, her
eyes wide open and terrified. She was speechless. Nahum
pointed to his thin, bare chest.

"Now watch carefully," he whispered frantically, "look.
This is where the bullet has entered. He's taken the bullet
full in the throat. It goes in here and out there. On the way,
it cuts his windpipe. The veins are severed as well. And
blood starts to flow here, down, inside, straight into his
lungs."

His pale fingers sketched the course of the wound on his
chest, and the feverish lecture raced on.

"And from the windpipe, here, all the blood pours into
the lungs. A hemorrhage like this nearly always causes suffocation and death."

"That's enough. Shut up. Please, stop it."

"They suffocate, simply because there's no room for air
if the lungs are full of blood. Now they are bringing him in
from the field straight to me, in the clinic. His face is blue,

he's choking, vomiting blood, spitting blood, his clothes are full of blood, his beard is full of blood, his eyes have rolled up and you can only see the whites. But I don't panic. I take a knife, a rubber tube, and a pocket light, and I cut his windpipe. Like a butcher, except that I'm doing it to save his life at the last moment. I'm not looking for decorations or prizes. I save his life because we are all brothers-in-arms. Very low down I cut his windpipe—look here, watch—farther down—here. And I insert the rubber tube through the severed windpipe right into his lung. Like this."

Bruria sat upright, her neck taut, as if mesmerized, under a spell, watching the pale, nimble fingers running over the thin chest like sewing needles, as if searching for some invisible opening. She was silent. Nahum went on without a pause, his voice choking and feverish.

"Now I'm gripping the end of the tube in my mouth. I start sucking the blood out of his lungs to give him a chance to breathe, so he won't die of suffocation. Watch, sucking and spitting, sucking and spitting, not pausing for a moment, devotedly, lovingly. And watch, now I'm breathing into his lungs, like this, in-out, in-out, like saving a drowned man."

Gradually, without her realizing it, Bruria's breathing changed as well. She began to follow the rhythm of the orderly's breathing. There was a short silence.

"He's recovering now," Nahum shouted suddenly. "I can see his eyes moving. And his knees. He's showing signs of life now."

Bruria opened her mouth as if to weep or to cry out, yet she neither wept nor cried out, but went on breathing deeply.

"Now he's already breathing by himself—not through his nose or his mouth, but through the tube that I inserted in his lung. Look. Spitting blood. That's good for him. Choking. That's a good sign, too. He won't die on us now. He's going to live. Here, open his blurred eye for a moment. Look. This one. The left. Close it. Pale. Now you can go down on your knees beside the stretcher and take his hand in yours and try to talk to him. He won't be able to answer you, but perhaps he can hear you. I'm going now. Yes. Don't try to stop me, I don't need any thanks. I've done my duty. I'm going, the ambulance is honking outside and the doctor has arrived. An unknown orderly has taken it upon himself to carry out a difficult operation under field conditions and has saved the life of a national hero. Itcheh and I will embrace on the front page of the newspaper. You don't owe me anything. Far from it. You'll get married, live happily ever after. I've only done my duty. And I shall continue to love you both from a distance. Good-bye, good-bye, I'm off, I'm going, good-bye."

Nahum said good-bye, but he did not go. Instead he sank down, exhausted, on the camp bed at Bruria's feet. He began weeping softly. She placed a comforting hand on his shoulder. The room was filled with a pale, sickly light from the unshaded yellow bulb. A sheaf of blank forms lay on the top of a steel filing cabinet in the corner of the room. Here and there pieces of women's clothing were scattered; perhaps underwear, too; Nahum did not dare to look, just buried his head in Bruria's lap and rubbed his burning cheek. She stroked his hair, staring into space and saying over and over again, "That's enough, enough, enough."

The first sounds came unexpectedly, as if prematurely. Bruria had anticipated a thundering salvo, but the battle opened with tentative, stammering shots, cautious and very soft.

"The orchestra is tuning up. Soon it will start," said Nahum.

"Relax," said Bruria, "relax, little baby. You may put your head in my lap as long as you're quiet and don't talk and don't cry any more. You baby. You don't understand anything, anything at all. And what you say is all nonsense. They won't bring Itcheh back to this camp at all. They'll take him straight to the hospital, you won't have a chance. The best surgeons are standing by at the hospital tonight. No sucking blood out of lungs through a rubber tube. They have an operating room, proper instruments, and they will save Itcheh a thousand times quicker and better than you could. You're just a little boy. You don't stand a chance. Stop making me laugh. Just your head, I said, keep still, you're tickling me. Relax. Like that. Good boy. Quiet. Hush. And don't touch me. Let me see your hand. You little fledgling. Maybe Itcheh will take you along on a mission some time, and you can save each other to your hearts' content, because I've had enough now, I've had enough of all of you and I don't care what happens, I just want the time to pass. Put your glasses on the table. Yes. Now I can touch you. Relax. I'll sing you a lullaby. I can persuade Itcheh to take you on the next mission. He'll even make a combat orderly out of you. When Itcheh recovers from the wound in his throat I'll tell him that you were a good boy and you didn't want him to die and you even wanted to save his life. I shall tell him that you didn't say anything and you just lay quietly. Yes. Like this."

The big damp stains on the ceiling were like shadowy monsters. At intervals a little mouse scuttled across the room, hid between the cracks in the tiles, and then appeared again from an unexpected corner. Bruria took off her sandal and threw it at the mouse; she missed. At that moment the ominous distant sounds were renewed. Long bursts of machine-gun fire split the silence. A mortar broke into a thick, angry cough. Sounds like thunder rolled in the darkness outside.

Nahum said: "I can breathe into his lungs quickly and violently, blow him up, burst him. I can pull out the rubber tube and he'll turn blue again and suffocate. But I won't do either of those things. I'll save him if you'll just stop insulting me. And don't sing me to sleep, I mustn't sleep now, I must be ready at any moment to run to the clinic and carry out the operation and save him for you. And don't push me; I'm stronger than you. It will be a gift, and I've earned my reward by saving his life and bringing him back to you alive."

Now the long-range artillery was heard. The enemy batteries on the mountain slopes started shelling the settlements close to the border and lighting up the sky with tracer shells. The demolition squads obliterated Dar an-Nashef house by house, while the spearhead units were still burning out obstinate pockets of resistance. The thunder of the guns tore apart Nahum's pleading. "You'll be the death of me," said Bruria. She groaned and gave in. The young man streamed with sweat and his eyes rolled up. She stretched out her hands to her sides as if awaiting crucifixion and said, "At least get it over with quickly." As it turned out, these words were nqt necessary.

The frantic sound of automatic fire was scattered in all directions. Dim, faraway salvos echoed in the background. A violent explosion drowned the bursts of machine-gun fire. Gradually the sounds of the battle settled into some secret rhythm; wave upon wave of humble, diffident queries, and thick, hoarse crashes in reply. The strident wail of strings swallowed by the dizzy boom of percussion. At last this rhythm was broken, too. A glittering cataract of blazing sound rose up and roared to the dark horizons. Then the final spasmodic bursts, until they, too, died away. Silence came and pieced together the fragments with gentle, merciful patience. The orderly left the room without another word and hurried to the clinic to prepare the operating instruments that were kept in a sterile pack for use in emergency. The stillness of the night descended on the plain. Soon the crickets and the jackal packs returned to their evil ways.

# 5

Our commander said: "That was sharp and to the point. Just like in the training manuals. No problems. No obstacles. Neat as a Bach fugue. Run along now, girls, and open up a bottle of arak for the maestro."

Parched, dirty, and overflowing with husky elation, Itcheh began shooting off joyful bursts of gunfire into the sky.

"Got it!" he roared. "Got mutton, potatoes, arak, everything we need, and no more Dar-bloody-Nashef! There's not a cat left there! No cat, not even a dog! Not one son-of-a-bitch is left! Where's that whore Bruria, where is she! And all the p-r-r-retty girls, where are they!"

He suddenly stopped roaring when the orderlies dragged the corpse of Yonich off the tailboard of the truck and carried it to the lighted clinic. The body was wrapped in a dirty blanket, but Nahum turned it up for a moment and saw that the eyes were wide open in hurt surprise as if they had made a fool of him again. Even his strange smile seemed to have softened. The smiling half of his face had not relaxed, but the other half had conformed to it. Nahum turned to Itcheh.

"What have you done to Yonich?"

"Why are you looking at me, why me?" cried Itcheh self-righteously. "His name was written on the first bullet. He was killed before things even got started. A volley missed me by a couple of yards, and he was standing in the way." As he spoke, Itcheh began stripping off his belt and weapons and equipment, pulled off his crumpled shirt, and asked quietly, "Where is she, where is she hiding?"

"How should I know?" said Nahum.

"Then go and find her for me and bring her here. You've got five minutes," commanded Itcheh hoarsely and wearily. "And before you do that, get me a drink of water."

Nahum obeyed.

He poured a cup of water, handed it to Itcheh, waited till it was empty, refilled it, waited again, then rinsed the cup in the sink and ran off to look for Bruria.

Almost without hesitation he went to the place where the shadows were darkest, behind the storehouses on the hillside. There he saw Bruria, leaning against the wall. The buttons of her blouse were open, one breast protruded from her brassiere, and Rosenthal, the operations officer, was holding the nipple between two fingers and whispering playfully. But she was not laughing or moving. She stood there as if asleep on her feet or as if all was lost and there was no purpose left. This sight filled Nahum with a silent, heart-rending anguish. He did not know why; he knew only that it was all a mistake, all of it, from beginning to end. He turned and went back to Itcheh.

"She isn't here at all," he lied. "She's gone away. The two of them were seen going off in a jeep before you got back. She isn't here."

"OK," said Itcheh very slowly. "I see. He's taken her with him to Jerusalem. She could at least have waited to see if I'd been killed or not."

Nahum trembled and said nothing.

"Come on, pal," Itcheh went on, "come on. Let's find ourselves a jeep. Have you got a cigarette you can spare? No? Never mind. We'll go after them. How long ago were they seen going out? An hour? Half an hour? We'll catch them this side of the Hartuv turn. One crisis after another to-night. Come on, get in, let's go. Pity it's so late. Rosenthal can start hanging a white flag on his jeep. What did you say? I thought you said something. Come on, let's get after them. No time for coffee. Pity about that little guy. He just went out there and got himself killed. Pointless. Next time I'm not tak-ing anyone who isn't essential. The man who makes jokes about death is a bastard, the man who doesn't is a bigger bastard. Say something. Well? Nothing to say? Talk. Say something. At least tell me what your name is. I've forgotten your name. I know you work in the store, but just now I've forgotten your name. I'm tired. Hey, look how fast we're go-ing. A hundred and twenty, a hundred and thirty, at least. And we're not even at top speed yet."

The night road was deserted and cheerless. Far away, on the slopes of the eastern mountains, the night sky reflect-ed the dying flames of the ruined enemy village. And in the irrigation channels of the orchards the black water flowed noiselessly and was swallowed up in the soil of the plain.

# 6

Nahum leaned back in the worn seat of the jeep and turned to look at Itcheh. He saw only a mane of hair and a thick beard. For a moment he was reminded of his Bible classes and the prophet Elijah, wild and jealous, slaughtering the prophets of Baal on the slopes of Carmel. He, too, figured in Nahum's imagination, as a faceless giant, all beard and mane. Itcheh controlled the vehicle with sleepy violence, one hand on the wheel and the other resting wearily on his knee. His heavy body leaned forward, like that of a rider clutching at his horse's neck. Is it really possible that he se-cretly suffers from bad eyesight? The jeep tore up the road, zigzagging, screeching, and whining. Stormy gusts of wind slapped their faces with blasts of intoxicating scents from the orchards.

One after another the lights of the villages along the Coastal Plain slipped away and were hidden, hastily fleeing behind the backs of the travelers. Here and there were civilians who had left their beds and gathered beneath a lamp in the main street of their sleepy settlements, exchanging speculations and waiting for the light of the approaching day and the early-morning news broadcast, to discover the meaning of the noises in the night and of the fire reflected in the sky. Itcheh and Nahum did not pause to give explanations, nor did they slacken their speed. Once, at a dark road junction, Itcheh braked sharply at the sight of a suspicious figure standing at the roadside, wrapped in an overcoat or a blanket, as if lying in wait. Itcheh picked up the submachine gun that lay at Nahum's feet and swung the muzzle toward the figure. "What's up?" he demanded. The headlamps picked out a young man, a rabbinical student, dressed all in black. Only his face and his socks were white. The student wore spectacles and looked helpless. He gabbled something in Yiddish, and Nahum was surprised to hear Itcheh answer him in Yiddish, patiently and quietly. Then the man blessed them and they went on their way. The jeep sprang into motion, raced across the curve of the road and onward, to the edge of the incline, toward the hills of Jerusalem.

They met no one else that night.

Itcheh did not speak, and Nahum asked no questions. Quiet joy and secret longing filled his heart. He knew the truth and Itcheh did not. Itcheh was driving the jeep like a madman and he was driving Itcheh. The road began to twist. The willing jeep attacked the curves furiously, with squeals of burning hatred. Nahum asked softly:

"What kind of a man are you, Itcheh, what are you really made of?"

The sharp wind swallowed his words. Itcheh must have heard something else, for he answered a quite different question:

"From Rumania. I was born in a place very near Bucharest. You could even say it was a suburb of Bucharest. In the war we escaped to Russia and got split up there. Some died, some disappeared, and a few went back afterward to Rumania. My little sister and I traveled across Poland and Austria to northern Italy, and then Youth Aliya came and took us from there to Israel, to the young people's training farm run by the religious movement. We grew up there. There are still one or two of the family living somewhere in Russia, but I've no idea where. Not that it matters to me now."

"I suppose you'll be a professional soldier," said Nahum. "In ten years you'll be a colonel at least. And then a great general."

Itcheh glanced at the orderly in surprise.

"Not likely! In another year or so I shall be discharged. I'm saving up to buy a share in the bus cooperative, and I've got a good chance of playing center-forward for Petah-Tikva. Not now. Some time. I've still got a lot to learn. It may be there'll be professional soccer in this country one day, and then I'll be in the pink. I'll marry off my sister and live like a human being at last."

"And you haven't lived like a human being up to now?"

"Like a dog," said Itcheh with weary anger.

"Tell me, what were you saying in Yiddish to that guy?"

"I asked him what the matter was. He said he'd heard shots and was scared. I told him the Arabs should be scared, these days it isn't the Jews who need to be scared of gunfire at night. And I took half a pack of cigarettes off him in exchange for my sermon. Do you want one? No? We'll catch them this side of Castel and take care of that Rosenthal once and for all. We'll take Bruria with us to Jerusalem. Do you know Jerusalem? Will we find a café open before morning?"

"It's a dead city," said Nahum. "Everything's dead in Jerusalem at night. In the daytime, too, for that matter. Anyway, we won't catch them at Castel or anywhere else if we don't go faster. A lot faster. Rosenthal will take her to his house and straight into his bed, and we'll be standing like a pair of idiots in the dark in the middle of Jerusalem, not knowing which way to go. We'll look like Laurel and Hardy! So step on it, Itcheh, faster, fast as you can, step on it!"

Itcheh hit the accelerator furiously. The engine gathered up its last reserves of strength. The speed intensified, sullen, brooding, whining, roaring. And Nahum was filled with dread and longing. He knew where Bruria was now, and where the bastard Rosenthal was, and Itcheh did not know. He was making the mighty Itcheh race along the road in the night on a fool's errand, and Itcheh did not know. Even now he was savoring the scent of her skin, the scent of strong plain soap, and the taste of her fingers on his neck, and Itcheh did not know. He put his hand into the pocket of his shirt and fingered the instruments, the sterilized lancet, the bandages, the vial of morphine, the rubber tube, all that would be necessary for an emergency operation when the jeep plunged into a crevice at the side of the mountain road. This, too, was something Itcheh did not know and could not know. Here at his right hand sat the man who would save his life in a little while. A grim and demanding assignment, which Nahum would fulfill, to perfection. An unknown orderly has performed an operation at night by flashlight and has saved the life of a national hero. Resourcefulness. Dedication. Cool nerves. Comradeship. Expertise. Also—in a whisper, a movement of the lips without sound—love, too.

Then one of the headlights suddenly went out: it flickered a few times, hesitated, gave in, and went dark. Still the jeep galloped eastward by the light of one blazing Cyclops' eye that stunned the shadows in the hills. Like a phantom the jeep raced on, spurred to ever greater efforts at Itcheh's hands; he was hunched over the wheel, biting his lips and ramming the accelerator down to the floor hard. He will be seriously injured, Bruria, critically injured, but I won't let him die. I'll operate and I'll bandage him with devotion, and I'll disregard my own injuries. You will owe his life to me, and I shall go away humbly. Itcheh is just an ignorant, overgrown bear cub: he knows nothing, understands nothing. Listen: he's started humming to himself; he has no idea what's going to happen to him in a moment.

Perhaps Itcheh remembered the pale student whom they had met on the way up from the plain and his Yiddish entreaties. Perhaps he remembered other places and other times. He was intoning a melancholy song to himself:

> "Our Father, our King, have mercy and hear us,
> For we can do no-o-thing.
> Show us ki-indness and grace,
> And sa-ave u-us. . . ."

"Amen," whispered Nahum Hirsch fervently. And his eyes filled with tears.

Near the Shaar-Hagay junction, where the Jerusalem road touches enemy territory in the Latrun salient, the travelers were struck by a blast of cold air: the air of Jerusalem, chilling and full of the fragrance of pine. The engine began to groan, coughed hoarsely a few times, spluttered, and fell silent, silent as the lifeless things of which the night is full.

# 7

Itcheh rose from his seat, heavy and weary, and opened the hood. Nahum took out the pocket light that was to have been used for the emergency operation and trained it on the interior of the engine. He watched Itcheh grappling with the sparkplugs, blindly pulling and pushing, angrily thumping the metal panels with his fist, tightening a screw with strong fingernails, tugging at wires mercilessly, perhaps aimlessly. This only added to the insolence of the engine. Suddenly, without warning, the other headlight gave out, and the machine went dead. Itcheh snatched the torch from Nahum and hurled it with a wild gesture into the rocks at the side of the road.

"Screw everything," he said.

Nahum nodded his head as if to say: Yes, of course, absolutely. But now total darkness had descended on them, and Itcheh could not have seen this movement. Nahum used up match after flickering match. With the last match they both lit cigarettes from the pack that Itcheh had taken from the student on the way.

First Itcheh cursed the engine, then Nahum, Bruria, women in general, heaven and earth. Most of the curses were Russian and ruthless, some were Arabic. Itcheh cursed the Arabs, too, long and hard, Finally he cursed himself. Then he fell silent. His voice was hoarse from all the shouting he had done before the raid, during the battle, and after the return to camp. Now all he could manage was a pathetic, desperate croak. He settled himself on the hood of the dead jeep like a hairy mountain. And he lay there without sound or movement.

Then, when the eyes of both men had begun to adjust a little to the clinging darkness, Itcheh picked out a dark, brooding mass across the border near Latrun: the dim, straggling profile of the Trappist monastery, beyond the cease-fire line, on enemy soil.

"That's a building," Itcheh croaked faintly.

"It's a monastery," explained Nahum brightly. A burning desire to teach suddenly filled his heart. He was wide awake, far from all weariness, feverish. "It's the Trappist monastery. The monks have taken a vow to be silent forever. Till the day they die."

"Why is that?" asked Itcheh in a whisper.

"Because words are the root of sin. Without words there are no lies. It's simple, isn't it. They live there cheek by jowl and never exchange a word among themselves. Imagine what a divine silence that must be. Whoever wishes to join must take a vow. It's like an army. You swear an oath of silence."

"I can't understand it," croaked Itcheh.

"Of course you can't understand. All you can do is destroy a village without knowing anything about its people or its history, without wanting to know. Just like that. Like a mad bull. Of course you don't understand. What do you understand? Fucking and killing, that's what you understand. And soccer. And shares in the bus cooperative. You're a wild animal, not a human being. A wild, stupid animal. They're deceiving you all the time. Rosenthal fucks Bruria, so do the officers, the MPs, even someone like me. Do you think she's in Rosenthal's jeep on the way to Jerusalem? Is that what you think? Because you're a wild animal, not a human being, that's why you think they're all exactly like you. They aren't all like you. They don't all trample and kill everything that moves. The opposite. They're all laughing at you. Rosenthal is fucking Bruria for you, and he's fucking you, too. I fucked her, and now I've fucked you, too. Why did you run like a madman, tell me? Why did you grab a jeep and a submachine gun and me, and start running like a bull on the rampage? I'll tell you why. Because you're not a human being, that's why. Because you're a stupid wild animal. That's why."

Itcheh said with what was left of his voice, "Tell me more about the monastery."

Nahum Hirsch, the thin and bespectacled medical orderly, lifted his knee and rested the sole of his boot on the wheel of the jeep. He smoked and felt power throbbing in his veins like wine.

"'The dust of dead words has clung to you. Purify your soul with silence.' Rabindranath Tagore wrote that, the Indian poet and philosopher. Now, of course, I shall have to start at the beginning and explain to you what a poet is and what a philosopher is and what an Indian is. But who's got the time and patience to make a human being out of you? It's a waste of words. Anyway, it won't help you. Very well, then. Latrun takes its name from a fortress that stood here in the Middle Ages. The Crusaders built a fortress here to control the most convenient route from the Coastal Plain to Jerusalem—the Bet Horon road, that is. Latrun is a corruption of the name of that fortress: Le Touron des Chevaliers— The Tower of the Knights. *Touron* means tower. Like *tour.* La Tour Eiffel. There's a tower in chess, too. We call it *tora.* Are you asleep yet? Is that too much for one lesson? No? There are some scholars who claim another source, an even older one, for the name Latrun: Castellum Boni Latronis, meaning the castle of the good thief who was crucified with Jesus of Nazareth. Have you ever heard of the Crucifixion, of Jesus, the good thief? Have you ever read a book in your life? Answer me. What's the matter with you? Don't you feel well? Answer me!"

Itcheh said nothing.

The lights of faraway settlements twinkled in the darkness. The enemy outposts in Latrun, where news of the destruction of Dar an-Nashef must have arrived by now, pointed spasmodic searchlight beams at the thick woods that grew on the slopes of the Judean hills. A single shot, derisory almost, rolled between the hills and set up a long echo.

"Hey, isn't it a bit dangerous to stay here like this all night?" asked Nahum, suddenly afraid.

Itcheh said nothing.

"Tell me, isn't this too dangerous? Should we start

walking? Maybe there's a settlement or a kibbutz somewhere around here."

Itcheh turned his bearded face for a moment, glanced at
Nahum Hirsch, and looked away. He did not speak. Nahum
urinated behind the jeep. Suddenly he was scared, afraid of
being separated from Itcheh in the dark. He said in a clear
voice, grinding his teeth, "What a lump of shit I am! What
a miserable bastard!"

Itcheh said nothing.

Then came the first signs of the approaching day, softening the dark masses and sharpening the edges. There was
a glimmer of light in the east, like a halo, like a dream of
grace. If there are such things as mercy or grace, thought Nahum, that is their color. Bruria will go to the shower to wash
away the sweat and the tears, and then she'll sleep. They
will bury Yonich—or, as they like to say—they'll lay him to
rest. If only there were a little rest for someone like me. If
only there were rest for Itcheh; he's tired to death now. After
all, everybody needs rest. If only a little. I can't take any
more of this. I need silence.

Suddenly the voices of the jackals rose in triumph on
every side. From enemy territory the voices came, piercing
the steep wadis and spreading over the plains of the belea-
guered land. The enemy searchlights moved back and forth
haphazardly, sullenly. Now the light swept down the road
and passed the dead jeep and the two lost soldiers, now it
stopped and retraced its steps to search among the thorns
and bushes. A little night predator was caught in the shaft
of light. He froze, stunned, his hide bristling. His mangy fur
quivered with mortal terror. A moment later he darted off
and fled into the depths of the darkness.

But soon the darkness betrayed those who had made it
their refuge, fading gradually from the peaks of the eastern
hills, the lands of the enemy.

1962

# Strange Fire

*Night spread his wings over the peoples of the world. Nature spun her*
*yarn and breathed with every turn of the wheel. Creation has ears, but in*
*her the sense of hearing and that which she hears are one thing, not two.*
*The beasts of the forest stir and search for prey and the beasts of the*
*farm stand at the manger. Man returns home from his labor. But as soon*
*as man leaves his work, love and sin are digging his grave. God swore to*
*create a wo.ld and to fill the world. And flesh shall draw near to flesh ...*

—*Berdichevski,* Hiding in the Thunder

# 1

At first the two old men walked without exchanging words.

On leaving the brightly lit and overheated clubroom
they helped each other on with their overcoats. Yosef Yarden maintained a dogged silence, while Dr. Kleinberger let
out a long series of throaty coughs and finally sneezed. The
speaker's words had left them both in a state of depression:
All this leads nowhere. Nothing ever comes out of these discussions. Nothing practical.

An air of weariness and futility hung over the sparsely
attended meetings of the moderate Center Party, of which
the two friends had both been members for many years.
Nothing will ever come of these meetings. Precipitate action
is dragging the whole of the nation into an orgy of arrogant
affluence. The voice of reason, the voice of moderation, the
voice of common sense, is not heard and cannot be heard in
the midst of this jubilation. What are they to do, the few men
of sense, no longer young, the advocates of moderate and
sober statesmanship, who have seen before in their lifetime
the fruits of political euphoria in all its various forms? A
handful of men of education and good sense cannot hope to

put a stop to the intoxication of the masses and their jubi-
lant, lightheaded leaders, all of them skipping with yells of
triumph toward the abyss.

After some thirty paces, at the point where the side
street opened into one of the majestic and tranquil boule-
vards of the suburb of Rehavia, Yosef Yarden stopped, thus
causing Dr. Kleinberger to stop as well without knowing
why. Yosef Yarden fumbled for a cigarette and, after some
difficulty, found one. Dr. Kleinberger hastened to offer his
friend a light. Still they had not exchanged a single word.
With delicate fingers they shielded the little flame from the
wind. Autumn winds in Jerusalem blow strongly, ferociously. Yosef thanked his companion with a nod of his head and
inhaled smoke. But three paces farther on, the cigarette went
out, for it had not been properly lit. Angrily he threw it down
on the sidewalk and crushed it with the heel of his shoe.
Then he thought better of it, picked up the crumpled cigarette, and tossed it into a trash can that the municipality of
Jerusalem had placed on the iron pole of a bus stop.

"Degeneracy," he said.

"Well, really, I ask you," replied Dr. Kleinberger, "is
that not a simplistic, almost vulgar definition for a reality
that is by definition complex?"

"Degeneracy and arrogance, too," insisted Yosef
Yarden.

"You know as well as anyone, my dear Yosef, that a
simplistic definition is a form of surrender."

"I'm sick of this," said Yosef Yarden, adjusting his scarf
and the collar of his coat against the freezing daggers of the
wind. "I'm sick of all this. From now on I shall not mince
words. Disease is disease, and degeneracy is degeneracy."

Dr. Kleinberger passed his tongue over lips that were always cracked in winter; his eyes closed like the embrasures
of a tank as he commented:

"Degeneracy is a complex phenomenon, Yosef. Without
degeneracy there is no meaning to the word 'purity.' There
is a cycle at work here, some kind of eternal wheel, and this
was well understood by our Sages when they spoke of the
evil side of human nature, and also, on the other hand, by
the Fathers of the Christian Church: apparently degeneracy
and purity are absolute opposites, whereas in fact one

draws the other out, one makes the other possible and makes it flourish, and this is what we must hope for and trust in in this decadent age."

An arrogant wind, sharp and chilly, blew in the streets of Rehavia. The street lamps gave out an intermittent yellowish light. Some of them had been smashed by vandals and hung blind on top of their posts. Birds of the night had nested in these ruined lamps.

The founders of the Rehavia quarter planted trees and laid out gardens and avenues, for it was their intention to create amid the sun-bleached rocks of Jerusalem a pleasant and shady suburb where the piano might be heard all day and the violin or the cello at nightfall. The whole neighborhood basks beneath a cluster of treetops. All day the little houses stand sleepily on the bed of a lake of shadow. But at night dim creatures roost in the foliage and flap their wings in the darkness, uttering despairing cries. They are not so easy to hit as the street lamps; the stones miss their mark and are lost in the gloom, and the treetops whisper in secret derision.

And surely even these opposites are not simple but complex; in fact, one draws the other out and one cannot exist without the other, et cetera, et cetera. Dr. Elhanan Kleinberger, a bachelor, is an Egyptologist with a modest reputation, particularly in the European state from which he escaped by the skin of his teeth some thirty years ago. Both his life and his views bear the mark of a brilliant stoicism. Yosef Yarden, an expert in the deciphering of ancient Hebrew manuscripts, is a widower who is shortly to marry off his eldest son, Yair, to a girl named Dinah Dannenberg, the daughter of an old friend. As for the birds of the night, they roost in the heart of the suburb, but the first fingers of light drive them away every morning to their hiding places in the rocks and woods outside the city.

The two elderly men continued their stroll without finding anything further to add to the harsh words they had heard and spoken before. They passed by the Prime Minister's office on the corner of Ibn Gabirol Street and Keren Kayemet Street, passed the buildings of the secondary school, and paused at the corner of Ussishkin Street. This crossroads is open to the west and exposed to the blasts of cold wind blowing in from the stony fields. Here Yosef Yarden took out another cigarette, and again Dr. Kleinberger gave him a light and shielded it with both his hands like a sailor: this time it would not go out.

"Well, next month we shall all be dancing at the wedding," said the doctor playfully.

"I'm on my way now to see Lily Dannenberg. We have to sit down and draw up a list of guests," said Yosef Yarden. "It will be a short list. His mother, may she rest in peace, always wanted our son to be married quietly, without a great show, and so it will be. Just a modest family ceremony. You will be there, of course, but, then, to us you are like a member of the family. There's no question about that."

Dr. Kleinberger took off his glasses, breathed on them, wiped them with a handkerchief, and slowly replaced them.

"Yes. Of course. But the Dannenberg woman will not agree to that. Better not deceive yourself. She's certain to want her daughter's wedding to be a spectacular event, and the whole of Jerusalem will be invited to bow down and wonder. You will have to give in and do as she wishes."

"It isn't that easy to make me change my mind," replied Yosef Yarden. "Especially in a case where the wishes of my late wife are involved. Mrs. Dannenberg is a sensitive lady, and she is certainly aware of personal considerations."

As Yosef Yarden said that it would not be easy to make him change his mind, he began inadvertently to squeeze the cigarette between his fingers. Bent and crushed, the cigarette still did not go out but continued to flicker. Dr. Kleinberger concluded:

"You're mistaken, my friend. The Dannenberg woman will not do without the big spectacle. Certainly she's a sensitive lady, as you so admirably express it, but she's also an obstinate lady. There is no contradiction between these two qualities. And you had better prepare yourself for a very tough argument. A vulgar argument."

A mutual acquaintance, or perhaps one whose silhouette reminded the two friends of a mutual acquaintance, passed by the street corner. Both put their hands to their hats, and the stranger did the same but pressed on without stopping, hurrying, head bowed, against the wind. And he vanished in the darkness. Then a hooligan roared past on a motorcycle, shattering the peace of Rehavia.

"It's outrageous!" fumed Yosef Yarden. "That dirty gangster deliberately opened up his throttle, just to disturb the peace of ten thousand citizens. And why? Simply because he's not quite sure that he's real, that he exists, and this buffoonery gives him an inflated sense of importance: everybody can hear him. The professors. The President and the Prime Minister. The artists. The girls. This madness must be stopped before it's too late. Stopped forcibly."

Dr. Kleinberger was in no hurry to reply. He pondered these words, turning them this way and that during a long moment of silence. Finally he commented:

"First, it's already too late."

"I don't hold with such resignation. And second?"

"Second—yes, there is a second point, and please pardon my frankness—second, you're exaggerating. As always."

"I'm not exaggerating," said Yosef Yarden, teeth clenched in suppressed hatred. "I'm not exaggerating. I'm just calling the child by his name. That's all. I've got the cigarettes and you've got the matches, so we're tied to each other. A light, please. Thank you. A child should always be called by his name."

"But really, Yosef, my very dear friend, but really," drawled Dr. Kleinberger with forced didactic patience, "you know as well as I do that usually every child has more than one name. Now it's time to part. You must go to your son's future mother-in-law, and don't you be late or she'll scold you. She's a sensitive lady, no doubt about that, but she's hard as well. Call me tomorrow evening. We can finish that chess game that we left off in the middle. Good night. Take the matches with you. Yes. Don't mention it."

As the two elderly men began to go their separate ways, the children's shouts rose from the Valley of the Cross. Evidently the boys of the Youth Movement had gathered there to play games of hide-and-seek in the dark. Old olive trees make good hiding places. Sounds and scents rise from the valley and penetrate to the heart of the affluent suburb. From the olive trees some hidden current passes to the barren trees, which were planted by the landscape gardeners of Rehavia. The night birds are responsible for this current. The weight of responsibility infuses them with a sense of deadly seriousness, and they save their shrieking for a moment of danger or a moment of truth. In contrast, the olive trees are doomed to grow in perpetual silence.

# 2

Mrs. Lily Dannenberg's house lies in one of the quiet side streets between the suburb of Rehavia and her younger and taller sister, the suburb of Kiryat Shemuel. The hooligan who shattered the peace of the entire city with his motorcycle did not disturb the peace of Mrs. Dannenberg, because she had no peace. She paced around the house, arranging and adjusting, then changing her mind and putting everything back in its original place. As if she really intended to sit at home and quietly wait for her guest. At nine-thirty Yosef means to come over to discuss with her the list of wedding invitations. This whole business can bear postponement; there is no need for haste. The visit, the wedding, and the list of guests, too. What's the hurry? In any case, he will arrive at nine-thirty precisely—you can count on him not to be a second late—but the door will be closed, the house empty and in darkness. Life is full of surprises. It's nice to imagine the look on his face—surprised, offended, shocked as well. And nice to guess what will be written on the note that he will certainly leave on my door. There are some people, and Yosef is one of them, who when they are surprised, offended, and shocked become almost likable. It's a sort of spiritual alchemy. He's a decent man, and he always anticipates what is good and fears what is not.

These thoughts were whispered in German. Lily Dannenberg switched on the reading lamp, her face cold and calm. She sat in an armchair and filed her fingernails. At two minutes to nine her manicure was complete. Without leaving her chair she switched on the radio. The day's reading from the Bible had already finished, and the news broadcast had not yet begun. Some sentimental, nauseatingly trite piece of music was repeated four or five times without variation. Lily turned the tuning knob and passed hurriedly over the guttural voices of the Near East, skipped over Athens without stopping, and reached Radio Vienna in time for the evening news summary in German. Then there was a broadcast of Beethoven's *Eroica.* She turned the radio off and went to the kitchen to make coffee.

What do I care if he's offended or shocked? Why should I care what happens to that man and his son? There are some emotions that the Hebrew language isn't sufficiently developed to express. If I say that to Yosef or his friend Kleinberger, the pair of them will attack me, and there'll be a terrific argument about the merits of the Hebrew language, with all kinds of unpleasant digressions. Even the word "digression" does not exist in Hebrew. I must drink this coffee without a single grain of sugar. Bitter, of course it's bitter, but it keeps me awake. Am I allowed one biscuit? No, I'm not allowed to eat biscuits, and there's no room for compromise. And it's already a quarter past nine. Let's go, before he appears. The stove. The light. The key. Let's go.

Lily Dannenberg is a forty-two-year-old divorcee. She could easily claim to be seven or eight years younger, but that would be contrary to her moral principles, so she does not disguise her true age. Her body is tall and thin, her hair naturally blond, not a rich tint but deep and dense. Her nose is straight and strong. On her lips there is a permanent and fascinating unease, and her eyes are bright blue. A single, modest ring seems to accentuate the lonely and pensive quality of her long fingers.

Dinah won't be back from Tel Aviv before twelve. I've left her a little coffee in the pot for tomorrow morning. There's salad in the fridge and fresh bread in the basket. If the girl decides to have a bath at midnight, the water will still be hot. So everything is in order. And if everything's in order, why am I uneasy, as if I've left something burning or open? But nothing is burning and nothing's open and already

I'm two streets away heading west, so that man Yosef isn't likely to meet me by chance on his way to the house. That would spoil everything. Most young Levantines are very attractive at first glance. But only a few of them stand up to a second look. A great spirit is always struggling and tormented, and this distorts the body from within and corrodes the face like a rainstorm eating limestone. That is why people of spiritual greatness have something written on their faces, sometimes in letters that resemble scars, and usually they find it hard to keep their bodies upright. By contrast, the handsome Levantines do not know the taste of suffering, and that is why their faces are symmetrical, their bodies strong and well proportioned. Twenty-two minutes after nine. An owl just said something complicated and raucous. That bird is called *Eule* in German, and in Hebrew, I think, *yanshuf.* Anyway, what difference does it make? In exactly seven minutes, Yosef will ring the doorbell of my house. His punctuality is beyond doubt. At that precise moment I shall ring the doorbell of his house on Alfasi Street. Shut up, *Eule,* I've heard everything you have to say more than once. And Yair will open the door to me.

# 3

A person who comes from a broken home is likely to destroy the stability of other people's homes. There is nothing fortuitous about this, although there is no way of formulating a rule. Yosef Yarden is a widower. Lily Dannenberg is a divorcee whose ex-husband died of a broken heart, or jaundice, less than three months after the divorce. Even Dr. Kleinberger, Egyptologist and stoic, a marginal figure, is an aging bachelor. Needless to say, he has no children. That leaves Yair Yarden and Dinah Dannenberg. Dinah has gone to Tel Aviv to pass the good news along to her relatives and to make a few purchases and arrangements, and she will not be back before midnight. As for Yair, he is sitting with his brother, a grammar-school student, in the pleasant living room of the Yarden household on Alfasi Street. He has decided to spend the evening grappling with a backlog of university work: three exercises, a tedious project, a whole mountain of bibliographical chores. Studying political economy may be important and profitable, but it can also be wearisome and depressing. If he had been able to choose, he might have chosen to study the Far East, China, Japan, mysterious Tibet, or perhaps Latin America. Rio. The Incas. Or black Africa. But what could a young man do with studies such as these? Build himself an igloo, marry a geisha? The trouble is that political economy is full of functions and calculations, words and figures that seem to disintegrate when you stare at them. Dinah is in Tel Aviv. When she comes back, perhaps she'll forget that unnecessary quarrel that we had yesterday. Those things I said to her face. On the other hand, she started it. Dad has gone to see her mother, and he won't be back before eleven. If only there was some way of persuading Uri to stop sitting there picking his nose. How disgusting. There's a mystery program on the radio at a quarter past nine called *Treasure Hunt*, broadcast live. That's the solution for an uncomfortable evening like this. We'll listen to the program and then finish the third exercise. That should be enough.

The brothers switched on the radio.

The antics of the night birds do not abate until a quarter past nine. Even before the twilight is over, the owls and the other birds of darkness begin to move from the suburbs to the heart of the city. With their glassy dead eyes they stare at the birds of light, who rejoice with carefree song at the onset of the day's last radiance. To the ears of the night birds, this sounds like utter madness, a festival of fools. On the edge of the suburb of Rehavia, where the farthest houses clutch at the rocks of the western slope, the rising birds meet the descending birds. In the light that is neither day nor night the two camps move past each other in opposite directions. No compromise ever lasts long in Jerusalem, and so the evening twilight flickers and fades rapidly, too. Darkness comes. The sun has fled, and the rear-guard forces are already in retreat.

At nine-thirty, Lily had meant to ring the doorbell of the Yardens' house. But at the corner of Radak Street she saw a cat standing on a stone wall. His tail was swishing, and he was whining with lust. Lily decided to waste a few moments observing the feverish cat. Meanwhile the brothers were listening to the start of the mystery program. The first clue was given to the studio panel and the listeners by a jovial fellow; the beginning of the thread was contained in a song by Bialik:

> Not by day and not by night
> Quietly I set out and walk;
> Not on the hill or in the vale,
> Where stands an old acacia tree ...

And at once Yair and Uri were on fire with detective zeal. An old acacia tree, that's the vital point. Not on the hill or in the vale, that's where it starts getting complicated. Yair had a bright idea: Maybe we should look the poem up in the big book of Bialik's poetry and find the context, then we'll know which way to turn. He pounced on the bookcase, rummaged around, found the book, and within three minutes had located the very poem. However, the lines that followed did not solve the puzzle, but only tantalized the hunters still further:

> The acacia solves mysteries
> And tells what lies ahead ...

Yes. I see. But if the acacia itself is the mystery, how can it be expected to solve mysteries and even tell the future? How does it go on? The next stanza is irrelevant. The whole poem's irrelevant. Bialik's no use. We must try a different approach. Let's think, now. I've got it: the Hebrew word *shita* isn't only the name of a tree. It also means "method." *Shita* is a system. These inquiries would do credit to that buffoon Kleinberger. Well, then, let's think some more. Shut up, Uri, I'm trying to think. Well, my dear Watson, tell me what you make of the first words. I mean "Not by day and not by night." Don't you understand anything? Of course you don't. Think for a while. Incidentally, I don't understand it yet, either. But give me a moment, and you'll see.

The doorbell rang.

An unexpected guest stood in the doorway. Her face

was set, her lips nervous. She was a weird and beautiful woman.

An alley cat is a fickle creature; he will abandon anything for the caress of a human hand. Even at the height of rutting fever he will not turn away from the caress of a human hand. When Lily touched him, he began to shudder. With her left hand she stroked his back firmly, while the fingers of her right hand gently tickled the fur of his neck. Her combination of tenderness and strength filled the animal with pleasure. The cat turned over on his back and offered his stomach to the gentle fingers, purring loudly and contentedly. Lily tickled him as she spoke.

"You're happy. Now you're happy. Don't deny it, you're happy," she said in German. The cat narrowed his eyes until two slits were all that was left, and continued purring.

"Relax," she said, "you don't need to do anything. Just enjoy yourself."

The fur was soft and warm. Thin vibrations passed through it and ceased. Lily rubbed her ring against the cat's ear.

"And what's more, you're stupid as well."

Suddenly the cat shuddered and stirred uneasily. Perhaps he guessed or half-sensed what was coming. A yellow slit opened in his face, the wink of an eye, a fleeting glimmer. Then her fist rose, made a wide sweep in the air, and struck a violent blow at the belly of the cat. The creature took fright and leapt away into the darkness, collided with the trunk of a pine tree, and dug in his claws. From the murky height he hissed at her like a snake. All his fur stood on end. Lily turned and walked to the Yardens' house.

"Good evening, Yair. It seems you're free. And on your own."

"Uri is here and we . . . but isn't Dad on his way to see you?"

"Uri here, too. I'd forgotten about Uri. Good evening, Uri. How you've grown! I'm sure all the girls must be chasing you. No, you needn't invite me inside. I just came to get something straight with you, Yair. I didn't mean to intrude."

"But Mrs. . . . but Lily, how can you say that. You're always welcome. Come in. I was so sure that just now you'd be at your house drinking coffee with Dad, and suddenly . . ."

"Suddenly your dad will find the door locked and the windows dark, and he won't understand what's become of me. He's disappointed and worried—which makes him look almost agreeable. Pity I'm not there among the trees in the garden, secretly watching him, enjoying the expression on his face. It doesn't matter. I'll explain everything. Come on, Yair, let's go out, let's go for a little walk outside, there's something I need to straighten out with you. Yes. This very evening. Be patient."

"What . . . Has something happened? Didn't Dinah go to Tel Aviv, or . . ."

"She went like a good little girl, and she'll come back like a good little girl. But not until later. Come on, Yair. You won't need your coat. It isn't cold outside. It's pleasant outside. You'll have to excuse us, Uri. How you've grown! Good night."

In the yard, near the pepper tree, she spoke to Yair again: "Don't look so puzzled. Nothing serious has happened."

But Yair already knew that he had made a mistake. He should have brought his coat, in spite of what Lily had said. The evening was cold. And later it would be very cold. He could still excuse himself, go back, and fetch his coat. Lily herself was wearing a coat that was stylish, almost daring. But to go back to the house for a coat seemed to him somehow dishonorable, perhaps even cowardly. He put the thought aside and said:

"Yes. It's really pleasant out here."

Since she was in no hurry to reply, Yair had time to wonder if there really were acacia trees in Jerusalem, and if so, where, and if not, perhaps *shita* should be taken as a clue to the verb *leshatot*—"to jest." Who knows, maybe the treasure's hidden in one of the wadis to the west or the south of Rehavia. Pity about the program. Now I'll never know the solution.

# 4

After a brief moment of astonishment and confusion and a few indecisive speculations, Yosef Yarden made up his mind to go to Dr. Kleinberger's house. If he found him at home he would go in, apologize for the lateness of the hour and the unexpected visit, and tell his friend about this strange incident. Who would have thought it? And just imagine the look she would have given me if I had been a few minutes late. And there I was, standing and waiting, ten o'clock already, two and a half minutes past. If something had happened to her, she would have phoned me. There's no way of understanding or explaining this.

"And for the time being you have avoided a vulgar and possibly painful argument," said Elhanan Kleinberger, smiling. "She wouldn't have given in to you over the guest list. She'll send invitations all over the city, all over the university. To the President of the State and the Mayor of Jerusalem. And really, Yosef, why should you expect her to give up what she wants in deference to what you want? Why shouldn't she invite the Pope and his wife to the wedding of her only daughter? What's the matter, Yosef?"

His guest began to explain, patiently:

"Times are not easy. In general, I mean. And remember, all these years we have been preaching, both in speech and in writing, the need to 'walk humbly.' Yair's mother wanted an intimate wedding, a small circle of relatives, and that is a kind of imperative, at least from the ethical point of view. And ... then there's the cost. I mean, who wants to go into debt for the sake of a society wedding?"

Dr. Kleinberger felt that he had lost the thread. He made coffee, set out milk and sugar. And at this point he also took the opportunity to add something to his previous remarks concerning the interplay of opposite extremes. The conversation soon diversified. They discussed Egyptology, they discussed Hebrew literature, they conducted a scathing inquiry into the workings of the municipality of Jerusalem. Elhanan Kleinberger has a great flair for linking together Egyptology, his professional field, and Hebrew literature, which is his heart's love, as he puts it, and of which he is a passionate lover, as he also puts it. In general, Yosef is used to having his views overruled by those of his friend, although he tends on most occasions to reject the particular wording adopted by Elhanan Kleinberger. So their arguments end with the last word going to Yosef Yarden and not to his old friend.

Were it not for the cold, the two friends would have gone out together to stand on the balcony and gaze at the starlight on the hills, as was their habit in summer. The Valley of the Cross lies opposite. There old olive trees grow in bitter tranquillity.

In passionate, almost violent hunger, the olive trees send out their tendrils into the blackness of the heavy earth. There the roots pierce the rocky subsoil, cleaving the hidden stones and sucking up the dark moisture. They are like sharpened claws. But above them the green and silver treetops are caressed by the wind: theirs is the peace and the glory.

And you cannot kill the olive. Olive trees burned in fire sprout and flourish again. A vulgar growth, quite shameless, Elhanan Kleinberger would say. Even olives struck by lightning are reborn and in time clothe themselves with new foliage. And they grow on the hills of Jerusalem, and on the modest heights on the fringes of the Coastal Plain, and they hide away in the cloisters of monasteries enclosed within walls of stone. There the olives thicken their knotted trunks generation after generation and lasciviously entwine their stout branches. They have a savage vitality like that of birds of prey.

To the north of Rehavia lie sprawling suburbs, poor neighborhoods with charming streets. In one of these winding alleyways stands an old olive tree. One hundred and seven years ago an iron gate was erected here and the lintel was supported by the tree. Over the years the tree leaned against the iron, and the iron bit deep into the trunk like a roasting spit.

Patiently the olive began to enfold the iron wedge. In the course of time it closed around it and set tight. The iron was crushed in the tree's embrace. The tree's wounds healed over, and the vigorous foliage of its upper branches was in no way impaired.

# 5

Yair Yarden is a young man of handsome appearance. He is not tall, but his shoulders are powerful and his torso is trim, well proportioned, and athletic. His chin is firm and angular, with a deep dimple. Girls secretly long to touch this dimple with their fingertips, and some of them even blush or turn pale when they feel the impulse. They say, "And what's more, he thinks he knows a thing or two. He's about as brainy as a tailor's dummy."

His arms are strong and covered in black hair. It would be wrong to say that Yair Yarden is clumsy, but there is a certain heaviness, a kind of slow solidity, perceptible in all his movements. Lily Dannenberg would have called this "massivity" and returned to her theme of the inadequacy of the Hebrew language, with its dearth of nuances. Of course, Elhanan Kleinberger is capable of refuting such barbed comments and of suggesting in the twinkling of an eye a suitable Hebrew adjective, or even two. And at the same time he will come up with a Hebrew expression to fit the word "nuance."

It may be that this fascinating "massivity" with which Yair Yarden is endowed will change within a few years into the patriarchal corpulence for which his father is noted. A sharp eye may detect the first signs. But at present—Lily has no intention of disguising the truth—at present, Yair is a handsome, captivating youth. The mustache gives a special force to his appearance. It is blond, droopy, sometimes flecked with shreds of tobacco. Yair is studying economics and business management at the university; his whole future lies before him. Romantic follies, kibbutzim, and life in border settlements hold no attraction for him. His political views are temperate; he has learned them from his father. To be precise, Yosef Yarden sees in the political situation a wasteland of degeneracy and arrogance, whereas Yair sees a wide-open prospect before him.

"Will you offer me a cigarette, please," said Lily.

"Of course. Here you are. Please take one, Lily."

"Oh, thank you. I left mine at home, I was in such a hurry."

"A light, Lily?"

"Thank you. Dinah Yarden—a name almost as musical as Dinah Dannenberg. Perhaps a little simpler. When you have a child you can call him Dan. Dan Yarden: like something out of a ballad about camels and bells. How much time are you going to give me, how long will it be, before you make me a grandmother? A year? A bit less? You needn't answer. It was a rhetorical question. Yair, how do you say 'rhetorical question' in Hebrew?"

"I don't know," said Yair.

"I wasn't asking you. It was a rhetorical question."

Yair began scratching the lobe of his ear uneasily. What's the matter with her? What's she up to? There's something about her that I don't like at all. She isn't being sincere. It's very hard to tell.

"Now you're searching for something to say and not finding it. It doesn't matter. Your manners are perfect, and for heaven's sake, you're not in front of a board of examiners."

"I wasn't thinking of you as a board of examiners, Lily. Not at all. I mean, I . . ."

"You're a very spontaneous boy. And quick and witty replies don't matter to me. What interests me is, rather, your . . . how shall I put it, your *esprit.*" And she smiled in the dark.

Chance led them to the upper part of the suburb. They reached the center of Rehavia and turned north. A passerby, thin and bespectacled, definitely a student of extreme views and crossed in love, passed in front of them with a transistor radio in his hand. Yair paused for a moment and turned his head, straining to catch a fragment of the fascinating program that Lily had interrupted. Not on the hill or in the vale, where stands an old acacia tree. Thanks to her he had gone out of the house without a coat, and now he was cold. He did not feel comfortable, either. And he had missed the climax of the program. Time to get to the point, and get it over with.

"Right," said Yair. "OK, Lily. Are you going to tell me what the problem is?"

"Problem?" She seemed surprised. "There's no problem.

You and I are going for a stroll on a pleasant evening because Dinah has gone away and your father isn't at home. We are talking, exchanging views, getting to know each other. There are so many things to talk about. So many things that I don't know about you, and there may even be things that you would like to know about me."

"You said before"—Yair scratched his ear—"you said there was something that you—"

"Yes. It's just a formality and really quite unimportant. But I would like you to sort it out as soon as possible. Let's say tomorrow or the day after, at the latest by the beginning of next week."

She put out her cigarette and refused the offer of another.

Many years ago a famous architect sketched the plan of Rehavia. He wanted to give it the character of a quiet garden suburb. Narrow shady lanes like Alharizi Street, a well-tended boulevard called Ben-Maimon Avenue, squares like Magnes Square, full of the pensive murmur of cypresses even at the height of summer. An enclave of security, a sort of rest home for fugitives who have suffered in their lives. The names of great medieval Jewish scholars were given to the streets, to enrich them with a sense of antiquity and an air of wisdom and learning.

But over the years, New Jerusalem has spread and encircled Rehavia with a noose of ugly developments. The narrow streets have become choked with motor traffic. And when the western highway was opened and the heights of Sheikh-Badar and Naveh Shaanan became the heart of the city and the state, Rehavia ceased to be a garden suburb. Demented buildings sprouted on every rock. Small villas were demolished and tenements built in their place. The original intentions were swept away by the exuberance of the new age and the advance of technology.

The nights give back to Rehavia something of its plundered dreams. The trees that have survived draw a new dignity from the night and sometimes even act like a forest. Weary, slow-moving residents leave their homes to stroll at dusk. From the Valley of the Cross a different air arises, and with it a scent of bitter cypresses and night birds. It is as if the olive groves rise up and come into the lanes and the courtyards of houses. By electric light, book-laden shelves appear through the windows. And there are women who play the piano. Perhaps their hearts are heavy with longing or desire.

"That man on the other side of the street, the one feeling the sidewalk with his stick," said Lily, "that's Professor Shatski. He's getting old now. I don't suppose you knew Professor Shatski was still alive. I dare say you thought he was something out of the last century. Perhaps you'd have been right. He was an elegant and venomous man who believed in mercy, and in his writings he demanded mercilessly that all men show mercy to all men. Even the victim should show mercy to his killer. Now he's blind."

"I've never heard of him," said Yair. "He isn't exactly in my field, as they say."

"And now, if I may just ask for one more cigarette, let's talk about your field, as they say."

"By all means. Take one. I'm curious to know about the formality that you started talking about before."

She narrowed her eyes. Tried hard to concentrate. Remembered moments of pain that she had lived through long before this clumsy cavalier was born. She felt a momentary nausea and almost changed her mind. But after a while she said:

"It has to do with an examination. I want you to have a medical examination as soon as possible, certainly before we announce the wedding officially."

"I don't understand," said Yair, and his hand stopped halfway to his ear. "I don't understand. I'm a hundred percent fit. Why do I need an examination?"

"Just a screening examination. Your mother died of a hereditary disease. Incidentally, if she had been examined in time, she might have lived a few years longer."

"I had a physical two years ago, when I started at the university. They said I was as healthy as an ox. I know very little about my mother. I was young then."

"Now, Yair, don't go making a big fuss over a little examination, OK? There's a good boy. Just for my peace of mind, as they say. If you knew any German, I'd make you a present of all the economics books that Erich Dannenberg left me. He's someone else that I'm sure you don't remember. A new leaf, as they say. I shall have to think of some other present for you."

Yair said nothing.

As they walked up Ibn Ezra Street, they were confronted by an elegantly dressed old woman.

"There is a personal link that joins all creation. God is angry and man does not see it. One meaning to all deeds, fine deeds and ugly deeds. They that walk in the darkness shall see a great light. Not tomorrow—yesterday. The throat is warm and the knife is sharp. To all of creation there is one meaning."

Yair moved away from the madwoman and quickened his pace. Lily paused for a moment without speaking, then caught up with him. A poisonous, twisted sort of expression spread over her face like a disease. And then passed. In Jerusalem they called the elegant woman "One Meaning." She had a startlingly deep voice and a German accent. From a distance the madwoman of Rehavia blessed the two who were walking by:

"The blessing of the sky above, and the blessing of the water beneath, from Düsseldorf to Jerusalem, one meaning to all deeds, to those that build and those that destroy. Peace and success and full redemption to you and to all refugees and sufferers. Peace, peace, to near and far."

"Peace," replied Lily in a whisper. From there until they reached the Rothschild School, not a word was said. Yair was humming or murmuring to himself, "Not by day and not by night . . ." and then he stopped.

Lily said, "Let's not quarrel over this examination, even though it may sound to you like a whim. Your mother died only because of negligence, and as a result your father was left alone again and you became an orphan."

Yair said, "All right, all right, why make an issue of it?" Then, with a slow realization, he began to see the significance of something she had said. He put his tongue to the edge of his mustache, caught a fragment of tobacco, and said:

"Again? Did you say that my father was left alone again?"

Now Lily's voice had a cold and authoritative sound to

it, like that of a clerk at an information counter:

"Yes. Your father's second wife died of cancer when you were six. Your father's first wife did not die of cancer; she left him. She was divorced. Soon you will be a married man yourself, and it's time your father stopped hiding elementary facts from you as if you were still a child."

"I don't understand," said Yair, hurt. "I don't understand—you say my father was married before?"

In his puzzlement he raised his voice beyond what was appropriate to the time and place. Lily was anxious to restore things to their proper level.

"Your father was married for four months," she said, "to the woman who later married Erich Dannenberg."

"That's impossible," said Yair.

He stopped. He took out a cigarette and put it between his lips but forgot to light it. Then for a moment he forgot his companion and forgot to offer her a cigarette. He stared into the darkness, deep in thought. At last he managed to say:

"So what? What has that got to do with us?"

"Be a dear," Lily said, smiling, "and give me another cigarette. I left mine at home. You're right. I myself find it hard to believe that there ever was, or could have been, such a marriage. I myself can hardly believe what I've just told you. But you should know, and you must learn what there is to be learned from that episode. Now, please light the cigarettes, mine and yours. Or give me the matches and I'll light them. Don't let it upset you. It happened in the past. A long time ago. And it lasted less than four absurd months. It was just an episode. Come on, let's walk a little farther. Jerusalem is wonderful at this time of night. Come on."

Yair began to follow her northward, lost in thought. And she was filled with a savage joy. A car honked and she ignored it. A night bird spoke to her and she did not answer. She watched her shoes and his on the sidewalk. And she took the lighter from his distracted fingers and lit both the cigarettes.

"And I was never told anything about it," said Yair.

"Well, you've been told now. That's enough. Relax. Don't get yourself all worked up," said Lily warmly, as if to console him.

"But it's ... it's so strange. And not very nice, some-how."

She touched the back of his neck. Caressed the roots of his hair. Her hand felt warm and comforting to the boy. They walked on, out of Rehavia and into the neighboring quarter. The winding streets became sharp-angled alleyways. And there in front of them was the olive tree, embracing and crushing the iron gatepost.

# 6

Elhanan Kleinberger and Yosef Yarden were engrossed in their game of chess. A lamp styled in the shape of an old Ba-varian street lamp shed a dim light on the table. On the bind-ings of the scholarly books danced gold letters which gave back a light still dimmer than the one they took from the lamp. All around stood Dr. Kleinberger's bookshelves, set out along the length and height of the walls of the room, from floor to ceiling. One special shelf was devoted to the Egyp-tologist's stamp albums. Another was reserved for Hebrew literature, Elhanan Kleinberger's secret love. In the few spaces among the rows of books there were African minia-tures, vases, primitive statuettes of a crudely erotic style. But these statuettes also served as vases, holding colored paper flowers that never wilted.

"No, Yosef, you can't do that," said Dr. Kleinberger. "In any case, you have no choice now but to exchange your knight for my rook."

"Just a moment, Elhanan, give me a chance to think. I still have a small advantage in this game."

"A temporary advantage, my friend, a temporary ad-vantage," replied Dr. Kleinberger playfully. "But think, by all means. The more you think, the better you will appreciate just how temporary your advantage is. Temporary and irrel-evant." He leaned back comfortably in his armchair.

Yosef Yarden thought hard: Now I must concentrate. What he says about the weakness of my position is just tactics in a war of nerves. I must concentrate. The next move will decide the game.

"The next move will decide the game," said Dr. Kleinberger. "Should we call a ten-minute break and have a cup of tea?"

"A Machiavellian suggestion, Elhanan, and I don't hesitate to call the child by his name. A diabolical suggestion designed to upset my concentration, and you have succeeded in doing that already. Anyway, the answer is: no, thank you."

"Did we not say before that every child has more than one name, Yosef? We were talking about that only two or three hours ago. It seems that you have already forgotten our conversation. Pity."

"I have already forgotten what I was intending to do to you. To your rook, I mean. You've succeeded in distracting me, Elhanan. Please, let me concentrate. Look, so. Yes. I am here and you are there. What do you say to that, my dear doctor?"

"For the time being I don't say anything. All that I will say is: let's break off for a moment and listen to the news. But after the news I shall say 'check,' Yosef, and then I shall say 'checkmate.' "

It was nearly midnight when the two men parted. Yosef bore his defeat with dignity. He consoled himself with the glass of brandy that his host offered him, and said:

"At the end of the week we shall meet at my house. On my territory you will be the loser. You have my word on it."

"And this," said Dr. Kleinberger, laughing, "this is the man who wrote that eloquent article 'Against the Politics of Revenge' in *The Social Democrat*. Sleep well, Yosef."

Outside were the night and the wind. An ill-mannered owl urged Yosef to hurry up. I forgot to phone her to ask what happened. Better wait until tomorrow. She will phone and apologize and I won't accept her excuses. At least, not right away.

# 7

The acacia solves mysteries / And tells what lies ahead, / I shall ask the acacia tree / Oh, who is my bride to be?

The insistent tune takes no account of circumstances and will not leave Yair alone. Already he has whistled it, hummed it, and sung it, and still the song gives him no peace.

Lily has questioned Yair about his professors, about his studies, about the girl students who were sure to be mad with grief at the thought of his forthcoming marriage.

Yair was thinking: That's enough. Let's go home. What she's told me isn't necessarily true. And even if it is true, so what? What does she want? What's the matter with her? Time to put a stop to all this and go home. Besides, I'm cold.

"Perhaps," he said cautiously, "perhaps we should start heading back home. It's late, and there's a dampness in the air. It's cold as well. I don't want it to be my fault if you catch a chill."

He gripped her arm, just above the elbow, and began gently drawing her toward a street corner lit by a lamp.

"Do you know, my dear child," she said, "the amount of patience that is required of a man and a woman to prevent their marriage from turning into a tragedy after a few months?"

"But I think ... Let's talk about that on the way home. Or some other time altogether."

"For the first few months there is sex and sex is all that matters. Sex in the morning, at midday, and at night, before and after meals, instead of meals. But after a few months you suddenly begin to have a lot of time to sit and think— and you think all kinds of thoughts. Infuriating habits come to the surface, on both sides. And this is when subtlety is required."

"It'll be all right. Don't worry. Dinah and I ..."

"Who said anything about you and Dinah? I'm talking in general terms. Now I can also tell you something from my personal experience. Put your arm around my shoulders. I'm cold. Yes. Don't be so shy. Be a nice boy. Like this. I'm going to tell you something about Dinah and something about you, too."

"But I already know."

"No, my child, you don't know everything. I think you should know, for example, that Dinah is in love with your outward appearance and not with you. She doesn't think about you. She's still a child. And so are you. I don't suppose you have ever once been depressed. Don't answer me now. No, I'm not saying that you're a crude boy. Far from it. I just mean you're strong. You're straightforward and strong, as our young people should be. Here, give me your hand. Yes. Don't ask so many questions. I asked for your hand. Yes. Like this. Now, squeeze my hand, please. Because I'm asking you, isn't that reason enough? Squeeze. Not gently. Hard. Harder. Harder still. Don't be afraid. You're afraid of me. There, that's good. You're very strong. Have you noticed that your hand is cold and mine is warm? Soon you'll understand why. But stop whining and trying to persuade me to go home all the time, or I'll begin to think I came out for a walk with a spoiled toddler who just wants to go home and sleep. Look, child, look at the moon peeping out from behind the clouds. Do you see? Yes. Just relax completely for a few moments. Don't say anything. Hush."

The dim wailing of jackals is heard from far away. Words flee from him. Something other than words now strives to assert itself but finds no outlet. A sharp and mischievous wind rises from the desolation on the fringes of the town and comes to play in the stone-flagged side streets. Windows are shut. Shutters closed. Drains with iron gratings. A long procession of trash cans frozen on the sidewalk. Cats prowl on the mounds of Jerusalem stone. Lily Dannenberg is sure that the things that she has said to Yair Yarden are "educational." She tries hard to keep to the rhythm of events, lest everything be wasted. But the blood is pounding in her temples, and some inner agitation urges her to go racing on without drawing breath. Here among the houses there is no acacia solving riddles. The two walkers emerge from the side streets and pass through the market of Mahaneh Yehuda toward Jaffa Road. Here Lily leads the young man to a cheap café that caters to the all-night taxi drivers.

Beneath the electric light the moths are singeing their wings in token of their love for the yellow bulb. Mrs. Dannenberg orders black coffee without sugar or saccharine. Yair asks for a cheese sandwich. He hesitates and asks for a small glass of brandy as well. She lays her hand on his broad brown hand and carefully counts his fingers. In a state of mild dizziness he responds with a smile. She takes his hand in hers and raises the fingers to her lips.

# 8

In this taxi drivers' café in the Mahaneh Yehuda district there was a certain driver, a giant named Abbu. All day he sleeps. At midnight, like a bear, he wakes up and goes out to prowl Jaffa Road, his kingdom. All the taxi drivers willingly defer to him, for he is strong and goodhearted, but a hard man, too. Now he was sitting at one of the tables with three or four of the younger members of the flock, showing them how to load the dice in the game of backgammon. When Yair and Lily came into the café, Abbu said to his young cronies:

"Here come the Queen of Sheba and King Solomon."

And when Yair said nothing and Lily smiled, he added:

"Never mind. Health is what matters. Hey, lady, are you letting the kid drink brandy?"

His fellow drivers turned to look. The café proprietor, a tubercular and melancholic man, also turned to watch the approaching scene.

"And as for you, little boy, I'm damned if I understand what you're playing at. What is this, is it Grandma's Day today? Giving your grandma a treat? What are you doing going around at night with a vintage model like that?"

Yair leapt to his feet, his ears reddening, willing and ready to fight for his honor. But Lily motioned him back to his seat, and when she spoke her voice was warm and happy.

"There are some models that a man of experience and taste would sell his soul for—and not just his soul, but any number of these newfangled toys of today, all tin and glass."

"Touché!" said Abbu, laughing. "So why not come over to my place and get a good hand on your wheel, an experienced hand with clever fingers, how about it? Why go around with that slip of a boy?"

Yair sprang up, his mustache bristling. But once again she got in first and snuffed out the quarrel before it began. A new light danced in her eyes.

"What's the matter with you, Yair? This gentleman doesn't mean to insult me but to make me happy. He and I think exactly the same thoughts. So don't lose your temper, but sit down and learn how to make me happy. Now I am happy." And in her happiness the divorcee pulled Yair toward her and kissed the dimple in the middle of his chin. Abbu said slowly, as if about to faint at the sweetness of the sight:

"Lord God of Hosts, where, oh, where have you been all this time, lady, and where have I been?"

Lily said:

"Today is Grandson's Day. But maybe tomorrow or the day after, Grandma will need a taxi, and maybe Grandpa will be around, or he will discover where the Queen of Sheba is enthroned and bring her tribute of monkeys and parrots. Come on, Yair, let's go. Good night, sir. It's been a great pleasure meeting you."

As the couple passed the drivers' table on their way to the door, Abbu murmured in a tone of reverent awe:

"Go home, young man, go home and sleep. By God, you're not fit to touch the tip of her little finger."

Lily smiled.

And outside Yair said angrily:

"They're a gang of thugs. And savages."

# 9

The tips of her little fingers were pressed in the flesh of his arm.

"Now I'm cold, too," she said, "and I want you to hold me. If you know by now how you should hold me."

Yair embraced her around the shoulders in anger and shame, emotions that breathed violence into his movements.

Lily said, "Yes. Like that."

"But ... I think, anyway, it's time we turned around and headed back. It's late," he said, unconsciously gripping the lobe of his ear between thumb and forefinger. What does she want from me? What's the matter with her?

"It's too late now to go home," she whispered, "and the house is empty. What is there at home? There's nothing at home. Armchairs. Disgusting armchairs. Erich Dannenberg's chairs. Dr. Kleinberger's. Your father's. All the miserable people. There is nothing for us there at home. Here outside you can meet anything and feel anything. Owls are bewitching the moon. You're not going to leave me now, outside in the night with those wild thugs of drivers and all the owls. You must stay and protect me. No, I'm not raving, I'm perfectly rational and I'm almost frozen to death; don't leave me and don't say a word, Hebrew is such a rhetorical language, nothing but Bible and commentaries. Don't say another word to me in Hebrew, don't say anything at all. Just hold me. To you. Close. Like this. Please, not politely, please, not gently, hold me as if I'm trying to get away from you, biting and scratching, and you're not letting me go. Hush. And that wretched *Eule* can shut up as well, because I shall hear and see nothing more because you have covered my head and my ears and gagged my mouth and tied my hands behind my back because you are much stronger because I am a woman and you are a man."

# 10

As she spoke, they walked through the Makor Baruch quarter toward the Schneller Barracks, approaching the last of the dirt paths and the zoo in North Jerusalem, which lies on the frontier between the city and enemy territory.

The treasure hunt had come to nothing. Nobody had interpreted correctly the clue of the old acacia tree, and the treasure was not found. Uri was asleep curled up in the armchair

when Yosef Yarden returned from his visit to Dr. Kleinberger. The house was in chaos. In the middle of the table
lay an open volume of Bialik's poetry. All the lights were on.
Yair was not at home. Yosef Yarden roused his younger son
and sent him off to bed with a scolding. Yair must have gone
to the station to meet his fiancée. Tomorrow I will let Lily
apologize for not being home tonight. She will have to apologize profusely before I agree to accept her excuses and forgive her. The most disagreeable thing was the quarrel with
Kleinberger. Naturally I had the last word in the argument,
but I have to admit that I was beaten, just as I was in the
chess game. I must be honest. I don't believe that our
wretched party will ever succeed in shaking off its apathy
and depression. Weakness of heart and weakness of will
have eroded all the good intentions. All is lost. Now it's time
to sleep, so that tomorrow I won't be sleepwalking like the
majority of people. But if I get to sleep now, Yair will come
home and make a lot of noise. Then I won't be able to sleep
until morning, which means another dreadful night. Who's
that shouting out there? Nobody's shouting. A bird, perhaps.

Dr. Elhanan Kleinberger had also put out the light in his
room. He stood at one end of the room, with his face to the
wall and his back to the door. The radio was playing late-
night music. The scholar's lips moved silently. He was trying, in a whisper, to find the right word for a lyric poem.
Unbeknownst to anyone, he was composing poetry. In German. He, the passionate lover of Hebrew literature and the
defender of the language's honor, whispered his poetry in
German. Perhaps it was for this reason that he concealed
what he was doing from even his closest friend. He himself
felt that he was committing a sin and was guilty of hypocrisy
as well.

With his lips he strove to put ideas into words. A wandering light flickered among the dark shelves. For a moment
this light danced on the lenses of his spectacles, creating a
flash as of madness or of utter despair. Outside, a bird
screeched with malicious joy. Slowly, and very painfully,
things became clearer. But still there were things for which
no words existed. His frail shoulders began to shake in

choking desire. The right words would not come; they only slipped by and eluded him like transparent veils, like fragrances, like longings that the fingers cannot grasp. He felt that there was no hope for him.

Then he switched on the lamp again. Suddenly he felt a vicious hatred for the African ornaments and the erotic vases. And for words.

He stretched out his hand and casually selected a scientific volume from one of the bookshelves. The title shone in gold letters on the leather binding: *Demons and Ghosts in Ancient Chaldee Ritual.* All words are whores, forever betraying you and slipping away into the darkness while your soul yearns for them.

# 11

The last wood. In its center stands the Jerusalem Biblical Zoo, and its northern flank marks the frontier between Jerusalem and the enemy villages across the cease-fire line. Lily had been married to Yosef Yarden for less than four months, and he was a delightful youth, full of dreams and ideals. All this happened many years ago, and still there is no peace. It is the way of flesh to hold its grudges, and it is the way of the moon to hover with calm and cold insolence in the night sky.

Within the zoo is a nervous silence.

All the predators are asleep, but their slumber is not deep. They are never totally free from smells and voices borne on the breeze. The night never ceases to penetrate their sleep, sometimes drawing from their lungs a low growl. Their hide bristles in the frozen wind. A tense vibration, a ripple of fear or of nightmare, comes and goes. A moist, suspicious nose probes the night air and takes in the unfamiliar scents. Everywhere there is dew. The rustling cypresses breathe a sigh of quiet sorrow. The pine needles whisper as they search in the darkness, thirsty for the black dew.

From the wolves' cage comes a sound. A pair of wolves in heat, lusting for each other in the darkness. The bitch bites her mate but his fury is only redoubled. In the height of their fever they hear the cries of the birds and the vicious growl of the wildcat.

A blue-tinted vapor rises from the valleys. Strange lights twinkle across the border. The moon sheds her light upon all and shrinks, enchanted, in the whiteness of the rocks: cancers of shining venom in beams of sickly, primeval light.

Moon-struck jackals roam the valleys. From the murky groves they call to their brothers in the cages. These are the lands of nightmare, and perhaps beyond them lie those gardens that no eye has seen, and only the heart reaches out to them as if wailing: Homeward.

Out of the depths of your terror lift up your eyes. See the tops of the pine trees. A halo of pale-gray light enfolds the treetops like a gift of grace. Only the rocks are as dry as death. Give them a sign.

1964

# A Hollow Stone

## 1

The next day we went out to assess the damage. The storm had ruined the crops. The tender shoots of winter corn had been wiped off the fields as if by a gigantic duster. Saplings were uprooted. Old trees lay writhing, kissed by the terrible east wind. Slender cypresses hung limply with broken spines. The fine avenue of palm trees planted to the north of our kibbutz thirty years earlier by the founders when they first came to these barren hills had lost their crowns to the storm: even their dumb submission had not been able to save them from its fury. The corrugated iron roofs of the sheds and barns had been carried far away. Some old shacks had been wrenched from their foundations. Shutters, which all night long had beaten out desperate pleas for help, had been broken off by the wind. The night had been filled with howls and shrieks and groans; with the dawn had come silence. We went out to assess the damage, stumbling over broken objects.

"It isn't natural," said Felix. "After all, it's spring."

"A typhoon. Here. A real tornado," added Zeiger with mingled awe and pride.

And Weissman concluded:

"The loss will come to six figures."

———

We decided on the spot to turn to the government and the movement for help. We agreed to advertise for volunteer specialists to work with us for a few days. And we resolved not to lose heart, but to make a start on the work right away. We would face this challenge as we had faced others in the past, and we would refuse to be disheartened—this is the substance of what Felix was to write in the kibbutz newsletter that weekend—and above all we must keep a clear head.

As regards clarity, we had only to contemplate the polished brilliance of the sky that morning. It was a long time since we had seen such a clear sky as on that morning when we went out to assess the damage, stumbling over broken objects.

## 2

A limpid crystal calm had descended on the hills. Spring sunlight on the mountains to the east, benign and innocent, and excited choruses of birds. No breeze, not a sign of dust. We inspected each part of the farm methodically, discussing, taking notes, making decisions, issuing immediate instructions. Not wasting a word. Speaking quietly and almost solemnly.

*Casualties:* Old Nevidomsky the night watchman, slightly injured by a falling beam. Shoulder dislocated, but no bones broken, according to the doctor at the district hospital. *Electricity:* Cables severed at various points. First priority, to switch off the current before letting the children come out to play, and to inspect the damage. *Water:* Flooding in the farmyard and no water in the nursery. *Provisions:* For today, a cold meal and lemonade. *Transport:* One jeep crushed; several tractors buried in wreckage. Condition impossible to ascertain at present. *Communications:* Both telephones dead. Take the van into town to find out what has happened in other places and how much the outside world knows of our plight.

Felix saw to the dispatch of the van and proceeded to the nursery. From there he went on to the cowsheds and chicken coops. Then to the schoolhouse, where he gave instructions for lessons to be resumed not later than ten o'clock "without fail."

Felix was animated by a passionate energy, which made his small, sturdy frame throb. He stowed his glasses away in his shirt pocket. His face took on a new look: a general, rather than a philosopher.

The farmyard was full of hens, unconcernedly scrabbling hither and thither, just like old-fashioned chickens in an old-fashioned village, as if oblivious that they had been born and bred in cages and batteries.

The livestock showed slight signs of shock: the cows kept raising their foolish heads to look for the roof, which had been carried off by the wind. Occasionally they uttered a long, unhappy groan, as if to warn of worse things still to come. The big telegraph pole had fallen on Batya Pinski's house and broken some roof tiles. By five past eight, the electricians had already trampled all over her flower beds rigging up a temporary line. First priority in restoring the electricity supply was given to the nurseries, the incubators for the chicks, and the steam boilers so there would be hot meals. Felix asked to have a transistor radio brought to him, so that he could follow developments elsewhere. Perhaps someone should look in on Batya Pinski and one or two invalids and elderly people, to reassure them and find out how they had weathered the terrors of the night. But social obligations could wait a little longer, until the more essential emergency arrangements had been made. For instance, the kitchens reported a gas leak whose source could not be traced. Anyway, one could not simply drop in on people like Batya Pinski for a brief chat: they would start talking, they would have complaints, criticisms, reminiscences, and this morning was the least suitable time possible for such psychological indulgence.

The radio news informed us that this had been no typhoon or tornado, but merely a local phenomenon. Even the nearby settlements had hardly been touched. Two conflicting winds had met here on our hills, and the resulting turbulence had caused some local damage. Meanwhile the first volunteers began to appear, followed by a mixed multitude of spectators, reporters, and broadcasters. Felix delegated three boys and a fluent veteran teacher to stem the tide of interlopers at the main gate of the kibbutz, and on no account to let them in to get under our feet. Only those on official business were to be admitted. The fallen telegraph pole was already temporarily secured by steel cables. The power supply would soon be restored to the most essential buildings. Felix demonstrated the qualities of theorist and man of action combined. Of course, he did not do everything himself. Each of us played his part to the best of his ability. And we would keep working until everything was in order.

# 3

Condensation on the windows and the hiss of the kerosene stove.

Batya Pinski was catching flies. Her agility belied her years. If Abrasha had lived to grow old along with her, his mockery would surely have turned to astonishment and even to gentleness: over the years he would have learned to understand and appreciate her. But Abrasha had fallen many years before, in the Spanish Civil War, having volunteered to join the few and fight for the cause of justice. We could still remember the eulogy that Felix had composed in memory of his childhood friend and comrade; it was a sober, moving document, free from rhetorical hyperbole, burning with agony and conviction, full of love and vision. His widow squashed the flies she caught between her thumb and forefinger. But her mind was not on the job, and some of the flies continued to wriggle even after they were dropped into the enamel mug. The room was perfectly still. You could hear the flies being squashed between her fingers.

Abrasha Pinski's old writings were the issue of the moment. Thanks to Felix's energetic efforts, the kibbutz-movement publishing house had recognized the need to bring out a collected volume of the articles he had written in the thirties. These writings had not lost their freshness. On the contrary, the further we went from the values that had motivated us in those days, the more pressing became the need to combat oblivion. And there was also a certain nostalgia at this time for the atmosphere of the thirties, which promised a reasonable market for the book. Not to mention the vogue for memories of the Spanish Civil War. Felix would contribute an introduction. The volume would also contain nine letters written by Abrasha from the siege of Madrid to the committed socialist community in Palestine.

Batya Pinski sliced the dead flies at the bottom of the mug with a penknife. The blade scraped the enamel, producing a grating yellow sound.

At last the old woman removed the glass cover and poured the mess of crushed flies into the aquarium. The quick, colorful fish crowded to the front of the tank, their tails waving, their mouths opening and closing greedily. At the sight of their agile movements and magical colors, the widow's face lit up, and her imagination ran riot.

Fascinating creatures, fish: they are both cold and alive. A striking paradox. This, surely, is the longed-for bliss: to be cold and alive.

Over the years Batya Pinski had developed an amazing ability. She was capable of counting the fish in her aquarium, up to forty or fifty, despite their perpetual motion. At times she could even guess in advance what course an individual fish or a shoal would take. Circles, spirals, zigzags, sudden totally capricious swerves, swoops, and plunges, fluid lines that drew delicate, complicated arabesques in the water of the tank.

The water in the tank was clear. Even clearer were the bodies of the fish. Transparency within transparency. The movement of fins was the slightest movement possible, hardly a movement at all. The quivering of the gills was unbelievably fine. There were black fish and striped fish, blood-red fish and fish purple like the plague, pale-green fish like stagnant water in fresh water. All of them free. None of them subject to the law of gravity. Theirs was a different law, which Batya did not know. Abrasha would have been able to discern it over the years, but he had chosen instead to lay down his life on a faraway battlefield.

# 4

The illusion of depth is produced by aquatic plants and scattered stones. The green silence of the underwater jungle. Fragments of rock on the bottom. Columns of coral up which plants twine. And on top of a hill of sand at the back of the tank is a stone with a hole.

Unlike the fish, the plants and stones in the aquarium are subject to the law of gravity. The fish continually swoop down on the stones and shrubs, now and then rubbing themselves against them or pecking at them. According to Batya Pinski, this is a display of malicious gloating.

As a procession of blood-red fish approaches the hollow stone, Batya Pinski rests her burning forehead against the cool glass. The passage of the live fish through the dead stone stirs a vague power deep inside her, and she trembles. That is when she has to fight back the tears. She feels for the letter in the pocket of her old dressing gown. The letter is crumpled and almost faded, but the words are still full of tenderness and compassion.

"I feel," writes Abramek Bart, one of the directors of the kibbutz-movement publishing house, "that if we have been unfair to the beloved memory of Abrasha, we have been even more unfair to the minds of our children. The younger generation needs, and deserves, to discover the pearls of wisdom contained in the essays and letters of our dear Abrasha. I shall come and see you one of these days to rummage, in quotation marks of course, through your old papers. I am certain that you can be of great assistance to us in sorting through his literary remains and in preparing the work for publication. With fraternal good wishes, yours," signed by some Ruth Bardor for Abramek Bart.

The old woman held the envelope to her nose. She sniffed it for a moment with her eyes closed. Her mouth hung open, revealing gaps in her teeth. A small drop hung between her nose and upper lip, where a slight mustache had begun to grow during these bad years. Then she put the letter back in the envelope, and the envelope in her pocket.

Now she was exhausted and must rest in the armchair. She did not need to rest for long. It was enough for her to doze for a minute or two. A stray surviving fly began to buzz, and already she was up and ready for the chase.

Years before, Abrasha would come and bite. Love and hate. He would burst and collapse on her, and at once he would be distracted, not here, not with her.

For months before his departure the tune was always on his lips, sung in a Russian bass, shamelessly out of tune. She recalled the tune, the anthem of the Spanish freedom-fighters, full of longing, wildness, and revolt. It had swept their bare room up into the maelstrom of teeming forces as he enumerated the bleeding Spanish towns that had fallen to the enemies of mankind, counting them off one by one on his fingers. Their outlandish names conveyed to Batya a resonance of unbridled lechery. In her heart of hearts she disliked Spain and wished it no good; after all, that was where our ancestors had been burned at the stake and banished. But she held her peace. Abrasha enlarged on the implications of the struggle, expounding its dialectical significance and its place in the final battle that was being engaged all over Europe. He considered all wars as a snare and a delusion; civil wars were the only ones worth dying in. She liked to listen to all this, even though she could not and did not want to understand. It was only when he reached the climax of his speech—describing the iron laws of history and averring that the collapse of reaction would come like a thunderbolt from the blue—that she suddenly grasped what he was talking about, because she could see the thunderbolt itself in his eyes.

And suddenly he was tired of her. Perhaps he had seen the tortured look on her face, perhaps he had had a momentary glimpse of her own desires. Then he would sit down at the table, propping up his large square head with his massive elbows, and immerse himself in the newspaper, abstractedly eating one olive after another and arranging the pits in a neat pile.

# 5

The kettle whistles fiercely as it passes boiling point. Batya Pinski gets up and makes herself some tea. Since the storm died down, at about four o'clock in the morning, she has been drinking glass after glass of tea. She has still not been out to inspect the damage. She has not even tried to open the shutters. She sits behind her drawn curtains and imagines the damage in all its details. What is there to see? It is all there before her eyes: shattered roofs, trampled flower beds, torn trees, dead cows, Felix, plumbers, electricians, experts, and talkers. All boring. Today will be devoted to the fish, until the premonition is confirmed and Abramek Bart arrives. She always relies unhesitatingly on her premonitions. One can always know things in advance, if only one really and truly tries and is not afraid of what may emerge. Abramek will come today to see the havoc. He will come because he won't be able to contain his curiosity. But he won't want to come just like that, like the other good-for-nothings who collect wherever there's been a disaster. He will find some excuse. And then he'll suddenly remember his promise to Batya, to come and rummage in and sort through Abrasha's papers. It's half past eight now. He will be here by two or three. There is still time. Still plenty of time to get dressed, do my hair, and get the room tidy. And to make something nice to serve him. Plenty of time now to sit down in the armchair and drink my tea quietly.

She sat down in the armchair opposite the sideboard, under the chandelier. On the floor was a thick Persian carpet, and by her side an ebony card table. All these beautiful objects would shock Abrasha if he were to come back. On the other hand, if he had come back twenty years before, he would have risen high up the ladder of the party and the movement; he would have left all those Felixes and Abrameks behind, and by now he'd be an ambassador or a minister, and she would be surrounded by even nicer furnishings. But he made up his mind to go and die for the

Spaniards, and the furnishings were bought for her by Martin Zlotkin, her son-in-law. After he married Ditza he brought all the presents, then took his young bride away with him to Zurïch, where he now managed a division of his father's bank, with branches on three continents. Ditza ran a Zen study group, and every month she sent a letter with a mimeographed leaflet in German preaching humility and peace of mind. Grandchildren were out of the question, because Martin hated children and Ditza herself called him "our big baby." Once a year they came to visit and contributed handsomely to various charities. Here in the kibbutz they had donated a library of books on socialist theory in memory of Abrasha Pinski. Martin himself, however, regarded socialism the same way he regarded horse-drawn carriages: very pretty and diverting, but out of place in this day and age, when there were other, more urgent problems.

# 6

On the eve of Abrasha's departure Ditza was taken ill with pneumonia. She was two at the time; blonde, temperamental, and sickly. Her illness distracted Batya from Abrasha's departure. She spent the whole day arguing with the nurses and pedagogues and by evening they had given in and allowed the sick child to be transferred in her cot from the nursery to her parents' room in one of the shabby huts. The doctor arrived from the neighboring settlement in a mule cart, prescribed various medicines, and instructed her to keep the temperature of the room high. Meanwhile Abrasha packed some khaki shirts, a pair of shoes, some underwear, and a few Russian and Hebrew books into a knapsack and added some cans of sardines. In the evening, fired with the spirit, he stood by his daughter's cot and sang her two songs, his voice trembling with emotional fervor. He even showed Batya the latest lines dividing the workers from their oppressors on a wall map of Spain. He enumerated the towns: Barcelona, Madrid, Málaga, Granada, Valencia, Valladolid, Seville. Batya half-heard him; she wanted to shout, What's the matter with you, madman, don't go away, stay, live; and she also wanted to shout, I hope you die. But she said nothing. She pursed her lips like an old witch. And she had never since lost that expression. She recalled that last evening as if it had been re-enacted every night for twenty-three years. Sometimes the fish moved across the picture, but they did not obscure it: their paths wound in and out of its lines, bestowing upon it an air of strange, desolate enchantment, as though the widow were confronted not by things that had happened a long time previously, but by things that were about to happen but could still be prevented. She must concentrate hard and not make a single mistake. This very day Abramek Bart will step into this room, all unawares, and then I shall have him in my power.

The cheap alarm clock started ringing at three o'clock. He got out of bed and lit the kerosene lamp. She followed him, slender and barefoot, and said, "It's not morning yet." Abrasha put his finger to his lips and whispered, "Sssh. The child." Secretly she prayed that the child would wake up and scream its head off. He discovered a cobweb in the corner of the shack and stood on tiptoe to wipe it away. The spider managed to escape and hide between the boards of the low ceiling. Abrasha whispered to her: "In a month or two, when we've won, I'll come back and bring you a souvenir from Spain. I'll bring something for Ditza, too. Now, don't make me late; the van's leaving for Haifa at half past three."

He went out to wash in the icy water of the faucet that stood twenty yards downhill from the shack. An alarmed night watchman hurried over to see what was going on. "Don't worry, Felix," Abrasha said. "It's only the revolution leaving you for a while." They exchanged some more banter in earnest tones, and then, in a more lighthearted voice, some serious remarks. At a quarter past, Abrasha went back to the shack, and Batya, who had followed him out in her nightdress, went inside with him again. Standing there shivering, she saw by the light of the kerosene lamp how carelessly he had shaved in his haste and the dark: he had cut himself in some places and left dark bristles in others. She stroked his cheeks and tried to wipe away the blood and dew. He was a big, warm boy, and when he began to hum the proud, sad song of the Spanish freedom-fighters deep in his chest, it suddenly occurred to Batya that he was very dear and that she must not stand in his way, because he knew where he was going and she knew nothing at all. Felix said, "Be seeing you," and added in Yiddish, "Be well, Abrasha." Then he vanished. She kissed Abrasha on his chest and neck, and he drew her to him and said, "There, there." Then the child woke up and started to cry in a voice that was almost effaced by the illness. Batya picked her up, and Abrasha touched them both with his large hands and said, "There, there, what's the trouble."

The van honked, and Abrasha said cheerfully, "Here goes. I'm off."

From the doorway he added, "Don't worry about me. Good-bye."

She soothed the child and put her back in the cot. Then she put out the lamp and stood alone at the window, watching the night paling and the mountaintops beginning to show in the east. Suddenly she was glad that Abrasha had cleared the cobweb from the corner of the shack but had not managed to kill the spider. She went back to bed and lay trembling, because she knew that Abrasha would never come back, and that the forces of reaction would win the war.

# 7

The fish in the aquarium had eaten all the flies and were floating in the clear space. Perhaps they were hankering after more tidbits. They explored the dense weeds and pecked at the arch of the hollow stone, darting suspiciously toward one another to see if one of them had managed to snatch a morsel and if there was anything left of it.

Only when the last crumbs were finished did the fish begin to sink toward the bottom of the tank. Slowly, with deliberate unconcern, they rubbed their silver bellies on the sand, raising tiny mushroom clouds. Fish are not subject to the laws of contradiction: they are cold and alive. Their movements are dreamy, like drowsy savagery.

Just before midnight, when the storm had begun to blow up, the widow had awakened and shuffled to the bathroom in her worn bedroom slippers. Then she made herself some tea and said in a loud, cracked voice, "I told you not to be crazy." Clutching the glass of tea, she wandered around the room and finally settled in the armchair facing the aquarium, after switching on the light in the water. Then, as the storm gathered strength and battered the shutters and the trees, she watched the fish waking up.

As usual, the silverfish were the first to respond to the light. They rose gently from their haunts in the thick weeds and propelled themselves up toward the surface with short sharp thrusts of their fins. A single black molly made the rounds of its shoal, as if rousing them all for a journey. In no time at all the whole army was drawn up in formation and setting out.

At one o'clock an old shack next to the cobbler's hut collapsed. The storm banged the tin roof against the walls, and the air howled and whistled. At the same moment the red swordfish woke up and ranged themselves behind their leader, a giant with a sharp black sword. It was not the collapse of the shack that had awakened the swordfish. Their cousins the green swordfish had weighed anchor and gently set sail into the forest, as if bent on capturing the clearing abandoned by the silverfish. Only the solitary fighting-fish, the lord of the tank, still slept in his home among the corals. He had responded to the sudden light with a shudder of disgust. The zebra fish played a childish game of tag around the sleeping monarch.

The last to come back to life were the guppies, the dregs of the aquarium, an inflamed rabble roaming restlessly hither and thither in search of crumbs. Slow snails crawled on the plants and on the glass walls of the tank, helping to keep them clean. The widow sat all night watching the aquarium, holding the empty glass, conjuring the fish to move from place to place, calling them after the Spanish towns: Málaga, Valencia, Barcelona, Madrid, Cordova. While outside the clashing winds sliced the crowns off the stately palm trees and broke the spines of the cypresses.

She put her feet up on the ebony card table, a present from Martin and Ditza Zlotkin. She thought about Zen Buddhism, humility, civil war, the final battle where there would be nothing to lose, a thunderbolt from the blue. She fought back exhaustion and despair and rehearsed the unanswerable arguments she would use when the time came. All the while her eyes strayed to another world, and her lips whispered: There, there, quiet now.

Toward dawn, when the wind had died away and we were going out to assess the damage, the old woman fell into a half-sleep full of curses and aching joints. Then she got up, made a fresh glass of tea, and began to chase flies all over the room with an agility that belied her years. In her heart she knew that Abramek Bart would definitely come today, and that he would use his promise as an excuse. She saw the plaster fall from the ceiling as the pole fell and broke some of the roof tiles. The real movement was completely noiseless. Without a sound the monarch arose and began to steer himself toward the hollow stone. As he reached the arched tunnel he stopped and froze. He took on a total stillness. The stillness of the water. The immobility of the light. The silence of the hollow stone.

# 8

Had it not been for Ditza, Batya Pinski would have married Felix in the early nineteen-forties.

It was about two years after the awful news had come from Madrid. Once again a final war was being waged in Europe, and on the wall of the dining hall there hung a map covered with arrows, and a collection of heartening slogans and news clippings. Ditza must have been four or five. Batya had got over the disaster and had taken on a new bloom, which was having a disturbing effect on certain people's emotions. She always dressed in black, like a Spanish widow. And when she spoke to men, their nostrils flared as if they had caught a whiff of wine. Every morning, on her way to the sewing room, she walked, erect and slender, past the men working in the farmyard. Occasionally one of those tunes came back to her, and she would sing with a bitter sadness that made the other sewing women exchange glances and whisper, "Uh-huh, there she goes again."

Felix was biding his time. He helped Batya over her minor difficulties and even concerned himself with the development of Ditza's personality. Later, when he had submitted to the desires of the party and exchanged the cowsheds for political office, he made a habit of bringing Ditza little surprises from the big city. He also treated the widow with extreme respect, as if she were suffering from an incurable illness and it was his task to ease somewhat her last days. He would let himself into her room in the middle of the morning and wash the floor, secreting chocolates in unlikely places for her to discover later. Or put up metal coat hooks, bought out of his expense allowance, to replace the broken wooden ones. And he would supply her with carefully selected books: pleasant books, with never a hint of loss or loneliness, Russian novels about the development of Siberia, the five-year plan, change of heart achieved through education.

"You're spoiling the child," Batya would sometimes say. And Felix would word his answer thoughtfully and with tact:

"Under certain circumstances it is necessary to pamper a child, to prevent it from being deprived."

"You're a sweet man, Felix," Batya would say, and occasionally she would add, "You're always thinking of others. Why don't you think about yourself for a change, Felix?"

Felix would read a hint of sympathy or personal interest into those remarks; he would stifle his excitement and reply: "It doesn't matter. Never mind. In times like these one can't be thinking of oneself all the time. And I'm not the one who's making the real sacrifice."

"You're very patient, Felix," Batya would say, with pursed lips.

And Felix, whether shrewdly or innocently, would conclude, "Yes, I'm very patient."

Indeed, after a few months or perhaps a year or two, the widow began to soften. She permitted Felix to accompany her from the dining hall or the recreation hall to the door of her room, or from the sewing room to the children's house, and occasionally she would stand and listen to him for half an hour or so by one of the benches on the lawn. He knew that the time was not yet ripe for him to try to touch her, but he also knew that time was on his side. She still insisted on wearing black, she did not temper her arrogance, but she, too, knew that time was on Felix's side; he was closing in on her from all sides, so that soon she would have no alternative.

It was little Ditza who changed everything.

She wet her bed, she ran away from the children's house at night, she escaped to the sewing room in the morning and clutched her mother, she kicked and scratched the other children and even animals, and as for Felix, she nicknamed him "Croakie." Neither his gifts and attentions nor his sweets and rebukes did any good. Once, when Felix and Batya had begun to eat together openly in the dining hall, the child came in and climbed on his knee. He was touched, convinced that a reconciliation was coming. But he had just started to stroke her hair and call her "my little girl" when suddenly she wet his trousers and ran away. Felix got up and ran after her in a frenzy of rage and reformist zeal. He pushed his way among the tables trying to catch the child. Batya sat stiffly where she was and did not interfere. Finally Felix snatched up an enamel mug, threw it at the elusive child, missed, tripped, picked himself up, and tried to wipe the pee and yogurt off his khaki trousers. There were smiling faces all around him. By now Felix was acting secretary general of the Workers' Party, and here he was, flushed and hoarse, with a murderous gleam showing through his glasses. Zeiger slapped his belly, sighing, "What a sight," until laughter got the better of him. Weissmann, too, roared aloud. Even Batya could not suppress a smile as the child crawled under the tables and came to sit at her feet with the expression of a persecuted saint. The nursery teachers exclaimed indignantly, "I ask you, is that a way to carry on, a grown-up man, a public figure, throwing mugs at little children in the middle of the dining hall, isn't that going too far?"

Three weeks later it came out that Felix was having an affair with Zeiger's wife, Zetka. Zeiger divorced her, and early in that spring she married Felix. In May Felix and Zetka were sent to Switzerland to organize escape routes for the survivors of the death camps. In the party Felix was regarded as the model of the young leadership that had risen from the ranks. And Batya Pinski started to go downhill.

# 9

When Abramek comes, I'll make him a glass of tea, I'll show him all the old papers, we'll discuss the layout and the cover, and eventually we'll have to settle the problem of the dedication, so that there won't be any misunderstanding.

She picked up the last photograph of Abrasha, taken in Madrid by a German Communist fighter. He looked thin and unshaven, his clothes were crumpled, and there was a pigeon on his shoulder. His mouth hung open slackly and his eyes were dull. He looked more as if he had been making love than fighting for the cause. On the back was an affectionate greeting, in rhyme.

Over the years Batya Pinski had got into the habit of talking to herself. At first she had done it under her breath. Later, when Ditza married Martin Zlotkin and went away with him, she started talking out loud, in a croaking voice that made the children of the kibbutz call her Baba Yaga, after the witch in the stories they had heard from their Russian nurses.

Look here, Abramek, there's just one more point. It's a slightly delicate matter, a bit complicated, but I'm sure that we can sort it out, you and I, with a bit of forethought. It's like this. If Abrasha were still alive, he would of course want to bring his own book out. Right? Right. Of course. But Abrasha isn't alive and he can't supervise the publication of the book himself. I mean the color, the jacket, the preface, that sort of thing, and also the dedication. Naturally he would want to dedicate the book to his wife. Just like anybody else. Now that Abrasha isn't with us any more, and you are collecting his articles and his letters and bringing out his book, there isn't a dedication. What will people say? Just think, Abramek, work it out for yourself: what will people make of it? It's simply an incitement to the meanest kind of gossip: poor fellow, he ran away to Spain to get away from his wife. Or else he went to Spain and fell in love with some Carmen Miranda or other out there, and that was that. Just a minute. Let me finish. We must kill that kind of gossip at all costs. At all costs, I say. No, not for my sake; I don't care any more what people say about me. As far as I'm concerned they can say that I went to bed with the Grand Mufti and with your great Plekhanov both at once. I couldn't care less. It's not for me, it's for him. It's not right to have all sorts of stories going around about Abrasha Pinski. It's not good for you: after all, you need a figure you can hold up as an example to your young people, without Carmen Mirandas and suchlike. In other words, you need a dedication. It doesn't matter who writes it. It could be you. Felix. Or me. Something like this, for instance: First page, QUESTIONS OF TIME AND TIMELY QUESTIONS, collected essays by Abraham brackets Abrasha Pinski, hero of the Spanish Civil War. That's right. Next page: this picture. Just as it is. Top of the next page: To Batya, a devoted wife, the fruits of my love and anguish. Then, on the following page, you can put that the book is published by the Workers' Party, and you can mention Felix's help. It won't hurt. Now, don't you argue with me, Abramek, I mustn't get upset, because I'm not a well woman, and what's more I know a thing or two about you and about Felix and about how Abrasha was talked into going off to that ridiculous war. So you'd better not say anything. Just do what you're told. Here, drink your tea, and stop arguing.

Then she sighed, shook herself, and sat down in her armchair to wait for him. Meanwhile she watched the fish. When she heard a buzzing, she leapt up and swatted the fly on the windowpane. How do they get in when all the windows are closed. Where do they come from. To hell with the lot of them. Anyway, how can the wretched creatures survive a storm like that.

She squashed the fly, dropped it into the aquarium, and sat down again in her armchair. But there was no peace. The kettle started boiling. Abramek will be here soon. Must get the room tidy. But it's all perfectly tidy, just as it has been for years. Close your eyes and think, perhaps. What about.

# 10

We were recovering hour by hour.

We tackled the debris with determined dedication. Buildings in danger of collapse were roped off. The carpenters fixed up props and blocked holes with boards. Here and there we hung flaps of canvas. Tractors brought beams and corrugated iron. Where there was flooding we improvised paths with gravel and concrete blocks. We rigged up temporary powerlines to essential points until the electrical system could be repaired. Old kerosene heaters and rusty cooking stoves were brought up from the stores. The older women cleaned and polished them, and for a while we all relived the early days. The bustle filled us with an almost ecstatic joy. Old memories were brought out, and jokes were exchanged. Meanwhile Felix alerted all the relevant agencies, the telephone engineers, emergency services, the Regional Council, the Department of Agricultural Settlements, the headquarters of the movement, and so on and so forth. The messages all went by jeep, because the telephone lines had been brought down by the storm. Not even our children were idle. To keep them from getting under our feet, Felix told them to catch the chickens, which had scattered all over the village when their coops had been damaged. Happy hunting cries arose from the lawns and from under the trees. Panting, red-faced gangs came running eagerly from unexpected places to block the escape routes of the clucking hens. Some of these sounds managed to penetrate the closed shutters, windows, and curtains into Batya Pinski's room.

What's the matter, what's so funny, the widow croaked to herself.

By the same afternoon all essential services were operating again. A cold but nourishing meal had been served. The nurseries were light and warm once more. There was running water, even if the pressure was low and the supply intermittent. After lunch we were able to draw up a first unofficial assessment of the damage. It transpired that the worst-hit area was the group of old shacks at the bottom of the hill, which had been put up by the founders decades previously. When they had folded up the tents that they had pitched on the barren slope and installed themselves in these shacks, they had all known at last that they were settling here and that there was no going back.

Years later, when the successive phases of permanent buildings had been completed, the old wooden shacks were handed over to the young people. Their first inhabitants were a detachment of young refugees who had arrived from Europe via Central Asia and Teheran to be welcomed by us with open arms. They were followed by a squadron of underground fighters that later produced two outstanding military men. From this group of huts they set out one night to blow up a British military radar installation, and it was here that they returned toward dawn. Later, after the establishment of the state, when the task of the underground had been completed, the tumbledown huts became a regular army base. This was the headquarters of the legendary Highland Brigade during the War of Independence, where the great night operations were planned. Throughout the fifties the shacks housed recent immigrants, paramilitary youth groups, students in intensive language courses, detachments of volunteers, eccentric individuals who had begun to come from all over the world to experience the new way of life; finally they were used as lodgings for hired laborers. When Phase C of the building program was drawn up, the huts were scheduled for demolition. In any case they were already falling down: the wooden walls were disintegrating, the roof beams were sagging, and the floors were sinking. Weeds were growing through the boards, and the

walls were covered with obscene drawings and graffiti in
six languages. At night the children came here to play ghosts
and robbers among the ruins. And after the children came
the couples. We had been about to clear the site to make
way for the new development when the storm anticipated
us, as if it had run out of patience. The carpenters searched
the wreckage, salvaging planks, doors, and beams that might
be reused.

Felix's short, stocky figure was everywhere at once, almost as if he were appearing simultaneously in different
places. His sober, precise instructions prevented chaos, re-
duplication, and wasted effort. He never for a moment failed
to distinguish between essential and trivial tasks.

For seventeen years Felix had been a public servant,
secretary general, chairman, delegate, and eventually even
a member of Parliament and a member of the executive committee of the party. A year or so earlier, when Zetka, his
wife, was dying of cancer, he had given up all his public po-
sitions and returned home to become secretary of the kibbutz. Social and financial problems that had seemed
insoluble for years suddenly vanished at his return, as if by
magic. Old plans came to fruition. Unprofitable sections of
the farm took on new life. There was a new mood abroad.
A few weeks earlier, ten months after Zetka's death, Felix
had married Weissmann's ex-wife. Just two days before the
storm, a small, stern-faced delegation had come to prepare
us to lose him once more: with new elections coming,
our party would need a strong man to represent it in the
Cabinet.

The telephone was working again after lunch. Tele-
grams of concern and good will began to pour in from all
over. Offers of help and sympathy from other kibbutzim, in-
stitutions, and organizations.

In our kibbutz calm reigned once more. Here and there
police officers confabulated with regional officials, or an ad-
viser huddled with a curious journalist. We were forbidden
by Felix to talk to the press and the media, because it would
be best for us to put forward a unanimous version when the
time came to make our claim for the insurance.

At a quarter past one old Nevidomsky was brought home from the hospital, with his dislocated shoulder carefully set and his arm in an impressive sling, waving greetings with his free hand. At half past one we were mentioned on the news; again they stressed that it had been neither a typhoon nor a tornado but simply a limited, local phenomenon: two conflicting winds, one from the sea and the other from the desert, had met and caused a certain amount of turbulence. Such phenomena were of daily occurrence over the desert, but in settled areas they were infrequent, and the likelihood of a recurrence was remote. There was no cause for alarm, although it was advisable to remain on the alert.

Batya Pinski switched off the radio, stood up, and went over to the window. She peeped outside through the glass of the shutters. She cursed the kitchen crew who had neglected their duty in the confusion and forgotten to send her her lunch. They should know better than anyone how ill she was and how important it was for her to avoid strain and tension. Actually she did not feel in the least hungry, but that did nothing to diminish her indignation: They've forgotten. As if I didn't exist. As if it wasn't for them and their pink-faced brats that Abrasha gave his life in a faraway land. They've forgotten everything. And Abramek's also forgotten what he promised; he's not coming today after all. Come, Abramek, come, and I'll give you some ideas for the jacket and the dedication, I'll show you the havoc the storm has wrought here, you're bursting with curiosity and dying to see it with your own eyes, only you have no excuse, why should the director of the party publishing house suddenly drop all his work and come goggle at a disaster like a small child. So come, I'll give you your excuse, and I'll also give you some tea, and we'll talk about what we have to talk about.

She leapt across the room, spotting some dust on the bookshelf. She swept it away furiously with her hand. She stooped to pick up a leaf that had fallen from a potted plant onto the carpet. Then she drew Abramek Bart's letter from her dressing-gown pocket, unfolded it, and stared briefly at the secretary's signature, some Ruth Bardor, no doubt a painted hussy with bare thighs, no doubt she's shaved her legs and plucked her eyebrows and bleached her hair, no doubt she wears see-through panties and smothers herself in deodorants. God damn her. I've given those fish quite enough food for today; they'll get no more from me. Now here's another fly; I can't understand how they get in or where they hide. Perhaps they're born here. Kettle's boiling again. Another glass of tea.

# 11

After the embarrassing episode in the dining hall in the early forties, some of us were glad that the affair between Batya Pinski and Felix had been broken off in time. But all of us were sad about the change that took place in Batya. She would hit her child, even in the presence of other children. None of the advice or discussions did any good. She would pinch her till she was black and blue and call her names, including, for some reason, Carmen Miranda. The girl stopped wetting her bed but instead started to torture cats. Batya showed the first signs of asceticism. Her ripe, heady beauty was beginning to fade. There were still some who could not keep their eyes off her as she walked, straight and dark and voluptuous, on her way from the sewing room to the ironing room. But her face was hard, and around her mouth there played an expression of disappointment and spite.

And she continued to discipline the child with an iron hand.

Some of us were uncharitable enough to call her a madwoman; they even said of her: What does she think she is, a Sicilian widow, that cheap melodramatic heroine, that Spanish saint, that twopenny actress.

When the founders of the kibbutz moved into the first permanent buildings, Batya was among them. Zeiger volunteered to build her an aquarium in her new house. He did this out of gratitude. Zeiger was a thickset, potbellied, hirsute man. He was always joking, as if the purpose of life in general and his own life in particular was amusement. He had certain fixed witticisms, and his good humor did not desert him even when his wife did. He said to anyone who cared to listen: I am a mere proletarian, but Felix is going to be a commissar one day, when the revolution comes; I'd live with him myself, if only he'd have me.

He was a short, stocky man, who always smelled of garlic and tobacco. He moved heavily and clumsily like a bear, and there was an endearing lightheartedness about him— even when he was accidentally shot in the stomach during illegal weapon-practice in the old days. We were fond of him, especially at festivals, weddings, and parties, to which he made an indispensable contribution.

Ever since his wife left him, he had maintained a correspondence with a female relative, a divorcee herself, who lived in Philadelphia and whom he had never set eyes on. He used to call on Batya Pinski in the evenings, and she would translate the relative's letters from English into Yiddish and his comical replies from Yiddish into English. Batya had taught herself English from the novels she read in bed at night. He always apologized at the end of each visit for taking up her valuable time; but it was he who dug the flower bed in front of her new house, and raked it and mulched it and brought her bulbs and seedlings. His distinctive smell lingered in the room. Little Ditza loved to ask him riddles; he never knew the answers, or if he did he pretended not to, and she always laughed at his amazement when she told him.

One day he came with aluminum frames, panes of glass, a folding ruler, a screwdriver, and a sticky, smelly substance which he referred to as *kit* but which Batya taught him to call putty.

"An aquarium," he said, "for fish to swim in. It's aesthetic. It's soothing. And it doesn't make a noise and it doesn't make a mess."

And he set to work.

Batya Pinski took to calling him Ali Baba. Willingly accepting this nickname, he responded by calling her "the Contessa from Odessa."

It was perhaps because of this nickname that little Ditza began to address Zeiger as Pessah. Even though his real name was Fischel, we all came to call him Pessah, so that even in the kibbutz newsletter he was referred to as Pessah Zeiger.

Firmly but carefully he fitted the panes of glass into the soft bed of putty. At intervals he employed a tool that fascinated both Batya and Ditza: a diamond glass-cutter.

"How can we thank you for this beautiful present?" Batya asked when the aquarium was finished.

Zeiger pondered a moment or two, breathed out a gust of garlic and tobacco, winked to himself, and suddenly shrugged his shoulders and said, "*Chort znayet*," which is to say, the Devil alone knows.

The fish were brought in a jar and put into the aquarium with a great deal of fuss. Ditza had invited all her friends to a "fish party," which did not please Batya. That evening Zeiger brought, in addition to the letter from his relative in Philadelphia, a small flask of brandy.

"Won't you offer me a drink?" he said.

Batya poured him a drink and translated the letter and his reply.

That evening we were celebrating the Allied victory. World War II was over, and the monster had been vanquished. We flew the Zionist and socialist flags from the top of the water tower. In the nearby British army camp there was a fireworks display, and in the small hours of the morning the soldiers came in army trucks to join in the singing and dancing. The girls of the kibbutz saw fit to consent for once to dance with the British soldiers, despite their smell of beer. The dining hall was decorated with slogans and with a large portrait of Josef Stalin in uniform. Felix delivered a passionate oration about the pure new world which was about to be built on the ruins of the defeated powers of darkness. He pledged to us all that we would never forget those who had sacrificed their lives in this struggle, here and on distant frontiers. Then he pinned the victory badge printed by the Workers' Party onto Batya's lapel, shook her hand, and kissed her. We rose to our feet, sang the Zionist anthem and the "Internationale," and danced all night. At ten past three Zeiger seized Batya's arm, dragged her almost forcibly out of the corner of the dining hall where she had been sitting silently all evening, and saw her to her room. His voice was hoarse and his white shirt was clinging to his back, because between dances he had taken it upon himself to act like a clown, as if this had been an old-fashioned Jewish wedding. When they got to Batya's door Zeiger said:

"That's it. You've had more than enough. And now, good night." He turned to go.

But she ordered him to come inside and he obeyed her. She took off his sweaty shirt. When he asked if he could wash his face, she said neither yes nor no, but instead she switched on the light in the aquarium and turned off the overhead light. He began to apologize or to plead but she cut his stammering short by pressing him to her, sweaty, steaming, unwashed, and embarrassed, and conquered him in silence.

# 12

In a small village run on sound principles there are no secrets, nor can there be any.

Just before six o'clock in the morning, the neighbors saw Zeiger emerge, subdued, from Batya Pinski's door. By seven o'clock the news had already reached the sewing room. Some of us, including Felix and his wife, Zetka (who had previously been married to Zeiger), saw a positive aspect to this new development: after all, the whole situation had been unnatural and full of unnecessary tensions. Now everything would be much simpler. Martyrdoms, Mediterranean tragedies, emotional arabesques were irreconcilable with the principles according to which we guided our lives.

Even these people, however, could not accept what ensued with equanimity. Zeiger was the first, but he was not the last. Within a matter of weeks, news had spread of various peripheral characters' finding their way to Batya Pinski's room at night. She did not even turn up her nose at refugees, or at eccentrics like Matityahu Damkov. Her silent, noble melancholy had turned into something better left unnamed. And her face was becoming ugly.

Within a year or two even little Ditza was going around

with soldiers and birds of passage. We were unable to devote our full attention to this unhappy episode, because the struggle to drive out the British was reaching its climax, and then regular Arab armies invaded the country; they reached the very gates of our kibbutz, and we repelled them almost barehanded. Finally all was calm again. Hordes of refugees poured in from all directions. Zeiger's relative, a middle-aged woman, also came, as a tourist, and dragged him back to Philadelphia with her. We were all sorry to see him go, and there were some who never forgave him. Felix accepted a central party position and graced us with his presence only on weekends. As for Batya, her last embers died. Ditza ran away again and again to the pioneering camps and the newly emerging settlements in the desert; again and again she was brought back. Her mother took to her room. She announced that her condition would not permit her to work any more. We did not know what this condition was, but we decided not to ask too many questions. We left her alone. We were all relieved when Ditza finally married Martin Zlotkin, the son of the well-known banker. Batya accepted the marriage and the presents of expensive furniture from the young couple calmly. It was the fish that were now in the center of the picture. The electric kettle was always on the boil. It seemed as though it was all over for her, when the matter of Abrasha's literary remains came up and it was decided to publish his collected essays along with his letters from Madrid. Just as Felix had promised at the victory celebrations: we would not forget our comrades who had sacrificed their lives. And Felix it was who, despite all his commitments, did not forget, and made the kibbutz-movement publishing house finally tackle the job. The widow waited day by day. The fish swam across the picture without blurring it. They were cold but alive, they were not subject to the law of gravity, since they could hover effortlessly in the water. Last night's storm will bring Abramek Bart; but it's two o'clock already, and he hasn't come yet. A man like him will be able to understand the delicate matter of the dedication; he won't make any difficulties.

# 13

But I can't receive him in my dressing gown. I must get dressed. I must tidy the room, if it's not tidy enough already. I must get out the best china, so that I can serve the tea properly. And open the shutters. Let some fresh air in. Freshen up the biscuits, too. But first of all, get dressed.

She went to the sink and washed her face repeatedly in cold water, as if to mortify her flesh. Then she ran her bony fingers over her face and hair in the mirror and said aloud, There, there, you're a good girl, you're lovable, don't worry, everything's all right.

She put a little makeup on and brushed her gray hair. For an instant she caught a glimpse in the mirror of the old witch the children called Baba Yaga, but at once she was replaced by a noble, lonely woman unbowed by her suffering. Batya preferred the latter, and said to her: No one else understands you, but I respect you. And the book is dedicated to Batya, a devoted wife, the fruits of my love and anguish.

Just as she pronounced these words she heard the squeal of brakes in the clearing in front of the dining hall. She leapt to the window, still disheveled because she had not had time to put the hairpins in place; she flung the shutters open and thrust her head out. Abramek Bart, director of the publishing house, got out of the car and held the door open for the secretary general of the movement.

Felix appeared from nowhere to greet them both with a warm yet businesslike handshake and a serious expression. They exchanged a few words and walked off together to inspect the damage and the reconstruction work, which had been proceeding ceaselessly since early in the morning.

# 14

She finished getting ready. She put on her burgundy-colored dress, a necklace, and an unobtrusive pair of earrings, dabbed a few drops of perfume behind her ears, and put the water on to boil. Meanwhile the blue daylight poured in through the open windows. Children and birds were shrilling joyfully. The streaming light seemed to dull the water in the aquarium. The old Spanish tune came back to her lips, and a warm, deep voice emerged from her chest. The song was compelling and full of longing. In the old days, in the distant thirties, the Spanish freedom-fighters and their sympathizers all over the world had been forever humming it. Abrasha could not stop singing it the night he left. A decade or so later, during the Israeli War of Independence, it had acquired Hebrew words. It was sung around the campfire among the old shacks by pale-faced soldiers who had recently fled from Europe. Night after night it had drifted among the kibbutz buildings and had even reached Batya Pinski:

> The first dish to be served
> Is your beloved rifle
> Garnished with its magazines. . . .

Suddenly she made up her mind to go outside.

Bursting out among the fallen trees and broken glass, she saw the sky peaceful and clear over the hills, as if nothing had happened. She saw Matityahu Damkov, his bare back glistening with sweat, mending a water pipe with silent rage. And farther away she could see the empty spot where the wooden shacks, the first buildings of the kibbutz, had stood. Workers were rooting among the wreckage. A few goats grazed peacefully.

She reached the clearing in front of the dining hall at the very moment when Felix was escorting his guests back to their car. They were standing by the car, presumably running over the main points of their discussion. Up to that moment Felix had kept his glasses in his shirt pocket; now he put them on again while he jotted down some notes, and at once he lost the look of a general and regained his habitual appearance of a philosopher.

Finally they shook hands once more. The visitors got into the car and Abramek started the engine. As he began to maneuver his way among the beams and scattered planks, Batya Pinski darted out of the bushes and tapped on the window with a wrinkled fist. The secretary general was momentarily alarmed and covered his face with his hands. Then he opened his eyes and stared at the terrifying figure outside. Abramek stopped the car, rolled the window down a fraction, and asked:

"What's up? Do you need a lift? We're not going to Tel Aviv, though. We're heading north."

"Don't you dare, Abramek, don't you dare leave out the dedication, or I'll scratch your eyes out and I'll raise such a stink that the whole country will sit up and take notice," Batya screeched without pausing to draw breath.

"What is this lady talking about?" asked the secretary general mildly.

"I don't know," Abramek replied apologetically. "I haven't got the faintest idea. In fact, I don't even know her."

Felix immediately took command of the situation.

"Just a minute, Batya, calm down and let me explain. Yes, this is our Comrade Batya Pinski. That's right, Abrasha's Batya. She probably wants to remind us of the moral obligation we all owe her. You remember what it's about, Abramek."

"Of course," said Abramek Bart. And then, as if assailed by sudden doubts, he repeated, "Of course, of course."

Felix turned to Batya, took her arm gently, and addressed her kindly and sympathetically:

"But not now, Batya. You can see what a state we're all in. You've chosen a rather inconvenient moment."

The car, meanwhile, was disappearing around the bend in the road. Felix took the time to see Batya back to her room. On the way he said to her:

"You have no cause to worry. We'll keep our promise. After all, we're not doing this just for your sake, there's no question of a personal favor to you; our young people need Abrasha's writings, they will be the breath of life for them. Please don't rush us. There's still plenty of time; you've got nothing to worry about. On the other hand, I gather you didn't get your lunch today, and for that you have reasonable grounds for complaint. I'll go to the kitchen right away and tell them to send you a hot meal: the boilers are working again now. Don't be angry with us, it hasn't been easy today. I'll be seeing you."

## 15

There was still the aquarium.

Now the fish could get the attention they deserved. First of all the old woman inspected the electrical fittings. Behind the tank there was concealed a veritable forest of plugs and sockets, of multicolored wires, of switches and transformers which kept the vital systems alive.

From a tiny electrical pump hidden underneath the tank, two transparent plastic tubes led into the water. One worked the filter, and the other aerated the water.

The filter consisted in a glass jar containing fibers. The water from the bottom of the tank was pumped up into the filter, to deposit the particles of dirt, uneaten food, and algae, and returned to the tank clear and purified. The aerator was a fine tube that carried air to the bottom of the tank, where it escaped through a perforated stone in a stream of tiny bubbles which enriched the water with oxygen and inhibited the growth of algae. These various appliances kept the water clear and fresh, and enabled the fish to display their array of breathtaking colors, and to dart hither and thither with magical swiftness.

A further electrical fixture without which the aquarium could not function was the heating element, a sealed glass tube containing a finely coiled electric wire. The glowing coil kept the water at a tropical temperature even on rainy days and stormy nights. The light and warmth worked wonders on the gray-green forests of water plants in the depths of which the fish had their home. From there shoal after shoal emerged to pursue a course that was unpredictable because subject to unknown laws. The quivering tails suggested a heart consumed by longing, rather than mere pond life. The fish were almost transparent; their skeletons were clearly visible through their cold skins. They, too, had a system of blood vessels; they, too, were subject to illness and death. But fish are not like us. Their blood is cold. They are cold and alive, and their cold is not death but a liveliness and vitality that makes them soar and plunge, wheel and leap in mid-course. Gravity has no power over them.

The plants and stones emphasize this by contrast. The sight of a school of swordfish swimming gently through the hollow stone arouses a grave doubt in the widow's mind. Is death a possibility, and if so, what need to wait, why not plunge in this very instant.

She presses her burning forehead against the glass. It feels as though the fish are swimming into her head. Here is peace and calm.

Breadth distracts the mind from depth. Depth also exists. It sends wave upon wave of dark stillness up toward the surface. And now the surface of the water reflects the crest-shorn palm trees.

The daylight fades and the windows darken.

Now she will close the shutters and draw the curtains. The kettle will boil again. More tea—this time in one of the china cups she has brought out specially. The fish are clustering around the underwater lamp as if they, too, can sense the approach of night.

A blue-tinged crystalline calm descends on our hills. The air is clear. The day's work is done. May she repose in peace. May the fish swim peacefully through her dreams. May she not be visited in the night by the crest-shorn palm trees. A last procession passes through the hollow stone. Darkness is coming.

1963

# Upon This Evil Earth

## 1

Jephthah was born at the edge of the desert. At the edge of the desert his grave was also dug.

For many years Jephthah roamed the desert in the company of wandering tribesmen close to the borders of the land of Ammon. Even when the elders of Israel came down to seek him in the desert and raised him to be judge of Israel, Jephthah did not leave the desert. He was a wild man. It was for his wildness that the elders of the congregation chose him as their leader. All these things befell in lawless times.

Jephthah was judge for six years. He was victorious in every war he fought. But his countenance was ravaged. He did not love Israel and he did not hate his enemies. He belonged to himself, and even to himself he was a stranger. All the days of his life, even when he sat within his own house, his eyes were narrowed as if for protection against the dust of the desert or the dazzling light. Or else they were turned inward, because nowhere around could he find.

Indeed, on the day of his victory over the Ammonites, when he returned to his father's estate and the people shouted for triumph and the daughters of Israel sang: Jephthah has slain, Jephthah has slain, the man stood as if in a daze. One of the elders of the tribe who was present thought in his heart: This man is deceptive; his heart is not here with us but far away.

His father's name was Gilead the Gileadite. His mother was an Ammonite harlot named Pitdah daughter of Eitam. He named his daughter Pitdah after her. Toward the end of his days, when he was drawing near to death, Jephthah thought of those two women as one.

His mother Pitdah had died when Jephthah was a young man. His brothers, his father's sons, drove him out into the desert because he was the son of another woman.

In the desert bitter-hearted wanderers gathered around him, and he became their leader because he possessed the attributes of lordship. He knew how to speak to them either in a warm voice or with cold malice, at will. Moreover, when firing an arrow, taming a horse, pitching a tent, the man seemed to move slowly, as if weary or sluggish, but this was deceptive, like a dagger reposing in folds of silk. He could say to a man: Rise, come, go; and the man would rise or come or go, although Jephthah the Gileadite made not a sound, only his lips moved. He spoke little because he did not like words and did not trust them.

For many years Jephthah dwelled in the mountains of the desert, and even when he was surrounded by tumultuous throngs of men he was always alone. One day the elders of Israel came down to ask him to fight for them against the Ammonites. They gathered up the hems of their robes because of the dust of the desert and went down on their knees before the wild man. Jephthah stood facing them, listening in silence, and he surveyed their broken pride as though it were a wound. Sorrow suddenly took hold of him, not sorrow for the elders, perhaps not sorrow at all, but something resembling gentleness, and gently he said to them:

"The son of a whore will be your leader."

And voicelessly the elders echoed:

"Our leader."

All this took place in the desert, outside the land of the Ammonites, outside the land of Israel, deep in the silence amid shifting surroundings: sand, mist, low scrub, white mountains, and black boulders.

Jephthah defeated Ammon, returned to his father's estate, and fulfilled his vow. He was certain that he was being confronted with a test, a test that he would withstand. As soon as he had bound his daughter he would be told: Lay not thine hand upon the girl.

Afterward he returned to the desert.

He had loved Pitdah and trusted the night sounds that filled the desert every night. Jephthah the Gileadite died in the mountains in the place which is called the Land of Tob. Some men are born and come into the world to see with their own eyes the light of day and the light of night and to call the light light. But sometimes a man comes and traverses the length of his days in gloom and at his death he leaves behind him a trail of foam and rage. At Jephthah's death his father dug a grave and over it he said:

"He judged Israel for six years by the grace of God."

And then he added:

"The grace of God is vanity."

For four days every year, the daughters of Israel go to the mountains to lament Pitdah daughter of Jephthah. An old blind man follows them at a distance. The dry desert winds snatch the tears from among his wrinkles. But all the winds cannot take away the salt, and it dries, scorching, on the old man's cheeks. To the mountains go the daughters of Israel to send forth their wailing to the desert, lands of fox and asp and hyena, wide expanses eaten by white light. Bitterhearted men, wanderers of the Land of Tob, hear their weeping in the night and respond from the distance with a bitter song.

# 2

The place of Jephthah's birth was at the edge of the land. The estate of Gilead the Gileadite was at the far end of the tribe's patrimony. Here the desert licked at the sown land, and sometimes it would penetrate into the orchards and touch both men and cattle. In the morning, as soon as the sun burst over the eastern mountains, it would begin to scorch the whole land. At midday it fell like blazing hail and smote everything with outpoured wrath. At the end of the day the sun descended westward to burn the mountain heights to the west. The boulders changed color and took on from a distance the semblance of desperate movement, as though they were being roasted alive.

But at night the land was calm. Cool breezes spread over it gently, like a caress. Dew covered the boulders. The night breeze was merciful. This mercy was transitory, and yet it returned ever and again, like the cycle of birth and death, like wind and water, alternating hatred and longing, a shadow that came and went.

Gilead the Gileadite, the lord of the estate, was a tall, broad man. The sun had scorched the skin of his face. He strove with all his might to subdue his spirit, but even so he was a tyrant. His words always left his mouth reproachfully or in a venomous whisper, as though whenever he spoke he had to silence other voices. If he laid his strong rough hand on the head of one of his sons, on the neck of his horse, or on a woman's hips, they knew without looking that it was Gilead. Sometimes he would touch an inanimate object, not because he wished to say or do anything, but because he was smitten with doubts: the substantiality of all things suddenly filled him with wonder. And sometimes he sought to handle things that cannot be touched—sounds, longings, smells. When night came Gilead would sometimes say suddenly: Night has come. Such words are surely unnecessary. In the evening he would summon his household priest to read to him from a holy book, and he would shrink and listen. Even in trivial matters he would turn to God and ask for the birth of a bull calf or the repair of cracked earthenware pitchers. At times he would laugh for no reason at all.

All these things inspired great fear in his servants. Whenever loud hoarse laughter burst from him in the fields at midday in midsummer, the slaves laughed with him out of fear. Or sometimes in the night Gilead was suddenly overcome by a cold hatred of the cold starlight, and he would shout aloud and assemble all the men and women in the courtyard. Before their eyes he would stoop and pick up a large stone, and his eyes shone white in the dark as though he meant to hurl the stone and fell a man. Then slowly and painfully, as though the breath were being squeezed out of him, he would bend and replace the stone in the dust of the courtyard, as gently as if he were placing glass on glass, taking great care not to hurt the stone or the dust or the silence of the night, for the nights in that place were quiet, and any sounds that passed through them were like dark shadows moving silently beneath the surface of the waters.

Gilead's wife was the offspring of priests and merchants, and her name was Nehushtah daughter of Zebulun. She was white as chalk and timorous. In her youth in her father's house, she had known dreams and darkness. She was passionately fond of small objects, little creatures, buttons and butterflies, earrings, morning dew, apple blossom, cat's-paws, soft lamb's wool, slivers of light shimmering in water.

Gilead took Nehushtah to wife because he thought he detected in her signs of an inner thirst which nothing in the world could ever quench or assuage. Whenever she said, "Look, a stone," or "Look at that valley," she seemed to be saying, "Come, come." He yearned to touch this thirst the way a man may suddenly ache to feel some idea or desire with his very fingertips. And Nehushtah followed after Gilead because she saw in him sorrow and strength.

Nehushtah longed to dissolve his strength and penetrate his sorrow and at the same time submit to them. However, Gilead and Nehushtah were unable to do all these things to each other because, after all, body and soul are no more than body and soul, and living men and women are not able to plumb their depths. A few months after she arrived at Mizpeh of Gilead she was already in the habit of standing alone at the window pleading with her eyes, hoping that across the wilderness and the mountains she might descry the plains of black earth from which she had been brought here to the desert. In the evenings she said to him:

"When will you take me."

And Gilead would answer:

"But I have already taken you."

"When shall we ride away from here."

"All places are the same."

"But I cannot endure any more."

"Who can. Bring me wine and apples and leave me, go to your room or sit at the window if you like; just stop staring into the darkness like that."

After years went by, after she had given birth to Jamin, Jemuel, and Azur, Nehushtah fell ill and seemed to be in the grip of a sensuous decay. She was already white as chalk, and her skin grew ever finer. She hated the desert that blew in at the window of her room all day long and at night whispered to her, "Lost lost," and she also hated the savage songs of the shepherds and the lowing of the beasts in the courtyard and in her dreams. Sometimes she called her husband a dead man and her children orphans. And sometimes she would say of herself, Surely I, too, have long been dead, and she would sit for three days at the window without tasting food or water. The place was very remote, and from the window she could see by day only sand dunes and mountains and at night stars and darkness.

Three sons did Nehushtah daughter of Zebulun bear to Gilead the Gileadite: Jamin, Jemuel, and Azur. She was white and her skin grew ever finer. She could not endure the man's moods. If she complained and wept, Gilead would raise his voice and shout and dash the pitcher of wine to clattering smithereens. If she sat silently at the window stroking the cat or playing with earrings and brooches on her lap, Gilead would stand and watch and laugh hoarsely, exuding a shaggy smell. At times he would take pity on her and say:

"Perhaps the king will hear of your sorrow. Perhaps he will send chariots and horses to take you to him. Perhaps today or tomorrow torches will appear in the distance and the outrunners will arrive."

And Nehushtah would say:

"There is no king. There are no outrunners. Why should anyone run. There is nothing."

At these words Gilead would be filled with compassion for her and terrible anger at himself and at what he had done to her, and he would beat his chest with his fists and curse himself and his memory. In the midst of his compassion he would suddenly despise her, or himself and his compassion for her, and he would shut himself up and hide his face. For many days she would not see him, and then one night toward the dawn, when she had despaired of him, he would come and throw himself upon her in love. In his lovemaking he would purse his lips like a man straining to break an iron chain with his bare hands.

He was a moody and hopeless man. At night, if the torchlight fell on his face it looked like one of the masks with which the pagan priests covered their faces. It may happen that a man traverses all the days of his life like an exile in a strange land to which he did not choose to come and from which he cannot escape.

In the winter Gilead was filled with melancholy. He would lie on his back for a day or a week with his eyes fixed on the arched ceiling, staring blankly and seeing nothing. Then Nehushtah would sometimes enter his bedchamber and fondle him with her pale fingers as if he were one of her pet animals. Her lips were as white as a sickness, and he yielded his body to them as a weary traveler yields himself to a harlot in a wayside inn. And upon both of them there was silence.

But when mounting vigor roused his body against him, Nehushtah took refuge in her innermost chamber, and Gilead would storm into the women's quarters to relieve on the maidservants the pressure of the boiling venom. All night long the quarters were alive with wet sounds and low tremulous moaning and the squeals of the maids, until the dawn, when Gilead would burst forth and rudely awaken the household priest. Cowering at his feet, he would sob: Unclean, unclean. Then, with the tears still wet on his face, he would knock the priest flat on his back with a punch, and out he would rush to saddle his horse and gallop away into the eastern hills.

In the women's quarters there was a little Ammonite concubine named Pitdah daughter of Eitam, whom the Gileadites had snatched in the course of one of their raids on the Ammonite settlements beyond the desert. Pitdah was a strong, slender girl whose eyes were shaded by thick lashes.

If she directed her green-eyed gaze at her lord's lips or at his chest, if she stood facing him in the courtyard with her fingertips fluttering over her belly, he would tremble and curse the little servantgirl. Bellowing aloud, he would clasp both her hands in one of his and bite her lips until the two of them screamed together. Her hips were never still, and even when she came and stood at the stable door to inhale the smell of horses' sweat, they seemed to be dancing to a secret inner rhythm. Fire and ice sparkled green in the pupils of her eyes. And she always walked barefoot.

In time it transpired that the Ammonite woman practiced sorcery. This was disclosed by her rivals, who had seen her at night brewing herbs in the night with a gleam in her eye. Pitdah called to the dead at night and summoned them to her, because she had been dedicated from her childhood as a priestess of Milcom the god of Ammon. The trees in the orchard rustled secretively in the darkness and the doors of the house shrieked in the wind. She worked her magic in the cellars at night and the brew bubbled and boiled and the woman's shadow quivered and flickered over rotting saddles and casks of wine, on wooden threshing sledges and iron chains.

When her doings came to light, Gilead ordered her to be given a leather flask of water and sent away into the desert to the dead to whom she called at night, for it is written: Thou shalt not suffer a witch to live.

But at first light the lord saddled his horse and rode out and brought her home. He cursed her gods and struck her face with the back of his rough hand.

Pitdah blew in his face and cursed him and his people and his God. A hot green sparkle glinted in the pupil of her eye.

Suddenly they both laughed and went inside. The door closed behind them while outside the horses neighed.

Gilead's wife Nehushtah urged her three sons against the Ammonite woman because she could endure no more. She rose from her bed and stood at the window in her white robe, with her back to the room and her sons and her face to the desert, and she whispered to them, You see your mother dying before your eyes and you are silent: do not be silent.

But Jamin and Jemuel feared their father and would not raise a finger.

Only Azur, the youngest of her sons, hearkened to her and plotted against the Ammonite servantgirl. This Azur devoted all his days to the dogs of the estate. He it was who fed and watered them, taught them tricks, and trained them to go straight for the throat. In Mizpeh of Gilead they said of him: That Azur understands the dogs' tongue and can howl or bark in the dark like one of them. Azur had a small gray wolf cub that ate from his dish and drank from his cup, and both of them had sharp white teeth.

One day at the beginning of autumn, when Gilead had gone away to another field, Azur set his dogs on Pitdah the Ammonite concubine. He stood in the shade of the house and let out a guttural growl when Pitdah went past, and the dogs, with the wolf cub in their midst, darted from the dungheap and almost tore her apart.

At nightfall Gilead returned home and gave his son Azur over to a cruel slave, shriveled and shorn, to take him out to the desert, as shall be done to a murderer.

In the night the wild beasts howled, their eyes gleaming yellow in the darkness beyond the stockade.

This time, too, Gilead set out on horseback at the end of the night and brought his son back. He struck and cursed his son just as he had struck and cursed his concubine.

After these things it came to pass that the Ammonite woman cast a spell upon the boy Azur: for forty days he howled and barked and could not speak a word.

Upon her lord Pitdah also cast a dark spirit, because he had spared Azur and she did not forgive him this pardon. A brooding gloom fell on the master of the house which only lifted when he consumed large draughts of wine.

When Pitdah bore Jephthah, Gilead the Gileadite shut himself up in the cellar of the house for four days and five nights. All through these nights he clinked cup on cup, drained them both, and filled them again. On the fifth night he collapsed on the ground. In his dream he saw a black horseman with a lance of black fire, mounted on a black horse, while a floating woman who was neither Pitdah nor

Nehushtah but a stranger held the reins; horse and rider followed her silently. Gilead did not forget this dream, because he believed, like some other men, that dreams are sent to us from that place from which man comes and to which he returns through his death.

When the child Jephthah grew old enough to leave the women's quarters and walk about in the courtyard, he learned to hide from his father. He would shelter in a haystack until the heavy man had passed and his sinister footsteps had receded, so that he should not find him. Until Gilead disappeared the infant would chew straw or hay or his own finger and whisper to himself: Quiet, quiet.

If the child was so absorbed in his dreams that it was too late for him to hide, Gilead the Gileadite would catch him and wave him aloft between his frightening hands and moo at him, and he smelled sweaty and shaggy, so that the child howled with pain and fear and planted his tiny teeth in his father's shoulder in a vain effort to free himself from the powerful grasp.

# 3

Jephthah was born facing the desert. The estate of Gilead the Gileadite was the last of all the tribe's patrimony. At its fringe began the desert, and beyond the desert was the land of the Ammonites.

Gilead the Gileadite possessed flocks of sheep, and he also had fields and vineyards whose margins were yellowed by the desert. The house was surrounded by a high stone wall. The house itself was also built of black volcanic stone. An ancient vine sprawled over its walls. On summer days people seemed to come and go through a thicket of vines; the foliage was so dense that the stone walls of the house could not be seen in summer.

Toward morning sheep bells could be heard, and the shepherds' pipes spread vague enchantments, the water whispered quietly in the irrigation channels, and a gray light shone in the wells.

There was calm toward morning over all Gilead's estate.

Within the calm rippled a suppressed yearning. The shade of large trees concealed chilly twilight.

But every night dark, impassive shepherds guarded the farmstead against bears and nomads and Ammonite marauders. All night long torches flamed on the rooftop and a pack of lean hounds lurked in the darkness of the orchards. The household priest flitted like a dark shadow along the fences in the night, conjuring evil spirits.

From his earliest childhood Jephthah knew all the sounds of the night. He knew them in his blood, sounds of wind and wolf and bird of prey, and human sounds disguised as wind and fox and bird.

Beyond the fence lived another world, which silently yearned by day and night to raze the house to the ground, gnawing slyly and with infinite patience, like a stream slowly eating away at its banks. It was unimaginably soft and quiet, softer than a mist, quieter than a breeze, and yet ever-present: powerful and invisible.

Black goats kept the boy company; he led them to pasture and watched them all day long munching the sparse grass, risking their lives on the sheer crags of the narrow strip of pasture that survived among the rocky ravines, for the place was on the edge of the desert. He was also accompanied by emaciated dogs, his brother Azur's dogs. They were rough dogs, and savagery always lurked beneath their obsequiousness. Wild birds also flocked to Jephthah, shrieking their reproaches in his ears.

Early in the morning birds screeched in the distance. In the evening, as twilight fell, the crickets shrilled as though they had an urgent, fearful message to deliver. In the dark Jephthah heard a fine stillness pierced occasionally by the cry of a fox or jackal, punctuated by a hyena's laughter.

Sometimes desert nomads raided the estate at night. In the darkness Gilead's shepherds lay in wait for the foe, who came as softly as a breath; if he slew he stole silently away, and if he was slain he died as silently. In the morning they would find a man lying on his back under the olive trees, his

hand perhaps still clutching the haft of the knife that was
sunk in his flesh and his eyes turned inward. Shepherd or
foeman alike.

Seeing the whites of the corpse's bulging eyes, Jephthah
would say to himself: A corpse turns his eyes inward, perhaps there he finds other sights to see.

Sometimes Jephthah dreamed of his own death, and he
seemed to feel strong, kindly hands bearing him down to the
plain. Softly, sweetly, a light drizzle touched him, and a little
shepherd girl said: Here for a while we shall sit and rest until after the rain and the light.

In the summertime the vegetation ran riot in the orchards and the ripening fruit filled out with moisture. Powerful juices coursed through the veins of the apple trees. The
vine shoots seemed to shudder with the pressure of pent-up
sap. Goats sported wantonly and the bull bellowed and
raged. In the women's quarters and in the shepherds' booths
there was heavy panting; toward dawn the boy could hear
in his slumber a sound like a dying beast's groans. Women
also occupied his dreams: Jephthah was filled with longing
for delicate forces he could not name, not silk, not water, not
skin, not hair, but a yearning for a warm, melting touch,
hardly a touch at all, perhaps river-thoughts, smells, colors,
and not that, either.

He did not like words and therefore he was silent.

In his dreams on summer nights in his youth, he forced
his way gently upstream.

In the morning, when he rose, he took the dagger and
slowly, patiently tested with it everything he found in the
courtyard: Dust. Bark. Wool. Stone. Water.

Jephthah did not display his father's moods. He was a
strong, finely shaped boy; colors, sounds, smells, and objects
attracted him much more than words or people. When he
was twelve he could handle an ax, a ewe, a cudgel, or a bridle. As he did so, a controlled excitement could sometimes
be discerned in him.

And now the hatred of his brothers Jamin, Jemuel, and
Azur began to close in all around him. They wished him ill
because he was the son of another woman, because of his

haughty silence, and because of the arrogant calm that seemed at every moment to be concealing stubborn, secretive thoughts which brooked no sharing. If ever the brothers invited him to join in their games, he played with them without saying anything. If he won a contest he did not boast or gloat, but merely shut himself up in a silence which increased their hatred sevenfold. And if one of the brothers defeated Jephthah, it always seemed as though he himself had voluntarily renounced the victory out of calculation or contempt, or because he had lost his concentration in the middle of the game.

The three brothers, Jamin, Jemuel, and Azur, were solidly built, broad-shouldered youths. In their own way they knew joys and laughter. Jephthah, on the other hand, the son of the other woman, was slim and fair. Even when he laughed he seemed withdrawn. He had a habit of fixing his gaze on others and refusing to look away. A fleeting yellow spark would flash in his eyes, compelling others suddenly to yield.

Because of Pitdah's spells, or perhaps because of fear of their father, the brothers did not dare to mistreat Jephthah as they wished. They merely hissed from a distance in a whisper: Just you wait.

Once Pitdah said: Weep, Jephthah, cry out to our god Milcom, he will hearken and protect you from their whispering hatred.

But in this matter Jephthah did not heed his mother. He did not weep to Milcom god of Ammon but merely bowed low and said to his mother: As my lady mother says. As though he considered Pitdah to be the lady of the house.

She wanted to bring down on her son the blessing of Milcom god of Ammon, because she foresaw that she would die and that the boy would be left alone among strangers. And so she brewed her potions at night and fed them at night to Jephthah. When her fingers touched his cheek he would tremble.

In his heart Jephthah had no faith in these potions, but neither did he refuse to drink them. He loved their strange, pungent smell, the smell of his mother's fingers. And she would speak to him of Milcom, whom the Ammonites worshiped with wine and silk. Not like your father's god, a barren god who afflicts and humiliates those who love him. No, Milcom loves marauders, he loves those who are merry with wine, he loves those who pour out their hearts in song, and the music that blurs the line between ecstasy and rage.

Of the God of Israel Pitdah said: Woe to those who sin against him and woe to those who worship him in faith; he will afflict them both alike with agonies because he is a solitary god.

Jephthah observed the stars in the summer sky over the estate and the desert. They seemed to him to be all alone, each star by itself in the black expanse, some of them circling all night long from one end of the sky to the other, while others remained rooted to one spot. There was no sorrow in all the stars, nor was there any joy in them. If one of them suddenly fell, none of the others noticed or so much as blinked, they simply went on flickering coldly. The falling star left behind it a trail of cold fire, and the fiery trail also faded and gave way to darkness. If you stood barefoot and strained to listen, you might hear a silence within the silence.

The household priest who taught the other brothers also taught Jephthah to read and write from the holy scriptures. Once Jephthah asked the priest why God was more merciful to Abel and Isaac, Jacob, Joseph, and Ephraim, and why he preferred them to their elder brothers, Cain, Ishmael, Esau, and Manasseh: surely all the evil in the scriptures came from God himself, surely it was to him that the blood of Abel cried from the earth.

The household priest was a corpulent man with small, anxious eyes. He was constantly shrinking from the wrath of the lord of the house. The priest replied to Jephthah that the ways of God were wonderful and who could say to God why or wherefore. At night Jephthah dreamed of God coming heavy and shaggy, a bear-God with rapacious jaws who growled at him panting gasping and panting as though he were throbbing with lust or boiling rage. Jephthah cried out in his dream. People occasionally cried out in their sleep in Gilead's house, and at the end of their cries there was silence.

Milcom, too, crept into Jephthah's dreams on those summer nights. Warm currents coursed luxuriantly through his veins as the silken fingers touched his skin and sweet juices washed through him to the soles of his feet.

Next morning Jephthah would appear solitary and withdrawn in the great courtyard, skipping from shadow to shadow, and the yellow glint had even faded from the pupils of his eyes.

When Jephthah was a boy of about fourteen, he began to be favored with signs. As he walked alone in the fields or followed the flocks down into one of the gullies, he was beset by signs, and he felt that it was to him alone that they were directed, that he was being called. But he could not discover what the signs were or who was calling him. Sometimes he fell on his knees as the household priest had taught him and struck his head on the rock and pleaded aloud: Now, now.

In his mind he weighed the love of God against the love of Milcom. He found the love of Milcom very easy, it came to him at almost no cost, like the love of a dog. You play with it for a moment and you have won its heart; it will come close, lick your hand, and perhaps even guard your sleep in the field.

But to ask for the love of God Jephthah did not dare, because he did not know what. If a momentary pride flared up inside him and he made a mental comparison, saying: I am the youngest, I am like Abel and Isaac and Jacob, sons of their parents' old age, at once he would recall that he was the son of another woman, like Ishmael, who was the son of the Egyptian woman.

One day the lord told his household that God must be approached not in the way that a butterfly approaches a flower but as it approaches the fire.

The boy heard these words and he also put them to the test.

He began to seek out dangers with which to challenge himself. He tested himself on the mountain crags, in the shifting sands, in the well. He even pitted himself against a wolf. One night he went out alone and unarmed to find the wolf and fight it at the mouth of its lair, and with his bare hands he broke the beast's back, and returned home from the test merely bitten and scratched. He was trying to court God's favor, and in the autumn he even trained himself to pass his hand through the fire without crying out.

Some of these acts were seen by the household priest, and he went and told the lord that the Ammonite was passing his hand through fire. Gilead heard the priest out, then his face clouded with rage, he gave a wild laugh, cursed the priest, and gave him a blow that sent him sprawling.

That night Gilead the Gileadite gave orders for the concubine's son to be found and brought to him. A fire was burning in the hall, because it was a cold desert night and the air was dry and biting. The walls of the hall were hung with saddles, iron chains, shields, threshing sledges, and spears of polished bronze. All these objects caught the firelight and reflected it gloomily.

Gilead fixed his gray eyes on the other woman's son and stared at him long and hard. He could not recall why he had sent for him at night, or why the dogs were barking outside in the dark. At the end of his silence Gilead said:

"My son, I am told that you pass your hand through the fire and that you do not cry out when you do it."

Jephthah said:

"That is the truth."

Gilead said:

"And why should you do such a wrong and painful thing?"

Jephthah said:

"To prepare myself, Father."

"Prepare yourself for what?"

"I do not know for what."

As Jephthah spoke to his father he looked at the broad, rough hand that rested heavily on an earthen tray. At the sight of his father's hand his own pale, thin hand filled with fear and longing. Perhaps he imagined that his father might speak to him lovingly. Perhaps he imagined that his father might ask for his love. At that moment, for the first and only time in his whole life, Jephthah suddenly yearned to be a woman. And he did not know what. In the brazier the fire blazed and sparks of firelight glowed dully on the bronze weapons hanging on the walls, and in the lord's eyes, too, a certain spark gleamed.

Gilead said in a whisper:

"Very well, put your hand in the fire and let us see."

Jephthah looked entreatingly into his father's face, but Gilead the Gileadite's face was hidden in the flickering light and shadow, for the tongues of fire in the brazier were darting restlessly hither and thither. The boy said:

"My father's word is my command."

Gilead said:

"Put your hand in now."

Jephthah said:

"If you will love me."

As he put out his hand his teeth showed as if he were laughing, but Jephthah was not laughing.

Suddenly his father shouted:

"My son, do not touch the fire. That is enough."

But Jephthah did not want to hear, and he did not avert his eyes. The fire touched the flesh, and beyond the fence the desert stretched to the most distant hills.

After this episode Gilead said to Jephthah his son:

"You are tainted as your father is tainted. And yet I cannot bring myself to hate you."

Then the lord poured wine from the earthen pitcher into two rough cups and said:

"Jephthah, you will take wine with me."

And because neither the man nor the boy could trust words or liked words, half the night passed before either of them spoke another word.

Finally Gilead rose to his feet and spoke.

"Now, my son, go. Do not hate your father and do not love him. It is an ill thing that we must be each of us son to a father and father to a son and man to a woman. Distance upon distance. Now, don't stand there staring. Go."

# 4

After these things it sometimes happened that father and son rode out together toward dawn in the open country. They would cross the bed of the ravine and mount the slope that led up to the expanse of broad sands, and very slowly, as though riding in a dream, they would traverse the parched plateau. Stubborn, forlorn shrubs sprouted here and there among the crevices of the rock. They seemed less like plants than like the loins of the barren boulders. A baneful white light beat mercilessly down. When they had ridden far away, a fitful conversation might flare up between them.

Gilead might say:

"Jephthah, where do you want to go."

And Jephthah, his eyes narrowed against the brutally blazing light, would reply, after a silence:

"To my own place. Home."

Then Gilead, with a hint of a smile fleeting across his stony face, would ask:

"Well, why don't we turn around and ride for home."

And Jephthah, himself almost smiling, his voice remote and abstracted:

"That is not my home."

"Then where is your home, what home do you want to go to."

"That, Father, is what I do not yet know."

After this exchange, silence would close in once more. But now they were both within the same silence and not in two separate silences. The boy would be full of love, and lovingly he would stroke his horse's mane. Once, when they came to the valley of black basalt, he asked his father:

"What is the desert trying to say, what thought is the wasteland, why does the wind come and why does it suddenly drop, with what sense must a man hear the thronging sounds, and with what sense may he hear the silence?"

To which Gilead replied:

"You for yourself. I for myself. Every man for himself."

And after a moment he added, this time with a shadow of compassion in his voice:

"There is a lizard. Now it has gone."

And with that they both relapsed into their shared silence.

As they rode back to the farm, Gilead the Gileadite might stretch out his broad, rough hand and suddenly hold his son's bridle for a moment or two. And they rode close together.

Then he would let go as they came through the fence. Jephthah would be dismissed to join the other youngsters in the farmyard, while Gilead would go into the house.

During the last winter Pitdah sometimes came to Jephthah's bedroom at night. Barefoot, she would come and sit on the edge of his bed, whispering spells. She was given to laughing suddenly, a soft, warm laugh, until the boy could no longer contain himself and laughed along with her, without making a sound. Or else she would sing him gentle Ammonite songs about the vast expanses of water or the buck in the vineyards or about suffering and grace.

She would take his hand in hers and draw his fingers slowly up her arm slowly over her shoulder slowly around her soft neck. And she would entice him to Milcom god of pleasure, whispering rapid strange words, the secret of his own flesh and everything of which flesh was capable. And she also entreated him to flee from the desert to the places of shade and water before the desert succeeded in parching his blood and his flesh.

Jephthah had never set eyes on the sea in his life, he did not know its smell or the sound of its waves in the night, but he called his mother, Sea, sea.

One night, after she had left him, Jephthah had a dream. The bald, shriveled steward came and sheared a ewe closely, then sheared her again until her skin showed pink and sickly, crisscrossed with countless veins, and the servant sheared her yet again and slaughtered the ewe, not by the throat but by the belly, and black blood gushed and bubbled and stuck to Jephthah's skin in his dream and then God came heavy and iron-shouldered clad in a bearskin and he was hot and parched. On a carpet of vine leaves Milcom lay wrapped in silk and jewels, and Jephthah saw God force his way into the silk as a ram forces his way with bloodshot eyes into a ewe stooping submissively as if stupefied by the powerful rage unleashed against her.

Jephthah woke from this bad dream drenched in sweat. He opened his eyes and lay trembling feverishly and saw darkness, and he closed his eyes and again saw nothing but darkness and he started to whisper a prayer which he had learned from the household priest and still he saw darkness and he tried singing his mother's songs but still the darkness did not release him and he lay on his bed as though petrified because he imagined that while he was dreaming they had all, his father and mother, the priest and the maidservants, the sheep and the shepherds and his stepbrothers and the farmdogs and even the wandering nomads outside, been carried off dead and he was left all alone by himself and outside in the dark the desert stretched to the ends of the earth.

One night at the end of that winter Pitdah died. The maidservants said, The Ammonite whore has died by her sorcery. So she was buried on the following day in the plot reserved for outcasts.

On the horizon at the end of the plain that morning a gray sandstorm rose up tall and furious in the distance, and all the air was filled with dust and the smell of a gathering tempest. All the land was covered with a fine ash. And meanwhile the household priest tossed earth onto the dead woman's grave and uttered a dark oath: Leave us now and go to the accursed place from which you were taken and do not return to us either in the dark or in a dream, lest the curse of God pursue you even in your death and the demons of destruction hound you. Go, go, accursed one, go and never return, and let us have rest. Amen.

At the sound of these words the boy Jephthah picked up a small stone and touched his lips with it, and suddenly he pleaded out of the depths: God love me and I will be your servant, touch me and I will be the leanest and most terrible of your hounds, only do not be remote.

After the burial the sky closed in. Massive, dark shapes sped in succession on the wind, as though sent to crash against the wall of mountains to the east or to break through that same mountain wall. Later still, white flashes struck and then the low thunder rolled. The house built entirely of black volcanic stone stood in the midst of the storm looking as though it had already been burned.

Jephthah returned from the burial ground and entered the house. Pressed against the dark wall in the shadow of the entrance hall stood his three half-brothers, Jamin, Jemuel, and Azur, as though awaiting his return. He passed between them in the narrow hall, and their chests almost brushed his shoulders as he passed, yet not one of them moved or stirred. Only the wolflike look in their eyes groped at Jephthah's skin as he passed between them in the entrance to the house. He did not speak and the brothers did not speak to him, they did not even speak to one another, not a whisper passed among them. All day long the three of them paced up and down the passages of the house; every footfall gave an impression of supreme delicacy, even though the brothers were generally clumsy men.

Jamin, Jemuel, and Azur paced up and down the house on tiptoe all day long, as though their brother Jephthah were dangerously ill.

Toward evening their mother Nehushtah left her bed and her bedchamber and went to stand at a window. But contrary to her habitual custom, she did not look through the window to see what was outside, but stood with her back to the window and her eyes on the orphan boy. With a chalk-white hand Nehushtah daughter of Zebulun stroked her hair. She said to her sons:

"From now on he, too, is an orphan cub."

And the sons said:

"Because his mother is dead."

She added in a whisper:

"You are all large and dark, but one of you is quite different, fair and very thin."

And Jamin, the eldest, said:

"Thin and fair, but not one of us. The night is falling."

———

That same night Nehushtah his stepmother suddenly came to see Jephthah in his room on the rooftop. She opened the door and stood barefoot in the doorway, just as Pitdah used to come barefoot, but between Nehushtah's white fingers there was a white candle, and its flame was trembling violently. Jephthah saw her wan smile as she came close to his bed and passed a cold, damp hand across his brow. She whispered to him:

"Orphan. Go to sleep now, orphan."

He did not know what to say to her.

"You are mine now, thin little orphan cub. Go to sleep now."

With her fingertips she touched the curls on his chest for a moment. Then stopped.

When she left the room the stepmother blew out the lamp. She took both the lamp and the candle out with her when she went. It was dark.

All night long the storm raged outside. The wind hurled itself drunkenly against the walls of the house. The pillars groaned and the wooden ceiling whistled and creaked. In the yard the dogs went mad. The terrified cattle moaned and wailed in the darkness.

Jephthah stood watching at the door until dawn in case they came. He gripped his knife between his teeth. He imagined that beyond the door he could hear soft footsteps padding up and down, the whisper of cloth rubbing against stone, a rustling sound on the topmost stair. And outside a hyena laughed, a bird screeched, iron clanged at the edge of the shadows. The house and the farm stood strange and sinister.

At first light Jephthah slipped out through the window of his room and shinned down the vine with his knife between his teeth. He stole bread, water, a horse, and a dagger from the empty farmyard and fled to the desert to escape from Jamin, Jemuel, and Azur his brothers, his father's sons.

Gilead the Gileadite, the lord of the property, had not appeared at the graveside of his servant Pitdah in the plot reserved for outcasts, nor after the burial, in the evening or the night.

The sun rose and the storm ceased. The desert sand drank up all the puddles of water and once more became arid and brilliant in the terrible light.

The whiteness of those wide expanses rose uncompromising and merciless.

Only in the crannies of the rocks did a little water still remain, dazzled by the blinding sunlight. For a moment Jephthah imagined that the hollows of the stones were clutching the remains of last night's lightning. He had seen all these sights before in his dreams. Everything, the mountains, the sand dunes, the wind, and the dazzle, everything called out to him, Come, come.

After a few hours, when his horse had carried him well away from his father's house, his mind suddenly cleared. To the Ammonites. It was time for him to go to the children of Ammon. With the Ammonite bands he would return when the right time came and set fire to the whole farm. As the fire consumed everything, Jephthah the Ammonite would emerge through the flames carrying the unconscious body of the old man in his arms. He would lay him down among the embers and ashes and crouch over him to give him water and dress his wounds. When Gilead had lost his wife, his farm, and his sons, what would he have left except his last son, who had saved his life.

And then they could both set out together to look for the sea.

The following night, by the light of a clay lamp, the household clerk wrote in the household records: Jephthah shall have no inheritance in his father's house because he is the son of another woman. And the household clerk wrote further in the household records: Darkness and wrath surely beget wrath and darkness. This whole affair is evil: evil is he who has fled and evil are those that remain. Evil will also be our latter end. May God forgive his servant.

# 5

Jephthah dwelled for many days among the Ammonites in the city of Abel-Keramim. From his childhood he spoke their language and knew their laws and their songs, because his mother had been an Ammonite woman who was snatched by the Gileadites when they raided the Ammonite settlements beyond the desert.

Indeed, in Abel-Keramim he also discovered his mother's father and all her brothers, who were great men, and they adopted Jephthah and took him into the palaces and temples. The Ammonite princes honored and exalted Jephthah, because the sound of his voice was cold and lordly and a yellow glint sometimes appeared in his eye, and also because he was very sparing in his use of words.

They said:

"This man was born to be a leader."

And they also said:

"Truly it seems that this man is always at rest."

And also:

"It is very hard to know."

When shooting arrows or carousing, Jephthah sometimes seemed to those around him to be moving slowly, almost wearily or with a slight hesitancy. How deceptive this was: like a knife reposing between folds of silk.

He had the power to say to a stranger: Rise, come, go; and the man would rise or come or go, although Jephthah made not a sound, only his lips moved. Even when he turned to one of the elders of the city and said, Now speak, I am listening, or, Do not speak, I am not listening, the elder felt an inner compulsion to reply; Yes, my lord.

He was loved by many women in the city of Abel-Keramim. Like his father Gilead before him, he was endowed with powers of sadness and powers of silent dominion. Women longed to dissolve the power and penetrate the sadness and also to submit to them. At night, between the silken sheets, they whispered into his ear: You

stranger. When his skin touched theirs they would cry out.
And he, mute and remote, knew how to extract from them
a gushing melody, as well as slow, tormented tunes, a fer-
vent arching and swelling beyond endurance, patiently sailing upstream night after night to the very limit of the soul.

In those days Gatel ruled over the children of Ammon.
He was a boy king. When Jephthah came before King Gatel
the king looked at him as a sickly youth looks at a racing
charioteer, and asked him to tell him stories: let the stranger
tell the king stories to sweeten his sleep at night.

And so Jephthah sometimes came to King Gatel at the
end of the day to tell him about rending a wolf barehanded,
about the wars of shepherds and nomads, about whitening
bones in the desert at midday, about the terror of the night
sounds that rise from the desert at the middle watch.

Sometimes the king would plead, More, more; sometimes he would implore, Don't leave me, Jephthah, sit here
till I fall asleep, because of the dark; and sometimes he
would suddenly burst out laughing feebly like a haunted
man, unable to stop unless Jephthah laid a hand on his
shoulder and said to him: That's enough, Gatel.

Then the king of the Ammonites would stop laughing
and turn his pitiful blue eyes on Jephthah and beg, More,
more.

In the course of time King Gatel made Jephthah his con-
fidant and was always watching attentively for the yellow
spark which did or did not glint in Jephthah's eye.

The elders of Ammon looked askance on all this: A
young slave has come to the city out of the sand dunes, and
now the king is under his spell, and must we watch and say
nothing.

King Gatel was an assiduous reader of the chronicles of
ancient times. He had set his heart on being like one of those
mighty kings who had brought many lands under their dominion. But because he loved words with all his being and
always paid more attention to the words in which his chronicle would be written than to the victorious deeds themselves, he was smitten by serious doubts about even simple
questions. If he had to select a new groom, or order the construction of a new turret, or in general to choose between

two different courses of action, he would torment himself with doubts all night long because he could always see both sides of the problem.

If ever Jephthah deigned to hint which was the better course or which would end badly, Gatel would be overcome with gratitude and affection, of which he was unable to express to Jephthah even the smallest part, because it is the way of words to delude the man who courts them.

He would say:

"Let's ride to Aroer or Rabbat-Ammon to see if the figs are ripe yet."

Then he would add:

"Or perhaps we shouldn't, because the stars do not favor a journey today."

Or else:

"I had a pain in my ear and in my knee all night. And now I have a toothache and a bellyache. Tell me another story about that boy you told me about, the one who could speak the language of the dogs. Don't leave me."

And so it came to pass that King Gatel fell in love and confusion, and would stamp his foot with longing if Jephthah did not come to the palace in the morning. And within the palace a secret enmity was hatched. People said to one another:

"This will lead to no good."

Abel-Keramim was a large and happy city. Its wines flowed abundantly, its women were round-hipped and sweet-scented, its servants were eager and merry, its maidservants were easygoing, and all its horses were swift. Chemosh and Milcom had showered the city with delights. Every evening the trumpets sounded for banquets, and at night sounds of players and musicians rose up and rows of torches blazed in the squares of the city until morning light appeared and the caravans set out through the city gates.

Jephthah did not stand aloof from the pleasures of Abel-Keramim. He tried everything and saw everything, but he touched it all with his fingertips only, because his heart was far away and he said to himself: Let the Ammonites play before me. Three or even four women flocked to him in the same night, and Jephthah loved to revel with them and enjoy them one by one while they enjoyed each other in unison and he would enter among them a scourge of lust a rod of rage and sometimes after all the sound and fury they would sing him Ammonite songs about expanses of water or bucks in the vineyard or suffering and grace while he lay back among them awash on a sea like a dream-swept child. At first light he would say to them all, Now, go, that's enough. And he would sit at the window watching the fingers of light and the pallor of the mountains and the distant conflagration and finally also the sun.

The summer came and went. The autumn winds snatched at the treetops. Old horses suddenly reared and whinnied. Jephthah sat at the window and remembered his father's house. He suddenly longed to be sitting in the stable with the household priest and his three brothers Jamin, Jemuel, and Azur while the priest read to them from a holy book and outside the water ran in the channels, the orchards were cloaked in wintry sadness, and the scent of autumn rose from the vineyards as the vine leaves fell. The longing pierced and stung him with the sharpness of an arrow until his soul was writhing in torment.

He rose and stood at the window while, behind him on his couch, one of the beautiful women lay sleeping, her hair covering her face, breathing peacefully. It sounded to him like a soft evening breeze, and all of a sudden he could not remember who she was, or even whether he had already been with her or if he still had to go to her, and why.

Jephthah sat down on the end of the bed and began singing his mother's songs to the sleeping woman. But his voice was rough and the song came out bitter and rasping. He reached out and touched her cheek with his fingertips, and she did not wake up. He rose and returned to the window and saw dark clouds hurrying eastward in a panic, as though something were happening beyond the eastern horizon and he must arise and go there at once, now, before it was too late. But he did not know what the place was or why it might be too late or who it was who was calling him to go, and he only said to himself:

"Not here."

And then Jephthah also thought: My brother Azur is not Abel and I am not Cain. O Lord of the asp in the desert, do not hide yourself from me. Call me, call me, gather me to you. If I am not worthy to be your chosen one, take me to be your hired assassin: I shall go in the night with my knife in your name to your foes, and in the morning you may hide your face from me as you will, as if we were strangers. You are the lord of the fox and the vulture and I love your wrath and I do not ask you to lift up the brightness of your countenance toward me. Your wrath and barren sorrow are all I want. Surely anger and sadness are a sign to me that I am made in your image, I am your son, I am yours, and you will take me to you by night, for in the image of your hatred am I made, O lord of the wolves at night in the desert. You are a weary and a desperate God, and whomsoever you love, him will you burn with fire, for you are jealous. I say to you cursed be your love, O God, and cursed be my love of you. I know your secret for I am in your secret: you paid heed to Abel and his offering but in your heart it was Cain, Cain, that you loved, and therefore you spread your wrathful care upon Cain and not upon his simplehearted brother. And you chose Cain and not Abel to be a fugitive and a vagabond upon the face of this evil earth, and you set the seal of your image upon his brow to wander to and fro in all the land and to stamp your seal the seal of a barren God upon people and hills, O God of Cain, O God of Jephthah son of Pitdah. Cain is a witness and I am a witness to your image, O lord of the lightning in the forest of the fire in the granary of the howling of maddened dogs in the night, I know you for you are in me. I the son of the Ammonite woman loved my mother, and my mother clove to my father out of the depths, and out of the depths my father cried to you. Give me a sign.

The city of Abel-Keramim stood at the crossroads of the caravan routes, and as dusk fell long lines of caravans from afar passed under its gates, laden with all the riches of Egypt, spices and perfumes and copper from Assyria, glassware from Phoenicia, fragrant game from the land of Edom to the south, from Judea grapes and olives, wines from the Euphrates, silk from Aleppo, little blue-eyed boys from the blue isles of the sea, Hittite harlots, bracelets, myrrh, and concubines; by nightfall everything was gathered within the walls, the heavy gates were barred, and the whole city was filled with torchlight and tumult. Sometimes the golden domes caught flashes of light and seemed to sparkle with blood and fire and all the temples overflowed with strains of ecstatic music.

Jephthah wallowed in wine, women, and court life. Despite all this luxury, his visage appeared as if scorched by fire. On his couch at night he was caressed by the fairest women of the city; they sipped his wintry powers like dazed birds. Their lips fluttered among the hair of his chest and they whispered to him: You stranger. He said nothing, but his eyes turned inward because nowhere around could they find.

In the course of time jealousy began to swell in the city. The notables of Ammon were jealous because of their wives and daughters, and also on account of the king. The elders said in their council: Ammon serves King Gatel, and King Gatel is like a woman in the hands of Jephthah the Gileadite, and this Jephthah is not one of us but belongs only to himself.

These words even reached the ears of the king, who already despised himself for his love of Jephthah. Sometimes at night he would say to himself, Why do I not have this fair-haired man killed.

But he hesitated, because he could see both sides of the question.

When the words of the elders reached his ears, and rumor whispered that the king was like a harlot before the stranger, his eyes brimmed with tears. All the days of his youth he had dreamed of waging great wars like one of the mighty kings of old, but he did not know how to make war, and whenever he so much as set foot outside his palace the sunlight made his head reel and the very smell of a horse always made his teeth chatter. Therefore he summoned Jephthah one day and said to him: Take men, chariots, and lances, take horses and horsemen, take priests and magicians, and go to the land of Gilead to conquer the land into which your mother was carried to servitude. If you refuse to go that will prove that the elders are right, that you are not one of us but a stranger. I am the king and I have spoken. Fetch me a glass of water.

That night Jephthah dreamed of the desert. In his dream he was climbing a crag in the desert and was trapped halfway up the rock face, because it was as smooth as Sidonian glass and he could neither climb up nor go down but only close his eyes, because beneath his feet there was a sheer drop onto the sharp white rocks far below. The wind howled all around him like a wild beast. Just then he felt a woman's hand caress his back, and her touch weakened his grip on the rock face, and he yearned to give up and to go to where she was calling him. In the depth of the cave there was a damp wind and the light was grim and lurid, but the woman was there at his side and there was stillness, cool water, and rest.

When he woke up in the morning he knew that his stay in the land of Ammon was at an end and that the time had come for him to leave. Outside the city reached up toward heaven with all its palm trees and gold-domed towers. When the morning light touched the gold the whole city began to blaze. This was a sadness Jephthah had not expected. He had innocently supposed that a man could simply get up and go without looking back. He almost changed his mind. It was as if the city were clutching at his robe with sharp claws of longing and would not let him go.

But King Gatel sent urgent word: Where is my war, I have waited a whole day now and there is no war or anything, what are you waiting for, Jephthah.

Jephthah delayed no longer.

He rose and fled to the desert.

He did not go alone, but took with him the daughter whom one of the women had borne to him.

Pitdah was seven years old when she was taken out of the city into the desert on the back of her father's horse. She was an Ammonite, like her mother. She had passed her childhood among maidservants, eunuchs, and silks. Jephthah had lived in Abel-Keramim for ten years.

When they left the city by the Dung Gate Pitdah laughed for joy, for she loved riding; she fondly imagined that she was being taken out into the desert for a day's ride and that at evening she would be brought back to her mother and the cat. But when the first night broke on her in the wilderness, she was alarmed and began to scream and stamp her feet, and she cursed her father and even kicked the horse with her strong little legs. Her mouth, pursed with rage, was a pitiful spectacle.

She did not stop screaming until the sounds of the desert soothed her to sleep.

In the morning Jephthah gave her a little pipe he had made from a reed. Pitdah could play the songs of Abel-Keramim which the harlots and concubines sang in the squares of the city at night. Some of them were the same songs his mother Pitdah had sung to him. As she played Jephthah could hear the water running in the channels in the orchards on Gilead's farm. His heart went out to her whenever she said the word Father. And he rode very slowly, and to take her mind off the heat and the discomfort of the journey he told her story after story, about the barehanded slaying of the wolf and about his brother Azur who could understand the language of dogs. That day Jephthah used more words than on any other day in his whole life.

After a few days Pitdah stopped asking for her mother and her home. He revealed to her that their goal was the sea. When she asked what that might be, he replied that the sea was a vast hilly land where the hills were made not of sand but of water. When she asked him what was there he replied that perhaps there was peace. And when she wanted to know why the earth did not soak up the sea in an instant as it soaks up all water, he did not know what to answer and only said:

"Now cover your head from the sun."

Pitdah said:

"When will we reach the sea like you said."

Jephthah said:

"I don't know. I've never been there. Look, Pitdah, a lizard; now it's gone."

Sometimes when she looked up at her father there was a tired light in her eyes. She might have been sick from the sands and the sun, or perhaps she was merely alarmed. At night he would enfold her in his cloak to protect her against the biting cold.

When the moon began to wane, Jephthah and his daughter arrived at a cave in the mountains in a place called the Land of Tob. There was a spring there, and several oak trees which cast a deep, soft shade. Beside the spring there were some mossy stone troughs, where desert nomads gathered to water their mangy flocks. They pitched their black goat-hair tents on the slope of the hill. That was where Pitdah learned to collect sticks and to make a fire at the entrance to the cave. Jephthah would go hunting and bring back a roebuck or a tortoise, which he would roast in the fire.

At night they saw a hollow moon rolling gently along the line of mountain peaks as though cautiously testing the surface of the desert before flooding it with silvery pallor. In the moonlight the jagged mountains looked like thirsty jaws.

Early in the morning Pitdah would go down to the troughs to fetch water, and, returning barefoot to her father, she would wake him up by splashing handfuls of cold water in his face. After he was up she played on her pipe, while Jephthah sat silently absorbing the music as though it were wine.

The desert nomads who roamed the Land of Tob were all malcontents or outcasts. Jephthah joined them. Cadaverous women hugged the girl and fussed over her all day long, because in the Land of Tob no child was ever born. Its inhabitants wandered restlessly between the desert plains and the mountain ravines. Sometimes the Land of Tob was raided, either by Ammonite troops or by bands of Israelites bent on killing the nomads. These nomads were desperate men: some were killers and some were fleeing from killers; some were haters whose hatred the settled lands could not contain, others were hated men with hounds on their heels; there were also soothsayers, and dreamers who lived on roots and herbs so as not to increase suffering in the world.

Above the land there stretched a sky of molten iron; the earth was copper-colored, parched and cracked. But the nights in the Land of Tob were powerful and heady like black wine. A blessed coolness descended calmly over all each night, bringing relief to the outcasts, to the mangy flocks, and to the desperate wasteland itself.

One day Jephthah and his daughter were brought before the chieftain of the nomads.

He was a lean, shriveled old man; his face was like aged leather, and only the line of his jaw retained a vestige of strength or ruthlessness. Jephthah stood before him in the gully of a lifeless riverbed. He was silent because he chose to hear first the words that the old chieftain would address to him. The old man, too, sprawled drowsily on his gray camel, waiting for the stranger to speak. For a long while they were both silent, each testing the strength of the other's silence with stubborn patience, while a circle of thin women surrounded them at a distance.

The chieftain sat like a lizard in the sun, without flickering an eyelid. In front of his camel Jephthah stood rooted to the spot with a face of stone. At his feet his daughter Pitdah scrabbled and burrowed in the sand, trying to discover where the ants came from. Everything was still. Only the shadow of the two men, the one mounted on his camel and the other standing on his feet, moved gently, as the sun climbed higher into the white sky. It was a long silence. Finally the old man spoke, in a parched voice:

"Who are you, stranger?"

Jephthah said:

"I am the son of Gilead the Gileadite, my lord, by an Ammonite servant woman."

"I did not ask your name or your father's name; I asked, who are you stranger."

"I am a stranger, as you say, my lord."

"And why have you come to this place. You have been sent by the Ammonites or by the Israelites to spy on us and to betray us to our mortal foes."

"I have no part in Israel, or any inheritance among the children of Ammon."

"You are a desperate man, stranger. I can see that your eyes are turned inward like the eyes of a desperate man. Whom do you worship."

"Not Milcom."

"Whom do you worship."

"The Lord of the wolves in the desert at night. In the image of his hatred am I made."

"And the girl."

"My daughter Pitdah. And she is growing more like the desert every day."

"You are a warrior. Come out with us to kill and plunder, like one of these young men. Come out with us tonight."

"I am a stranger, my lord. I have lived out my life among strangers."

# 6

Jephthah found favor among the wandering men of the Land of Tob.

In the course of time he fought with them against their attackers and joined them in several raids on the settled lands, for these nomads hated all house dwellers. They slipped by night through the fences of the farms and flitted like ghosts within. The slain died silently and the killers stole as silently away. They came with knives or daggers. And with fire. By morning charred embers smoked in the ruins of the farm, in the land of Ammon or of Israel. And Jephthah rose ever higher among them because he was endowed with the attributes of lordship. He had the power to impose his will on others without a movement, by his voice alone. As always, he spoke little, because he did not love words and he did not trust them.

One night the Jephthahites stole into the farm of Gilead the Gileadite, on the border of the land of Gilead, at the edge of the desert.

Shadowy shapes scurried along the paths of the estate, among the dark orchards and the dense foliage of the vineyards, to the door of the house that was built of black volcanic stone. But Jephthah did not allow the house to be burned with its inmates, because a sudden longing rose within his hatred and he recalled the words his father had spoken on a faraway night and a faraway day. You are tainted as your father is tainted. You for yourself. I for myself. Every man for himself. There is a lizard; now it has gone.

He knelt on all fours and drank from the irrigation channel. Then he gave a shrill birdlike whistle, and his men gathered and slipped away into the wasteland without setting fire to the farm.

The nomads raided Ammon and Israel alike. Every man's hand was against them, and anyone who found them would slay them. They slept all day in crevices, crannies, and caves, with the dark shapes of their meager flocks scattered in the shade of the oak trees beside the mossy rockhewn troughs. Lean black-robed women watched over the flocks by day, while the sun dissolved everything with its white-hot hatred. And by night the nomads emerged from their hiding places to raid the settled lands. On their return they sang a bitter song, like a long-drawn-out wail. Occasionally a man would let out a shout in the middle of the song, and suddenly fall silent.

Pitdah, too, found favor in the eyes of the nomads. She was a darkly beautiful girl, and her movements were always dreamy, as if she were made of a fragile substance, as if even the ground beneath her feet and the objects between her fingers were all longing to break and she had always to be careful.

The bitter women adored Pitdah, because no child was ever born in the Land of Tob. She would play her pipe to the hillsides and the boulders even when there was no one to hear her. Whenever Jephthah heard her playing in the distance, it seemed to him like the sound of the wind in the vineyards on his father's estate, the plashing of the water as it ran in the channels in the shade of the orchard. Pitdah dreamed even when she was awake, and Jephthah's heart went out to her if she told him one of her dreams or if she suddenly said to him: Father.

He loved her savagely. But he was careful whenever he stroked her hair or hugged her shoulder because he would recall how his father Gilead had held him when he himself was a small boy. He would say:

"I shall not hurt you. Give me your hand."

And the girl would reply:

"But I can't help laughing, because of the way you're looking at me."

He loved her savagely. Whenever he chanced to think of a strange man coming one day to take Pitdah away from him, his blood rebelled in his veins. Some short, fleshy man might clasp Pitdah in his hairy arms, reeking of sweat and onions, licking and biting her lips, groping downwards with clumsy fingers toward her delicate recesses. At the sight of his bloodshot eyes she laughed aloud, and he cooled his burning brow with the flat of his dagger and whispered to her: Play, Pitdah, play; and he sat listening to the music like a man going blind until the rage subsided and only a dry sadness remained like a taste of ashes in his throat. Sometimes the power of his love made Jephthah bellow wildly like his father Gilead before him, and sometimes he yearned to be able to brew her potions in the night and conjure away the threatening evil.

Jephthah and the nomads could see her growing before their eyes. When she was not gathering firewood or watering the flocks with the gaunt women, she would sit in a gully playing with pebbles from the brook, building towers, walls, castles, turrets, and gates, and suddenly she would destroy them all with glee and burst out laughing. She would also weave wreaths of thistles, when the thistles were in flower. She seemed to be in a dream, and her rounded lips were slightly parted. Sometimes she would hold up in her sun-darkened hands a whitening bone she had found, and sing to it, and blow on it, and even touch it to her hair.

She knew how to carve little figures from branches of shrubs, a galloping horse, a resting lamb, a black old man leaning on a stick. Sometimes odd occurrences that were no laughing matter made Jephthah's daughter laugh warmly. If a woman was tying bundles onto a camel and the camel was startled and all the bundles fell off, Pitdah would erupt in soft, low laughter. Or if one of the nomads stood with his back to her and his head bent motionlessly forward, as if he were sunk deep in thought as he pissed among the rocks, she would laugh uncontrollably and would not stop even if the man lost his temper and shouted at her.

If one of the men suddenly stared at her sideways, with gaping eyes and parted lips and the tip of his tongue protruding between his teeth, Pitdah would laugh aloud. And if Jephthah caught sight of the man staring at his daughter and his eyes began to flash cold rage, Pitdah would move her eyes back and forth between them as though drawing a line, laughing louder than ever. Even when he shouted, That's enough, she could not stop laughing; sometimes she would infect him with her laughter and he could not stop, either. The young nomads interpreted all this as a sign of happiness, but the women considered it something that would not end well. The nomads' wives taught Pitdah to weave and cook and milk goats, and to tame a stubborn billy goat. The girl could do all these things easily, and her thoughts always seemed to be far away.

Once she said to her father Jephthah:

"At night you go out to fight and you win, and in the daytime you sleep, and then even the flies on your face are stronger than you are."

Jephthah said:

"Everybody has to sleep."

Pitdah said:

"Snakes never sleep; they can't even close their eyes, because they have no eyelids."

Jephthah said:

"It is written in the holy writings that the snake is more cunning than any other beast of the field."

Pitdah:

"How sad to be more cunning than any other beast of the field. And how sad never to sleep and never to close your eyes and dream at night. If the snake was really cunning, it would find a way to close its eyes."

"What about you."

"I love watching you sleeping on the ground after your

night fights, with the flies walking all over your face. I love you, Father. And I love myself, too. And the places where you never take me, where the sun sets in the evening. You have forgotten the sea, but I remember. Now, put this cloak over your head and moo, and I'll watch you and laugh."

In his dreams Jephthah saw a procession of princes and powerful men coming to ask him for his daughter's hand. Their faces were crooked; like dogs they must be chased away with a stick or a stone, because Pitdah was not for them. Very slowly and heavily his father Gilead appeared in Jephthah's dreams, and he, too, put out his broad, rough hand to touch Pitdah and she ran away from him and hid behind the troughs and he ran after her and Jephthah cried out in his sleep. Or else the boys appeared, Azur and Jamin and Gatel and Jemuel, and they surrounded Pitdah in his dream with hundreds of white fingers to tear off her clothes and she laughed with them and he screamed at the sight of them because they had no eyelids and their eyes were wide open and gaping at her not closing not blinking and they closed around her and he woke up with a cry and found that he was holding the dagger and his hand was shaking.

Touch me, O God, you have not touched me yet, how long shall we wait for you. Reach out for me with your hand and with fingers of fire. Here I am before you upon one of the mountains, holding the lamb for a burnt offering, and behold the fire and the wood, but where is the knife. I shall desire your shadow all the days of my life. If you appear in the mountain I shall be burning dust. If you shine forth in the crescent moon or in the reflection of the moon in water, there your servant will be in the white sands or in the depths of the water. If the dogs howl and pour out their hearts in their howling, that is a sign that you are loving and wrathful. Send me your wrath, O God, and let me be touched by it, surely you are a solitary God and I, too, am all alone. You shall have no other servant before me. I am your son and I shall bear witness all my life to your inscrutable terrors, O Lord of the wildcat stalking the lifeless riverbeds by night, night after night.

In the course of time Jephthah became the chieftain of the nomads. He spoke little, and when he did speak his voice was very soft. Anyone who wanted to hear him had to lean toward him and listen attentively.

At that time the king of Ammon invaded the land of Israel. He conquered all the cities and farms and made slaves of their inhabitants. Some managed to escape, but the rest were under the sway of King Gatel. The king never left his palace, but passed his time filling scroll after scroll with orders for his generals, and also writing the *Book of the Wars of King Gatel.*

One day Jephthah's three brothers, Jamin, Jemuel, and Azur, came to the desert to the Land of Tob, to the place where Jephthah dwelt. They were fleeing from the Ammonites and they had come here because Jephthah's fame had spread all over the land, as he and his nomad band, the Jephthahites, snapped at the heels of the Ammonite army, robbing the caravans and flouting the king's guards like a bird playing with a bear.

Jephthah did not conceal his identity from his brothers. But neither did he fall on their necks and weep. With the passage of the years his two eldest brothers had become even coarser. Jamin, the eldest, was now a heavily built, corpulent man who resembled neither his father nor his mother but looked more like the household priest. Jemuel could not rid his face of an obsequious smile accompanied by a lecherous wink, which seemed to be saying, Come over to my house, my friend, and let's have an orgy. Only the youngest brother, Azur, had developed the speed and sharpness of an arrow in flight; he resembled his half-brother the son of the Ammonite woman, rather than the two sons of Nehushtah daughter of Zebulun.

When the three brothers had bowed down and prostrated themselves before the nomad chief, Jephthah said:

"Rise, fugitives. Do not bow down to me. I am not Joseph and you are not the sons of Jacob. Stand up. At once."

Jamin, the eldest, spoke as though reading from a written text:

"My lord, we have come to tell you that the Ammonite foe has conquered your father's estate. And now our father is an old man and cannot fight against them. We, your servants, say to you: Arise, Jephthah, rescue your father's house and your father's land, for only you and no other can defeat the Ammonite serpent."

They pleaded with Jephthah and Jephthah said nothing. He merely ordered that they be accepted into his band. Day by day they said to him: How long will our lord tarry. He did not answer them and he did not rebuke them. In his heart he said, O God, grant me a sign.

The Jephthahites harried the armies of Ammon. Fear and panic seized the city of Abel-Keramim at night because of the Jephthahites who raided the caravans. Jephthah's men were as swift and cunning as their lord. His footsteps at night were like a breeze or a caress. He sent silent-knived assassins by night to the Ammonite captains. Gatel's soldiers were seized by terror whenever they heard at night the sound of a breeze or a wolf or a bird of prey, lest it be Jephthah's nomads in the night making the sound of bird or wolf or breeze. The Jephthahites penetrated the walls of Rabbat-Ammon and infiltrated the squares of Abel-Keramim and its temples: they entered the city by day with the caravans, disguised as merchants, by night they sowed panic, and in the morning they were borne away by the wind and were no more, and time and again Gatel sent forth his army to pursue the wind. In the book of his wars King Gatel wrote:

"Surely this is the way of the fainthearted, to strike and to flee. Let them come by the light of day, let us meet face to face, and I shall crush them and have peace."

But the Jephthahites did not choose to come by daylight. Day by day the lord of the nomads went out and stood alone on the hill, with his back toward the camp and his face toward the wilderness, as though waiting for some sound or scent.

Then King Gatel sent word to Jephthah:

"You are an Ammonite, Jephthah. We are brothers. Why are we fighting each other? If you choose, come and I shall place you in my second chariot, and none shall lift up hand or foot without your word in all the cities of Ammon and of Israel."

By the hand of his adjutant Azur the nomad chieftain sent back word to Gatel king of Ammon saying:

"Gatel, I am not your brother or your father's son. You know that I am a stranger. I do not fight for the Israelites, I fight for one you do not know. In his honor I shall put you to the sword and your enemies, too, for I have been a stranger all the days of my life."

# 7

Pitdah dreamed a dream one night in her tent in the Land of Tob. In her dream she was a bride in a bridal gown. The maidens were dancing around her with lyres and timbrels, and there were bracelets on her arms.

When she told her father about this dream he flew into a panic. He shook her by the shoulders and whispered frantically: Tell me who was your bridegroom. As he pleaded with her his hands twisted her shoulders violently, and she suddenly started to laugh, as she often laughed, without cause. Then he slapped her face wildly with the back of his hand and shouted: Who was your bridegroom.

Pitdah said:

"You are looking at me like a murderer."

"Who was it, tell me who it was."

"I couldn't see his face in the dream, I could only feel his hot breath on me. Look at you, you've got foam on your lips, leave me alone, go and wash your face in the brook."

"Who was it."

"Don't you hit me again or I'll laugh aloud and the whole camp will hear."

"Who was it."

"But you know who my bridegroom is. Why did you shout at me, why are you trembling so."

She stood laughing and he stood facing her wearing a dazed look. His eyes were closed and his lips said to him:

Of course I knew, why was I so startled. They were still standing there when the elders of Israel rode down to prostrate themselves at Jephthah's feet.

He opened his eyes and saw them coming, and he also saw his father Gilead riding with them. He was just as broad and heavy and ugly as in the old days, only his beard had turned gray.

The elders of Israel raised the hems of their cloaks because of the dust of the desert. They fell flat on their faces before the chief of the nomads. Gilead alone did not bow or prostrate himself before his son. Then a delicious bubbling joy began to course through Jephthah's veins, such a joy as he had never known before and would never know again.

With an effort he controlled his voice as he addressed the elders:

"Arise, elders of Israel. The man to whom you are bowing down is a harlot's son."

But they remained on their knees and would not stand up; they merely looked at one another, not knowing what. At the end of the silence Gilead the Gileadite said:

"You are my son, who will save Israel from the Ammonites."

Jephthah contemplated their broken pride distantly as though it were a wound. Then he was touched by sorrow, not the sorrow of the elders, perhaps not sorrow at all, but something that was not far removed from gentleness, a taste of scorched earth. Gently he said to them:

"I am a stranger, O elders of Israel. No stranger should go before you in your wars, lest the camp be unclean."

At this the elders rose. They said:

"You are our brother, Jephthah, you are our brother. See, today we have made your father Gilead judge of Israel and you, our brother, shall be the captain of our army, you shall fight for us against the Ammonite; as captain of your father's army you shall be our commander, you shall have power over all your brothers, Jephthah, because from your earliest youth you have known the skills of war. To this day the story is told around the shepherds' campfires how you tore a wolf with your bare hands."

"But surely you hate me, elders, and when I have

crushed the Ammonite for you you will chase after me like a rebellious slave and my father here will put me in irons because he is the judge of Israel and I am a stranger, a nomad and a harlot's son."

"You are my son, Jephthah. You are my boy who put his hand into the fire without crying out and who tore a wolf with his bare hands. If you come back and fight the Ammonites for us I shall bless you before all your brothers, and you shall be the one who leads the people out and brings them in all the days of my life."

"Why do you not leave me alone, elders. And you, too, judge of Israel: stop pleading with me. You are not children: why are you playing these games. Go while you can and save your hoarheads, and take your priests and all your scribes with you. Only leave me alone. I can see through your plot. Jephthah will not be the warhorse of Israel, and this old man will not ride on my back."

Then Gilead the Gileadite spoke, with lips pressed tight together as though he were straining to break an iron chain.

"Your father will not judge Israel. You shall fight and you shall judge."

The elders were silent; their tongues failed them at the sound of these words.

Jephthah spoke quietly, like a fox, and as he spoke the yellow spark glimmered in his eye.

"If you are really and truly appointing me to be judge of Israel this day, then swear to me now in the name of our God."

"As God hears and witnesses: you shall be judge."

"A whore's son shall be your leader," Jephthah said, and he laughed so loudly that the horses were alarmed.

And the elders soundlessly repeated:

"Our leader."

"Then clap this old man in irons at once. The judge of Israel commands you."

"Jephthah, my son—"

"And cast him into the pit. I have spoken."

The following day Jephthah inspected his army and appointed captains and commanders. He dispatched his brothers Jamin and Jemuel to assemble speedily all the fighting men among the tribes of Israel. And he sent his adjutant Azur the Gileadite with a message to Gatel king of Ammon:

"Get out of my land."

At nightfall on the following day, the judge of Israel commanded a large tent of honor to be pitched in the middle of the camp, and he ordered his father Gilead to be brought up from the pit and installed in this tent and furnished with wine and servant girls. To his daughter Pitdah he said: If the old man dashes the wine pitcher to the ground and smashes it, tell the servants to hurry and bring him a fresh one quickly. If he breaks the second let them fetch him another, because this old man sometimes takes a fancy to the sound of breaking glass. Let him smash to his heart's content. Only do not dare to enter the tent yourself; stop laughing now. Go."

Gatel king of Ammon was driven to distraction by the Jephthahites who picked off his soldiers by day, and by night seemed to be swallowed up by the earth. He sent his army after them, but it was like chasing the wind. He became a laughing stock in Moab and in Edom a byword: the fly bites and the bear dances.

Gatel sent Jephthah a message by the hand of Azur his adjutant: Leave me alone, Jephthah. You are an Ammonite; why should you harm me; surely I loved you deeply. But Jephthah knew Gatel's mind, he knew that he had set his heart on being like one of the mighty kings of old but that even the smell of horses in the distance was enough to make him feel giddy. Calmly the judge of Israel waged a war of words with the king of Ammon by means of envoys who passed to and fro: to whom did the land really belong, whose forefathers had settled it first, what was written in all the chronicles, who was in the right and who had justice on his side. Eventually Gatel came to imagine that it was a war of scrolls that he had to wage, and he multiplied scroll upon scroll.

The elders of Israel came to the judge's tent saying: In God's name, go, the time is passing, the Ammonite is devouring all the land, if you delay longer what will there be left to save for us. Jephthah listened and said nothing. The elders spoke further to the judge: Send word to the Edomite and to the Arab, send to Egypt and to Damascus, we cannot manage alone, for Ammon is too strong for us. And still Jephthah said nothing.

But to himself he said:

"Grant me but one sign more, O God, and I will offer you their carcasses strewn upon the field as you love, O Lord of the wolves in the night in the desert."

One night Pitdah saw another dream. Her bridegroom came in the darkness and said to her in a still small voice: Come, my bride, arise, for the time has come.

In the morning Jephthah listened to her dream, and this time he was silent but his face grew very dark. He had been stalked by dreams all the days of his life. And like his father Gilead before him he believed that dreams come from that place from which man comes and to which he returns through his death. To himself he said: Now is the time. And the girl laughed aloud.

One hour later the trumpet sounded.

All the camps assembled on the rocky slope, and the sun played on the lances and shields. The elders of the tribes were in a panic, searching for the right words to prevent him from launching their whole force against the walls of Ammon in one swoop, for great was the strength of Ammon, and Israel might never recover from this disaster; surely the wild man had resolved to dash the head of Israel against the stone walls of Ammon. But the judge of Israel rose and left the tent in the midst of their entreaties and stood at the entrance facing the troops, and this time his daughter Pitdah was standing at his side. He placed his hand on her shoulder and the voice of his dead mother seemed to ring in his voice as he said: O God, if you will surely deliver the children of Ammon into my hand, then it shall be that whatever comes forth from the doors of my house to meet me when I return in peace from the children of Ammon shall surely belong to God, and I will offer it up as a burnt offering—

"He will deliver the children of Ammon into your hands. Now, you, my maidens, make ready my bridal gown," said the darkly beautiful girl. The people cheered and the horses neighed, and she laughed and laughed and never stopped.

Jephthah the Gileadite emerged from his hiding place in the Land of Tob and pounced on Ammon to raze its walls to the ground, for great was the strength of Ammon. Sweeping through the villages, he toppled the towers and fired the temples, flattened the turrets and shattered the golden domes and gave the wives, concubines, and harlots as food to the fowls of the air.

By the time the day reached its heat Gatel had been put to the sword and Ammon had been smitten from Aroer until you come to Minnith, even twenty cities, and as far as Abel-Keramim, with a very great slaughter, and by nightfall Ammon was defeated and Gatel was slain and still Jephthah was silent.

# 8

The days of a man's life are like water seeping into the sands; he perishes from the face of the earth unknown at his coming and unrecognized at his passing. He fades away like a shadow that cannot be brought back. But sometimes dreams come to us in the night and we know in the dreams that nothing truly passes away and nothing is forgotten, everything is always present as it was before.

Even the dead return home in the dreams. Even days that are lost and forgotten come back whole and shining in dreams at night, not a drop is lost, not a jot passes away. The smell of wet dust on an autumn morning from long ago, the sight of burned houses whose ashes have long since been scattered by the wind, the arched hips of dead women, the barking at the moon, on a distant night, of remote ancestors of the dogs that are with us now: everything comes back living and breathing in our dreams.

As if in a dream Jephthah the Gileadite stood at the entrance to his father's estate, within the fences of which he was born, in the shadows of whose orchards he had first felt the touch of a hand, and from which he had fled for his life many years before: not a drop was lost, not a jot had passed away. The fences and orchards stood before him as of old, and the vine still covered all the walls of the house so that the black volcanic stones could not be seen through its embrace. And the water ran in the channels and beneath the trees there was cool dark longing.

Like a man possessed by a dream Jephthah stood looking up to the house, only half-seeing the darkly beautiful one coming out to meet him with songs. And after her came the maidens with timbrels and the shepherds with pipes and his father Gilead, a broad, bitter man. And Jamin, Jemuel, and Azur were also on the path, and their mother Nehushtah daughter of Zebulun could be seen all white in a white dress through the window with pale laughter on her lips. And all the dogs were barking and the cows were lowing and the household scribe and the household priest and the bald-headed steward, all as in a dream, nothing was left out.

And the maidens followed after her, dressed in white and playing their timbrels and singing: Jephthah has slain, Jephthah has slain; and the people cheered and the torches blazed over all of Mizpeh of Gilead.

As she came out she seemed to be floating, as if her feet disdained to touch the dust of the path. As a gazelle comes down to water so Pitdah came down to her father. Her bridal gown gleamed white, her eyelashes shaded her eyes, and when she looked up at him and he heard her laughter he saw fire and ice burning with a green flame in her pupils. And the maidens sang: Jephthah has slain slain slain, and Pitdah's hips moved restlessly as though to the rhythm of a secret dance and she was slender and barefoot—

Drowsily the judge of Israel stood facing the entrance to his father's estate. His face was parched and weatherbeaten, and his eyes were turned inward. As though he were deathly tired. As though in a dream.

The cheering of the people grew louder as Gilead was carried out on a litter by Jamin, Jemuel, and Azur, and the troops shouted: Happy is the father, happy is the father. The whole of Mizpeh of Gilead was lit up by torches, and the noise of the timbrels was a riot of joy.

Beautiful and dark was Pitdah as she placed the victor's wreath on her father's head. Then she put her hands silently over his eyes and said:

"Father."

As his daughter's fingers touched his eyelids, Jephthah felt like a sunbaked boulder in the desert that is suddenly splashed with cold water. But he did not want to wake from his slumber.

He was tired and thirsty, and his unwashed body was still smeared with blood and ashes. For a moment he missed the city he had burned that day, Abel-Keramim, reaching up to heaven with its many towers topped with golden domes, the sun touching the gold in the mornings, and the sickly boy king pleading with him: Jephthah, don't leave me, tell me a story because of the dark, and the caravans coming in through the gates of the city in the evening twilight with the music of camel bells, and women's lips fluttering on the hair of his chest and whispering: Stranger, and the lights at night and the music, and his sword piercing the throat of the ailing king and emerging steaming from the back of his neck, and Gatel saying with dying lips: What an ugly story, and the city in flames and burning women throwing themselves off the rooftops and the smell of roasting flesh and the screaming—

Silently he stood without moving at the entrance to his father's estate, and his eyes were closed.

Then the old man Gilead raised his hand to silence the singers and players, and the cheering crowds so that the judge of Israel could speak to the people.

All the people stopped to listen. Only the torchlight trembled in the silent breeze.

The judge of Israel opened his mouth to speak to the people, and suddenly he collapsed on the ground, howling like a wolf that has been pierced by an arrow.

My lady mother, his lips said. And one of the elders of the tribe who was present thought in his heart: This man is deceptive; he is not one of us.

# 9

She asked him for two months, and he, as though he had forgotten everything, said to her:

"Leave this place, go to another country and never come back to me."

The girl laughed and answered:

"Put this cloak over your head and eyes and moo, and we'll watch you and laugh."

And he, lost among his longings, said:

"Look, Pitdah, on the fence, there's a lizard. Now it's gone."

For two months she wandered in the mountains and her maidens followed after her. The shepherds fled at their approach. If she passed through one of the villages, the villagers hid indoors. Silently they went clad in white along moonswept ravines. What was the message of this ghostly pallor, dead silver light on dead hilltops. No wild beast touched them. Olive trees twisted with age did not dare to scratch their skin. Their footfall was muffled by the dust like the rustling of leaves in the breeze. With what sense must one listen to the many sounds, and with what sense listen to stillness. Man and woman, father, mother, and son, father and mother and daughter, a pair of brothers, winter, autumn, spring, and summer, water and wind, all are merely distance upon distance, and whether you scream or laugh or remain silent, everything without exception will be absorbed into the stillness of the stars and the sadness of those hills.

Pitdah was dark and beautiful as she walked and laughed in her bridal wreath, and wretched nomads who saw her from a distance said: She is a stranger, the daughter of a stranger, no man may approach her and live.

When two months had passed she returned. Jephthah had set up an altar on one of the mountains, and the fire and the knife were in his hand. In later times the wandering tribesmen would speak around their campfires at night of the great joy they had both shown, she a bride on her marriage couch and he a youthful lover stretching out his fingers to the first touch. And they were both laughing as wild beasts laugh in the dark of night, and they did not speak, only Jephthah said to her, Sea, sea.

You have chosen me out of all my brothers and dedicated me to your service. You shall have no other servant before me. Here is the dark beauty under my knife; I have not withheld my only daughter from you. Grant me a sign, for surely you are tempting your servant.

Afterward the night beasts shrieked among the rocks and the barren desert stretched to the tops of the distant hills.

# 10

Six years did Jephthah the Gileadite judge Israel. He sank up to his neck in blood, and he provoked Gilead against Ephraim to destroy Israel, just as he had spoken in his youth to Gatel king of Ammon saying: I have no part in Israel nor any inheritance among the children of Ammon; I shall put both you and your enemies to the sword, for I have been a stranger all the days of my life.

And after six years he tired of judging and returned alone to the desert. No man approached him, for there was a deathly fear upon all the nomads of the Land of Tob. Only his half-brother Azur would come down and leave him bread and water at a distance. And the lean hounds always came down with him.

For a whole year Jephthah dwelt alone in a cave in the Land of Tob. He studied all the night sounds which came up from the wilderness when the desert bristled, until he could utter them all himself, and then he decided: Enough.

In the chronicle of the household the household scribe wrote:

*And after him Ibzan of Beth-lehem judged Israel. And he had thirty sons and thirty daughters.*

1966
1974–75